TRYST SIX VENOM

PENELOPE DOUGLAS

BERKLEY ROMANCE

New York

BERKLEY ROMANCE
Published by Berkley
An imprint of Penguin Random House LLC
penguinrandomhouse.com

Copyright © 2021 by Penelope Douglas LLC
"Bonus content" copyright © 2021 by Penelope Douglas LLC
Excerpt from *Five Brothers* copyright © 2024 by Penelope Douglas LLC
Penguin Random House supports copyright. Copyright fuels creativity, encourages diverse
voices, promotes free speech, and creates a vibrant culture. Thank you for buying an authorized
edition of this book and for complying with copyright laws by not reproducing, scanning,
or distributing any part of it in any form without permission. You are supporting writers
and allowing Penguin Random House to continue to publish books for every reader.

BERKLEY and the BERKLEY & B colophon are registered trademarks
of Penguin Random House LLC.

Library of Congress Cataloging-in-Publication Data

Names: Douglas, Penelope, author.
Title: Tryst Six venom / Penelope Douglas.
Description: First Berkley romance edition. | New York : Berkley Romance, 2024.
Identifiers: LCCN 2023034731 | ISBN 9780593641989 (trade paperback)
Subjects: LCGFT: Romance fiction. | Novels.
Classification: LCC PS3604.O93236 T79 2024 | DDC 813/.6—dc23/eng/20230814
LC record available at https://lccn.loc.gov/2023034731

Tryst Six Venom was originally self-published, in a different form, in 2021.

First Berkley Romance edition: April 2024

Printed in the United States of America
1st Printing

PRAISE FOR THE NOVELS OF PENELOPE DOUGLAS

"Penelope Douglas showcases [their] knack for creating compelling central characters and thus reversing all our expectations about them. [They] deliver a multilayered love story that strikes every emotional chord along the way—a story that is beautifully complicated, infinitely angsty, and completely impossible to put down."

—Natasha Is a Book Junkie

"Beyond addictive! Visceral and cuttingly edgy, *Punk 57* will own you from the first page to long after you turn over the last. Penelope Douglas slays it!"

—Katy Evans

"Douglas launched this series and held nothing back. They delivered a medley of emotions I never thought I could feel at once. I was afraid, intrigued, anxious, and enamored. A must-read!"

—B.B. Reid

"*Credence* consumed me with its sinfully unique taboo story and gorgeous imagery. Truly a one-of-a-kind book that I can't recommend enough."

—Carian Cole

"The seductive tug highlighted by the character-driven storyline held me in its grasp until the very end. Douglas's ability to draw such powerful emotions from the reader is truly fascinating."

—Abbi Glines

"Misha and Ryen's fiery romance will have your heartstrings twisted in knots and have you wanting a pen pal of your own. They're fire and ice, and I couldn't get enough." —H. D. Carlton

"Penelope Douglas does many things very well. One of the best of those things is their ability to make something taboo seem irresistibly satisfying. With *Birthday Girl*, they twist the older man / younger woman taboo and make it compelling, sensual, and a wonderful treat."

—Eden Butler

TITLES BY PENELOPE DOUGLAS

The Fall Away Series

BULLY

UNTIL YOU

RIVAL

FALLING AWAY

THE NEXT FLAME
(includes novellas *Aflame* and *Next to Never*)

Stand-Alones

MISCONDUCT

BIRTHDAY GIRL

PUNK 57

CREDENCE

TRYST SIX VENOM

The Devil's Night Series

CORRUPT

HIDEAWAY

KILL SWITCH

CONCLAVE
(novella)

NIGHTFALL

FIRE NIGHT
(novella)

To Abigail

Unless I'm reading an assignment or doing a paper or taking a test, I'm thinking about you.

—V. C. Andrews, *Secret Whispers*

Dear Reader,

This book deals with emotionally difficult topics, including abuse, bullying, homophobia, suicide, self-harm, violence, body shaming and fatphobia, sexual assault, emotional and physical abuse, eating disorders, and outing. Anyone who believes such content may upset them is encouraged to consider their well-being when choosing whether to continue reading.

PLAYLIST

"All the Things She Said" by t.A.T.u.

"Beautiful Is Boring" by Bones UK

"Blank Space" by I Prevail

"Blood in the Cut" by K.Flay

"Bravado" by Lorde

"Carry On Wayward Son" by Kansas

"Celebrity Skin" by Hole

"Cool Girl" by Tove Lo

"Crimson and Clover" by Joan Jett & the Blackhearts

"Death" by White Lies

"Dirty Mind" by Boy Epic

"Fall" by The Bug, Inga Copeland

"Fuqboi" by Hey Violet

"Girls Like Girls" by Hayley Kiyoko

"Graveyard" by Halsey

"Hatefuck" by Cruel Youth

"Head Like a Hole" by Nine Inch Nails

"Heart Heart Head" by Meg Myers

"Holy" by Zolita

"Hypnotic" by Zella Day

"I Don't Wanna Be Me" by Type O Negative

"Swish Swish" by Katy Perry

"Take Me to the River" by Kaleida

"The One I Love" by Scala & Kolacny Brothers

TRYST
SIX
VENOM

1

Clay

Want to bet my mother is about to have a meltdown? I'm sure it's after nine. She should be home, flushing out any calories she consumed today, and finishing up step five of her skincare regimen instead of waiting for me at the dress shop right now.

I'm so late.

Confetti flies in the air, and I reach down, grabbing three more rolled-up T-shirts out of the bucket as the parade float bounces and sways under us.

"More shirts!" I yell over to Krisjen to restock.

The crowd cheers on both sides of the street, and I jump down off the step, stopping at the edge as I hold my hand to my ear.

Come on. Let me hear it!

"Ah!" little girls scream.

"Hi, Clay!" tiny six-year-old Manda Cabot squeals at me like I'm a Disney princess. "Hi!"

She waves at me as her twin sister, Stella, holds up her hands, ready to catch.

A comfortable breeze blows through the palms lining Augustine Avenue, grazing my bare legs in my jean shorts as the potted pink lantanas hang on the street lamps lining the road and fill the air with their scent.

Just your typical balmy Florida winter evening.

"We want a shirt!" Stella cries.

I shoot my arm up in the air, my white T-shirt with the word BIG shining in bold silver letters.

I smile, shouting, "You wanna be a Little?"

"Yeah!" they cry out.

"Then I need to hear it!" I move my feet, doing a little dance move. "Omega Chi Kappa! Come on!"

"Omega Chi Kappa!" they shout. "Omega Chi Kappa!"

"I can't hear you!"

"Omega Chi Kappa!" they scream so loud their baby teeth damn near shake.

Oh my God. So adorbs. I hope I have daughters.

I throw them both an underhand toss and resume dancing to the music as the truck pulls us at a crawl, our float in the middle of a long line of floats, all celebrating the annual Founder's Day.

"See you in a few years!" I tell them. "Be good and study!"

"Yeah, we only take the best!" Amy Chandler shouts next to me.

Followed by Krisjen's chirp at my other side, "Be best!"

I snort, turning around to grab some more shirts. Balloons dance in the air along the sidewalks, and I toss some more bundles, the tingles in my head helping me play my part as I dance our choreographed little number in sync with Krisjen to "Swish Swish."

The rest of our girls walk in front of or alongside the float, dancing along with us in the street, and every eye on us makes the hair on my arms rise. The attention always feels good. Rolling my hips, arching my back, and shaking my body, I know one thing for sure. I'm good at this.

Our sorority is the biggest in any high school in the state, and while it's service- and academic-based, because that's what gets us into college, we're popular for other reasons. We look good doing what we do.

Whether it's washing cars to raise money for cat saliva research, hosting the football team's annual pancake breakfast, or helping clean Angelica Hearst's house and do her laundry because she just had baby number four from daddy number four and she's overwhelmed—bless her heart—we get it done Instagram-style.

Krisjen and I falter in our steps, laughing as we grab some more shirts and toss them to our future little sisters out there in the crowd.

"You see how drunk they are?" Krisjen says under her breath.

I follow her gaze, seeing her boyfriend, Milo Price, smiley and sweaty in his backward baseball cap and flushed cheeks, which is his tell that he'd had beer tonight.

Callum Ames stands next to him, grinning with his arms folded over his chest, watching me like something that's already his.

Maybe. I'll look good on his arm at the debutante ball, nevertheless.

I swipe my water bottle out from underneath the papier-mâché clown fish and take a swig, the burn already intoxicating as it courses down my throat. Just the taste eases my nerves.

"I'm going to kill him," Krisjen gripes.

"Wait until after the ball," I tell her. "You need a date."

Taking the bottle out of my hands, she throws back a swallow as I grab her shirts and toss them to waiting hands.

Music and laughter surround us, and the confetti gun shoots another bomb into the air—blue, pink, silver, and gold—fluttering like snow.

"God, that stuff is good." She hands me the bottle back. "Goes down like water."

"As long as you don't drink sixty-four ounces of this a day, got it?" I down another swallow and cap my new favorite brand of vodka, disguised in my Evian bottle.

She scrunches up her face in a smile, her apple cheeks perfect and her long chestnut hair in a messy bun on the top of her head. "What would I do without you?"

I chuckle. "The only thing any of us need is a little love"—I lean in, whispering—"from the right bottle."

She laughs, and we both hop down from the float, leaving Amy to handle it, while we join the girls in the last chorus of the dance.

My head floats a few feet above my neck, the "help" we just drank giving me just the right buzz that I'd sweat off in twenty minutes, but enough to put a spring in my step.

I'm so late. This parade is taking so much longer than I'd hoped, and Lavinia's will close soon. I dance faster as if that'll speed up the vehicles in front of us.

Callum and Milo follow, Callum's dark blond hair blowing in the breeze as I step and tease him with my eyes. Little girls cheer us on, looking up at me like I'm something special, while a couple guys hover close together, staring at me and whispering between them.

I move in ways our facilitator will certainly hear about on Monday, but I don't care. I rub in their face something they'll never get.

Because even at twelve, strutting down a pageant stage in a bikini, I knew what my power was. There's never been any confusion.

"We love you, Clay!" some of my classmates scream as I lead the group and finish the dance.

I close my eyes, soaking up all the phone cameras recording us and the pictures of Clay Collins that would survive long after I'm gone. Images that will show who I am far louder than I can ever say in words.

Homecoming queen.

Prom queen.

Omega Chi sweetheart, and something nice to look at.

That's me.

I open my eyes, immediately seeing myself in the window of a parked car at the curb. I bring up my hand, pushing the lock of blond hair back in place.

We all have to be something, I guess.

A re you sure you have to go?" Krisjen says from the back seat of Callum's Mustang. "Have you even slept the past twenty-four hours?"

I climb out of the passenger side seat and shoot her a look as Milo sits next to her, hanging his arm around her.

I slept last night. Minus a couple hours to finish readying the float.

I close the door and lean on the convertible, meeting Callum's blue eyes as he sits in the driver's seat. "Get her home safe?" I ask.

God knows, Milo's too dumb to do it.

"Maybe," he taunts.

"Then *maybe* I'll think about letting you take me to the light-house party." I swing my bag over my shoulder and dig inside, pulling out a wipe to clean the sparkly Greek letters off my cheeks.

He sits there, that confident gleam in his eyes like everyone wants to be near him, and he'll wait for me to realize that.

"Come here," he says.

Slowly, I lean in, giving him ninety, so he only has to give me ten and still look like the man. He kisses me, coming in again and again, his wet tongue grazing my bottom lip before he pulls back.

Holding back so I'll beg for more.

"You were amazing tonight, babe," Milo slurs, squeezing Kris-jen. "You both were."

I hold Callum's eyes as I stand upright again. "Thank you for coming."

"I think they liked it," he says. "You dancing for me."

Yeah, okay. I smile, backing away toward the dress shop.

He shifts the car into gear, takes off, and I spin around, wiping off my mouth.

I hate kissing. Wet and slobbery tongue like a damn slug flopping around my mouth.

I pull open the door to Lavinia's on the Avenue and stroll in, tossing the wipe out on the sidewalk behind me.

The streets of St. Carmen still buzz with foot traffic, cafés, and local hot spots swarming with people enjoying a quiet night with friends alfresco. The parade ended more than an hour ago, and even though it took us that long to get our gear cleaned up and Amy's father to get the float clear of the gridlock, I'm still not done for the day.

I walk into the boutique, gowns displayed on mannequins as I cross the white carpet and pass the reception desk, my mother sitting in the lounge area.

She spots me. "Talk tomorrow," she says into her phone.

"I'm here now," I tell her, knowing she's going to whine.

"I've been waiting over an hour." She rises from the white-cushioned, high-back chair and sticks her phone into her handbag. "Call next time."

I chuckle under my breath as I keep walking and she follows. "Like I can control how fast the parade moves," I mumble.

Her chunky gold-and-pearl bracelet jingles as she enters the dressing area behind me, and I set my bag down next to the chair near the floor-length mirrors. I glance at her in the reflection, noticing my gold necklace draped across her tanned chest, visible in her flowing, deep V-neck blouse.

Coiffed golden hair, perfectly tailored black slacks that hug her three-spinning-classes-a-week ass, and squeaky clean, right down to her trimmed cuticles. My mother's body hasn't seen a carb other than champagne in at least twelve years. Pretty sure it's in cryofreeze at this point, simply relying on eggs and hair spray to animate.

In ten minutes, I'm on the riser in front of the mirror and wearing the debutante gown my mother had designed for me.

"Oh, Lavinia," she says, holding her hands to her cheeks as she circles me. "You've outdone yourself. It's exquisite. I love it. The detail . . ."

I look away from my image in the mirror, clenching my jaw as hard as I can to contain myself.

My mother rushes up to me as the older lady remains back, taking in her work and looking for any final fixes.

"Clay?" my mom urges me. "What do you think?"

I look down at her, struggling to keep my emotions from bubbling up my throat. I fold my lips between my teeth, about to burst. She doesn't care what I think. She wants me to lie.

"It's, um . . ." I choke on the words, a snort escaping. "It's so beautiful. I'm speechless."

And I can't do it anymore. Laughter pours out of me as I take in the big, fat hoopskirt monstrosity in the mirror that makes me look like Scarlett fucking O'Hara, complete with puffed sleeves and some dumbass ruffle around the waist. I'm tempted to look for the stains of Lavinia's tears of laughter all over the dress as she sewed this bullshit.

I hunch over, my stomach tight as I try to rein it in.

My mother glares at me.

"I'm sorry," I gasp, fanning myself. "My emotions are running wild. I've waited so long for this." I plant my hand to my heart, recovering. "Lavinia, can you bring me some gloves and a pearl necklace? I need the whole picture. I'm so excited. Thank you."

The corners of her eyes crinkle with a tight smile, but she nods, quickly leaving the room to fetch the accessories.

It's not technically her fault. My mother approved the design.

The two of us alone, my mother steps up on the riser in front of me and twists the bodice, jerking it until it's straight.

"I thought for sure I'd look like a cupcake," I tell her, trying to catch her eyes. "Now, I almost *wish* I could say that I looked like a cupcake. You know that white stuff that spills out of a heroin addict's mouth when they're overdosing? That's what I look like."

She meets my eyes, her blue slightly paler than mine as she continues to yank at the dress. "You chose your homecoming gown," she points out. "And you'll choose your prom dress. The debutante ball is mine."

I knew I should've gotten this over with two years ago when she wanted me to.

My body jerks as she situates the dress on me, and I stare over her shoulder and into the mirror. The back of her blond head can easily be me in twenty years.

"You won't be able to tell me from everyone else," I say, coming as close as I can to begging her.

Every other debutante will be wearing white, and while the fabric is rather pretty on mine—lacy with pearl accents—the design is embarrassing. All the debutante dresses reek of Stepford.

"That's kind of the point," my mom says. "Tradition. Solidarity. Community. Unity. You're coming out as a member of society, and a society functions on standards." She smooths her hands down the fabric, pressing out any wrinkles. "You need to learn that rocking the boat puts everyone onboard in danger."

But that's what boats are built for.

I sigh, not sure why I decided to let her have this one. I get my way because my mother picks her battles, and any battle with me that lasts more than three minutes is too much effort.

I could fight her on it. Maybe I still will.

"Do you need a Valium or something?" she asks.

I laugh under my breath and look away. Gigi Collins, everyone. Chairwoman, socialite, and school board president.

She puffs my sleeves, and then presses a hand to my stomach. "Hmm."

"What?"

She purses her lips and walks around me, inspecting. "I was going to have her take it down to a four, but a six is already a squeeze, isn't it?"

Heat spreads down my skin, and I clench my jaw.

Her phone rings from her bag on the chair, and she heads for it, waving me off. "We'll leave it, I guess."

Picking up her bag, she digs out her phone and answers it, walking past me and leaving the room.

I rub my eyes, listening to her chatter out in the waiting area about whether or not we should have a crêpe station for my school's Easter brunch in two months.

Looking up, I stare at my huge skirt in the mirror, bored with this entire look that'll live forever and come back to haunt the shit out of me in years to come.

I don't want my daughter to laugh when she sees pictures.

I lift up the skirt, cringing at the white stockings and fugly satin heels, and then I spin, taking in the back of my gown and the obnoxious corset lacing that should really be buttons instead.

God, I should've taken that Valium. Why the hell do I want to make her happy when she's out to hurt my feelings like this?

But I know why. In a few months, I'll be off to college. Away from everything. Graduating. Gone.

Everyone will be leaving. *Everyone* . . .

Standing straight and tall, I face the mirrors again, but then a door slams shut somewhere in the shop, and I freeze.

It wasn't the front door. That door has a bell over it. This was the rear one—heavy and thick—the click of the latch so loud I can hear it from here.

My heart beats faster, and in a moment, her eyes on my back warm my skin.

Everyone . . .

I look up, meeting Olivia Jaeger's eyes as she leans against the archway leading into the dressing room, staring at me.

And all of a sudden, my skin is too hot.

She holds canvas bags stuffed with tulle and ribbon, her aviators sitting on top of her head as she clearly struggles to hold back her amusement.

Her shift ended over an hour ago. I thought she was gone for the night.

"Come here," I tell her.

She loses the bags and comes around my front, facing me. I gaze down at my classmate, my teammate, and the only thing I ever look forward to anymore.

"Pin the hem," I order her. "It's still dragging, so bring it up another quarter of an inch."

Hands on her hips, she hesitates like it's a choice, and then drops to her knees, pulling a pin off the cushion secured to her wrist.

But before she grabs the dress, I pull it away from her. "Wash your hands first."

I shake my head as she shoots me a look. I mean, really. If she's learned anything crossing the tracks into St. Carmen every day to attend one of the most prestigious schools in the state the past three and a half years, it should be some common sense. They certainly teach that at Marymount.

Rising, she walks over to the round table and pulls a wipe out of the package, cleaning her fingers. The Jaegers were born with grease under their nails, so better to be safe than sorry.

In addition to mowing the lawns and trimming the hedges of St. Carmen, her brothers also partially own a dump of a restaurant in their neck of the woods, sell drugs, fix cars and motorcycles, and dabble in loan-sharking.

Okay, maybe the "sell drugs" part is only a rumor. The whole family is sketchy, though. Especially with the power they wield as the unofficial patrons of Sanoa Bay, their hidden little community in the swamps.

Tryst Six, they're called. There are six siblings, and I can only assume the *Tryst* part comes from their mother, Trysta. They even have an adorable little logo. Insert eye roll.

Approaching me again, Olivia drops down, blowing the lock of hair that came loose from her ponytail out of her face, and folds the hem, pinning it up.

The hair falls back in her face, and my fingers tap my leg, fighting the urge to move the lock behind her ear for her.

"Hurry up," I tell her.

I tip my head back and smooth my own hair into a fist high on the top of my head, twirling it into a bun and holding it there. I check myself in the mirror.

Her fingers tug gently at the fabric as she moves to the next spot, and my heart beats harder, every pore on my body cooling with a sudden sweat.

I let my eyes fall again, watching her at my feet.

Her jean shorts. The dusky olive skin of her toned legs glowing in the light of the chandelier. I trail my gaze over her messy jet-black ponytail and the red tint of her lips as she bites the bottom one, concentrating on her task. Her black-and-white-checkered flannel flaps open, and I pause at the low V of her gray T-shirt underneath as it dips between the smooth, poreless skin of her chest.

I tip my chin up, looking in the mirror again. Is she even wearing a bra, for Christ's sake?

She lifts up my skirt to just past my ankles and steals a peek. "You should lose the stockings," she tells me, going back to pinning. "And the shoes, too, for that matter."

I turn a little, jutting out my shoulder and trying to decide if the dress looks better with my hair up or down. "Imagine what the world would have to come to for me to take fashion advice from a white trash, rug-sucking, swamp rat like you," I reply.

Her black leather calf-high boots are kind of cute and all, but I'm pretty sure everything she's wearing is whatever she could scrounge up from someone's hand-me-downs.

I feel her eyes on me, and I look down, seeing a little gleam in them. Kind of amused, but mostly a warning that she's making a mental note of all the shit I say to her for a rainy day.

I'm shakin', Liv. Really, I am.

"If I take off the stockings," I explain, "I won't be properly dressed. The women in my world are ladies, Olivia."

"You'll feel it on your legs, though." She looks back down to her task. "It'll change how you carry yourself."

"What will? The sticky, noxious sweat of Florida in springtime on my naked thighs?"

The debutante ball is in late April. The humidity will be a nightmare, despite the air-conditioned banquet hall hosting it. Like she knows anything.

"Afraid I might be right?" she taunts.

I roll my eyes. *Please.* The only thing I'm afraid of is wasting time.

But I stand there, letting my hair fall down my back again, and watch her. I'm not sure why, but I kick off my heel and set the ball of my foot on her knee.

Prove it, then.

Tipping her head back, she looks up at me, her honey-brown eyes unblinking.

"I can't bend over in this dress," I tell her.

Fisting the skirt in my hands, I start to pull it up, past my knees, and up my thighs to where the garter secures the stockings.

She holds my gaze for another moment, and then she reaches up, unfastening the clips.

Her fingertips brush the skin on the inside of my leg, and my flesh pebbles, chills breaking out everywhere. I draw in a sharp breath, and she darts her eyes up to mine, as still as me.

"I don't have all day," I chide, trying to hide my reaction.

Her chest rises and falls slowly, and then she peels the stocking down my leg and off my foot, followed by the other one, both of my shoes lying strewn on the floor with the nylons.

Walking to a nearby shelf, she scans the heels and grabs a pair, pointing to the chair near the mirror.

Indulging her, I step off the riser and have a seat as she plops down on the floor and searches for my right foot under the dress.

I hike up the skirt again as she slips the heel on, almost amused that she refuses to look. I know she wants to. My legs are one of my best attributes. She's looked at them before.

It's amazing she's endured me as captain of the lacrosse team this year, especially when she's probably the better player, and I haven't made anything easy on her.

But that's how it is. Effort, focus, hard work . . . they mean very little when you're lucky like me. Saints don't mix with swamp trash, and while Reva Coomer may be the coach, I'm the leader. Everyone follows me.

I gaze at her as she straps the heels on me, the tiny mole on her face, between her ear and the hollow of her cheek, bringing out the gold in her skin. I've never noticed that before.

She puts my foot back down, and I draw in a breath, standing up and heading back to the riser again. The dress rubs against the sensitive skin of my legs, now bare, and it's as if every inch of my body is alive and aware of itself.

Almost like I'm naked in my bed, only feeling the sheets.

Holding up my skirt, I look in the mirror, the gold heels with the thin jeweled straps making my skin glow, and I fight not to smile, because they feel and look worlds better than the other shoes.

However . . .

"They don't go with the dress," I tell her.

But I'm hardly surprised she's so bad at this, given the shit she wears.

I reach around my back, trying to untie the corset.

"You're right," she says. "You need a new dress now."

I almost snort. Well, we agree on that.

Unable to reach the laces, because the corset is too tight for me to move, I twist around, planting my hands on my hips.

"Unlace it."

She steps up, pulling the bow and loosening the corset, so I can push it down and off my body.

"Tell Lavinia to call me when the alterations are done," I instruct, "and tell her to take it down a size."

"It fits you perfectly."

"To a four, please," I snip as I pick the dress up off the floor. "And remove this flower." I grab the one at the center of the bodice. "Are we repurposing wedding dresses from 1982 or something?"

But she's not paying attention. She stands back and stares at me, and when she turns and checks my reflection in the mirror, I follow her gaze.

The simple hoop skirt wraps around me, thin and absent of bows and ruffles and lace, while the strapless white bustier hugs my breasts almost too tightly and covers my stomach, leaving an inch of skin between that and my skirt.

If it weren't obvious that they were undergarments, they might be kind of hot.

"I could make it for you," she says. "But better."

She moves in, placing a hand on my tummy, and I ignore the skip in my heart.

"Maybe a little see-through here with some embroidery," she explains, "piece them together and add some layering to give it dimension. Tighten up the bodice with some light and subtle gold and pink accents to complement the shoes . . ."

I envision it in my head as we look at me in the mirror.

For some reason, I have no doubt she'll pull it off if I let her, and I'd even love it.

If I let her.

She turns her eyes on me again, standing in front of me and looking up and down my attire. "We can keep it this same shade of white. It's a perfect color, really." She meets my eyes, looking at me dead-on. "You won't even see the cum stain when he drunk-ejacs all over you in the back seat of the car after the ball," she says.

The ever-present knot in my stomach pulls tighter, and I hold her gaze, unfaltering. *Excuse me?*

"Because ladies in your world don't talk about those things." A smile curls the corner of her mouth as she inches in, whispering, "You just go home in tears and do things with a pulsating shower-head that God didn't intend for sweet, little southern girls to do, right?"

My blood runs ice cold, and I grit my teeth, the heat of her breath an inch away, falling across my lips as I curl my fingers into fists.

"Try it tonight," she says, staring at my mouth. "You might like it."

She snatches the dress out of my hand, and I suck in a breath as I watch her not miss a beat as she steps backward off the riser and leaves.

God, I hate her. I watch her disappear, no comeback or witty response spilling out of my mouth before she's gone, and I'm left standing there and feeling stupid.

Drunk-ejacs . . . Is she serious? I don't even have a detachable showerhead.

I raise my eyes to the mirror again, the excitement I want to feel for the ball or the prom or anything coming out as nothing but a hard beat in my chest that makes me sick instead. And it's almost like she knows that. Like she knows something's wrong.

Liv Jaeger has been a bloody nuisance since the day I met her, but sometimes I'm not even sure what bugs me so much about her. She stays in her lane, doesn't she?

But I love pushing her. I love it like nothing else.

Tearing off the undergarments and kicking them to the side, I dig in my bag for the Valium and tap out two pills into my hand. Throwing my head back, I pop them into my mouth and dry swallow before quickly dressing.

I have to get out of here.

Pulling my gray hoodie out of my bag, I slip it on and take my gear, creeping out to the lobby. My mom stands out front on the sidewalk, conversing rather robustly on the phone still. Someone must not be down with the whole crêpe idea, I guess.

I sneak out through the back, pushing through the alley door, and don't see Lavinia or Liv as I make my escape.

Pulling out my Evian bottle, I finish off the rest of the vodka, tossing it into a dumpster as I pass.

I hate her. The ball will be special. I'll have fun. This is who I am. I'm lucky.

I inhale, filling my lungs as I pull my hood up and put my head down, moving through the dark streets. I turn off my phone so my mom can't track me, and tuck my hands in my center pocket.

I cross Bainbridge Park, spotting a couple of guys loitering by the bathrooms. The skateboarder who sells smack nods to me, and I nod back, passing him. I head down the hill to Edward Street.

Stopping in front of the large, cream-colored stucco house decorated like a cottage, I look around and see the empty, dim street, lit only by lamplight. No cars drive through the neighborhood. All the families inside their homes.

Pulling my hood lower, I sneak around the side of the house, see the basement light on, and squat down, pushing open one of the windows, slipping inside before I'm spotted.

I step down, the freezers cooling the room making chills break out across my legs, and my nostrils instantly sting at the scent of the cleaning liquids used in here regularly.

I rub my thumb over the small tattoo on the inside of my finger, feeling like I'm exhaling for the first time all day. It's weird how that smell has become a comfort. Thanks to fantastic ventilation and industrial-strength deodorizers, I wouldn't even know there was a "decomp" in the cooler right now if I hadn't been here when he arrived a couple days ago.

I walk over to the table at the end of the row, feeling my heart start to hammer in my chest. A girl lies on the slab, her midsection covered with a sheet, and the puncture mark from embalming sits right below the rope burn around her neck. I'd read about her online today. Figured she'd be here by now.

Her wet red hair mats to her head, and I grip the side of the table, brushing her fingers. Her nails are covered in chipped pink nail polish that looks like a cheap brand you get at the grocery store.

"Did you know her?" I hear someone ask.

I don't have to turn around to recognize Sylvia Gates's voice. Owner of Wind House, the only funeral home in town.

I gaze at the girl's neck, swallowing the image of the moment she slipped the rope around it.

And what most likely drove her to it.

"She went to public school." I force my voice firm. "But I've seen her around town."

She's almost my age—a year younger, I think. *Did Liv know her?*

Mrs. Gates walks around the other side of the table, clean scrubs on. "You don't have to be here, Clay."

She's worried I'll get triggered, and then she'll have to explain to my parents why she lets me sneak in here at least once a week.

Fuck it. I don't want to be home, so . . . I pull off my hood and tie my hair back into a ponytail, ready to work as I draw in a deep breath and exhale.

I'll have to fix the nail polish. I'd love to change it altogether, but if she has it on, she must've liked it, so I suppose I should honor her style. I'm sure I have something equally hideous in my collection from when I was twelve that I can use.

I push up my sleeves and get to work, feeling my heart calm down again as I busy myself. But my thoughts still linger on *her*. What would Olivia Jaeger say if she saw me now?

Maybe it would be the one time she couldn't say anything.

Sometimes I feel like I want her to know me. Sometimes I don't want her to know anything *but* me.

And other times, I'm glad she doesn't have a clue.

2

Olivia

I climb off the back of the bike and unfasten the strap under my chin. "Thanks," I tell Iron.

I dump the helmet between my brother's legs, but he just sucks in a drag from his cigarette, looking around me—past me, beyond me—with his lids half hooded.

I clutch my backpack straps. "What?"

He hesitates a moment, looks down, and then shakes his head as he takes another puff. "I only approve of Macon paying for this place because I knew you wouldn't be interested in the guys ogling the short skirts."

The scent of the dogwoods lining the walkway up to the school wafts in the morning breeze, and although it's only March, I can tell they're about to bloom. The wind sweeps through the plumeria already decorating the campus, and students move across the circular driveway, while others climb out of cars dropping them off for various sports or club meetings before school.

Chills spread up my bare legs from the rare bite in the air. Rain is coming. "What about *women* checking me out?" I tease. "Worried about them?"

"Strangely, no." He looks amused. "They can't get you pregnant."

I scoff, looking right, and see a few students heading down the sidewalk toward us and the front of the school.

Clay Collins meets my eyes as she passes with her gray Fjäll-räven backpack, little pink octopuses drawn on the front pocket, and she tries so hard to look bored and intolerant. But the mischief playing on her lips warns me she had a lot of fun in the dress shop last night. We're not done.

We're never done.

Her gaze flicks to Iron, and I turn back to him, seeing his eyes lock on her as well, as he smokes the last of his cigarette. But whereas he's well aware of the shit she throws my way, he looks like he's entertaining ideas of all the things he could do with her in a dark room.

Or a back seat. Idiot.

"You approve of Macon paying for this place," I say, "so you can ogle Catholic girls in their short skirts when you drop me off every day."

"She has to be eighteen by now, right?"

I shake my head. "Hallmark Christmas movie heroines aren't your type."

"Everyone is my type when they're naked."

Gross. I back away, flipping him the middle finger. "See you after school."

But he shakes his head, stopping me. "Nope. Come here." He flicks his cigarette, the butt still burning as it lies in the school drive. "This could be it."

He holds out his arm, a warm, cocky smile on his mouth.

I sigh, half rolling my eyes before I come back in and embrace him.

This could be it. The Jaeger family creed. The Tryst Six warning, however you want to look at it.

Our parents' passing came as so great a shock that we make it a point to remind ourselves not to fight with each other now.

Not to waste time.

Not to leave anything unsaid.

This could be it. The last time we see each other.

"Be careful," I murmur in his ear, dropping my eyes to the tattoo on his neck. It's the same symbol that hangs on our wall at home in the garage and that adorns the leather bracelet all the Jaegers wear. A snake wrapped around an hourglass.

He holds me tight for another moment and then releases me. "You, too."

A look, a smile, and then he's off without a helmet on his head and his scab-marked elbows hanging out of his black T-shirt from the last time he rolled his motorcycle. I watch him until he pulls out of the driveway, turns right, and disappears down the street.

"Hi, Liv," someone calls.

I glance to see Maria Hoff walking past as I fit my earbuds into my ears.

I grunt and fall in line with the few other students making their way into the school. She's only being nice to me because there was a suicide with a public school student a couple days ago. Allison Carpenter—Alli for short. Everyone here seems to think every gay person knows each other, so she probably thinks I lost a friend.

I knew of Alli—small town and all—but I didn't know her. It was still awful what happened, though. And it happens too often.

But not to me. I'm almost done surviving them. Just a few more months.

I enter through the front doors, heading down the hallway. "¿Qué te gusta hacer?" I repeat with my Rosetta Stone app. "¿Qué te gusta hacer?" I push my tongue behind my teeth, trying to form the syllables with a pronunciation to match the voice on my phone. "Te . . . gusta . . . ?"

Damn Aracely. The next time some ex of my brother's calls me shit in Spanish, I want to know what they're saying. I guess I should be speaking it already. I'm one-fourth Cuban.

Or maybe an eighth, I'm not sure. The only thing my family prides themselves on is the other fourth—or eighth—of Seminole blood that keeps us on our land.

Blood that also came in handy when I applied to Marymount four years ago. A little diversity looks good on the school's yearly accountability reports, and even shaved a little tuition cost off for me when I won their scholarship.

I mean, I guess I didn't *win* it. I was the only one who applied for it, but still.

I breeze past my locker, around the corner, and push through the door to the women's locker room.

"¿Cual es son tu pasatiempos?" I repeat, opening my gym locker and hanging my backpack inside. I pull out my school skirt and black Polo, shaking out the wrinkles, and hang them on the hook inside, feeling the girls around me turn to quickly pull on their workout gear and cover themselves.

I'd learned a long time ago, even before Clay's mother and the rest of the school board forked over fifty grand for a complete re-model of the locker room showers to give us all private stalls "in the best interest of everyone," that it was best to just come up with a routine that put me in these situations as little as possible. I come to school in my leggings and tank top on workout days. I change in a stall after school before practices. I go home in my dirty gear afterward and shower there.

"¿Cual es son tu pasatiempos?" I say again, trying to act oblivious to the eyes on me ready and waiting to report to Father Mc-Nealty if I ogle their bodies like some hypersexual pervert.

I slip off my jacket and slide my phone into the leggings pocket on the side of my thigh before closing my locker.

"Tu pasa . . ." I enunciate my vowels to myself and make my way to the weight room.

School starts in an hour, but lacrosse has workouts on Mondays and Wednesdays. The football team is done for the year, the basketball team and baseball teams have the room on Tuesdays and Thursdays, and the swim team does most of their workouts in the pool.

Someone pops up to my side as I move past the showers. "Thin Mint?" she asks, and shoves a silver roll of cookies into my face.

I scowl, barely looking up to see Becks next to me. "That's not breakfast."

Of course, I hadn't had any yet, but I was pretty sure eating nothing was better than eating shit when I was about to work out.

"Come on. It can't be any worse than donuts. I mean, who decided what breakfast food should be breakfast food anyway?" Becks grabs two towels from the stand and tosses me one. "I mean, maybe ham doesn't go with eggs. Maybe eight Thin Mints is the same amount of carbs you'd find in a glass of orange juice. Maybe cereal was invented as a nighttime treat, but they cleverly decided, 'Hey, this is perfect for breakfast when people are in a hurry.'"

I cock an eyebrow. "Cereal was invented because John Harvey Kellogg believed Corn Flakes would stop Americans from sinning and masturbating."

Her laugh quickly turns to choking as she swallows down the wrong hole and coughs to clear her throat.

"H-how do you know that?" she asks, still laughing.

I shrug. "This is a really good school."

Her chest shakes as she laughs harder, and I slam the locker room door open. "Come on," I tell her. "We're already late."

And the coach isn't the one keeping time, either. The last thing I need this morning is a supersize cunt convo with our team captain. I had my dose last night.

Heading into the weight room, I hear the sounds of barbells clanging and weights dropping, and I snatch one of Becks's Thin Mints and stuff it into my mouth. She smiles and veers left, tossing the still half-full package into the trash can as I move ahead, down the center aisle, and toward the elliptical.

"¿Cual es son tu pasa . . . tiempos?" I mumble to myself, feeling eyes on me, but I refuse to look. "¿Tiempos?"

I jump on the machine, purposely not making eye contact with anyone, other than to check Becks and watch her pick up some baby weights in front of the mirrors, only actually completing three or four reps before she takes a selfie or starts talking to someone. She's gotten messed with on account of me from time to time, and I like to make sure I know when that's happening.

She would be a good friend if we had anything in common.

For now, we enjoy a camaraderie—the types of friends who navigate toward each other when our real friends aren't around. When there's a party and we need someone to talk to. Or someone to eat lunch with.

We don't call each other or text, but I'm glad I have her and a few like-minded individuals who make this place a little more bearable. Becks has money, but she doesn't use it as a shield to fling mud like Clay Collins and her friends.

After thirty minutes of cardio and moving through three more Spanish lessons, I walk over to a weight machine, adjust the notch for forty pounds, and pull down the bar behind me, working my shoulders.

"It's not hot yet," I hear someone say behind me. "But it will be."

I tap my earbuds, trying to initiate the next lesson. Did it pause? No sound comes through.

"None of those dresses are hot," Krisjen Conroy says. "I would've burned mine if it wasn't an heirloom."

"Heirloom or not, I'll burn the damn thing before Gigi Collins tries to force it on my daughter someday."

Clay. And that awful debutante gown I'd love to burn for her, but it was ever-so-amusing to see her trussed up in it last night.

"Is Callum escorting you?" Amy Chandler asks her.

"Someone has to."

I shake my head a little, like that will drown out their voices, tapping my earbuds again. What the hell?

"Come on," Krisjen says. "He likes you."

"And you're about to go off to college," Amy pants as she runs. "Live it up."

I tighten my fists around the bar, my arms wide as I bring it down slowly and then back up.

"I'll live it up," Clay says in a low voice, taunting, "with someone who makes sure the only way I can leave his bed when he's done with me is by crawling. Someone with a chest like a brick wall, and a cock, not a weewee."

A laugh bubbles up from my chest, but I stifle it quickly. I hate her, and I hate that I laugh at her sense of humor, but I also hate her boytoy, Callum, and the joke was at his expense, so I'm excused. My jaw relaxes.

Amy continues the fantasy. "Someone who smells like a sea god and is named . . ."

"Gabriel," Clay adds.

"Gabriel." Krisjen sighs, sounding dreamy.

"But 'Gabriel' wants an experienced woman," Amy warns her.

"Gabriel doesn't want to break me of another man's lousy technique," Clay fires back. "He'll teach me everything."

My teammates laugh at each other, and I just roll my eyes as I head for the chest press and lie back on the bench.

This Gabriel sounds like a gem. He'll make her into a real woman and teach the fragile little damsel how to take her man with silence and a smile. *God, she's pathetic.*

A picture of Clay Collins, naked and willing as she wraps her arms and legs around some beefy, sweaty, misogynistic shit-for-brains plays in my head, and I suddenly feel like I have hair on my tongue.

Without thinking, I lower my eyes from the ceiling, looking

straight over at her. Her blue eyes are already on me as she runs on the treadmill.

Why is she staring? Strands of loose blond hair bounce against her face, her skin glowing with a light layer of sweat, and for a moment, I can't move.

For a moment, she's beautiful.

"¿Cual es son tu pasatiempos?" a voice rings in my ears.

I startle, realizing the earbuds have kicked back on and my tutorial has continued. The pain in my arms blares, and I still have the barbell suspended above me, and I don't know how long it's been there.

I clear my throat, swallow, and bring the weights down and then quickly push back up as a cool sweat covers my back.

"¿ . . . Cual es son tu pasa . . . tiempos?" I mutter, trying to get my head back on track. "Ti-emp-os."

"What are you doing?"

I look up, pausing only a moment when I see it's Megan Martelle. She smiles down at me, a clipboard in one hand and her blond ponytail more white than Clay's golden. She assists in the P.E. department, having graduated last year; but for some reason, she remains part of the eighteen percent of Marymount graduates who don't advance to the Ivy League.

She still has time, though. Only nineteen and lots of people take a gap year.

I continue my rep, blowing out my mouth. "Trying to learn Spanish."

"All by yourself?"

"Yeah, why not?"

She cocks her head, studying me, and I don't know if it's the way her eyes linger or the smile she tries to hold back, but I drop my gaze, awareness prickling my skin.

"Yeah," she finally says. "Why not, I guess?"

Setting her clipboard down, she moves around behind me,

placing an underhanded grip on the bar for support. "Can I offer a suggestion?"

I meet her eyes, still aware of Clay's presence ten feet away.

"Widen your grip," she tells me, holding the bar as I push my fists out until they touch the weights. "And straighten out your wrists. You're putting too much pressure on them."

I do as she says, conversations going off around the room as I lower the bar again and raise it back up.

"Hurt a little more now?" she teases, looking down at me.

I nod. "Yeah."

"Good."

I keep going as she walks around me again, and then I feel her palm on my stomach. I warm under my skin.

"Press the small of your back into the bench, Liv," she instructs.

Her gentle hand makes my breath hitch.

"Feel that?" she asks, pressing harder as my back hits the bench. "It'll work your abs while you work your chest."

"Thanks."

And sure enough, I start to feel the burn in my tummy as I continue my reps.

Taking up position behind me again, she spots me as I lower the bar and push it back up, her perfume tickling my nose, and it's not at all unpleasant.

Footsteps still pound the treadmills, a constant thrumming in the background, and I suck in air, filling my stomach, before exhaling nice and slow. My body burns, my stomach cools with sweat, and I can feel a trickle between my breasts in my sports bra.

"I think it's great you're learning a new language," she says.

I look up at her, not stopping. "My brother's ex likes to yell at me in Spanish. I want to know what the bitch is saying."

She smiles, breathing out a laugh, and I drop my gaze to her plump, pink lips. They look like gum.

Her arms lower with me, and she presses down, holding me there. "Keep it down."

I hover the bar a couple inches above my chest, my elbows locked at a ninety-degree angle.

"Is that okay?" She raises her eyebrows in concern.

I nod, my muscles screaming a little. "Yeah."

Finally, she releases me, and I continue, raising the bar again.

"So many people our age don't have any ambition to grow," she says in a low voice, her eyes on my movements. "To keep learning."

She cocks her head again, meeting my eyes with a smile in hers, and there's something too soft in the way she gazes at me, and I'm pretty sure she wants my phone number.

The idea might be worth entertaining. She's pretty, and maybe I'm attracted to her.

I study her face, taking a moment. *Yeah. I'm attracted.*

But I'm also graduating in a few months. The last thing I need is to form an attachment. I've gotten through almost four years here without finding a reason to stay, even if I am somewhat intrigued by her.

I knew her when she was a student, after all. She was popular. Kind. Quiet. We spoke rarely, but things changed this year when she took the job here. All her friends are gone to college, and she seems to be looking for new ones. Without her comfortable alliances around, she's started to show other sides of herself. She's nice.

But there's something missing inside her. I don't know what it is.

Or maybe there's everything right about her and something missing inside me. I can't help it. I like crazy. She can be fire or ice, I don't care, I just need her to be one of them. And even better if it's both.

Something flies past us, splashing against the mirrors behind Megan, and water flies everywhere. I wince, drops hitting my hair, and I turn my face away, releasing the bar back to the power rack. Megan gasps. What the hell?

A water bottle falls into the tin garbage can, and I look down, seeing cool water droplets on my arm.

My heart leaps into my throat, and I turn my head, seeing Clay Collins approach.

She glares at Megan. "You're not *our age*," Clay corrects her. Then she picks up Megan's clipboard and tosses it at her. "We'll let you know when it's time to carry our shit onto the field this afternoon."

I stay lying on the bench, not budging from my back as I watch her work, almost amused as I take in her little power play.

Megan was a senior when we were juniors. An upperclassman. She's also one of our coaches. Does Clay take any of this into account before attacking? Not even a little.

Megan hesitates for a moment, probably gauging whether or not it's worth it to even try to report Clay's behavior. But in the end, she realizes, like we all do, that Clay might be a spoiled brat, but she's good at the long game. It's better to just hope this tantrum is the end of it, instead of enticing further retaliation.

Megan leaves, her wet ponytail dangling behind her, but she spares a glance back at me, a small, soft smile on her lips before she disappears through the doors.

Then I turn my gaze to Clay.

"What the fuck are you smiling at?" she asks me. "Your team spots you. Is that clear?"

I scoff as I sit up, grab my towel, and rise, meeting her eyes two inches from my face. "I wouldn't let you spot me a quarter for charity."

She may be my team captain, but the bitch has never had my back.

Becks lets a laugh escape from behind Clay, Clay's scowl hardening like she just made a promise in her head.

But I don't even blink as I slip around her and leave.

I know I should just lie low. Only four months left and all.

But as the home stretch shortens more every day, I care less and less.

Maybe I want to see if she has anything left up her sleeves.

I dare her.

I really do dare her.

I hurry down the aisle of the school's theater and push through the door. I dump my backpack against the wall, my blue-and-black plaid skirt brushing against my thighs as I break into a jog.

Jeremy Boxer and Adam Sorretti carry armfuls of wood and fabric, and a couple gallons of paint dangle from their fingers as I push past them and make for the cast list that I already see hanging on the bulletin board.

My heart races. *Come on.* The last eight hours of school, practice, and waiting were torture, but I'll be high as a kite for the rest of my life if one thing goes my way in the next two seconds.

I press my palm to the board to stop myself as I move my index finger down the list, not looking for my name first.

I stop, seeing *Mercutio,* and slide right, hoping but already knowing before I even see it.

Callum Ames.

I drop my arm, fighting the urge to cry as I stare at the roster and exhale hard. I trace the line from Mercutio to Callum three more times with just my eyes to make sure before it even occurs to me to scan the sheet for my name to see if I was cast in anything at all, despite losing the role I wanted.

And there I am. *Nurse* . . . . *Olivia Jaeger.*

I shake my head and turn away, holding back only a moment. *Fuck you.* I shoot off, my disappointment morphing into anger that I know won't do me any good, but I'm not letting her off the hook this time. I throw open Ms. Lambert's office door, finding it empty, and then stalk farther down the hall, step backstage, and see her leaning over a drafting table, sifting through designs.

I move around the table, standing opposite her. "Four years," I bite out, picking up at exactly where we left off the last time the theater director and I had this conversation.

She looks up at me, her short brown hair tucked behind her ears.

I continue. "Nearly four years of set designs and sewing costumes and completing whatever other menial task you asked of me," I tell her. "I've spent more time here than I have with my family."

"You got a part."

"The nurse?" I practically spit out.

"You didn't want Juliet."

"Romeo wouldn't have wanted Juliet if he'd spent more than one dance with her before marrying her!"

I'm yelling at a teacher, but I'm around her more than anyone, so I know she'll let me off the hook like a mom who still loves you even when you fuck up.

I grip the drafting table on both sides, drilling into her eyes with mine. "Mercutio is the most dynamic character in the play. To be able to reimagine him, I mean . . ."

And I trail off, not seeing the point in saying what I've said before. The opportunity to reinvent him would be a dream come true. What the hell could Callum Ames do other than look good in a codpiece? And even that's debatable.

She rolls her blueprints. "The administration won't allow a female to play a male's role."

"Why not? They spent hundreds of years playing ours."

She gives me a look like I'm not helping, and then heads over to another worktable.

I follow. "He's a skeptic, he's crude, he's hotheaded . . . He's the only one with potential for growth."

She laughs to herself. "A skeptic . . ."

Yes, a skeptic. I realize that's not fashionable in a Catholic school, but I think she's caught on to the fact that if it's "in," then I'm "out."

"Please," I ask, a vulnerability to my tone that I hate hearing from myself.

"No," she replies.

"I deserve this."

"No."

I stand there, watching her as she closes her laptop and gathers her travel mug and bags.

I can't play the nurse. I don't care if my part is small. It's not that.

But I know what I can do, and I'd put in my time. I know what I'm worth.

"Did you even ask them?" I charge.

Does the administration even know the opportunity I'd like?

She stops and looks up, straightening. The soft look in her eyes tells me she wants to make me happy, but . . .

She won't fight for me.

"No reimagined sets," she reiterates. "No reimagined costumes. No Mercutio."

She leaves, and I stand there, not frozen—just too tired to move. I wish she was telling the truth. I wish the administration really didn't have money for a *Romeo and Juliet* makeover, and really did hate the idea of a female Mercutio.

But I know what I know. The problem isn't my ideas. It's me. I've been the grunt backstage my entire high school career—paying my dues and showing them that no matter how dissenting the piercings on my ears, or how many times my family name is in the Police Beat section of the newspaper—

I want to be here. I will be here every day for as long as she needs me.

I love the theater. I want to be a part of that world onstage. I've put in my time—sewing costumes, building sets, being her right hand during auditions and rehearsals, and literally being the axis around which everything else spins on performance nights.

You need something pinned? Come here.

You forgot a line? Okay, which part do you play? I know them all.

Dorothy's almost up and she's missing? I saw her making out with the Tin Man in the wings. I'll go grab her.

I've pushed a wheelbarrow around in the background of *Fiddler on the Roof* and almost had actual lines as an understudy for North Winston when she played Miss Scarlet in *Clue*, but I'm kind of glad that never panned out. I wanted Mrs. White anyway.

Romeo and Juliet is my last chance—*was* my last chance—to prove what I can do before I'm inevitably rejected by the theater department at Dartmouth.

I hear the heavy stage door slam shut, the last few members of the crew clearing out, the only sound in the entire theater being the ever-present movement of the air-conditioning in the ducts above.

My phone is in my bag. I should call Iron to pick me up, but I'm not ready to go home yet.

Heading offstage, I wander down the hall, not really knowing where I'm going until I see the racks of costumes pulled from storage that sit outside the dressing rooms. Repairs need to be made, as well as some alterations for the actors wearing them this year, but I can't help sifting through the clothes, pushing each hanger to the left as I take in the same tired old shit. It isn't like my ideas are all that new, either. *Romeo and Juliet* has been re-adapted several times in *West Side Story, China Girl* . . .

Would Leonardo DiCaprio's version have been number one at the box office opening weekend if he'd been in tights?

Okay, perhaps, but the genius of that film was that it was revamped for a changing audience. Firefights, car chases, rock music, forbidden love . . . I'm not suggesting much that hasn't already been done.

I spot a long black coat—Victorian, with a fitted torso and calf-length skirt—mixed in with the Renaissance costumes, and I stop, studying it.

Pulling it off the rack, I hold it up, pause only a moment, and then grab the ruffle on the left shoulder, ripping it off. I do the same to the right side and slide the coat off the hanger, slipping my arms into it. I button it up, the bodice fitting perfectly, and then slip the rubber band off my wrist and pull my hair back into a high ponytail, teasing my hair. I dive into a dressing room and dab on some more eyeliner and dark shadow around my eyes, seeing the scene in my head. *New York. A cold night. White snow falling against a black sky.*

Prince Paris is in his penthouse somewhere in the city and horns honk in the distance, beyond the park, as Romeo's hair whips in the wind next to me.

My friend. I walk out to the stage, stand in the middle, and close my eyes.

My best friend. The true other half of his soul.

I swirl around the stage, Mercutio's famous monologue rolling off my tongue, because I've had it memorized for years. Mercutio is large—a one-person party—and she dominates every scene she's in, the coat spinning with me, my head tipped back, and my eyes still closed as the character slowly swells in my stomach. "This is the hag," I go on, feeling my eyes grow wild with fire as I gaze at my friend, "when maids lie on their backs, that presses them and learns them first to bear, making them women of good carriage." I sweat, inhaling and exhaling hard. "This is she." I shout, "This is she!"

"You're good," someone calls out.

I freeze, my breath stopping, and then I whip around, seeing Callum Ames standing behind me. He wears fitted black pants and a dark blue Polo, all of his dusty blond hair flopped to one side.

I narrow my eyes. "Better than you."

He grins, sliding his hands in his pockets. "I'm white, rich, and male. I'll succeed no matter what."

"You're male," I say. "You'll succeed no matter what."

He has zero interest in this play and not an ounce of talent. Why else did she give him this role?

He cocks his head, studying me. "Do you really think that's what stood in your way?" He steps toward me slowly. "Don't you think Lambert would've given that role to say . . . Clay, if she'd asked?"

I unbutton the coat but keep my eyes on him as he continues to move closer. Callum and Clay deserve each other. Both rotten human beings who won't realize the snake in the other as long as they distract themselves with how beautiful they are together.

Callum continues, "I have no doubt you'll pull yourself up out of the swamps and truly live a life that makes you happy, Liv, because you deserve it," he says, stopping a few feet before me. "You do. You're better than us, and don't think I don't know that."

I'm glad.

"But it won't be here," he tells me. "And it won't be soon."

I remain quiet, letting my eyes flit left and right to make sure he's alone. He always seems to travel with backup, and while he's never tried anything, he will.

"Why do you think Clay hates you so much?" he presses, but doesn't wait for an answer. "Because she knows this is the last time that she'll ever be more than what you are."

"She was never more or better."

"She would've gotten Mercutio," he retorts.

I clench my teeth, and I know he sees it, because his smile grows.

He's right. They wouldn't have said no to her, or probably anyone else at this school.

And I can lie to myself all I want and say that I need this part to get some experience under me before I apply as a theater major in college, but the truth is, I'm hungry. I want to be seen before I leave this fucking place.

By my brothers. By this school. I can't leave Marymount or St. Carmen a nobody.

Someday, I'm going to be a voice to others and relay how I barely had any friends. How Clay Collins made it so I never belonged here. How her mother renovated the fucking locker room showers three years ago so I didn't ogle their naked daughters.

"Do you want the role?" he asks.

I lift my eyes to his.

He tips his chin. "It's yours."

"If I consider your offer." I add the unsaid, because I know exactly where he's going with this. We've had this conversation.

But he just laughs quietly, dropping his gaze and inching closer. "Oh, you've had time to consider it," he taunts. "Now, I need an answer."

I gave you my answer.

"She's pretty," he whispers suddenly.

I pause.

"Soft, blond, young . . . Lips that taste like a milkshake, and that's not even half as good as the taste of her tongue."

My stomach coils and knots, wanting my boot in his face. Picturing that entitled smile covered in blood.

"And she'll want everything you do to her," he says.

I toss the coat on a nearby chair and start to move around him, but he steps in front of me and pulls a slip of paper out of his pocket, holding it up to me.

"You do this," he says, clarifying. "And I will get you this part."

He hands me the paper, and I hesitate, not for a second indulging his offer, but my curiosity has the better of me.

Unfolding the paper, I see it's a check. From Garrett Ames.

To the school.

In the note, it reads, *For the theater department.*

I stare at the twenty-five-thousand-dollar donation, which, I assume, is Callum's angle here. Lambert gets some play money for next school year if she lets me have the role I want. And Callum will take care of it, if I give him what he wants.

So this is how the world works, is it? I put on a sex show with some chick I don't know for a group of slobbering frat boys, and I'll live happily ever after?

Or will all my hard work and time and good intentions really just come down to how well I forever perform on the casting couch?

I feel Callum move around me as I study the check longer than I like. It's real. It's signed.

It's easy money to the Ames family. They wouldn't even notice it missing.

The stage hardens under my shoes, and I feel the heat of the spotlight that isn't even shining and the eyes of every seat filled.

I can picture it, it's opening night. The snow falls over my head, and I'm going to die one of the most powerful deaths ever written for stage.

God, I want it. I want a lot of things.

But you know what I want most of all? I really want Clay and Callum and everyone else to start paying their fucking bills.

"No one else from our school will be there?" I ask, playing along.

But he doesn't answer. I hear him exhale behind me, suddenly excited that I'm actually agreeing.

Idiot.

"Olivia . . ." he breathes out, and I think he's about to come.

"And it's just her?" I turn, questioning him. "Not you or anyone else, right?"

He nods, thrill lighting up behind his eyes.

All of a sudden, he holds up a copper key in my face, always ready. "Fox Hill," he tells me. "Don't lose it and be ready. I'll get you as my understudy, then the role, and then you pay up. Got it?"

Fox Hill is their country club, but it apparently also has a secret after-hours clubhouse where Callum Ames wants to use me to put on a show and impress his college buddies.

"I can't wait to see you go to work on her." He gives me that smile he gives all the girls. Like the one he gives Clay. "Make it hard. And hot. But if you don't show," he says, his tone suddenly stern, "it's open season on you, Jaeger, and your whole family."

"How do I know I can trust you to keep your end of the deal?" I ask.

He backs away. "When you have nothing, you really have nothing to lose, right?"

He smiles that fucking smug I-own-the-world-and-you-know-it grin before pivoting and heading down the stairs and off the stage.

I hold up the key, wondering if he's just stupid or too clever for me. Maybe I want the part bad enough. Maybe I do. My insides churn, not wanting to admit to myself that I'm not entirely sure how low I might sink in life if tempted. If you want something for so long, what price is too great?

But now I have the part.

And a key to his clubhouse.

I lift my chin, the wheels in my head starting to turn. And all without yet paying the toll.

3

Clay

I run my hands down my thighs, the flesh of my nipples hardening as the air touches them.

"Bravado" plays on my phone, and I close my eyes as I sit at the end of my bed in my underwear, feeling the weight of his text sitting on my bed next to me.

Now, he orders. Let me see your stomach.

I'd ignored the text from Callum last night, figuring I'd make up some excuse that I fell asleep or something. There was no way I was texting anyone pictures of myself.

I promise him that my clothes will look better off in person.

Eventually, he'll want me to prove it.

My mind drifts, the words coming again—against my neck in a whisper tucked away and hidden in tight spaces and dark places.

Just the two of us.

Now, he orders. Let me see your stomach.

But it's not his voice. I drop my head, breathing hard. It's not his voice I hear at all. My clit throbs, my nipples harden to pebbles, and I rub my thighs together, aching. "Goddammit," I murmur.

I push off the bed and yank my school skirt out of my closet. I pull it on, followed by a bra and a white blouse, before diving into my bathroom to straighten my hair and put on a little makeup.

I stare at myself in the mirror as I spread the lip gloss.

He'll feel good. He'll feel good when he stands behind me, his naked torso against my back. His eyes will peer over my head as his strong, muscular arms slip around my waist, and he'll take in the view of my body in the mirror, my shirt off for him. I can't wait for him to touch me. He's dying for it.

I dab some toothpaste onto a toothbrush and brush my teeth, imagining his hands gliding over my thighs and between my legs, and then I swish some mouthwash, locking on my gaze in the mirror.

You want him. You'll look so good together, and at night, under the sheets, he'll feel good, Clay. You'll love it. His golden skin and narrow waist. His broad shoulders and big eyes that make him look so innocent until he smiles and you can see the danger. Everyone wants him.

But as I rinse out my mouth and look up at him and try to see him on top of me, I see a taunting little dare looking *up at me* instead. Her amused eyes locked on mine as she lies on the weight bench.

A body smaller and softer than Callum's and lips I can feel between my teeth, because sometimes I want to bite her until she bleeds.

God, she pisses me off.

I open my mouth, letting the mouthwash fall out as I lean on the counter. My belly suddenly pooling with heat down low, and my mouth waters, nearly tasting her.

Liv. I breathe out, staring into the sink. Attention-seeking, rebel-without-a-clue, bitchy annoyance. I grip the edge of the counter.

I should just leave her alone. She's none of my business.

But confident people don't need to be loud, and it's not my responsibility to make her disdain for everyone around her easy. I won't stop pushing back until she runs from this place.

Shutting off the light, I grab my phone off the bed and fix the stuffed octopus propped up against my headboard. I have dozens tucked away in my closet and under my bed, but I only keep one out in the open.

I saw one in an aquarium in Orlando when I was about six—so beautiful and graceful—but I don't think I was obsessed until my father joked that they were actually aliens. My mother laughed about it, but as I grew up, I discovered there is a significant portion of the human population who really believe it. After that, I was hooked. The ability to do what no other creature can. Being that different from everything else around it. The allure of its secrets.

I don't know—they just called to me.

I slip on my flats, take my school jacket and backpack, and leave the room. Stepping into the hallway, I look right, seeing my parents' door closed at the end of the hall, but then I glance at the room right before it and make my way over.

Henry's name decorates the dark wood, spelled out in an arch in my little brother's favorite shade of blue. Sometimes I'll open the door. His smell still lingers. But I never go in. I like thinking he was the last to walk on the carpet or open the drawers of his dresser, even though I know my mom is in there frequently.

I'm just glad she's kept everything the same.

I touch his name, inhale and push down whatever is bubbling up in my chest, and head downstairs.

Detouring into the kitchen, I snatch a bottle of water from the fridge and the container of chicken salad that Bernie, our housekeeper, fixed for me, sticking them both into my backpack.

Putting on my blazer and heading through the foyer, I take my keys off the entryway table and move to the door, but I glance out the window panel on the side and see my father's car in the driveway. Morning dew glistens over the hood of his slate gray Audi.

I stop. I thought he was in Miami.

I drop my bag and twist around, a smile pulling at my lips. He's home so little anymore, business taking him to D.C., San Francisco, and Houston, but mostly Miami. It seems like he's there more than home the last few months.

One of the double doors to his office is cracked, and I squeeze the handle, peering my head inside.

"Hey," I say.

He sits behind his desk, light brown hair disheveled, tie loosened, and one leg wearing wrinkled gray pants and a shiny black shoe propped up on his desk. A stream of cigarette smoke snakes into the air above his head as he blows out a puff.

He pulls his foot off his desk, smiling, "Morning."

I saunter in, doing a playful little walk with my hands behind my back like I'm up to something, and swing around his desk, sitting on the arm of his chair and pull out a fresh cigarette from the marble box near his computer.

"When did you get in?" I ask as his arm goes around my waist, holding me steady.

For most trips, he flies, but Miami is close enough to drive.

"Just a couple of hours ago," he tells me, taking another drag. "Is your mom up?"

"I don't think so."

He watches me as I take his lighter off his desk. "Early start today?"

It's actually not as early as I usually leave. I think he just doesn't know my schedule anymore. Or what time school starts, or that we have service before first period a couple of times a month, or really anything else about me.

That's okay, though.

I light the cigarette before leaning back into his shoulder. "Morning Mass," I tell him, rolling my eyes.

He chuckles. "It wasn't my idea to send you to a Catholic school."

"Noted."

I take another puff, inhale, and then blow out smoke.

My dad shakes his head. "I'm a terrible father."

I laugh, holding up my cigarette. "Years down the road, I'll cringe when I think of the debutante ball, and I probably won't even remember my friends' names," I tell him, "but I'll smile when I remember sneaking cigarettes with my dad."

His mouth tilts up in a half smile, and the both of us take another drag at the same time, enjoying the morning silence for another moment.

"How are your classes?" he asks.

"Easy peasy."

"And your classmates? Is everything . . . happy?"

I turn away, watching the end of the cigarette burn orange. What's he going to do if I say no?

Parents ask these questions because they want to appear to care, but they don't want a problem. Not really.

"I should get going," I tell him instead, hopping off the chair and snuffing out the cigarette in the crystal ashtray.

I slip around his desk and hear the wheels of his chair move.

"You already got into Wake Forest," he calls after me. "Slack off a little. Enjoy your senior year."

But I can't. The biggest events of high school are just ahead of me. The fun is just starting.

"I'll be leaving again tomorrow morning," he informs me.

I stop at the door and turn my head. "Miami again?"

"Yes." He nods. "But I'll be back Monday afternoon."

Suspicions settle in, and I know just as well as my mother does why he'll be gone again. Over the weekend, when almost no one is in the office.

No one says anything about anything, though. We've splintered off since Henry's death, cultivating our own lives that consist of as many distractions as possible.

This house is just where we collect our mail.

"Travel safe," I tell him, his guilty eyes looking at me like he needs to say something.

But I'm gone before he has a chance.

———

A long time ago, I realized that it isn't my responsibility to fix my parents. My father can face the fact, at any time, that Henry would hate knowing how quiet the house is now. No smiles or food fights or watching Mom cry at the same part during *White Christmas* during our rewatch every single holiday season.

He can face the fact that, while one child is gone, he still has another. That I could be out doing who knows what while he's off in Miami or Austin or Chicago. I could be getting into drugs. Getting pregnant. Getting arrested.

Does he care? If he did, he'd be here.

I used to think it hurts him too much to be in the house, but we could've moved. Maybe it hurt him to be around my mother. In that case, he could've taken me with him sometimes.

But he just leaves, and it didn't take long to get the message. Neither of them wants this family anymore.

And honestly, I can't blame them sometimes. What's the point? You work for years—educating yourself, building, planning, working, loving—and leukemia sweeps through and ravages your ten-year-old son to death.

What's the point of any of this?

I enter the church, lockers slamming shut in the school hallway behind me. I stop, scanning the room.

She sits right off the aisle, about halfway down the pew, and something swims in my stomach, a small smile spreading my lips.

The truth is . . . there's no point to any of this. If being a lifelong Catholic school girl has taught me anything, the idea of heaven is as much of an abhorrence as the idea of hell. Who the fuck wants to be in church forever?

My mother has her shopping and her all-too-important schedule, and my father has another woman, both of them running as fast as they can from themselves, because they now realize there's no point in denying the sins that keep you feeling alive.

I stalk down the nearly empty row, drop my bag, and look at her. She turns her head, sees me and rises, grabbing her backpack, but I slide into the seat, grab her wrist, and yank her ass back down.

"Sit," I growl through my teeth, feeling heat rise up my neck as she crashes back into the wooden pew, her jaw flexing.

There's no point in denying myself any of this. I'm a bitch, but only to her, and only because it feels so good. Fuck it.

"Do something for me?" I ask her, keeping my voice low as students fill the rows around us, and the altar servers light the candles. "Move your ass a little faster than my grandmother down the field this Friday, or is that too much trouble?"

Liv doesn't look at me, just stares ahead as she lets out a quiet little laugh. "I haul ass down that field." Relaxing back into her seat, she hangs her elbows over the back of the pew, and her shirt creeps up a little. I spot the switchblade she keeps hooked over the waist of her skirt but hidden on the inside, which only I seem to know about. So far anyway. She goes on, "I'll never understand how a princess who can't pass a ball for shit and brags to anyone who will listen about being a Swiftie"—and she does air quotes—"'even before she went pop' is our team captain. Oh, wait. Yes, I do understand. Daddy is useful. When he's there."

My father didn't get me that position. She can think what she likes.

But I grin and turn toward the front of the church, my arm brushing hers.

"Swiftie?" I say. "Aw, you stalk my Twitter."

That was like four years ago when I said that.

But she just mumbles, "I couldn't care less about your Twitter and your twenty-eight followers."

"At least I don't lose a dozen every day," I retort.

Yeah, maybe I stalk her Twitter, too. And I don't have twenty-eight followers. I don't have as many as her, but it's more than twenty-eight.

"The world just doesn't like tattooed feminazis with hairy armpits," I tell her, my gaze catching the dimple on her cheek as she smirks, "who pass judgments like all the other constipated Captain Americas on social media who act like they really know anything when they're just angry their life sucks donkey nuts."

The dimple grows deeper, her matte red lips pursing to keep her amusement at bay. My heart thumps, and for a moment, I can't look away. Sometimes I get lost, looking at her. The shape of her nose that I'm kind of jealous of. How soft the lobe of her ear looks. The way she chews the corner of her mouth sometimes.

"Is everything okay?" someone says, snapping me out of it.

I turn my head, seeing Megan Martelle standing over us, holding a stack of collection baskets. Her blue eyes flit between Liv and me, knowing very well that this isn't a friendly conversation, but lucky for her, this isn't any of her damn business.

"Fine, thanks," I reply, my tone a big enough hint she'd have to be an idiot to miss.

But she looks to Liv instead. "Liv?"

Excuse me? It's not the name. It's how she says it. Like they know each other.

Liv must give her some gesture or something, because Martelle gives me one last look and then slowly leaves, continuing down the aisle toward the back of the church without another word.

What the hell is she thinking? Does she want to become my next hobby or something?

I reach down and pull my backpack closer before turning my eyes back to Liv to see if she's watching her leave.

But she's staring at me instead, amusement in her eyes.

"What the hell are you smiling at?" I demand.

She never loses her cool, and it pisses me off.

But she just replies, "You have a tattoo."

Her gaze drifts to my hand, and I squeeze my fingers together, covering it. All over again, I feel the needle carve into the inside of my middle finger on my left hand.

Fair enough. I'd mocked tattooed feminazis, an umbrella term I tossed her under, when, in fact, she doesn't actually have any tattoos. Not even the one of her family's little Sanoa Bay gang—the snake and hourglass that she wears on a bracelet around her wrist. Her brothers all seem to have it inked on them somewhere.

Her eyes hold mine, maybe waiting for a response or daring me for one, but the light coming in from the stained-glass windows catches the coppery glint of the strands in her dark hair, a lock hanging over her eye as the rest spills around her shoulders. A dozen or so little braids decorate her hair, none of the ends secured with rubber bands. She looks like a warrior girl in one of those futuristic dystopian movies.

And all of a sudden, nothing is hot anymore. It's just incredibly warm.

I squeeze my fingers tighter, the lines inked on the inside of my finger making the four quarters of an inch on a ruler, very few ever notice the lines, and those who do probably just assume I've leaked pen on myself.

Within that inch we are free. One inch.

"Clay?" she says, her tone different.

I don't realize I'm staring off until I bring my eyes back into focus and see the black of her Polo shirt. I lift my gaze, seeing a worried expression on hers.

Her eyes shift to my hand on the pew in front of us, and I notice that it's shaking.

"You okay?" she asks.

I inhale hard, angry at myself. *Why would I not be okay?*

She grabs my backpack. "You need one of your little blue pills?"

But I snatch the pack out of her hands and glare at her. "If you let her touch you," I bite out, changing the subject, "she will live to regret it. I don't even have to leave this seat to ruin her life."

Liv looks back at me, and I want to get closer—get in her face—because I want a reaction.

"She won't be able to take it," I growl in a low voice. "I will keep going until she *can't* take it."

I can ruin anyone's life from my phone. It would be fun. And easy.

"You're not embarrassing our team," I finally tell her.

Megan was flirting yesterday. There's no way in hell that's happening.

She holds my gaze and then draws in a breath, another fucking air of delight written all over her stupid fucking face. "I don't like women who chase me anyway," she says. "When I want them, they know."

A tingle spreads up my spine, and when I expect to feel anger at her boldness, something else comes over me instead.

When I want them, they know. How do they know? What does she do?

But she rises from her seat without elaborating. "Excuse me," she says, and takes her bag, trying to leave.

But I stomp down the kneeler, grab her wrist, and yank her to her knees. She sucks in a breath as she catches herself on the pew in front of her, and I pick up my backpack and rise.

"Sit your ass down," I grit out.

I don't stay to see her reaction. I spin around, ignoring the spying eyes from those around us, and leave the chapel just as Mass begins.

When I want them . . .

I blink long and hard. *Jesus.*

4

Olivia

Sit your ass down.

I startle, opening my eyes as the shadows of raindrops dance across my ceiling.

Shit. My bedroom comes into view, still dim from the sunless sky filtering through the windows, and the quick vibrations of my phone on my bedstand going off steadily.

Do something for me? I hear her say.

I squeeze my eyes shut, rolling over and burying my face in my pillow. Damn her.

The fabric cools my hot skin as sweat dampens my back. Her taunting voice—her whisper against my cheek—still rings in my ears.

I wasn't dreaming about her. God, please tell me I wasn't dreaming about her.

But I'm throbbing.

I search my brain, trying to remember anything before I woke, but all I feel is a cloud in my head. And the strain in my body. Pools of heat swirl in my stomach, the warmth between my thighs sensitive, I'm restless and relaxed at the same time. It's not unpleasant.

Reaching down between my legs, I touch myself through my shorts and underwear, instantly feeling the slickness.

I yank my hand away and sit up. *Jesus Christ.* That self-absorbed, shallow bitch . . . What the hell?

No. Absolutely not.

I'm over this. I've been over this for years now. She's straight. I knew that years ago when I first met her, had a crush, and couldn't stop thinking about her.

And she's cruel. I know that plain as day now. I can't even begin to contemplate what the hell my subconscious is thinking, but hate-fucking Clay Collins would be even less fun than bathing in lava.

You'd think with a local suicide that was probably the result of bullying, Clay Collins would back off. Alli Carpenter is dead. A queer girl who'd had enough.

Is that what Clay wants? What is her problem?

Picking up my phone, I check my social media, seeing I picked up a few new followers on Twitter.

I run across a trending tweet by Rev. John J. Williamson condemning a young new senator who happens to be homosexual. I shake my head, appeased by the comments on the thread condemning him instead. These guys are always the ones caught in motel rooms with fifteen-year-old boys.

Prick. I retweet, punching out the caption I **hope your daughters grow up and have wives**, and hit *Send*, and then I check texts.

One from Becks. Call me.

I don't talk on the phone. I text.

Another from Jonasy, Trace's ex, who thinks maintaining a relationship with the family will get her back into his bed. A new vintage shop opened in Little Cuba. Come with me!

Nope. When did she ever get the impression that I like vintage clothes? I might love wearing Macon's old motorcycle jacket with holes in the lining from when he was fifteen, but I'm pretty sure *old* does not equal *quaint*.

I toss the phone onto the bed and hop up, stretching and then pulling my hair free of my low ponytail, shaking out my hair.

"No!" I hear a bellow outside my door and twist my head to the sound. "Give it back now!"

I groan, closing my eyes and let my head fall back. *Trace and Dallas.* Twenty and twenty-one respectively, they were the youngest boys in the family, but still older than me. You wouldn't really know it, though, based on their behavior.

"It's too fucking early!" Dallas shouts back.

Then I hear squeaks against the hardwood floor, heavy footsteps, and then . . . a thud shakes the house, the shelves on my wall rattle, and my copy containing all of Henrik Ibsen's plays plummets to the ground. Another thud, and then almost a thunder that vibrates under my feet.

Jesus. I need air.

Whipping my door open, I find Dallas and Trace on the floor of the hallway, wrestling. Dallas is soaking wet and wearing a towel that's only a prayer from coming off his body, and Trace is just in jeans, laughing his ass off as they go at it.

"Enough!" I yell.

For God's sake. I grit my teeth, barreling past them and stepping over their bodies.

But hands grab my legs, and I barely have time to let out a scream before I'm falling backward and into waiting arms.

"Trace!" I yell, not even having to look to see who the culprit is. Dallas isn't the playful one, so I know it's not him.

Fingers dig into my stomach, and I hold back my laugh, kicking and squirming.

"Stop!" I growl as my brother tickles. "I'm not in the mood."

"You got sleep," Trace fires back. "I didn't get sleep."

Dallas pushes us off, clutches his towel closed, and disappears back into the bathroom, slamming the door.

"Come on." I fight Trace's hold, the scruff on his cheek stabbing my ear. "Coffee first. Please."

He's got this thing about moody people. People like Macon and

Dallas. People like me. He purposely pokes the bear and doesn't know when to stop.

We fight, and I kick, hitting the wall instead of him, the plaster cracking and a nice round dent appearing where there wasn't one before.

I used to feel bad, but the walls are covered in dents and holes from years of six Jaeger kids. Macon, the oldest and head of the house, won't know the difference.

"Let me go!" I bark, and elbow him in the gut.

His hold relaxes, and I scramble out of his arms, crawling and climbing to my feet, escaping.

But I hear his voice behind me. "Your turn to wash the bedding!"

I stop and turn my head, his short black hair sticking up all over the place, and his green eyes showing no hint that he'd had a sleepless night like he claims.

"I'm not touching your sheets," I tell him. "Put them in the washer yourself."

He bats his eyelashes, and I let out a quiet sigh. If I don't do his sheets, they won't get done. And why do I care? *No idea.*

"Don't make me touch your sheets," I plead.

But he just blinks up at me. "Coffee first," he says. "Coffee will help you feel better about it."

Whatever. I storm off, knowing I'll do it and knowing that he knows I'll do it.

I'm allowed to pout for a little while, though. If our parents were here, I might not feel obligated to give in to him, but Trace wasn't much older than me when we were orphaned. He thinks a woman will fill that void that not having a mom has left in him.

I step into the kitchen, the chipped blue-and-pink stucco walls shining with the light coming from the rusted old chandelier over the kitchen table. The shutters over the sink spread open, the white grate keeping out intruders, but letting in the smell and sound of the rain.

Macon leans against the stove, grease stains on his gray T-shirt and the leather peeling on the front of his steel-toe boots. He dries his hands and tightens the thin leather strap, identical to mine, around his wrist.

I walk for the moka pot. "Morning."

"It's almost noon." I hear him sip his coffee. "You'd never know I have five siblings with all the shit you all make me do around here by myself."

I hood my eyes, bracing myself as I pull the coffee beans out of the cabinet.

It's not noon. It's barely ten, and it's Saturday. "Coffee first, please," I say.

He's in a mood, probably been up since five a.m. and had time to self-talk himself into a nice little tizzy that we are the most ungrateful lot. Macon needs sex. Lots of it.

I pick up the pot but feel it's already full. *Ugh, thank you.* He brewed another pot.

I pour myself a cup and walk to the table, taking a seat opposite him. "I was at school late," I tell him, taking my first sip. "I guess the last few months of senior year aren't for relaxing after all."

"No, not for relaxing," Macon says, "any more than it's necessary to apply to Dartmouth when you're already going to Florida State."

I shoot my eyes up.

He reaches over the table, to the stack of bills waiting to be paid in the napkin holder, and plucks out a white envelope, tossing it to me.

I grab it, flipping it over to see the Dartmouth return address in the corner. The envelope is ripped open, and I can feel the letter inside.

"Congratulations," he tells me before I have a chance to read the letter.

I dart my gaze up to him again as I dig inside the envelope. "You opened my mail?"

But I don't wait for a response. Unfolding the piece of paper, I don't know if he's screwing with me, or if I really got in. My heart pounds as I start reading, taking in one word after the other, holding my breath for the shoe to drop.

It doesn't. I read the first couple of sentences over and over, reality slowly coming into view.

He's not lying. I got in. I exhale, smiling as I feel like I'm floating all of a sudden.

I got in. I got into an Ivy League school with a great theater department.

I'm going to Dartmouth.

I squeeze the paper, kind of wishing I could hug someone right now. But I'm the only person in this house happy about this.

"But what do I know, right?" Macon continues. "I'm just a poor, dumb redneck who'll never be more than this. I should be lucky to learn from you."

My smile slowly falls, and I look up, meeting his brown eyes. We're the only two kids—the first and the last—who got our mom's eyes, but that's all we have in common. I respect my oldest brother greatly. He takes care of things. He's reliable, honest, and strong.

I don't really like him much, though. He doesn't want me to go to Dartmouth. He doesn't talk to me other than to parent me.

"You're the one who pushed me," I tell him, setting the letter down. "You wanted me to get out of here. 'Be someone,' you said. 'Be remembered.' That's what you said." I can't help the scowl spreading across my face. "Dartmouth is ten times the school Florida State is, and you're still not happy."

It takes me less than three seconds to get angry at my family, but Macon just cocks his head, playing with me. "And what are you studying at Dartmouth?"

I shake my head. I'm not giving up the theater. It's *my* life, not his. "You want me close so you can reel me in."

"And you want to fly out of arm's reach where I can't."

He thinks theater is stupid. He thinks I'll wind up a middle-aged failure and realize too late that I can't go back and make the con-servative decisions he thinks I should make.

I'll be a failure if I stay.

"Eighteen won't make you an adult, Liv." He stares at me. "You still need raising. I was twenty-three and I still needed raising."

I fall silent, tired of going around and around with him about this. His situation was completely different. No one—no matter what age—would be ready to lose both their parents within two months of each other and also get saddled with raising and sup-porting five younger siblings.

Over the years, I became in awe of Macon, slowly realizing as I matured what it must have been like for him. He was a Marine, off seeing the world and living his life only for himself. He had freedom and opportunities.

One day, our dad had a heart attack that left him weakened until he finally passed one night. Two months later, my mom followed.

Macon had a choice. He could let us be split up and sent off to foster care, or he could be discharged and return home to pay more bills than he was capable of, feed bellies that were constantly hun-gry, and be chained to people who would continue to be dependent on him long after they'd turned eighteen.

His life was over, but he didn't hesitate. He came home.

Wailing hits my ear, and I let out a breath, bringing my mug back to my lips as the crying gets louder and louder.

Here comes exhibit A of what dependency looks like.

"You gotta take this kid," Army whines, coming into the kitchen and swinging his son over my shoulder and into my lap.

I shoot back, setting down my coffee, the scorching liquid sloshing onto my hand before I grab the kid and hang on to him.

I glare at my second-oldest brother as he passes me and heads to the fridge, no shirt, and his jeans hanging looser around his waist, because his five-month-old son still doesn't sleep through the night, and my brother forgets to eat just like he forgot to wear a condom.

"Army, come on," I bite out, hefting Dexter up and holding him close. "I've got chores and practice."

Army's brown hair, a couple shades lighter than mine, is matted on one side of his head, and bags darken the skin under his eyes. "I just need a shower," he assures. "Please? I'm dying. Damn kid cries all the time."

I meet Macon's gaze, both of us finding silent agreement in this one area. Army is twenty-eight, three years younger than Macon, and one of the most irresponsible people alive. We told Army that woman was no good, and now he's raising a kid alone.

Correction: not alone. We're helping him.

Which is why Macon will never be free. Who else will help my brothers pay for their weddings, support their kids, bail them out of jail, have a couch to crash on when their wives kick them out, or keep up the ancestral home?

A drop of water hits the kitchen table, and I look up at the leaky ceiling and move my coffee cup under the leak.

Macon has buried himself here to a point where there's more than just the six of us to worry about. Everyone in this community depends on Tryst Six.

"Besides," Army says, ruffling my hair as he moves behind me, "you've got the touch with him."

"I've got a vagina, you mean."

Iron sweeps through, pouring some coffee, and I quickly stuff the envelope back into the bill pile, because I'm not in the mood to talk about it anymore, and I don't want them to notice it.

"Put it out," Army yells at him. "Not in the house."

Iron nods, takes one final puff, and blows out the smoke, running the cigarette under the faucet. He tosses the wet butt into the trash.

Army walks toward the living room. "Two minutes."

"Arm—"

"Two minutes!" he yells back at me. "Ten, tops!"

And he disappears. I grit my teeth.

Iron follows him without a word, and I bounce Dexter up and down in my arms as I find my gaze traveling to Macon again, grease caked under his fingernails as he fists his mug.

It doesn't escape my notice that he's right. We're all just getting up and starting our day. He's filthy because he woke up hours ago. Probably already went to Mariette's to receive the deliveries of crawfish for the restaurant, got Trace's truck loaded for him to service lawns today, helped Mrs. Torres repair the pothole in front of her house that the city won't address, *and* fixed a motorcycle he's planning to flip.

"You should've gone to college, you know?" My words are quiet. Gentle. "You're the real brains in the family."

He doesn't say anything for a moment, and I'm afraid to look up.

"The hardest choices were never choices to begin with," he finally says. "That's life."

Still sucks, though. Why can't he just admit that it sucks? He has to want to be somewhere else. He has to know what wanting to leave feels like. He's not happy. Why does he pretend that he can't relate to me and to wanting something more?

"You're not paying forty thousand a year to learn how to playact." He pushes off the stove and I hear him empty his mug into the sink. "When you graduate in four years, you can do whatever the hell you want. Just get a degree you can use first."

And then a newspaper drops on the table in front of me, open to page fourteen and folded in half. "It's time for you to step up and help this family," he commands.

I lean over the kid in my arms and read the headline.

BLUE ROCK RESORT BREAKING GROUND

Blue Rock is Seminole land farther south. They're building a resort?

I scan the article, only reading a few paragraphs before I know enough not to have to finish the rest. Words like "eminent domain" and "job creation" jump out, confirming what everyone feared three years ago when the protests and lobbying started. As with everything, though, those with the most money win the long game, and those without lose the war.

We have nothing to do with Blue Rock, but if they can get Blue Rock, they can get Sanoa Bay. We're not a reservation, just a community of ancestral landowners who are lucky enough to be sitting off one of the few and most gorgeous reefs on the Florida coast.

They'll be coming for us next, and it'll be a piece of cake compared to Blue Rock.

I stare at the paper. "They can't do this."

"If the government determines that the land we're on is worth more revenue to the state in their hands instead . . ." Macon tells me what I already know. "If it means creating jobs that get the important people re-elected, then yes, they can. They will."

Light sprinkles hit my shoulders and legs, and I lick the water off my lips as I jog around the empty track. Normally, I hate running in the rain. My earbuds aren't waterproof, and music is the only motivation I have to stay in shape—that and the fact that more exercise means I can eat more guac—but today, I don't mind it. I need to think. I need silence.

Digging in my heels, I pick up the pace, an energy filling my legs that I'm not used to.

I have six months. Six months until I leave for Dartmouth and three months until I leave Marymount for good. I can figure this out. Macon doesn't have a plan B to keep our land, because he also doesn't have access to the developers on a daily basis.

I do. The developer—Garrett Ames—and the law firm—Jefferson Collins—in charge of the resort enterprise, are kicking eight, possibly nine families off their land in Blue Rock.

Collins and Ames.

I'm within arm's reach of their daughter and son every day right at this school. And I'm sick of these people never paying for what they take.

I'm tired of their kids doing the same.

I squeeze the copper key in my fist as I charge down the rust-colored clay track, the green field at the center glistening with rain as the wheels in my head spin and spin.

It's a key to Fox Hill.

It's a key to a private party.

It's a key to a lot of private parties, I'm sure, and not all of them hosted by Garrett Ames's idiot teenage son who doesn't have the good sense to sin with people who don't have a motive to hurt him.

Think, Liv. Think. How do I use this?

The sharp key cuts into my palm, but I just squeeze it tighter, seeing them in my mind. Seeing them lose and seeing us win.

Seeing Clay watch me walk away from her.

The rain picks up again, a little harder, and I feel drops pour down my legs and inside my white tank top, my black sports bra underneath seeping through my wet shirt.

There are usually a few cars in Marymount's parking lot on Saturday. Maintenance crews come to fix things when the students aren't here, teachers show up to get work done undisturbed, or the sports teams need the extra time to practice. But the whole place is abandoned today, the heavy clouds promising more shitty weather to come.

I have no idea why I'm here. I'm not hip on showing up to this place when I have to, let alone when I don't.

Sticking the key back into my pocket, I dig out the other key, the one to Dallas's old Mustang that the jerk let me take today, and fall to a walk as I head off the track and into the parking lot. He should just let me have the car. It sits on the street, collecting rust most days, but he's still under the impression he'll eventually have enough money to restore it.

"Clay, I'm not practicing in this!" someone yells.

I dart my eyes up, seeing Clay, Krisjen, and Amy in the parking lot. I pause midstep. *Great.*

I keep walking for my car, noticing Amy holding a raincoat over her head and scowling. Clay pulls lacrosse gear out of the back of her baby blue 1972 Ford Bronco convertible, seemingly unconcerned with the rain drenching her black leggings and sports bra.

She doesn't deserve that car.

"Let's go to the indoor center," Krisjen whines. "Please?"

"No, I wanna get dirty." Clay closes the tailgate and drops her stick to the ground, raindrops bouncing off the pavement around her bare feet.

"Clay, come on," Amy snips. "It's cold. And it's Saturday. I want to go shopping. I snagged my mom's black card."

I walk past them, not looking away when Clay sees me and holds my eyes.

The knot in my stomach is there, as it always is when I anticipate bullshit from her, but so is the skip in my heartbeat when I look at her.

I head to my car a couple spaces down, pulling my shirt over my head and wringing it out.

"I love you," Amy says, "but I'm just going to slip and break my ass out there."

"Get back here," Clay demands.

"And don't pull the captain card, either," Amy tells her, already walking away, "I'll see you tonight."

She walks off, and I see Krisjen follow her, giving Clay a shrug. "She's got her mom's black card."

Like limitless shopping is too much of a temptation to resist, and the fact that it's fraud is completely lost on them.

"You leave me alone out here and you owe me," Clay yells, "and owing me favors is painful."

"Meet you at your house at seven," Krisjen calls out, jumping into Amy's car.

I hear the engine start and the tires screech as Amy peels out of the flooded parking lot. I slide the key into the lock on the door, slowly turning it as Clay's eyes set fire to my back.

"Leaving?"

Chills cascade down my arms.

"Pity," she says. "You need the practice, too."

Just get in the car, I tell myself. People like her hate to be ignored.

"But it's always the shit talkers who don't bring it anyway." I hear a shuffle, and her alarm chirps, signaling she's locked her car. "I scored two goals the last game. Not you."

I open my door, almost smiling at her effort. She scored two goals because half the opposing team was down with strep throat and they were playing their backup goalie.

And I ran my ass down the field and intercepted both those balls before shooting them over to her so she could score. In four seasons, she's never known a win without me.

I stare at her back as she goes, the car key cutting into my palm so deep I think it draws blood. Reaching inside the car, I grab my stick, slam the door, and follow her. She's gonna get a taste of what it's like without me on her side.

I match her step for step, the entire way back to the track, and I know she knows I'm behind her, because she shoves her gear bag onto a bench with a little extra oomph, psyching herself up without even looking back.

"We play the whole field," she tells me, pulling her cleats out of her bag. "Whoever scores three goals first, wins."

"Lucky for you there's no one to pass to."

"You'll see how well I can pass when I shoot the ball into the net."

The corner of my mouth curls.

She props her foot onto the bench and slips one shoe on after the other, turning her head.

Let's see it, then. I push my hair over the top of my head again and start walking onto the field.

"No gear?" she shouts.

"Scared?"

She can protect her precious little face all she wants, but I hope she doesn't. I'd love to see blood coming out of her fucking nose.

We head straight for center field, both of us turning toward each other, ready to face off as she drops the ball between us.

"Whistle after three," I tell her, leaning down. "One."

She leans down with me, our eyes locked. "Two."

"Thr—"

But she charges, cutting me off and throwing her shoulder into me. I growl, crashing to my ass as she scoops up the ball and runs.

I should've known . . . I watch her ponytail swing as she flies down the field toward the goal, and I slam the ground with my fist, growling as I jump to my feet.

God, I hate her.

I bolt, charging after her, but she reaches the end of the field and launches the ball into the net. She doesn't celebrate as she grabs the ball back out of the goal and tosses it to me. I catch it, the rain spilling in my eyes as I barely notice her clothes sticking to her body.

"Again!" she demands.

Yeah, you got that right. Digging in my heels, I take up position back at the center, but I don't wait for her to be ready. I fling the ball down the field, but before she has a chance to move, I slam my body into her and rush past.

"Ugh!" she screams.

I run, picking up the ball and racing down the field, but in a moment, I feel her stick tapping harder and harder into my legs.

"Move your ass!" she yells. "Come on. Come on."

I tighten my fists around the damn stick, debating whether knocking her head off with my pole is worth the jail time.

I toss the ball, it lands in the net, and lightning flashes across the sky as her lips brush my ear. "I *love* how you move your ass for me."

I whip around, shoving her off, but she just laughs, digging the ball out of the net. She runs backward, her eyes gleaming. "Come on, baby. Do it."

I shake my head, but I do it. She rushes toward the other goal, and I race after her, but about midway down the field, a thought hits me.

This is what she wants. She doesn't need to win. She just wants me to sweat. I'm ten times the player she is, and she's enjoying this. She's got me on a leash.

Fuck her.

I jam my stick between her legs midstride. She stumbles, but before she falls, she grabs onto me and pulls me with her. *Shit!*

She cries out, I grunt, and our sticks fall to the wayside as I crash on top of her, my skull damn near hitting hers.

"Bitch!" she blurts out. She tries to shove me off, but I'm sick of her shit. I grapple for her wrists, pin them to the ground, and glare down at her.

"How desperate for attention you are," I spit out. "How shallow and small. I think you like engaging me. You like spending any time you can with me, don't you?"

She tips her chin up, closing her mouth but still breathing heavy through her nose, her jaw clenched. A lock of hair, darkened by rain, snakes under her left eye and across her nose.

I release her arms, but I don't move. "Come on." I hover over her, gazing down. "Hit me. Then I can hit you back and numb you like you want me to. Bullies are always in so much more pain than they inflict."

Her wrists remain pinned to the grass, her stubborn little chin unmoving and her eyes unwavering.

But I feel her, all the same. My legs around her body, my thighs hugging her . . . The cool, soft flesh of her wet legs presses against my calves.

All of a sudden, my smile falls, and I have no ambition to move. An amazing little buzz vibrates under my skin as I become aware of her body underneath mine.

Rain hits my skin like darts, but all I feel is the heat of her through our clothes.

She isn't moving away. Why isn't she trying to get away?

I leave her eyes, trailing my own down her neck, down her chest, her chilled nipples pressing against her bra, and down her stomach, feeling and seeing it shake in the inch between us, betraying the stone in her expression.

I shift my eyes back up to hers, a quiet laugh escaping my chest. She's scared of me. She's actually scared of me.

But why?

"Get off," she spits out.

I just laugh again, lowering my face to hers a little more. "Scared I'll like the position we're in and make a move?" I tease. "Or are you scared you want me to make a move?"

She pinches her eyebrows together, fucking quiet for once.

"Come on, it's just like being with a man, Clay," I mock, unable to hide my enjoyment as I lower my voice to a whisper. "You just open your legs."

I let my gaze fall to her lips, the wheels in my head starting to turn.

She's making no move to leave. I'm not holding her down.

"You just open your legs," I say again.

We lie in the field, in full view of anyone who decides to come by, but she doesn't seem worried about that.

It's pouring rain. We're alone.

Just the two of us.

And for a moment, I feel my heart stop. I'm just joking, but what if she does let her legs fall open? What will I do?

An invisible cord pulls at my hips, urging me to close the distance between us, but I won't. Even if the world falls off its axis and turns upside down, I'll never want her.

"You make me want to puke," she says quietly. "Dirty dyke."

"I bet your daddy likes it dirty," I retort. "In his fuckpad in Miami?"

Her face falls just a hair but enough, and I know I've touched a nerve. She's probably wondering how the hell I know about that? And does anyone else know?

I go on. "When he's not here trying to take away my family's land and kick the rest of Sanoa Bay off its ancestral home, that is," I explain. "I bet Callum Ames likes it dirty, too. When his family's not busy bragging about its long history of shipping every Seminole out of Florida."

I reach into my pocket, pulling out the copper key with the triangular head that opens a door at Fox Hill. I hold it between us, because while it represents a prime example of how those "with" victimize those "without" and how there are still men in this world who see women as something to be used, I'm not above using it to my advantage, either.

"When your men are not all busy, patting each other on the back for making St. Carmen clean and white," I continue. "When they're hidden away in places far from where their frilly, frigid wives and girlfriends who drink white wine and, like, decorate and shit . . ."

She stares at the key, a ton of questions probably racing through her mind, but her pride won't let her give in to ask me.

"Things you'll never have to know about," I tell her, "because you and your mother are dumb and boring and you can't understand the world beyond your own low level of perception." I stare down at her. "Everyone likes it dirty, Clay. Everyone likes it, period." I get in her face, and I feel my breath bounce off her lips. "Especially Callum Ames."

Her expression is unreadable, unchanging, but her chest moves up and down harder but not faster. Like she's feeling things but not angry.

"He's going to cheat on you," I point out. "Because women like you are displayed. A statue will never be good for anything else."

Water pools in her eyes, the blue looking like jewels, and I falter.

What the hell am I doing? This is the kind of shit she would say. I'm sinking to her level. This kind of behavior makes my world smaller, and I'm never cruel.

I catch sight of her wrists, still by her head, on the grass. The tattoo I saw the other day peeks out between her fingers.

An inch. That's what it looks like. Five lines, two of them smaller, looking like the quarter inch marks on a ruler. She hides the tattoo well enough that most people won't notice it, but not so well that she never sees it. It's important only to her.

What does it mean?

But then, she closes her fist, hiding it again.

I meet her eyes. What few tears she might've had there are now gone, and so is my fight. I don't give a shit what's underneath her layers. We all have problems and don't treat people like dogs, and I'm not giving Clay Collins the power to change me. I won't let her make me cruel.

Maybe I was an asshole just now, but she'll always be one.

I climb to my feet, grabbing my stick off the ground and wipe the water off my face. Without a word, I head off the field.

Walking past the bleachers, I pull out my key ring again, unlocking the women's locker room door. Staying late and coming in on weekends and vacations to sew costumes and build sets has its perks.

I stalk through the room, open another door, and step into the school hallway, my shoes squeaking against the terra-cotta tile. I pass the courtyard, rain hitting the palms and flower beds and splashing off the stone benches. I veer left toward the theater, and just then, I hear the locker room door swing open again, down the hall right behind me.

Jesus Christ. She hasn't had enough, I guess.

Diving into the theater, I climb up on the stage and head behind the curtain, down to the dressing rooms. I pull open the wardrobe in the hallway, seeing discontinued sets of school sweats and T-shirts sitting folded on the shelves. The theater director keeps the never-been-used, out-of-date overstock here for rehearsals when someone gets covered in fake blood, rain, or whatever else the production calls for.

Clay's footfalls hit the steps, and I grab my sizes and turn, leaving the cabinet open as I brush past her.

"What's the key for?" she asks.

I head back up to the stage, ignoring her, and pull off my shorts and tank top. Clothes drop to the table next to me, and I hear her start to strip her wet stuff.

"You wouldn't have shown me it if it wasn't important," she continues.

"Your dress is ready," I say, ignoring her question. "Unless you want me to fuck it up in all the ways your mother will hate. But it'll cost you."

She arches an eyebrow, tossing her wet leggings.

Will I really redesign her dress? If she pays, sure. I kind of like the idea of her wearing something I made, because she wouldn't if she didn't like it. Plus, she'll remember me every time she sees pictures of herself in it. For the next fifty years.

"What was that key?" she asks again, pulling on some dark gray sweats, matching mine. **MARYMOUNT** runs down the left leg in big yellow letters.

I don't answer her.

I pick up my sweats and lift my leg to put them on, but she

lashes out and pushes me. I chuckle, stumbling back, and drop the pants.

Darting out my hands, I shove her back. She stumbles but rights herself, squaring her shoulders.

I swipe my pants off the ground, not backing down. Clay doesn't lay her hands on me unless we're on the field. She might use the opportunity from time to time to be rough at practice, and the fact that she's upped her game off the field means she's desperate to get under my skin.

Because time is running out.

"What is that key for?" she demands again.

I shake out the pants again, dusting off any dirt from the floor. "It's to a party."

"When?"

"It's kind of a pop-up." My eyes go to the ceiling, trying to act casual.

"And you need a key to get in?"

"I guess so."

She snatches the sweats out of my hands, approaching me in her pants and sports bra. "And who will be at this party? Anyone I know?"

I laugh under my breath. What would she do if I told her right now? She'd believe it. Clay isn't stupid.

I narrow my eyes. *I don't want to tell her yet, though.*

"Megan Martelle?" she asks, inching in. "Is that who you're partying with?"

She's especially obsessed with our coach's assistant. Why?

When I say nothing, she backs away, a gleam in her eyes as she holds mine and digs in her duffel bag. Pulling out her phone, she starts tapping away. "Olivia Jaeger has a key to earn her A," she recites as she types. "To Martelle's apartment, so Teach can tongue her cunt all day . . ."

I take a step toward her. My enjoyment is gone.

She looks up, cocking her head. "That's only a hundred characters," she muses. "Still so much space."

A tweet has two hundred eighty. I tense. *She's not going to tweet that. She wouldn't.*

"What rhymes with 'strap-on'?" she inquires, an innocent pinch between her brows.

I lunge for the phone, ready to show her exactly how well she'd fare on my side of the tracks.

"Just because I don't fucking punch you doesn't mean I wasn't taught how," I growl. "Knock it off."

But she slips back, holding her phone. "Drop your bra," she tells me instead.

I lift my chin. What the hell is wrong with her?

"Drop your bra!" she bellows.

I startle, wincing. "Drop your phone."

I'll drop my bra for her, but no pictures.

She sets it down but grabs a Sharpie off the table, instead. Walking slowly, she stops in front of me, and I keep my eyes locked on hers as I reach behind me, unhook my black sports bra, and let it fall to the floor.

I hold back my flinch at the goddamn amusement written all over her face.

Let her make fun of me. Let her say what she's going to say. She doesn't want to send that tweet. Not really. This is what she wants. Me humiliated.

She doesn't do anything for several moments, almost as if she's trying to decide what to do at all, but then . . .

She lowers her gaze.

She stares at me, unblinking, and everything is hot under the scrutiny of her eyes. Her lips fall apart, and I don't think she breathes.

Chills spread over my skin.

"I didn't . . ." She trails off and then clears her throat. "I didn't realize your hips were wide enough to birth a full-grown line-backer." She uncaps the marker. "Your skirt hides it well."

Fuck you.

She sinks to her knees, watching me the whole time. "Should I let you keep your panties on?"

"Do you want me to take them off?"

Dare me. I stare at her, willing her to have the fucking guts.

But she draws in a deep breath, instead. "Your brother . . ." she says. "He was looking at me the other morning when he dropped you off, wasn't he?"

I clench my jaw.

"I didn't mind it. You want to take a picture of me for him?" She tsks. "Those Jaeger men . . . Definitely not the kind you marry, but that's kind of what's so hot about them."

What the hell is she talking about?

"Something hot about being used for something that feels so good?"

I study her, waiting for the fucking point.

"But Iron isn't in charge of the family. It's Macon, right?" She peers up at me. "Your oldest brother?"

I almost laugh. Messing with Macon will take a hell of a lot more than she has.

Her eyes fall down my legs and back up over my panties and up my breasts. "What would you do if I came out of his room one morning?" she nearly whispers. "Would you be angry? Would you warn him against me?"

Her wet hair clings to her shoulders, her soft lips and glowing skin so much more beautiful without makeup.

And an image of her sneaking out of my brother's room in a towel, after being in his bed, hits me, and I look away.

"Or would you wish I was in your room, instead?" she murmurs.

My chest caves a little, a picture of her nestled in my sheets coming unbidden to my thoughts.

I glare back. "I'd wish you well," I say calmly. "I have brothers to spare, and it looks like you need one."

Anger blazes in her eyes, her chest rising and falling in heavy breaths all of a sudden.

Take what you want from me, and do it in the next three months, bitch.

She yanks my panties down my legs, and I stumble with the force, feeling her strip them from my feet in moments.

I gasp, my hands going to cover myself, but I stop, begging her to remind me that I hate her and this school and need to get out of here. Let her push me until I'm running for the state line.

"Oh, exquisite," she coos.

Tears well in my chest. I can feel them rising to my eyes as the Sharpie digs into my skin. I look anywhere but at her.

"Just a few suggestions," she says, writing on me, "because poor or not, these things can be fixed."

She starts circling areas of my stomach, my inner thighs, and making notes on my calves and toes.

Nudging me around, she pushes me until I'm damn near prostrate over the table, but I take it, even as the bile rises up my throat and I'm dying to just kick her teeth in.

She won't get in trouble. She never did, so I stopped telling anyone, especially my brothers, because they would only get arrested for retaliating for me.

No. I will deal with this. When I know I can't get expelled.

She writes under my ass. "Some squats will take care of this."

Rising, she lifts each arm, shakes them to see if there's fat, and then circles the offending bits in marker so I can take note.

She marks the area under my belly button and my bikini line, and circles whatever muffin top she imagines is at my hips. She writes words I refuse to look down and read and inspects me with her hands, trailing and squeezing, accompanied by laughs here and there.

"I just can't get over the state of you," she gripes. "Jesus, you're an athlete. There's no excuse."

A golf ball swells in my throat, stretching it so painfully I can barely hold back the tears.

But even as the hurt grows and grows, so do the bricks inside me. *Keep going, Clay.* Please keep going.

She rises, caps her marker, and looks me dead in the eye, an inch between us. "You should thank me," she whispers. "Surviving me will give you all the tools you need when you leave me."

I look at her through the water in my own eyes, faltering. *Leave her?*

"Just like your mother left you," she says.

Excuse me? If she thinks she knows shit about my mother . . .

But she just shakes her head. "Trysta, right? Trysta Jaeger and her six kids that she left when she hung herself in her fucking bedroom."

I exhale hard, grinding my teeth together. I am nothing like my mother. I'm not abandoning Clay. I'll fucking run from her.

She backs away, tossing the marker onto the table, and grabs her bag, T-shirt, and phone. "Tell Lavinia I'll be in to pick up the dress on Tuesday."

And she spins around, heads offstage, and disappears.

I wait until I hear the heavy back door slam shut, and then I let out a breath.

A couple of tears spill to the floor as I glance down at my body. But I immediately look away before I can take in everything she did to me.

I pick up the sweats and pull them on as quickly as I can, followed by the T-shirt. I look around, finding my shoes, but . . .

I don't see my underwear.

Where the hell are my underwear?

I swing around left and again right, lifting up my wet clothes, but I don't see them anywhere.

My shoulders slump. She took them. What is she going to do with them?

Goddammit. I wipe my tears before any more can fall, take my stuff, and leave the theater, shoes in hand.

It's still raining outside, but I don't run to my car. My energy is gone. I walk.

She knows where to hit, doesn't she? She could do or say anything. She could have my brothers arrested with the slightest accusation.

She could have Martelle fired.

She could probably get Dartmouth to rescind my acceptance letter if she knew about it. All it would take is putting me in the path of scandal or arrest, and Dartmouth would wash their hands of me.

She didn't go for those kills, though. Putting herself in my house, at my table, in one of my brothers' beds . . . Home wouldn't even be safe for me anymore.

I drive through town, speeding because I'm anxious, but I don't want to go home.

Looking over, I see the dress shop ahead, the CLOSED sign hanging on the door. Without thinking, I swing right and pull into a parking space.

Leaving my shoes in the car, I grab my keys out of my backpack on the passenger seat and climb out of the car. I run to the shop, unlocking the door and diving inside.

Miss Lavinia must've decided to stay closed today with the weather, but I know she has calls forwarded in case someone has an emergency.

I twist the lock again, leaving the lights off as I trail to the workroom.

She offered to take me on as an apprentice last year, maybe run the shop together someday. While I guess I'm good at sewing, and I kind of enjoy designing, I only learned it as part of being as useful as I can be at the theater. It's not what I want to do forever.

I'm thankful for this job, though. At least it's not a drive-thru.

I step inside the large room, keeping the lights off, but light streams through the windows, rain pummeling the panes. There's a couch I want to crash on below the bulletin boards on the left wall, but I spot a dress lying on the table, pins stuck in the hem. Clay had wanted the length shortened.

Walking over, I pick up the dress, looking down at the Collins heirloom that I knew Clay's grandmother and mother had both worn. I'd seen the pictures.

Once in a while, after Lavinia is gone for the night, I try on some of the dresses I've altered. Sometimes I wonder if I'd have turned out more girly, if my mother had stuck around. By the time makeup and clothes started to interest me, she was gone and we were even poorer than when my parents were alive. A lot of what I owned before I could start making my own money was whatever no longer fit Trace.

I fist the neckline in both hands, bringing it to my nose, and smell the fabric.

Sometimes I wonder what it would feel like to be up on that riser as just a girl, excited for something special to happen to me, with my mom arguing with me about what to do with my hair.

Sometimes I wonder what it would be like to not be me. To live a life where every single step didn't have to be so hard.

I tighten my fists around the dress, breathing hard and shallow as my gaze grows hotter on the fabric. *Sometimes I wonder what it would be like to be Clay.*

And before I can stop myself, I stretch my arms wide, hard and fast, the ancient silk screaming as it tears in two.

5

Clay

"Miss Clay?" Bernie calls out. "Your mother—"

"Can call me if she needs me," I snap, racing up the stairs of my house.

I jog quickly past the housekeeper, carrying my duffel bag. I dive into my room, slamming and locking the door.

Ugh, that bitch. I hate her. So calm. So smooth. So patient.

I gulp, running my hands through my hair. *So beautiful with those tears in her eyes.*

Keeping the lights off, I drop the bag to the floor and fall into the door.

Why did I do that? Tears immediately spill down my face as I squeeze my eyes shut. *Too far. You went too far.* I've never laid my hands on her. Ever. I just . . .

I just . . .

It feels like there are hands on me instead. On my back and on my neck, pushing me down. Pushing my head down and keeping it down. The earth piles over my head, the dirt in my mouth and my nose, more and more every day, and I can't see me anymore. I'm small. I don't know who I am. I'm always mad. Bitter. Afraid.

That's all I am anymore.

I turn, pressing my forehead into the door and sob. Why did I do that to her? What does she matter anyway?

But even now, I still feel it. She's bigger than me. She glows, and I don't, and it's not like I even want to push her down and make her shrink. It's like . . .

It's like being in her orbit, I can feel the shine, too. I feel bigger with her close.

Stripping off my clothes, I head into my bathroom, unable to turn on the water and climb in fast enough. I'm supposed to help Mrs. Gates at the funeral home today, and I should go, because it's the only thing that puts my shit into perspective, but I just can't. I can't talk to anyone right now.

Wetting my hair and letting the hot water course down over my body, I can't make my muscles ease, everything still as tight as a rubber band.

But the peace feels good, and my breathing starts to even out.

I sit down in the bathtub, hugging my knees to my body.

I miss my dad. I miss Angsty Teen Tuesdays where my mom and I would alternate every week—her showing me teen movies from her day, and then me showing her some of mine—complete with Melted Milk Dud Popcorn and Mountain Dew.

I miss the pills when I try not to take them. It scares me how I miss them.

I notice an ache in my hand and realize my fingers are curled into a fist. I look down, slowly opening it, and find Liv's underwear in my hand.

I took them. I knew I took them, but I forgot they were there. My stomach flips, the shower wetting the black lace. Does she normally wear pretty things like this every day?

My knees still bent, I hold up the underwear with both hands, my head going places I don't understand. Does she sleep in them?

Does she sleep in *only* these? How many people have seen her in them? Has Megan Martelle?

A picture forms in my head of Liv wearing these, and I hear my voice again.

I just can't get over the state of you.

My eyes burn, thinking of all the insane shit I wrote all over her today. How I violated her.

She's not ugly. I hated that I couldn't find anything wrong with her, and I shouldn't have touched her. It hurt her.

I touched her skin, and she never said it was okay. My fingertips tingle, still feeling her smooth stomach and arms.

I grind the fabric between my fingers, the tornado inside my body raging again like it did when the shame and heartache of having her naked before me raged in the theater.

She'll hate me forever now. That's what I want, right?

I'd gone too far. I had to.

I lie back in the tub, the spray showering down on me. Leaning my head on my hand, I fist the underwear again and again, my gaze falling into a void in my head where I only see her.

In here with me.

Quiet with me.

Close with me.

Her head between my thighs.

I moan, my head falling back as I rub my pussy and roll my clit under my fingers through her panties.

"Fuck," I groan, the friction of her lacy fabric a little scratchy, but it feels so good.

Yes.

But then I open my eyes and stop, my body aching with need as horror sets in at what I'm doing.

A need I've never felt with Callum.

No. Tears well. *Fuck no.*

I squeeze the panties in my hand and fly to my feet, slamming my palm into the shower wall, and see Alli on that slab and what the world did to her for wanting something people didn't think she should.

I'll fuck him. I'll fuck him a dozen different ways, slow and fast, hard and gentle. And if that doesn't prove anything, I'll find someone else to give it to me.

Someone who's good. Someone who knows what to do with me. Someone not her.

After a few days, I'd convinced myself, as always, that she deserved it. Olivia acted like a bitch. Saying that shit about how I could use a brother now that I was down one? What a fucking pig.

When her mom went and hung herself two months after her father's death, have I ever brought that up? Did I ever use it against her? What I do to her doesn't even come close to how nasty that comment was yesterday.

And then she had the fucking gall to cry.

Grabbing the parking ticket that I got a year ago out of the glove box, I climb out of my car, carrying my purse, and slide the ticket under the windshield wiper before slamming the door.

I jump up onto the sidewalk, ignoring the sign that says no parking after four. My phone rings, and I pull it out of my purse, seeing Callum's name on the screen.

"Where are you?" he asks without a hello. "I waited after school."

"Picking up my debutante monstrosity," I tell him.

"Aw, you'll be beautiful."

I laugh under my breath. "Maybe underneath."

"Is that a taunt?"

"A dare," I retort, stopping at the door to Lavinia's. "A box of Cuban cigars that you can't get it off me on ball night."

He falls silent, and I wait, my hand on the door. Was that too bold?

Then, he finally asks, "Real Cubans?"

I smile. Despite my feelings for Callum being complicated, he knows how to play. "They're only illegal to poor people," I tell him.

I open the door, stepping inside.

"And if you win, what do you want?" he asks.

"A box of Cuban cigars."

A snort escapes him.

I walk into the shop, the crystal chandeliers glowing overhead, and I immediately cast a glance around, not seeing her. I'm not sure if I'm relieved or disappointed.

"Can't wait to see you in the dress," he says.

"Well, you're gonna have to, unfortunately." I sigh, seeing no one at the counter. "See you at school tomorrow."

"Bye."

I hang up, slipping my phone into my bag, and I'm about to call out for Lavinia, but she appears from the back room, her lipstick looking eggplant against her purple dress.

"Hi," I chirp.

"Clay!" She holds up her hand as if to stop me. "I want you to try on your dress before you take it, okay? Just to make sure."

Do I have to? I was hoping to only have to wear that damn thing one more time. On ball night.

"It's in the dressing room," she says. "Do you have time?"

"I . . ." But I can't think fast enough. "Sure."

I follow her to the dressing room, dropping my purse and closing the curtain after she leaves.

I don't have my underthings—the right bra or anything—so this shit won't fit like it's supposed to.

Which could work in my favor if Lavinia doesn't realize it and the dress isn't ready in time. I could borrow my mom's spaghetti strap silver Balenciaga instead. In a crunch, she won't make me cry by saying no.

I strip down, unzip the dress bag, but then Lavinia flips something over the drapes, a strapless bra with a quick "Here you go, honey!"

I hold in my groan. "Thank you."

Snatching the undergarment, I wrap it around my front, fitting my breasts into the cups, and reach behind me with both hands to try to fasten the hooks.

But there's no way I'm going to get them connected by just feeling. "Help," I call out.

I struggle with the clasps, sucking in my stomach and turning around so I can look behind me in the mirror to see what I'm doing.

But then the curtain suddenly opens, and I see Liv standing there in the mirror.

Where's Lavinia?

I stop breathing for a split second as she stares at me and I stare at her, and I don't know what she's going to do. I look for a Sharpie on her but don't see one.

Her black jeans hug her body like a second skin and her black T-shirt is cut off midway, her stomach tight and smooth as it peeks out. The white baseball cap she has on backward is almost blue from how many times it's been bleached, and I gaze at that dark tunnel between the hair that spills around her and her neck, an urge to just bury myself in . . .

I swallow, noticing the faint remnants of the Sharpie on her stomach.

"Where's Lavinia?" I ask, steeling my voice.

She cocks her head a little and her eyes instantly drop to my panties.

The black lace ones.

Hers.

She meets my eyes again, and then she steps in, closes the curtain, and yanks me around, fastening the corset.

"A little pent-up frustration over the separate shower stalls after freshman year?" I say. "Seizing your last chance to see me naked?"

"Nothing to see," she mumbles. "You still look the same as you did when we were fourteen."

I snarl a little. *I do not.*

I adjust my breasts inside the cups, my skin tingling at the touch of her fingers.

I clear my throat. "So, what happens if my father and Callum's father push your family out of Sanoa Bay?"

"What do you care?"

She jerks the corset tighter, and I dig my toes into the carpet to keep myself from falling.

"I care." I put my hands on my hips as she works. "You're my fun." *I like you around.*

She doesn't look up, and I can tell she won't. She's not giving an inch.

"You'll split up," I tell her, already knowing, but my chest hurts hearing myself say the words. "Macon will stay close to St. Carmen. He's rooted here with the businesses, right?"

She presses her lips together.

"Dallas, and maybe Trace, will join the military." I throw guesses out there, because what else do men who have zero direction or education do but go somewhere with job training, a guaranteed paycheck, and housing? "The rest will scatter."

Army Jaeger, I think, has a kid, and Iron has too many priors. The military won't take him.

"And you?" I press. "What will happen to you?"

"My plans won't change," she finally mumbles, finishing my hooks. "I'll still get the hell out of this shithole."

"And far away from me," I say.

She stands up straight, still behind me, and meets my eyes in the mirror. "You think you're a factor in any of my decisions? Dartmouth was always the plan. You don't matter."

Dartmouth?

New England? Has she ever been out of Florida?

I stare at her longer than I should, the wheels in my head racing, and I know she can tell I'm taken off guard.

I swallow the lump in my throat and drop my eyes, twisting the corset to make sure it's sitting straight.

You don't matter. That's what she said. She's just going to leave. She's already got plans. Like she's been waiting for the day to run and . . . *How can* . . .

I try to swallow again, but my mouth is dry.

Snapping out my hands, I unzip the dress bag and peel it away, a dress I don't recognize coming into view.

Huh?

Distracted from her news, I flip the bag back down to check the name, see that it's mine, and inspect the dress again.

This isn't my dress. It's even more hideous, if that's possible.

But then . . . I notice the silk. The same shade of chiffon that made up my dress, and I study it some more, taking in the lace and flowers, all mine but repositioned.

A halter-top neckline of bushy white flowers has been added, and sequins stick to the bodice like pinstriping, ending at the waist and giving way to the feathers adorning the skirt in a spiral formation.

A laugh bubbles up in my chest, but I hold it in. It's awful, and I absolutely adore it. She did this.

I contain my smile and look over my shoulder, seeing her watch me with a calm but amused expression. She's waiting for me to react.

She did this on purpose. She risked getting fired—hell, risked the wrath of my mother and grandmother—to get me back for the Sharpie incident.

She wants a rise out of me, and she's not going to get it. I couldn't be more pleased.

"Put it on me," I tell her, almost lightheaded from the high.

She stares at me, pausing only a moment before rolling with it. The next thirty seconds could be her last in this store, and she doesn't even seem to care. I'm more pleased I was significant enough for her to trouble herself. She must've spent the rest of the weekend on it.

I pull on the petticoat, and she takes the dress off the hanger, spreads the bodice open, and lowers it to my knees.

I step in, letting her pull it up my body and button the back while I drape the flowers around my neck and attach it to the dress.

But before I can fan out the dress and take a good look at myself, seeing what my mother will see and fantasizing about her reaction, I hear a screech behind us.

"What is this?"

We both stop and turn; Lavinia stands with her hand holding the curtain open.

"What is this?" she shrieks again, and then her eyes shoot to Liv. "Did you . . . ? Olivia . . . ?"

Laughter shakes my stomach, and I turn away to hide my smile. *Priceless.*

But a thought hits me at the same time. If she gets fired, I won't have access to her here. If she's willing to throw away a job to piss me off, then I'm not really winning anything.

Lavinia's eyes shoot up and down my body, taking in all her hard work fucked up, and then fixes a glare on Liv. "May I speak to you, please?"

And I know it's over for her.

Liv starts to leave the dressing room, but I brush past her and step out into the main room, up onto the riser. "I love it," I announce. "Ring it up."

"I will not," Lavinia fires back. "This . . . this . . ." She scans me

up and down again, like she's about to vomit. Then she shoots another glare to Liv, pointing to the back room where she can go fire
her in private. "Now!"

"Ring it up," I growl. "It's exactly what I wanted." I look to Liv,
rubbing it in her face. "The credit card is in my back pocket. Grab
it." And then to Lavinia again. "Olivia followed my orders. Don't
blame her. I want it paid in full."

Lavinia's mouth falls open like she's going to argue, but I cut
her off.

"I mean it," I say again.

And then I turn away, cutting off any further argument as I
check myself out in the floor-length mirrors, observing all angles.

Liv digs my mom's credit card out of the back pocket of my
jeans in the dressing room and shoots me a half-lidded look before
disappearing into the lobby. I hear Lavinia's hushed hissing and
stand there, trying to hear what she's saying to Jaeger, but I can't.

The bitch needs to shut up. I told her it was fine. I mean, it's not.
Liv's going to pay for this, and I don't need help punishing her.
She's my responsibility.

The hem of the dress is too short, the petticoat sticks out the
bottom, and the flowers around my neck itch. I hike up the skirt
and reach behind me, unzipping the petticoat and letting it fall to
the floor, stepping out of it. There's no way my mother will make
me wear this, and I'm half tempted to start cutting it into pieces so
it can't be salvaged for my future daughter. I could even blame Liv
for it. No one would think otherwise.

But . . . I won't go that far yet. She's finally playing, and I don't
want to actually get her in trouble before I can enjoy this.

"If this is the dress," someone says, and Callum appears behind
me, swinging me back into his arms, and I gasp. "I will absolutely
be peeling it off you as soon as possible."

I look up at him, feeling Olivia right outside the room.

He dips down, his breath on my lips as he hovers, not kissing me.

"Callum—"

"Shhh . . ." he tells me. "I snuck in."

"I thought you had a meeting of the Skull and Bones."

He grins, brushing off my teasing.

He's trying to get a head start in some fraternity before he goes to college next year. Schmoozing alumni and legacies. Milking connections that his father already made for him. I like that he's ambitious, even if whatever we have going won't last beyond graduation. He'll go to one school in the fall. I'll go to another.

And we both know neither one of us is waiting for the other while we're away.

"You can't see the dress." I stand back up and spin out of his arms.

But he pulls me back in, and I suck in a breath. He presses his body to mine, gazing into my eyes without blinking. "Undress for me," he whispers.

I still.

"Let me watch the dress come off and your clothes put back on," he murmurs, his nose brushing mine. "I won't touch you."

Part of me wants to. I like how slowly he moves, easing me into it.

He walks us backward into the dressing room and closes the curtain. "Every time I see you, I want third base already, Clay. Show me."

He moves over my lips, holding back just enough to make my skin tingle where his warm breath falls.

I want him. I look up into his eyes, picturing myself tearing his shirt off his body and what his skin will feel like against mine, but the tingles fade, and I inch up on my tiptoes, searching for his mouth. Chasing it. Fighting to get it back.

"Unbutton me," I pant.

I want him.

I want him to touch me and kiss me and take me home and sneak into my bed and . . .

He loses it. Grabbing my waist, he brings his mouth down on mine, backing me into the wall, and hikes up my skirt. He nestles himself between my legs, holding my knee at his waist.

His other hand works the buttons at my back.

"Five minutes, Clay," he says, jerking the buttons free until I feel the bodice loosen and slide down my torso. "How much damage can I do in five minutes?"

He covers my lips again and grinds into me, the twenty-four-hour scruff on his chin poking my face and lips. I scale my hands up his chest, his muscles tight and thick under his shirt, and I dive into his mouth deeper, waiting for the pulse between my thighs to need what he's doing. To like it. I'm tired of not fucking around like everyone else. I want my own guy.

I want someone touching me.

I want to search him out for more and not be able to control myself when we're together.

He forces my head back and kisses my neck, sucking and biting as he grips my ass and rolls his hips against my panties over and over again.

And I feel it. I freeze for a moment, the pulse on my clit starting to pump as the lace of Liv's panties rubs so good against my nub.

Heat spreads as I grow wet, and slowly, I close my eyes and let my arms fall away from his body. They hang at my side, images flashing like lightning behind my lids. So quick. So hot.

Skin. Wet skin. And her face is on fire, glowing and golden and covered with my mouth.

I moan, slipping my hand down her panties that I wear, rubbing my smooth skin and dipping my fingers inside and wanting her to watch me. To make her want me and make her happy.

"Goddamn, Clay," Callum growls, and he's stopped kissing me. I think he's watching.

But after a moment, lips land on me again, and I kiss so slow and gentle. With my tongue taunting and savoring her. Not him.

"Come home with me," he whispers in my ear. "Neither one of us can stop this."

My orgasm crests, and tears fill my eyes, grateful and gutted. I can come with him. Now I know how.

But God . . . What the hell is going on in my head?

I hear something and open my eyes, seeing Liv through the crack in the curtain. It lies open six inches, and she stands there, a stack of shoeboxes next to her on the table as she stares at us.

Her gaze falls, and I know she sees her underwear. She sees Callum Ames with his hands all over them, and I can't help the pleasure I feel in my stomach as I watch her watch me rub up on him a little more.

I linger on her chest, the faintest points of her nipples poking through her black T-shirt, the tan skin of her stomach peeking out the bottom. She's not wearing a bra, and my fingers hum, another moan escaping as I feel myself slide my hands up her shirt.

"Clay," he says again against my neck.

But I don't blink as I look at her. "The ball," I tell him. "After the ball. All night."

He can have me all night. I'll like it. I know I'll like it.

Liv's eyes narrow, the muscle in her jaw flexing, and I know she didn't hear me, she's probably just mad her plan to piss me off with the dress didn't work.

I matter, you brat. You don't. You can't just run from me. You'll leave here, but you'll do it knowing you never survived me. Not really.

We still have months, Jaeger. The fun is just beginning.

6

Olivia

I race down the field, sweat dripping down my back as the lights shine overhead. The crowd in the stands cheers or yells unintelligible orders like they'd be doing any better if they were out here.

Skidding to a halt, I whip around, find Clay, and pound my stick on the grass twice. "Here!" I shout.

She meets my eyes, both of us panting, and tosses the ball over to Ruby Ingram instead. I squeeze my fist around the stick, grit my teeth, and watch for all of two seconds before fucking Ruby loses the ball, and the other team speeds back down the field toward our goal with their prize.

Goddammit, Clay.

I dart off after the ball, shooting a glare at her before running past. What the hell is her problem? She wants to win, doesn't she? Does she think this makes *me* look bad? No. It's on her.

The attacker passes the ball, but I race ahead, scoop it up, and whip around, shooting it over to Amy. She runs, everyone changes directions, and I barrel after her, digging in my heels and on guard as I watch the ball go to Krisjen, who hesitates too long.

"Krisjen!" I bark. Her nervous eyes jerk to me and she flips her stick, only too happy to be rid of the damn thing. I catch it, run and swerve, and shoot. The ball hits the net, the goalie unable to react fast enough.

"Yeahhhhhhhh!" I hear my brothers roar from the stands in between whistles.

But I'm not happy. I walk up to Clay, slamming my shoulder into hers as others run around us. "Stop fucking up," I growl as I pass.

"What?" she taunts. "I just love watching you haul ass, is all."

Yeah, right. Her ponytail bounces as she runs ahead, and I almost wish Coomer would bench me. It's amazing how fast Clay can deplete my motivation.

Krisjen passes the ball to her, and she catches it, running toward me. I back up, holding my stick, ready to catch, but she shoots it over my head. Mercedes Peron goes for it, but an Eagle player knocks her into the ground. The ball rolls away.

I shoot daggers at Clay. *I'm going to kill her.* She's sabotaging this on purpose. Trying to prove no one needs me.

But just then, Clay pulls off her eyewear, wipes the sweat off her forehead, and looks anything but pleased with herself.

"Collins!" Coach shouts, but Clay refuses to make eye contact.

Mercedes holds out her hands, questioning Clay. "I thought you were passing it to Jaeger."

"Just shut up," Clay bites out.

The midfielders engage and Amy takes the ball, looking for Clay, but I rush over just as she shoots it, grabbing it with my stick and knocking Clay to the ground. I don't even look down to see her reaction, and I don't care if I get in trouble. I'm not letting her screw this up.

Racing down the field, I pass it to Amy, who passes it to Lena Marcus, who shoots and scores. I smile, backing up and ready for the ball to come back into play.

But when I look back, Clay is on the sidelines, Coomer giving her a good tongue-lashing. Clay stands there, her defiant little chin stern as always, and Megan stands near them, looking at me and biting back her smile.

I'm not smiling anymore, though. Clay isn't looking at the coach. She's looking at me, her breathing calm and even like she doesn't give a shit.

Why is she doing this? What does she want?

I don't have time to ponder too long, because play starts up again and it's pedal to the metal for the last twenty minutes of the game. Clay re-enters, avoiding me again and ignoring the coach, running the ball to the goal herself and securing our win at eleven over five.

I don't feel like celebrating, though. I just want to get out of here and away. Grabbing my shit, I walk for the parking lot, not staying for the coach's little talk after the game, and see Trace jogging up to me right before he lifts me into his arms. "O-liv-i-a!" he screams. "Ma bitch! Four goals!"

And despite my anger, I laugh as he swings me around.

He sets me down, and Iron brings me in for a hug. "Congratulations, kiddo."

"Thanks."

Dallas and Army walk up behind them, parents and everyone else on the bleachers slowly spilling into the parking lot to head home.

I look around. "Where's Macon?"

He said he'd come to this one.

But by the look in Army's eyes, I already know the answer. "Had to stay and get shit done, kid."

Yeah. I look away. *I know.*

"Come on." Trace nudges me, trying to cheer me up. "Mariette's. I'm starving."

"Me, too," Iron adds, taking my gear bag from me.

They pull me along, some of the girls leaving with their parents who came to watch, too, and others celebrating in the parking lot.

We pile into the truck, Iron tosses my bag into the bed, and Dallas starts the engine. I peer out the window as he shifts it into gear, seeing Clay leaning against the bus and scrolling through her phone.

It's not unusual until I notice our other teammates laughing with friends and getting hugs from proud parents. Don't Clay's parents usually come to the games? Thinking back, I guess I can't remember.

Maybe I should be less mad Macon never shows and just be grateful someone does.

"So, your birthday's soon," Army says from the front seat.

"Huh?"

He turns his head, looking at me. "The twenty-ninth. It's in a little over a week."

I wiggle my eyebrows. "What are you getting me?"

A car? Please say it's a car.

"A stripper," he replies.

Trace and Iron laugh, but I'm not impressed, because he's most likely not joking. "I have taste you can't afford."

"What are you talking about?" he replies. "Flamingo Flo's has top-notch ladies."

"Flamingo Flo's employs hillbilly meth-heads," I shoot back.

Army snorts, and everyone laughs again, knowing that's all too true, and I sit back, shaking my head.

But my smile fades a little. They're just joking, but they wouldn't be against it, either. Would they suggest getting me a stripper if I were into guys? No, they only feel the need to protect me from men, as if my relationships with women are less of a threat. As if they're not real.

They would never let a man give me a lap dance.

I stare out the window, the music blasting and Trace digging into the cooler between us and cracking a beer.

I'll miss them, but . . . I'm dying to leave here. To feel like I belong somewhere. To maybe meet someone.

I don't have anything here.

There's no one like me.

U p!" Army shouts.

Everyone lifts their glasses into the air, clinking as the cheap tiki torches around the patio of Mariette's burn in the evening air, and I smile, absolutely taking the shot of Patrón that Army lets me have, since Macon's not around.

"This could be it!" we all shout back in unison. "Salud!"

"Salud!" Army follows.

We shoot the tequila, my brothers laughing at me when I immediately chase it with a sip of Coke.

As long as they're around, I can typically have a drink or two, but the quick plummet from "I feel fantastic and love everyone" to "Oh my God, what have I done?" and wasting a whole day recovering from a hangover was a lesson I only needed to learn once. Ever since, I drink sparingly and almost never hard liquor.

But it's a special occasion tonight. I just scored four goals, I got into Dartmouth, my birthday is coming up, *and* the lawyer got Iron off with community service if he promises to also attend counseling.

As if a therapist is going to help my brother not slam any more waiters' heads into tables for getting smart with him. I wish I could say Iron risks his freedom for something more substantial, like money or power, but honestly, I'd think less of him if he were that shallow. The anger, I understand.

And he only uses it on others. Never his family.

We sit outside, the sea breeze beyond the swamp blowing through the cypresses and tupelos, the scent of the moss stinging my nostrils, but quickly calmed by the sand and salt following it.

Everyone slams their glasses down on the wooden table, the wind cooling my scalp and making the umbrellas flap overhead.

I dig into my ice cream sundae as Aracely drops two platters of crawfish onto the table and sits. She dated Iron, then Dallas, and now Army uses her to help with Dex, even though she's not his mother. We all know she's just in between brothers temporarily, so she just kind of sticks around as an honorary member of the family to help out. And to be a pain in my ass. Like the sister I never wanted.

Army fills his beer from the pitcher, and Dallas and Trace dig into the seafood, pinching off the tails, sucking the heads, and grabbing the meat with their teeth. In no time, the newspaper covering the table is littered with decapitated crawdads, and I laugh as Army shows his son how to peel a shell.

I stare at Dex, my smile faltering. I'm going to miss a lot when I do leave, won't I? His first steps and first words. And after I'm gone, who will be next? Trace, maybe? He's searching for his niche away from our older brothers.

Dallas, most definitely. All he's waiting for is someone to go first and give him permission to seek out the things Macon tells us we're selfish for wanting.

Army will marry someone to give Dex a mom, and Iron may end up in prison regardless of whether I stay.

But I look around the table at all the faces, the big smiles and bright eyes and how they look like they have everything they need, right here, right now, because we have each other.

It's not enough for me. It's never been enough. But I don't want it to change, either. When I come back home, I want to know they're here. All of them. On our land. Safe and sound.

The key sits in the bag on the back of my chair, weighing heavy on my mind.

I wish Macon was here. Not at home, avoiding us, too consumed with his responsibilities to enjoy his family.

I don't remember my father well. There are images. Feelings. That's it. I was too young, but when I think about what I do remember, it's almost as if he was another brother. He never disciplined me, yelled at me, or lost his temper. Iron and Dallas took the lead on that when I made a mess or failed a test or sassed back.

My father, I only saw at the end of the day. When he was tired. Relaxed. Happy to be home from work. I would sit with him on the recliner, eating popcorn and watching *Iron Man*. It was like spending time with Trace, my friends, or a grandpa you only spent minimal hours with once a month.

Macon had joined the military by the time I was old enough to remember anything. Significantly older than me, he was the one I feared when I should've feared my father. Here was this soldier I didn't know walking through our front door once a year, always lurking around the perimeter of a room, there but never quite present. He didn't smile as easily as Army or crack jokes like Trace. I never felt safe enough to wrap myself around his leg, torturing him until he gave me a brownie like I did with Dallas, and he was never around to protect me like Iron.

And while I knew he was my parents' first and was raised in our house, I started to wonder more as I grew older if he'd ever really lived with any of these people. I wasn't the only one he seemed cold to.

He reminded me of our mother. There was a cloud following them both, and you can still see it in his eyes, even now. There's something that wasn't as easy for them as it was for the rest of us.

And when I was eleven and he hit me, it devastated me more than losing both of my parents within eight weeks of each other just months earlier. I cried and cried, not because the spanking hurt, but because I felt hated.

Because he hated me.

At least that's what I thought until later that night when I found him sitting at the kitchen bar, his head in his hands as he quietly cried in the dark.

He never apologized, but he never did it again. And over time

I came to understand that my oldest brother was only twenty-three that night, and twenty-three is still so young. That he was suddenly in charge of three minors to feed and clothe, a mountain of debt, and the prospect that life would never be more than this for him. That even when we grew up, Iron would always be a problem, and Army and Trace would be bringing babies into the world they couldn't support on their own. Macon would be the one everyone turned to because he was the "adult." He always took care of us. You always felt lonely in a room with him, but you were never alone, and if we took anything into this world, it was that.

We didn't know if he loved us, but he would always stay.

I could rely on him like I never could my mother, and I craved his approval and respect like I never did with my father. I look around the table again, wishing he was here. What is he doing now? What does he do when he's alone?

"Fuckin' Saints think they own this place already," I hear someone say.

I blink, snapping out of my thoughts as I set my sundae aside. I look up, following my brothers' gazes.

Milo Price and Callum Ames eye us as they head up the sidewalk to the entrance of the restaurant, followed by Becks and Krisjen. Becks waves at me, offering a contrite smile that says she tried to talk them out of it. I don't wave back, but Aracely looks between us, and I can just tell this is all my fault. Somehow.

"They never will," Trace replies. "They will never own this place."

I yank over one of the trays and start in on what crawfish is left, wishing they were just here to eat, but I know they're not. Why else would they cross the tracks to dine at a mosquito-infested converted garage with rolls of paper towels instead of napkins on the tables and peeling linoleum floors?

Sanoa Bay is an unincorporated neighborhood of St. Carmen, but it may as well be the moon. They're Saints. We're Swamp. We share a zip code. That's it.

Aracely starts mumbling under her breath, and then she hikes up the volume, barking something in Spanish. I flick my gaze to Army and see he's already eyeing me. Like Macon, he speaks Spanish and understands her. Unfortunately, by the time Iron was born, our parents got tired and stopped raising their children bilingual.

But Army's face tells me she's talking about me. Like I didn't already know that.

"Just don't," I tell her.

She shrugs. "I wasn't talking to you."

"Yeah, every time you're not talking to me, you're speaking Spanish," I snap back. "They're not my friends, okay?"

I didn't invite them. Just because we go to the same school . . .

"You're with them more than you're home," she counters.

A bitter laugh catches in my throat, and I straighten up, looking around the table for support. "I'm at school. Or work. Or practice."

Iron sighs, trying to keep the peace. "It's okay."

But he says it to me as if I'm the asshole losing my temper here. She started it.

"I mean, what does she want from me?" I bark back at him. "Macon sent me to Marymount, I didn't want to go. I'm not one of them."

She spits something back in Spanish again and I can make out enough to hear, "Are you one of *us*?"

Gritting my teeth, I shove my chair and storm from the table as a couple of my brothers groan and Iron grumbles something to his ex.

Stepping into the restaurant, I ignore the looks in my direction and head for the bathroom, but think twice, needing fresh air instead. Heading right, I push through the double doors, seeing staff look up from their work, but I'm out the back door before Mariette has a chance to ask me what I'm doing in her kitchen.

Letting the door slam shut, I draw in a deep breath of thick air and fall back against the wall, the music of the locusts and frogs filling the night in the thicket beyond. Trees stretch high past the dirt road, and I can see the faint touch of moonlight on the water that still looks green despite how dark it is.

I stare ahead, lost in thought again.

My family thinks they're strong, but we're as brittle as a piecrust. With the knowledge that we're together, it gives us confidence, but leaving will diminish that just enough for Dallas to leave next. And then Trace and Army and Iron, and what will all of Macon's sacrifices be for?

I hate that he's asking me to stay, but I know why he feels owed. If I leave, I'll find success, but it'll be at the expense of my home. And I love my family.

Tears fill my eyes, and for the first time in my life, I realize what Macon must've felt when he left the Marines.

And I know exactly what would've happened to us if he hadn't. Where would I have been without him?

"Lost?" someone says.

I turn my head, seeing Megan approach. Her blond hair blurs, and I wipe my eyes, standing up straight and clearing my throat.

"No." I force a laugh. "You?"

"Not at all." She holds up a brown plastic grocery bag, one of Mariette's pie boxes inside.

Scratch what I said about the Saints crossing the tracks for no reason. The key lime pie here is the draw, they just always get it to go.

She stops in front of me, and I avoid her gaze until I blink away the rest of the tears.

"Don't cry," she whispers.

"I don't cry."

I put a smile on my face and finally raise my eyes, running my hand through my hair. A cool sweat dampens my back, and I slide my hands into my jean shorts pockets, watching her eyes drop for a moment to my cleavage that disappears down my loose tank top.

My skin pricks.

"What's wrong?" she asks, sounding genuinely concerned.

I shake my head. "I don't know."

I'm so confused, I don't know where to begin.

"Then, what's good?" she teases.

A laugh escapes me, and I lean against the wall of the restaurant again, relaxing.

Coming in close, she touches my face with her free hand and my heart skips, closing my eyes and liking it more than I want to. I'm a little vulnerable right now, and I'm kind of tempted to forget that she's an authority figure. Even if she is only a year or so older than me.

"So busy collecting stones." She tsks. "You're missing the diamonds."

Tears well again, and I know she's right. I have so many people who love me, and I'm whining.

"I just want to share joy with someone." My breathing shakes as tears spill through my closed eyes. "I don't want to be alone in everything I do. Fuck . . ."

School. Home. Work. The theater. There's always opposition, and I'm rarely the one in control.

"No one is on my side," I whisper, meeting her eyes.

It only lasts the span of a breath, but she holds my gaze and I stop breathing, her blond hair and blue eyes the only thing I see before she's on me. Her mouth melts into mine, and I only hesitate a moment before I slide my arms around her.

God . . .

I grip her slim waist, pressing my body into hers, and her groan vibrates down my throat as I squeeze my eyes shut and taste the heat on her breath. Intoxicated.

Or would you wish I was in your room instead? A voice carries me away.

Taking her face in one hand, I spin her around and back her

into the wall, her long, silky hair draping down her back, across to tickle my other hand.

I thread her hair through my fingers, feeling its soft silkiness, and nibble her mouth as a moan escapes me.

"Liv," she begs, her mouth trailing across my cheek and down my neck as she grinds into me.

I squeeze my eyes shut, gripping her hair at her scalp, the urge to go too hard overcoming me. God, I can't fucking stop. I take her throat in my hand and force her head back, sucking and biting her lips and relishing the feel of her body in my hands.

I'll show her what she gets for treating me like her fucking servant. For sabotaging all our team's hard work, and for never being kind to me.

And for letting that punk-ass frat boy touch her. What the hell does she see in him? He has an alarming array of pastel-colored Polo shirts, because he needs to let everyone know he's a white-as-fuck, roofie-jungle-juice-making Chad.

I kiss her hard, my blood boiling down my arms.

She whimpers, and I'm not sure if it's pleasure or pain. "Liv."

"Don't talk." I pull away and take her hand. "Get in the car."

I nod toward Dallas's Mustang and advance on her as she backs up toward it. Her steps are slow, as if she's unsure, but her chest rises and falls, and I know she wants it.

I don't look at her face.

The door opens, I climb in the seat after her and close the door, pulling her into my arms.

"We'll be seen," she murmurs against my lips.

I press my forehead to hers, running my thumb over her bottom lip and almost smelling that perfume that made me want to bury my nose in her skin the first time I saw her. "Sanoa is where secrets go to breathe," I tell her.

No one cares what we do here. *Here, you can have me all you want.*

"You won't tell anyone?" she asks.

Megan's worried about losing her job for fucking around with a student.

The girl in my head is worried about her boyfriend discovering what really makes her come.

"I won't tell anyone," I say.

And I pull her in, slipping my tongue into her mouth and my hand up her skirt.

She moans, the pulse in her neck throbbing against my fingers as she squirms.

"I've wanted you for so long," she tells me.

I pause, the spell starting to break. "Don't say that." I tip her chin down and force her eyes to me. "Say you hate me. Tell me to stop."

"But I . . ."

"Say it." I nudge her back against the door and hover over her. "Call me swamp trash and tell me to stop."

I dive into her neck as she stutters and tries to find the words that will please me, but she's confused.

"Say it." I grab the back of her neck, squeezing my eyes shut and rubbing her through her panties.

"Stop," she gasps. "I hate you, you fucking trash. I hate you."

I find her clit through the fabric, rubbing circles and hearing her moan again as she opens her legs wider.

"Yeah?" I lick her mouth. "But you're so wet. You don't want this?"

And I slip my finger inside, caressing her bare skin.

She gasps.

"Or this?" I taunt, sliding another one in.

"Stop." She kisses me back, breathing hard. "Ah, stop. No."

Mmm, no.

And all the while I'm trembling as she grabs for me and holds me close and wants me in our secret place where no one can see us, because I want it to be real, too. I want Clay Collins in this fucking car and to love me so much she can't stand it.

Just so I won't be alone anymore.

That's how pathetic I am. Fantasizing over a straight girl who believes I deserve nothing good in this world, because I think hate-fucking her would make me feel powerful. Because I don't love her and I don't like her, but I feel something about her, and whatever it is, it's strong, and I need it. I want to throw her down and put my teeth on her and feel hers on me, but at the end, make her come and kiss her mouth and let her finally know that there was one nice memory of me.

Oh, yeah. There was one.

I start to shake, and I can't catch my breath. I growl, pull off Martelle, and sit back in the seat, not sure if I'm angry for using her or disgusted that I tried to make her play the role of someone who will never deserve me.

There's no love here, but that didn't matter, did it? The hate turned me on. Jesus, I'm fucked up.

"Olivia?" I hear the leather seat grind under her weight as she sits up.

She reaches for me, but I pull away. "I'm sorry. I shouldn't have done this. This was wrong."

I don't know why it's wrong. It feels good. Clay probably let that jackass fuck her, and I know she doesn't love him, so why do I feel guilty?

Megan moves in closer. "Are you okay?"

But I swing open the door and climb out. "It's not your fault," I tell her, but I can't get away from her fast enough. "I'll see you at school."

And I leave the door open for her, quickly escaping back into Mariette's. The embarrassment settles over me of what she must think, but there's nothing I can do about it. She won't talk. I'm a student—and still technically a minor. I'm safe.

I slip into the employee restroom on the opposite wall to wash my hands and splash some water on my face, yanking two paper towels out of the dispenser.

I hold my eyes in the mirror as a tornado whirls around me that I can't seem to stop. *Have some damn control. You're better than this.*

It's just the pressure. The play and college and Clay . . . Lots at once.

And Callum. I'm just tired of taking it.

I swing open the door and walk through the kitchen, into the restaurant, and around the divider. I stop at Callum's table, Becks and Krisjen sitting in the booth opposite him and Milo. There's a round of sodas in front of everyone, and a basket of fries in the middle.

"You're not welcome here," I remind them calmly. "Not in the Bay."

They know this.

Callum looks up, a gleam in his eyes as he cocks his head. "We just want to eat," he tells me. "I hear your Cuban sandwich is the best around."

"Mariette?" I call out, pulling my blade out of my back pocket and leaving it sheathed at my side. "This table wants their order *to go.*"

Callum's eyes drop to the switchblade, trying to hold back his smile. "I would think you'd like to see more business in your neighborhood." He sighs. "I would think my understudy would be more grateful."

Oh, yes. I'm grateful for the scraps. Thanks for reminding me that nothing good comes unless by the good graces of the rich and beautiful.

"If it were up to me, you'd have the part," he taunts. "If it were up to me."

And his meaning isn't lost. It's not up to him. It's up to me and whether I use that key.

I slide the switch, the blade unsheathing, and I watch him watch the knife, ready.

"You know those clapping games little girls play?" I ask him.

"They seem silly and frivolous, but actually they teach motor coordination and dexterity."

The girls at the table stiffen as Milo watches in amusement, safely shielded by Callum.

I hear the screen door behind me swing open and shut, bouncing against the doorframe a couple of times.

I hold up the knife and lay my hand down on the table. "But I always liked the boys' game instead," I tell him. "You ever play stabberscotch?"

A couple of shadows fall over me, and Trace's body spray wafts through my nostrils.

"Thirty seconds." I balance the tip of the knife on my palm and then flip it, catching it. "If I don't cut myself, you take your fucking slugs and get out of here." I look at Krisjen, the nice one. "And that means you, too."

She keeps her mouth shut, simply looking to Callum to see what he's going to do.

"And Becks can stay," I add. She's the only one I really like.

But then Callum asks, "Why should I make a deal to stay when you know I don't have to leave?"

"As if you'll have to leave anyway, right?" I fire back. "I'm a loser. I'll lose."

He laughs, but it's a short nervous one, and he doesn't meet my eyes.

I smirk. "Scared?"

His gaze flickers to my brothers behind me, who stay quiet to see how this will play out, and he is caught between a rock and hard place. Lose and he has to leave. Or they'll make him leave.

And he's smart enough to know that I never play games, so I wouldn't play one unless I knew I could win.

So he does the only thing he can. "Not at all," he finally replies. "I'll take the bet."

Flattening my left hand on the table, I spread my fingers wide and dig the point of the blade into first position, on the outside of my thumb.

But just then, I feel something, and that perfume hits me before I even see her. Her hand slides underneath mine, and I still as Clay covers my back, her breath on my ear.

"Scared?" she whispers.

I almost shove her off, but fine. I forge ahead. "Start the timer," I tell Krisjen.

She brings up the app on her phone, hits the blue button, and I start, Clay's hand underneath mine, thinking her presence will make my little heart patter so badly I'll screw up. I'll take that bet.

One-two, one-three, one-four, one-five, one-six, one-six, one-five, one-four . . .

I move the knife back and forth, between my fingers, faster and faster, my brothers clapping behind me to help me keep time.

"Faster," Callum orders.

I move faster.

One-two, one-three, one-four, one-five, one-six, one-six, one-five, one-four . . . Moving through Clay's and my fingers and back again, the heat from her hand moving through mine and up my arm to my chest.

I dig faster and faster, and harder, but after a moment, all I feel is her eyes on my neck, and I swear she moves in closer, inhaling through her nose.

Smelling me.

And that's when I recognize the other scent on her. Vodka.

"Don't stop," she pants.

My eyelids flutter as her heart pounds against my arm.

The boys clap. Callum, Milo, Becks, and Krisjen watch the knife.

And even though Clay and I aren't alone, it feels like it. They don't hear her words.

"I dread the anticipation of pain more than the pain, don't you?"

she says in a low voice. "Most people don't know when it's coming. It's worse when you know it's coming."

She speaks so softly. It's not like her. What is she doing?

"Especially when you know it's there every day," she tells me.

I blink long and hard, heat flooding my body as the adrenaline rushes, because if I take my eyes off what I'm doing, I'm going to get hurt, but shit looks blurry now. *Goddammit.*

The girl is tail. That's it. She's a gutter human being and good for nothing else.

Her eyes linger on me, and I watch the timer, dropping to ten seconds left. *One-two, one-three, one-four, one-five, one-six, one-six, one-five, one-four . . .*

Her warm breath hits my neck. "Your skin looks like it's on fire," she whispers, and I swear I can feel her tongue.

Fuck. I groan, my stomach shaking, because she says it like she's in pain.

"Olivia," she pleads.

And my clit throbs, my hand trembles, and the knife slips, slicing right into the side of my middle finger.

Shit! Pain shoots through my hand, I drop the knife, and pull away, gritting my teeth.

Goddammit, Clay.

Laughter erupts at the table, and I turn back, seeing her slide onto Callum's lap, a self-satisfied smile on her stupid face.

I suck the blood off my finger, looking for any on hers, but it doesn't look like she was cut at all.

"She does have that effect on me, too," Callum says, pulling Clay back into his body by her throat and kissing her cheek.

I glare down at her. "You did that on purpose."

She leans forward, out of his hold, but his hands remain on her, roaming her back like she's his.

Clay plucks a fry out of the basket, and Krisjen's all smiles as she relishes her bestie's suave skill with the dyke.

"So what do we get now that we won?" Clay asks me, eating the fry.

"You get to stay," Trace replies behind me.

"We could stay anyway."

I pick up my blade, sheathing it and sticking it into my pocket.

"You know," Clay continues, "I will actually be sorry when my father levels this place. Just think . . ." She looks over her shoulder at Callum. "We're sitting right about the ninth hole, right? You've seen the blueprints?"

He nods, and Dallas steps forward, but I hold up my arm, keeping him back.

"Such a waste of good key lime pie," Milo offers.

"Well, the new community needs restaurants," Clay tells her. "We'll give Mariette a job."

And then she pins me with a look, and no matter what we do, they know they'll win. Not today, but eventually.

"A key lime pie!" Callum calls out to the server. "To go!"

They all start to get up, but I stop them. "Cancel that!" I tell Mariette. And I look at Clay. "Night Tide. You can cross the tracks."

This isn't her against me. It's Saints versus Swamp. Let's have some fun before everything is gone.

Clay hesitates. "The administration doesn't allow that. We have to stay in St. Carmen."

Night Tide is a senior tradition. A scavenger hunt around town. All night. There's usually unsanctioned drinking and a *secret* scavenger hunt that is also not allowed by the administration.

I give her a loaded look. "We won't tell."

Callum listens close as Clay ponders, her friends letting her make the call.

"All of us," she says.

I nod.

"All night."

I nod again.

"And we can go anywhere."

"You can try," I say.

I won't lose again.

"Deal," she says.

They rise from their seats, Callum dropping some money on the table as they filter past us toward the door.

But Clay stops at my side, speaking low and close again. "And you owe me a new dress," she says.

She leaves, and I smile to myself. *Yeah, good luck with that.*

"What are you doing?" Dallas yanks me around. "Macon won't agree to that."

I ignore him and leave the restaurant, passing Army, Iron, and Aracely without a word. I make the short trek down the road to my house, walking past the open workshop. Macon works on a motorcycle while a few of the local boys watch him with beers in their hands.

Safe in my room, I lock the door, plug my phone into the charger, and fall to my bed, keeping the room dark.

I stare above me, the streetlight outside glowing across the ceiling as some Kansas song vibrates through the walls from the garage. My white Christmas lights decorate my wrought-iron headboard and border the window frame, reminding me of spotlights in the dark of a stage.

I'm an actress, inside and out. For years, I played my part well, as if everything was according to script and I knew what was coming. No surprises.

But tonight, the snake inside uncoiled, and it felt good. My venom wasn't like hers, so I never thought it was deadly. I'd given Clay too much power the last four years.

I smile in the dark. *I'm poison.* I can be poison, too.

I take my pillow underneath my head and hug it to my chest, squeezing the fabric in my fists and burying my nose in it.

My desire for her earlier was nothing. Just confusion.

Maybe I'm still attracted to her like I was years ago, before I realized how hideous she was.

Or maybe I just hate her so much that I want her to see my power. A kiss that turns into a bite. A fight that turns into a fuck.

Any way I slice it, it isn't good. I've never been a violent person, and I don't want to hurt people.

I just . . . I don't know. She's changing me. I want to affect her.

Curling on my side, I hold the pillow, letting go of the worry and planning for tomorrow.

For Clay. For the key.

And for the reality that I don't want revenge or a fight. I want to have some fun.

I'm going to have fun on Night Tide.

"Liv?"

I stir, the fog in my brain lifting.

"Liv!" Two loud pounds hit my door, and I squeeze the pillow in my arms.

Sleep weighs heavy as I blink my eyes open, seeing a faint light stream through the windows.

Shit. I just lay down.

Didn't I?

Turning over, I look at the clock, seeing it's six fifty in the morning.

I shoot up, rubbing my eyes. *Oh my God.* I slept in my clothes.

I clear my throat. "I'm up!"

"Can you make me a lunch to take to work?" Army asks. "Please? I'm swamped."

Dex cries right outside the door, and I know he's talking about the baby.

I nod, even though he can't see me. "I'll be out in a minute."

Damn, it feels like I didn't sleep at all. I don't remember dozing off.

I straighten my arms, still wrapped around the pillow, and toss it off me.

The night before comes back, and I remember the deal I made with Clay.

I'm a little scared, but I'm a little excited, too. And my head is clearer now. She's not my enemy. She's not that important. It'll be an intense night, but I'll make sure the Saints aren't the only ones having fun.

My phone buzzes, and I grab it, climbing out of bed. I open my door, seeing Army walk with his kid down the hall. I close it again, stretching my arms above my head and feel the muscles and kinks crack in my back. I don't think I moved all night.

My phone buzzes again, and I hold it up, swiping the screen. My toolbar is filled with notifications.

I narrow my eyes. *What the hell did I miss while I slept? Damn.*

I pick one and click on it, my chest immediately caving as my stomach rolls and vomit rises up my throat.

"What?" I choke out.

Clay.

No.

7

Clay

"Have you seen her?" Amy asks, swiping her lunch card.

"Do I care?"

I follow, swiping mine, tossing it on my tray, and carrying my food to the lunch table. Krisjen follows, Milo stealing a handful of her fries as he passes. "Be careful, Clay," she says. "There's a reason Sanoa Bay has survived as long as it has. And a reason our parents don't want us over there."

"Please . . ." Amy chides her, sitting down next to Callum. "That video was priceless. Omega Chi supremacy."

I pull my sweater vest off over my head and set it down on the table, pulling my phone out of my bag and checking notifications. Heat dampens my forehead.

Posting that video was stupid. Jesus, what was I thinking? I'd just been so fucking hot after seeing her in that car, her sweaty paws all over Megan, that I whipped out my phone and started filming.

And then I went inside Mariette's and there was more confrontation. I can't stop thinking about her.

I'm always thinking about her. I just want her out of my head.

"Our money doesn't matter to them," Krisjen tells Amy.

"True power doesn't come from money," I bite back, sick of

Liv using that excuse as well. "It comes from doing things others won't. She threatened us. She challenged us. She brought this on herself."

Maybe.

And maybe I kinda went too far. I was angry when I came home last night, so I went to Wind House and worked on Mr. Green's makeup and watched Gates stitch a gash from a car accident victim that the morgue forgot to do.

But by one o'clock in the morning, it was still festering, so I just posted it. Fuck it. It was a reflex—a "close your eyes and just do it" moment that I quickly regretted—but what did she think was going to happen? I won't stop. I don't know why, but I can't, and I know she knows that. In fact, this should have gotten a lot uglier a long time ago.

What was I supposed to do? Just let her go? Just stop?

I haven't seen her all morning, but I know she'll show up at some point. Maybe tomorrow, with her head up, refusing to speak to me, taking the high road and not giving me the satisfaction of her attention and all that bullshit.

But then I hear Krisjen saying, "Clay."

And before I have a chance to turn around, someone shoves me, and I stumble, nearly falling. I spin around, spotting Liv just as her palm whips across my face. I whimper, my head jerking to the side and the tendons in my neck screaming. I tumble to the floor, shooting out my hands to catch myself.

"Ohhhhh!" someone howls.

"Bitch!" Amy shouts.

My cheek burns like it's on fire, but I shake my head clear and climb back to my feet. Amy rushes Liv, but I dart out and yank her back, shoving Liv in the chest.

"Come on!" I yell.

This is between her and me. Fucking finally.

Her eyes are like lightning, and she looks like she wants to take a bite out of me. I growl, charging her. She crashes into a table, grabbing juice and throwing it at me before we spill to the ground. My claws dig into her skin and her fingers are ripping my hair out of my scalp as we go at each other—hitting, tearing, squeezing, and raging.

I want to cry, I'm so happy. This is all I want. Everything I want. I don't want to ever do anything else.

Cheering fills my ears, she rolls on top of me, and I don't see anything but her.

I only feel her.

The cut at the corner of my mouth stings. I tongue it, slouching in the wooden chair as I gaze past Father McNealty's empty seat in his office.

God, it's better than a drug. The feeling swirling in my gut and my heart pounding like I'm dangling a hundred feet in the air, only holding on by a single hand.

She's better than a drug. I always knew she had it in her.

"If you ever come near me again," Olivia grits through her teeth in the chair next to mine, "I will cut you."

I look over at her. The orange juice she threw at me stains her white Polo, too.

But I almost smile, seeing the tear in her sleeve. I fought back, didn't I?

"Cut me?" I taunt, watching her as she watches me graze my hand up the inside of my thigh, dragging up my school skirt. "Where?"

I pretend to rub myself, moaning.

Her mouth twists into a snarl. "Cunt."

I turn away, smiling to myself. *Dyke.*

Sitting up straight, I hold up my nails, inspecting the damage. It took three teachers to pull us off each other. My only regret is that she didn't start this shit after school when we wouldn't have been interrupted. I'm in every bit as good of shape as she is. This could've gone on for hours.

The second bell rings, and now we're officially late for fifth period. Where the hell is he?

"They're going to research it, you know?" Liv says, and I can see her looking at me out of the corner of my eye. "Find out where that video came from, and when I take this online with my receipts, the entire fucking world will be calling for your head. Especially since I'm only seventeen."

Fuck. I forgot about that. She's a minor.

I pick at the chipped red nail polish, ignoring the skip in my heartbeat. "And who will believe you?" I turn my head, meeting her dark eyes under her long, black lashes. "I'm Clay Collins."

Blond and just like a bomb. Everything the administration loves to parade around in their recruitment brochures.

Her eyes narrow.

I look her up and down. "And you're a dumpster rat probably looking forward to a long and illustrious career turning tricks on the dirty floor of her shitty house."

Olivia launches out and grabs me by the back of my neck. I gasp.

I clutch the arms of the chair for support as she pulls us face-to-face, and I harden my jaw, looking into her eyes. The dark brown lights up with flecks of gold as she glares at me, and I can smell the peaches in her long black hair.

My heart pounds so hard. *Yes.*

Like a fucking drug.

She stares at me with fury, and I brace myself for impact when I know I should pull away.

But I don't want her to let me go. It took so long to get us here.

I hate Olivia Jaeger. I fucking hate her, and I'd happily never love anything if I could hate her my whole life. My eyes pool with tears, and I don't know why.

But I don't blink.

Come on. My chin trembles. *Come on.* I want this.

The juice she threw at me still drips from my skirt, and I close my eyes at the burn in my scalp where her fingers are curled into my hair under my ponytail. *Come on.* I open my mouth, feeling her everywhere. Almost tasting it.

Bitter but beautiful, like Valium on my tongue. That's what she's like.

I open my eyes, a tear spilling over, and I see her watching me, a mixture of anger and wariness in her eyes. Like she's unsure about something.

A voice carries in from the office, and Liv pushes me away, releasing me as the door to the headmaster's office opens.

I shake my head as I sit back in my chair. *Wimp.*

"Father McNealty is held up with the mayor," Mrs. Garrison tells us, remaining in the doorway. "He will speak to both of you in the morning, so don't think you're off the hook. Go to the locker room, change—"

I rise before she's finished, grab my cell phone off his desk, and walk past the old bag.

"And get directly to class," she yells after us as Liv and I walk through the office toward the door. "If I get another whiff of one more fight between you two, I'm calling your parents to pick you up!"

But we're already in the hallway, the door swinging closed behind us. I don't turn around, and I don't slow down, charging down the empty hallway as teachers drone on in their classrooms, and I descend the stairs, finding my way to the locker room.

Jaeger's on my tail the entire time, though, and I feel her eyes on my back. I hope she jumps me again.

I hope she does.

I push through the door, the offices and locker room empty as everyone is already outside. I stop at my locker and dial in the combination, throwing it open.

"Just had to be orange juice, didn't it?" I gripe, pulling my Polo off over my head. "Everything is sticky."

It's down in my goddamn socks. These saddle shoes are vintage. If she fucked them up, I'll make sure not even her lowlife brothers can protect her.

She digs in her locker—which is unfortunately in the same row, because Coach keeps lacrosse together—and I stalk over to the cabinet, pulling out a spare Polo.

"You know," I tell her, fumbling with a clean shirt, "if you didn't want everyone to see, then maybe you shouldn't have been practically fucking her in public."

"We weren't fucking," she growls, glaring at me. "As you and everyone else clearly saw. I guess if I didn't want people filming, I shouldn't have expected as much as some simple manners from a stupid, useless cow."

I slip my arms into the shirt. *Stupid, useless . . .*

But I pull it back off and throw it at her. "This should fit your fat tits. Take it."

She catches it, and I yank another shirt out of the cabinet, making sure it's a small.

She sets the shirt in her locker, checking her face in the mirror that hangs on the inside of the door. A trickle of dried blood coats the ridge of her ear, and I try not to look at her as she wipes it clean.

A tiny pang of guilt hits me, but I push it away. She made me bleed, too, didn't she? It's not my fault she has to line metal up her ear with all her dumb piercings. She came at me first.

I lick the cut at the corner of my mouth again, glancing over and watching her throw the bloody wipe on the ground, her lips twisted in anger.

But the fury is in her eyes, too, and I know she's still upset.

I pause, confusion seeping through. I know I deserved her anger. I'd have been furious, too. And I honestly wasn't going to post the video. That wasn't my plan originally, but . . .

I grind my teeth together and close my eyes, blinking long and hard. Olivia kissed that girl everywhere. *Everywhere.*

I stare off into my locker, the bra like sandpaper on my skin. I peel it off, dropping it to the floor.

I mean, if I did that with my boyfriend in a public place, I'd be a slut, right? I might even get into trouble, because sluts don't represent Marymount at lacrosse games.

Marymount girls are good girls. We're discreet.

And now she knows.

I stand there, the air grazing my bare breasts as she digs in her locker.

She brushes down her blue, green, and black plaid skirt as chills spread across my body. She tightens her high ponytail, fluffing up the messy hair and smoothing out the loose tendrils that hang around her ears, the posts and small rings there glinting in the lights as the flesh of my nipples hardens.

I can't look at her, but I see everything.

She stops moving and lets her head fall, both of us breathing in sync. Quiet and alone, but so crowded.

"Why do you want me to hurt you?" she asks, her voice suddenly soft.

I don't blink.

Why?

Why?

My chin trembles. *Because . . . at least it's something.*

At least I have that.

My brother's picture hangs inside my locker door, and I absently rub my thumb over the faint hidden tattoo on the inside of my middle finger. He would've been fourteen this month.

My insides shake, and I grab the prescription bottle, tapping out a ten-milligram blue pill. I pop it into my mouth, the bitter dust starting to dissolve on my tongue before I swallow.

I pull out a clean sports bra and pull it over my head, followed by the shirt as she takes off her dirty one. And I can't help but look.

The contours of her stomach are tight and smooth, and I slide my eyes down her legs, the curves on the backs of her thighs mesmerizing.

But then she holds her hand out to me, and I look up, seeing a package of wet wipes. I stare.

"You want them or not?" she barks.

"Piss off."

And she throws it. The package hits the side of my head, and I growl, letting it fall to the ground.

"There's a drop of blood on the back of your neck, dumbass," she tells me.

I almost laugh. What? Does she feel guilty about hurting me or something? It's not like she should. I got her good this morning, didn't I? That video had eighty-five thousand views before I took it down at three a.m.

But, of course, by then it had already done its damage. What's on the internet stays on the internet somewhere.

Jesus, what did I do?

I grab the package off the ground and pull out a wipe. "Where?"

She pauses a moment, staring at her locker, and then stalks over, taking it out of my hand. Pushing me back around, she wipes off whatever is on my neck, and my thighs are burning with her touch. *God* . . .

"It's going to take every ounce of pull I have to protect you," she says. "You know that?"

Protect me?

"Once my brothers find out what you did," she warns, "their women will rebuild your fucking face."

"I'm not scared of Tryst Six," I say over my shoulder.

My father eats that side of town for breakfast.

But then I hear the click of her blade behind me, and I stop breathing.

"Take out your phone," she tells me.

"What for?"

I turn around, meeting her eyes, both of us eye to eye.

Her arm hangs at her side, the blade in her hand. "Do it." She cocks her head, calm. "I'm sure you have notifications by now."

Notif—

What did she do?

I quickly turn around and grab my phone out of the locker, turning it back on.

It lights up, loads, and in a moment, I hear dings and see tabs pop up.

Clicking on one, I watch as YouTube loads, my heart pounding hard as the same video I posted—and deleted—starts playing again. The jewelry in Olivia's ear glimmers in the moonlight, and her flowing white tank top makes her slender neck look warm and tan as she bends it back for the girl to kiss.

The account is registered to Vaudevillian Vix—not me—and it already has seven thousand views.

I drop the wipes. "What did you do?" My eyes lock on her.

"You wanted it up, so it's back up."

"But I took it down," I growl.

Goddammit, I took it down. I look back at my phone, scrolling the comments. Why would she do this? When did she do this? Before the fight? After?

"They won't trace it back to you," she assures, walking back to her locker and tossing the knife in. "It came from my phone."

So why repost it then, if not to screw me over?

"Take it down." I charge over to her. "Take it down now."

I don't want people to see this. It was a mistake.

"You're not scared of Tryst Six?" She fixes her lip gloss in the mirror, extra red against her black shirt and black hair. "Well, I'm not scared of you, baby. Do what you will. Leave it up—forever if it gets you off." She turns and looks at me. "Every degrading comment and joke is for your pleasure, so enjoy it."

Son of a bitch!

I push her aside and pull her phone out of her locker. "Take it down now." I hold her phone out to her, but before she can take it, I pull it back and swipe the screen, trying to do it myself. "Unlock this!" I yell at her. "Goddammit, Jaeger!"

She pushes me back into the locker and grabs her phone. "Scared now?" she taunts. "Huh? Feel violated when you've lost control of your property? How does that feel?"

I raise my hand, pointing in her face and shouting, "Take it down!"

But she grabs my wrists and twists them behind me, and I whimper at the ache as she backs me up into the lockers again.

"Because why?" she whispers in my face. "Say it. You're afraid, aren't you?"

I shake my head. She presses her forehead into mine hard, but I push back, giving as good as I get while I try to wrangle my hands free.

"You're afraid because your life is sad, and you want to gut anything that's different." Her breath falls on my lips, and I feel a light layer of sweat cover my back. "Anything that makes you feel strong, because at least it's not dull, and it's too painful not to feel, isn't it? You're afraid of me because someday you're going to wake up and remember that that video is still there, but I'm not, am I? I'm gone, living, and you're not, because your brain is still in the fucking gutter."

A sob lodges in my throat, and my body shakes.

She shakes her head at me. "You're just afraid."

"I'm not afraid," I tell her. "I'm . . ."

But I swallow, pushing the word back down my throat.

I'm . . . Tears fill my eyes, and I tighten every muscle in my body, forcing myself to get my shit together.

But I'm lost. She's holding me, and I'm lost. She's not leaving. Not in six months. Not ever!

She stares at me, and I clench my fists behind me as our noses brush, and I hover a moment from her lips. "Livvy, I . . ."

She can't disappear. Time will stop. It has to. I can't see her go. I . . .

My mouth rests open, the need to feel her overtaking me. I can't . . .

I can't . . .

I can't stand it. I touch her mouth.

I layer my lips with hers—grazing, brushing, inhaling as she stops breathing and I just feel her and feel every inch of my body suddenly burn like a firework about to pop.

And then, all at once, we're in the shit.

She releases my hands, and we both grab onto each other as she pushes me into the lockers again, our arms and hands wrapping around one another as her mouth sinks into mine.

I moan. *Yes. Fuck, yes.*

Our legs thread together, the heat between her thighs hitting my center, and she slips her hands under my skirt, grabbing my ass through my panties as we go at each other, kissing and nibbling and grinding.

"Liv . . ." I whimper.

I lick her tongue and groan, kissing her hard and fierce and closing my eyes, because everything is spinning, and my body is on a roller coaster. I'm fucking flying right now.

She lifts my leg, and I can't stop. Grinding and panting as I slip my hand up her shirt, pulling down her strap, so I can get my hand inside her bra. She dives down to my neck, and I tip my head back, letting her have it all. I want her. I want to feel her and kiss her and touch her everywhere.

Our lips come back together, again and again, eating each other up, kissing frantically. I brush her nipple, and my clit throbs.

"You gotta be fucking kidding me," she whispers, shaken. "Are you kidding me right now?"

I know, all right? I know. I wasn't afraid. I was . . .

Jealous. I've wanted this since we were freshmen, that first day we met, before the fighting started.

And when I knew she liked me, I was so happy, but . . .

Ashamed. Tears spike my eyelashes, even with as happy as I am right now. I was so ashamed.

She brings one hand up, grabs the back of my neck, and takes my bottom lip between her teeth. I pause, savoring the fire blazing inside my body.

Our foreheads meet again. "We have to stop," I murmur.

I fumble and squirm, trying to push her away, damn near wrecked because I'm aching for this. I don't want to let her go.

But she doesn't let me. "No," she bites out in a whisper. Her mouth crashes down on mine again, and I can't fight. I hold her head, soaking up how soft she is. How beautiful she smells and how hot her mouth is.

I barely notice as she lifts up my skirt and yanks down my panties just enough to bare my sex, but then she fiddles with her own clothes between us, and in a moment, she's on me. Her pussy rubs against mine, and I pull away from her mouth to moan as she grinds on me, the friction of our skin agonizing.

Agonizing but perfect. It's hot and wet and . . .

She grips my ass, her head dipped into my shoulder as I wrap my arms around her neck and meet her rhythm, both of us fucking against the lockers.

"Ugh!" I cry out as she goes at me.

I'm consumed. This is what it feels like. This is what right feels like. It was always wrong before. Kissing someone. Letting them touch me. I never had that burn low in my belly.

I was never hungry.

Until her.

I sink into her mouth again, kissing, sucking, tasting . . .

At least there's this. I thought hating her was enough. If I couldn't have this, at least I had her attention. Even if it was bad.

At least I could destroy what I was going to lose anyway in three months when we graduated, and I couldn't look at her every day anymore.

But God, I do hate her. Her smile and her red lips. The way she smudges her dumb eyeliner, making her eyes look smoky and captivating, and her wild hair that always looks like it flew through the wind before she put it up in a ponytail.

Her olive skin, how her bracelets make music every time she moves, her chipped black nail polish, and those stupid biker boots with all the buckles she wears that make her legs so hard not to look at.

The way she rolls her skirt up, and I can't pay attention in Calculus.

I hate it all. How every part of her looks like it has a taste.

I whimper as our pace gets faster, and I feel and hear her breathe hard, in and out as the friction turns heavenly.

And this isn't even all we can do to each other. "God," I pant.

She hovers over my mouth. "Come to my shitty house tonight," she demands. "Sweat with me between the sheets?"

I nod. "Yeah."

I want to sneak out. Into a dark place with Olivia Jaeger and do things.

All night.

But then a voice pierces the air. "Oh, I know!" someone says.

I pop my eyes open, stopping. *What?*

Giggles and laughter follow, and I hear the creak of the locker room door.

Oh, shit. Ice courses down my veins as everything goes cold. This can't . . .

I can't . . .

Oh my God.

Another voice follows. "And then he was like . . ."

Fuck!

I push at Olivia. "Get off me."

She stumbles back, and I reach under my skirt, pulling up my underwear.

Jesus Christ. I'm just a world of stupid today, aren't I? Anyone could've seen us.

I step back over to my locker, avoiding Liv's gaze as I check myself in the mirror, righting my clothes again and tightening my ponytail.

I see the wet wipes on the floor and kick the package back over to her.

Sweat seeps out of my pores as girls round the corner just in time, and I look up, seeing Amy and Krisjen.

They stop, bags slung over their shoulders as their eyes dart from me to Olivia, noticing us there.

"Hey," Amy says.

Both of them stare at Liv, struggling to contain their smiles until Amy finally breaks down in laughter like the cat that ate the canary. Another punch of guilt hits me about the video. I cast a glance at Olivia and see her ignoring all of us as she pulls on a short, black leather jacket.

She won't meet my eyes.

"Are you okay?" Krisjen asks me, giving my back a sympathetic brush of her hand as she passes to her locker.

The knots in my stomach start to ease. I don't think anyone saw us.

The last time they saw me was when I was walked with Jaeger to the front office after the fight, so I'm sure they want to make sure I'm not in trouble.

"Are you kidding?" I steel my spine and swipe my finger under my eye, fixing my eyeliner. "Nothing is tastier than a piece of cake."

They both laugh at my jibe, and I dart my eyes up again, finally catching Olivia's.

Her head is turned toward me, staring at me with a mixture of pride and wrath.

Someone clears their throat, and I blink, seeing Amy turned toward Olivia.

"Would you mind?" Amy asks her.

Liv looks over her shoulder at her.

"I don't feel comfortable changing in front of you," Amy explains.

I clench my jaw.

But Liv remains silent.

It's on the tip of my tongue to dull the embarrassment for Liv and tell Amy no one wants to look at her pancake nipples, but . . .

I don't. Liv stands there for a moment, as if waiting for something, but I just ignore her and finish touching up my face.

Her locker door slams closed, and I jerk, seeing her move out of the corner of my eye and walk toward me.

She strolls past, knocking my shoulder with hers as she goes. "Don't cross the tracks."

And then she's gone, her threat hanging in the air as the locker room fills with the P.E. class coming in.

I almost laugh. She's rescinding her invitation for Night Tide, I guess.

Lucky for her, I love getting on her bad side.

8

Clay

C lay."

I draw in a breath, pulling my head out of the clouds where it always seems to be now, and turn around.

"Take these to the kitchen," my mother says.

I take the tray, the empty bowls on top clanking together as I carry them away.

Fondue with Father is one of the many dumb alliteration-inspired events Omega Chi sponsors every year, members of the alumni never missing an opportunity to sweep back into town to support the sorority and the school.

And maybe show off that new Birkin, of course.

I toss a glance over my shoulder, seeing poor Father McNealty drowning in a sea of moms, daughters, aunts, and grandmothers, all of them wanting to hear about how that new collection of first editions to the library they donated is making all the difference, or if their "hefty" contribution was used to buy new buses or the latest computers.

The latest computers . . . I shake my head, dropping the tray onto the counter and hearing a dish break just as I turn and leave. I keep walking.

The best athletic equipment, the highest-quality organic food in the cafeteria, the most state-of-the-art science lab . . .

On-site tutors, language learning, counseling, and college prep. Liv Jaeger benefits heavily from the people she loves to look down on. Her family makes no donations, and although our tuition is steep, it would never be enough to cover the overhead Marymount incurs if you figure in utilities, taxes, salaries, staff . . . These women here, however shallow to her, are necessary to the success of the school that helped her get into fucking Dartmouth.

I head to the back of the banquet hall and retrieve my backpack from one of the dressing rooms, digging out some jean shorts and a T-shirt.

So high and mighty, she is. Maybe if she'd ever acted a little more grateful . . .

She brought that video on herself.

So why do I regret posting it? I can't look at the comments online and what they're saying about her. That's why I took it down in the first place. I just wanted her to see that I had Megan Martelle's life in my hands. I wanted Liv to know that she wasn't powerful. That I am.

But really, I was just angry. Jealous. I want her, I can't have her, and I'm angry that I can't have her.

So I take it out on her.

I pull on my change of clothes, blowing out a breath and clearing my head. *But that's not it. I don't want her.* The affection felt good, and when you're starved for it, you'll take it from anywhere. That's all it is. I'm not bisexual. I'm straight.

I trust Liv not to talk, and I don't trust Callum. That's it. I'll trust him eventually. Or another man.

I swing my crossbody bag over my head with my money and phone in it and leave my clothes and backpack in the dressing room. My mother will bring it all home.

I head for the entrance, sneaking past the doors quickly so my mom doesn't catch me. It's almost six, already getting dark out, and I'm late.

But then I hear someone say, "Come here, darlin'."

I turn, seeing my grandmother sitting in a chair in the lobby. Her hair is as white as her pantsuit, and she clutches a cane, propping it up on the floor in front of her.

"Mimi." I walk over, absorbing the look from her that falls down my attire, assessing. "I was wondering where you were."

"Sure, you were," she retorts. But a smirk pulls at her lips, and I know she's teasing me.

Falling to the carpet at her feet, I sit down and lean against her leg, the dull hum of the party droning on in the next room.

"You knew I'd sneak out," I say. That's why she's sitting out here.

"It's Night Tide." She threads my hair through her fingers, and I hear laughter pour out of the banquet room. "I remember being unable to stand the anticipation when I was your age."

Mimi is still my age. She just hides it well.

"So, what's on the agenda tonight?" she asks.

I shrug. "Standard scavenger hunt, maybe some burgers . . ."

I used to love spending time with my mother's mother more than I did my actual mother, but I started to enjoy it less the older I got. Mimi's the reason my mom is the way she is.

I guard my words, because even though I may admire her ruthlessness, I also know I'm not safe from it. My grandmother is the most dangerous person I know.

"You be home at a decent hour." She caresses my hair. "It's not right for your mother to be home alone so much."

"She's never home," I tell her.

Mimi takes my chin and tips my eyes up at her. "A great deal has been asked of you in your young life, but you need to see the strength it's building, too." Her gentle eyes don't do enough to disguise the stern gaze underneath. "It's not enough to not be a burden, Clay. You need to be a comfort, and if you don't like that, that's too bad. You get in line. Your family needs you."

I almost nod, as always. It's better to just agree with my elders, because arguing wastes time, and I'm just going to do what I want to anyway, but something slips out of me that I don't feel like curtailing tonight. "A family doesn't live in that house anymore."

She thins her eyes, holding me closer. "Don't let them see," she says in a low tone.

"Who?"

"Everyone who is waiting with bated breath to see you unhappy." She releases me and tips her chin up, straightening her back. "Don't give that to them."

I've never given that to them. I never let my friends know how I hate being home. How my parents barely know each other anymore.

How they barely know me.

But I'm tired of the façade, and for a few stolen moments this week, I got a glimpse of what life was like without it. I was too high to reach.

I spot a cardboard tube on the table, *Biscayne Bay* written on the label featuring my father's letterhead. *Biscayne Bay?* He's working on a development called Palm Biscayne somewhere on our coast, but I've never heard of Biscayne Bay.

Bay . . . Not Sanoa Bay.

The gears in my head turn, and I'm afraid to ask. Nothing happens in this town without going through my grandmother, but I'm not sure I want to know. I was joking with Liv about Sanoa Bay being leveled for a golf course, because it's been a threat since we were born. No one ever thought it would actually happen.

I tuck the suspicion away for the moment and smile up at her. "We can't all be as strong as you, Mimi."

"You see what I want you to see."

Her eyes fall away from me, something else playing behind them. "Every woman has her secrets, Clay," she tells me. "We all have our sins, and I'm not special. You can have whatever you want, as many times as you want, for however long you want." She nudges my chin again. "As long as it stays a secret."

I can't hold back my smile. "I can't believe you're telling me that."

"Refusing yourself the things you need to feel alive only brings two consequences: detriment or death. We would break."

I stare at her.

"We can have what we want," she tells me again. "Quietly."

"What if it hurts to hide?"

"Oh, Clay." She shakes her head like I'm so naïve, but it's not in a way that offends me. "Everyone hides. The generations before you devoted their lives to building something that lasted. Working for the duty and legacy they inherited. It was important." She pauses before she continues. "But that inch—those quick minutes they carved out in the shadows—that's what they lived for."

My blood warms under my skin, the hair on my arms rising, and all of a sudden, the possibilities seem endless tonight. *An inch* . . . I rub the inside of my finger, brushing my tattoo. I got it on my birthday in December to remind me that there's a piece of myself I hate and love and it drives me nuts, but I need it, because it's the only thing I look forward to. That place I can escape to in my head where I can have the only thing I want anymore.

"As long as it stays secret," she points out again.

Yes.

"That is the price, I'm afraid."

I nod once. *I can live with that.* As long as I can have her. *Thank you, Mimi.*

She gives me her cheek, and I leave a quick peck before climbing to my feet and hurry out of the hall before my mother sees. Once outside, I send her a quick text, letting her know I'll be home late and to grab my stuff from the dressing room.

I'm about to text Callum that I'm ready and waiting, but I see a tattooed neck in a dark gray T-shirt straddling an old Triumph. I forget my phone and stare at the middle son of Tryst Six, cigarette smoke drifting into the air above his head.

He was the one checking me out last week when he dropped Liv off at school. I smile, tucking my phone back into my bag. *Oh, she'll hate this.* I walk up to him. "Hi."

Turning his head, Iron sucks on the cigarette, the end burning orange before he takes it out of his mouth.

He doesn't say hi back. He knows who I am.

"I'm Clay," I tell him anyway.

He faces forward, blowing out the smoke. "Yeah, I know."

Well, what a peach. Maybe he knows about the video. How could he not, I guess?

I take my chances anyway. "I'm doing a senior scavenger hunt. I need to take a selfie with a stranger."

He shoots me a look, taking another drag. "Is that school-sanctioned? Sounds unsafe."

I pull out my phone again. "Can I take a selfie with you?"

"No." He shakes his head, turning away again. "Like I said, I know who you are."

He doesn't really seem angry, though. Maybe she didn't tell her family about the video. Maybe he's just prejudiced because I'm a Collins.

I pass him and his bike, step into the street, and stick my thumb out, feeling my loose denim shorts slide down my hips as I move.

"What are you doing?" I hear him ask, a sudden edge to his voice.

"I need a ride across the tracks." A car passes, honking its horn, and I see it's some rusty old Honda filled with young guys. "I'm meeting Liv."

"Pretty sure Liv is the last person meeting you."

"Hey!" someone calls.

I look behind me to see that the Honda has stopped, one of the dudes poking his head out of the window.

I look back to Iron.

"Don't you have a driver or something?" he spits out. "Hitching is dangerous."

I back up toward the Honda, giving him a wicked smile.

"Oh, for Christ's sake, stop," he barks, rolling his eyes and taking up his bike. "I'll take you."

I grin wider and leap into a run, climbing on the bike behind him and taking the helmet he offers.

He starts the engine, the bike vibrating under me, and I watch the Honda pull off when I don't take their ride.

"You're good, kid." He looks over his shoulder, his sarcasm pretty thick. "I wish you'd use that brain for better rather than worse."

A car pulls up, and I see Krisjen peek her head out the back window. Milo sits next to her.

"Clay, let's go!" She looks up at me like *What the hell are you doing?*

Callum sits in the driver's seat, a small smile tilting his lips like he's ready for anything I have planned.

"I got a ride," I tell her.

I hear Iron groan, probably because there are witnesses now, and I wrap my arms around him, damn near laughing as my heart races.

"Clay!" Krisjen urges. "What the hell?"

But I just whisper to Liv's brother, "Go."

He shakes his head, his greasy brown hair kind of good-looking against his tan face. "My gut told me you were trouble," he grumbles. "Hold on."

He launches off, and a whimper escapes as my heart leaps into my throat. We fly forward, the moisture thickening the air as the clouds hang low, and I chance a look behind me to see the tires of Callum's car spinning and burning rubber as he sets off after us.

I squeeze Iron, the wind picking up with the speed, and I peer over his shoulder, watching as he flies us down the road, through the warehouse district, and onto Frontress Lake Drive, speeding along the canal and toward the tracks.

The bass from Callum's car booms on our tail, and I can tell he's gaining by how loud his Nine Inch Nails song is getting.

But not for long.

Iron grabs hold of my hands locked in front of him, holding me to him, as he kicks the bike up a gear, the front tire catches air, and we bolt ahead faster. I giggle—actually fucking giggle—in his ear, and I spot a little grin on his face, too.

Settling into the man's back, I watch as St. Carmen falls away, the lush lawns, boutiques, centuries-old churches, and the opulent edifices of the mansions tucked deep among the bald cypresses and strangler figs.

Green, gorgeous land lies beyond, the sky growing dark with the stars covered by clouds. My skin buzzes with something I hardly ever feel anymore.

Anticipation.

Henry would love this. I don't think he ever got to ride on a motorcycle.

"Iron, get her off your bike!" someone barks.

Iron pulls to an abrupt stop at the stop sign and I press into his back, looking over my shoulder to see Liv.

A pain hits my chest. I watch her cruise up next to us, her bike black, smaller, and older, but God . . . I rarely get to see her out of school clothes or lacrosse gear, and I can't take my eyes off her.

She puts her boots on the ground and scowls at her brother through her aviators. "This isn't a joke!" she yells at him.

And she flashes a glance back at Callum's car racing toward us.

My tongue feels like it's swelling so much I'll choke on it. Her legs in her tight black jeans. Her knees bare through the holes, her low-cut white top, and her faded leather jacket . . . Her hair wild and loose down her back, no helmet, and dog tags hanging around her neck. I notice the key she flashed on the lacrosse field last weekend hanging in between.

I loosen my hold on Iron, thinking about holding on to her instead. She'd fit perfectly.

"Aw, Jesus." She looks at me. "You ever experience a Cuban temper? You're about to."

I look behind me once more, seeing a Toyota Tacoma racing side by side with Callum, the cab filled with three long-haired individuals. Women?

I look at Iron. "A girlfriend?"

"Ex," he points out.

Oh, Jesus. I hop off his bike, climbing on behind Liv instead.

"Get off!" she yells, trying to shake me.

But I wrap my arms around her, feeling the switchblade hooked onto her jeans. "Scared of me?"

She breathes out a laugh. "I'm sick of you getting your way," she mumbles, more like she's arguing with herself than me. "What the fuck do I care if Aracely rips out all your hair?"

"My crew plays dirty." I hug her close. "Yours plays bloody. Don't worry, I know we won't win tonight."

"No, you won't."

"So, let's go," I say, and then whisper into her ear, "Just you and me for the next five minutes."

She turns her head away from my whisper, but I feel her chest cave and her stomach shake. I love feeling what I do to her.

"I hate you," she growls. But she revs the bike and takes off, and I smile, tucking my chin onto her shoulder.

Ditto.

I close my eyes, squeezing her until I'm sure she can't escape. The wind whips through my hair, and the scent of the palms hits my nose, and I wish it was day. I wish I could see the clouds.

Heat pools low in my belly, and I hug her with my thighs, aware of her everywhere.

Iron didn't feel like this. She smells like—I tip my nose up under her ear. Like one of those artisanal perfume oils popular in the hippie shops where they suck up all the oxygen, burning incense, and then wonder why they don't have any customers.

But I like it on her. She smells like cherry lollipops and . . . summer. I dip my nose in more, grazing her skin.

"Fuck me or cut it out, Clay," she says, throwing me another scowl over her shoulder. "Your bullshit isn't funny."

I keep my smile to myself. I pull my nose out of her neck, but I stay close as we cruise into the Bay. This neighborhood was incorporated into St. Carmen in 1942, but its residents only admitted that when they were forced to give their addresses on a job application. To them, Sanoa Bay still lives, and if anyone says they reside here, then you know their families have been rooted on the land since the sixteenth century. No one moves into this shithole by choice.

Liv zooms past overgrown properties and turns onto a muddy road, sporadic streetlights lining the dark path before we come to the village center, which is basically Mariette's, a small motel, a gas station, a bar, and an auto body shop where the kiddies can feed the alligators marshmallows while you wait for your oil change.

Past the shop is a long street, homes and dilapidated mansions of the old landowners, before they lost their land to St. Carmen, sitting hidden among the trees.

Liv stops the bike, a flurry of activity in every direction in the Bay. Lights decorate Mariette's, where groups of men and families enjoy dinner and beers, and the doors to the auto shop are open, their lights shining and "Crimson and Clover" pouring out from inside.

I hop off the bike and immediately head for the bar. "I need a condom from the men's room."

But before she even turns off the bike, she reaches out and grabs my arm. "Not from in there."

Why?

I cock my head. "Get your hands off me. You agreed to this."
Or better yet . . . "You *offered* this."

She holds my eyes for another moment and then finally releases
me. "Fuck it." She shakes her head, parking the bike. "Go."

Pivoting on my heel, I pull out my phone and bring up the list
in my notes. I hear her footfalls after me, but I make it to the door
before she can change her mind and grab me again.

I pull open the wooden door, some kind of classic rock playing
inside as the smell of cigarettes, fried food, and rotting wood hits me.

People turn and look, two ladies shooting darts, a few people at
the bar, and two pool tables filled with guys who clearly didn't
shower after work today. I pause for a moment, taking in the red
neon lighting around the bar and the plywood tables, their veneer
chipped and surrounded by mismatched chairs. I immediately picture my mother, clutching her handbag and refusing to sit for fear
of staining her white blouse.

The bartender—a skinny, bleached blonde with black roots,
dressed in a black T-shirt with some kind of tattoo around the
outside of her eye narrows her gaze. "Liv, what are you doing?" she
asks, sounding more like a warning than a question.

"She needs to, uh, use the bathroom," Liv tells her, humor in
her tone.

The woman takes me in for another moment and then sighs,
waving her hand. She resumes counting her register.

"You don't have to babysit me," I mutter over my shoulder. "I
know Sanoa Bay made their own list tonight. What's on yours?"

She doesn't respond, and I don't look back. Starting off, I spot
a hallway to the right and assume that's where the restrooms are. I
walk for it.

I would really love to know what's on her scavenger hunt. The
school uses a template they designed a generation ago, but they
fine-tune it every year, keeping up with the times and all. Since it's
school-approved, everyone "officially" plays from that one. If asked.

That doesn't mean any of us really use it, though. I still need to get that photo with a stranger, and there are plenty in here.

Sticking my hand inside my T-shirt, I use it as a glove, twisting the handle of the men's room door.

A twist knob on the restroom door. That's a good indication of the shitshow I'm going to find inside. *Unnnnnnnsanitaryyyyy.*

I open the door, the hinges whining as I look around. Three urinals cover the wall to my right, the porcelain stained after years of use, and two stalls, one without a door, sit across from them, reflected in the mirror.

Something bangs into a stall wall, and then I hear something else, but I don't see anyone.

Letting the door fall closed, I step farther inside. Liv enters behind me, and I'm not sure if she's protecting them from me or me from them, but whatever. My friends will find out where I've gone. They'll be here soon.

Panting hits my ears, followed by a woman's whimper, and I listen, hearing the screech of shoes across the tile and a steady rhythm start to hit the stall. The loose screws holding the walls in place clank as the pace speeds up.

People are fucking in here. Is this why she didn't want me in this dive?

I look at Liv. "Classy."

"At least they're not on YouTube."

They can be. I take out my phone, but she presses her hand down on mine, forcing it away. "Stop it," she mouths.

"Relax," I whisper. "I'm texting my friends where I am."

She releases me, leaning into the wall and putting her hand on her hip. I toss out a group text to Callum, Amy, Milo, and Krisjen, telling them where to find me. Hopefully that Aracely chick and her friends aren't holding them up.

I tip my head toward the condom machine, snapping a selfie as proof I was here, and then pull some change out of my bag. "So,

Iron is single?" I ask as I put away my phone. "Or is that girl in the pickup still claiming status?"

She hoods her eyes.

I slide my change into the machine and twist the old lever, the moaning from the stall growing heavier and louder. "You didn't tell them, did you?" I ask her.

On the one hand, you'd think she'd want to send all the muscle she could after me, or find some way to embarrass my family by broadcasting my behavior; but on the other hand, I understand why she didn't.

And I'd relied on that when I'd posted the video. Reporting me would only draw more attention to her, and Liv doesn't play the victim. Ever.

I pull the condom out of the machine and tuck it into my bag. "It wasn't that bad," I tell her, continuing to defend myself and I don't know why. "They didn't recognize Martelle."

"They recognized me," she retorts.

"So why put the video back up?"

"Because fuck you, that's why."

I stare at her, despising that I don't have a comeback.

"Was that what the locker room was all about?" She moves in closer. "You had somebody filming me again?"

We're both five-seven, but she feels taller somehow. Like she hasn't been thinking about it in the same way I have.

"Or maybe you came tonight to try to get me into the same position," she says, "so you could humiliate me some more?"

She thinks it was a ploy. Kissing her in the locker room.

She doesn't think it was real for me.

"Yeah, it's that easy with a queer, isn't it?" she taunts. "You think I'm just going to drop down and thank my lucky stars to fuck anything pretty, any time, any place, right? Because I'm desperate? Because gays are hypersexual, is that it?"

"I don't know . . . you seemed pretty into it," I whisper.

The woman's whimpers turn to cries, and his panting grows more ragged as we hold each other, our gazes locked.

"Turn me around," the girl tells him.

We listen as they shift positions and continue, Liv's lips so still as she watches me.

Her brown eyes hold mine, and I don't know if she's two seconds from pulling me into the empty stall or hitting me, but my heart thunders against my chest as the couple kisses and breathes, and I can feel the wet heat on their skin from here.

I stare at her, the world spinning around us, and we almost don't notice a man entering the room. He pauses briefly as he passes us before making his way for the urinals.

But I don't look away from her.

He pisses, and I see a smile peek out on her mouth as the steady stream fills the air and it makes me want to laugh, too.

Wow.

I take out my phone again. "I need a picture of a water feature."

But she snatches the phone. "Let's see the real list."

I grab for it, but she pulls the phone away, looking at the screen. "Seminole flag," she reads, and looks up at me. "The one at the lighthouse, I presume?"

I clamp my mouth shut.

The couple in the stall comes, and I hear the man at the urinal laugh, banging on the door twice as he zips up.

"Keeping the spark alive in there, Mr. and Mrs. Torres?"

The woman laughs, followed by the man's voice. "Eat me."

The guy walks away, washing his hands and smoothing back his hair. "Sounds like your wife beat me to it."

He passes us, stopping and speaking to Liv. "¿Está todo bien?"

Liv doesn't look at him, staying focused on me. "You expressed an interest in Macon?" she asks me.

Huh?

And then I remember teasing her about it in the theater.

But without waiting for my answer, she hands me back my phone and says to him, "Take her to my brother, will you?"

He looks at me.

"What?" I blurt out.

But he doesn't hesitate. Bending over, he sweeps me up and throws me over his shoulder, and I yelp, snatching my hands off his back, because he's all sweaty and wet.

"Let go of me!" I bellow, lifting up and glaring at Liv.

We're out the door in less than two seconds, and I flail, kicking and screaming. "Hey!"

"You wanted to know what was on the Bay list?" I hear Liv ask.

I lift my head up, breathing hard as the guy carries me outside and she follows.

"Only one thing," she teases, a wicked smile playing on her mouth. "You."

Me? What?

What the hell is she doing?

"Clay!" I hear someone call. I twist, looking around me, but I can't see shit.

"Clay!" Callum barks next.

I see shoes and hear splashes through puddles as my friends find me and follow.

"You're going to pay for this!" I growl at Liv.

"I've been paying since the day I met you," she retorts. "It's about time I enjoy it."

9

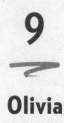

Olivia

Macon!" Santos calls out as if announcing the pizza's here. "Got some problems for you, man." And then under his breath, "As if you don't have enough already."

"Put her down now," Callum tells him, but no one listens.

We enter the body shop, Clay's party following close and yelling, creating a ruckus as Dallas, Trace, and Army head over to see what's up.

"Let me go!" Clay shouts.

The bar is only a hundred yards from the body shop, so it was as easy as carrying a sack of potatoes for my brother's friend.

Trace smiles wide, his plaid pajama pants hanging low on his hips with no shirt. He fits his baseball cap on backward, covering his messy hair. "Oh, I'm gonna enjoy this," he mutters, and then to Santos: "Drop her."

Dallas wipes off his hands, and the rest of the Sanoa Bay patriarchy with an average age of twenty-seven crowd around, leaving their hobby bikes and beer, ready to drip all their machismo at any given opportunity. Normally, I shun it, but it'll be useful tonight.

Santos flops Clay over and drops her on the old sofa, the brat shooting up, her eyes spitting daggers. I lean back against a worktable, ready for the show. She deserves this.

I can't believe I dropped my guard in that locker room. She just felt so good.

I watch her, every muscle primed and ready and the fire in her eyes. *God, she felt good.*

But she's not good. Emotions just bottled up over years without any outlet, and I was finally able to take them out on her and I guess it didn't matter how. That's all that was.

Macon steps out from underneath a car, grabbing the shop rag out of his back pocket as he looks around to see what the commotion is.

Taking one look at Clay, he turns away, bored. "Get 'em out of here."

But Trace steps up. "Oh, come on, Macon—"

But Macon twists his head, leveling Trace with the look we all know well. He shuts up.

"Liv said we were welcome tonight," Callum points out. He walks over and takes Clay's hand in his, pulling her to his side.

"My sister doesn't get to extend invitations," Macon tells him, tossing me a warning look.

I shrug. "What's the harm in letting them absorb some local color?"

"Keep it up." He wipes his hands. "You're gonna absorb my boot in your ass."

Yeah, yeah.

"Finish your fucking Night Tide on your side of the tracks," he tells them.

Clay stares, her eyes shifting between my brother and me, looking like she expects me to intervene, and why the hell would I do that? Honestly, they're lucky to get out of here unscathed. Macon is taking it easy.

"Come on, Clay." Amy pulls at her friend.

"It smells like shit over here anyway," Milo adds.

They start to drift toward the bay doors, but Clay refuses to budge. She pulls her hands free. "No."

"Come on," Amy urges. "I'm already fucking bored."

You mean scared, Amy? I hold in my laugh.

"I said no." Clay steps up toward my brother, and my heart stops for a moment. I stand up straight.

"So, what were you?" she asks him. "Navy? Air Force?" But she doesn't wait to hear his answer. "It's a free country. Everything you fought for."

"I fought to preserve democracy, not practice it." He still doesn't look at her. "Get the fuck off our land."

My eyes dart between them, Clay to my left and Macon to my right, alert. No one, except maybe family, speaks to him like that, and while I'm kind of enjoying it, she's going to find out why really soon if she's not careful.

No one leaves, the air in the shop thick with tension. Macon looks over, his dark eyes looking black under the bill of his cap. "If you don't move, I'll move you."

Clay glances to me. A slight urge hits to intervene, and if he touches her, I might, but . . .

But Macon is right. Clay is an extension of everything wrong with St. Carmen. How they bully us. Take from us. Shame us. Keep us poor and ignorant and pregnant, breeding more servants for them.

I'm tempted to throw the key to Fox Hill into Macon's hands right now and let Callum answer for it, but he'd just deny it. And even if Clay didn't believe him, she'd still take his side. I'm not going to waste the only card I have to play quite yet.

"Two things can happen here," Clay says as everyone listens. "One. We can refuse to leave, because we don't really have to. This isn't your property. Not for long anyway. Tryst Six's days are numbered."

Macon turns and listens, his gaze calm.

"So, out of anger," she continues, "which is all you really have, you'll kill me and then the rest of us so there are no witnesses."

Trace and Army laugh under their breath, a few of the other guys joining them.

But it's not completely impossible. The swamp cooks bodies down to a stew in no time, and Clay knows the stories out here.

"Or two, you'll rough us up," she tells him, "we'll complain to our parents, and a shitstorm will consume Sanoa Bay, risking lots of unwanted attention on your 'business.'"

She does the little air quote thing, because she knows those stories, too. The rumors of how Macon and Army sold to the college kids—Oxy, Molly, Adderall—to make ends meet after our parents died.

I never asked if it was true, and I never will. Macon doesn't allow drugs in our house or in Sanoa Bay, but I also know he'd do anything to feed us.

"Either way, it's not good for you," Clay goes on. "Because the power you have is an illusion, because you have no—and never will have any—money."

I swallow, kind of wanting to smile and puke at the same time. That's gonna piss him off. While I'm happy it's not me, I'm kind of glad someone is biting him back.

Everyone turns to Macon, waiting for his response, and I almost think he's at a loss for words, because he's quiet for several seconds.

Aracely and her friend Carissa hover next to Iron, and I can tell by the pinch of their lips that they both want Clay's scalp.

"Well," Macon replies, blowing out a heavy breath. "Shit. You were right." He looks at me. "She is smart."

I nod, bracing for what's coming. "Told you." I play along.

Aracely and her pals move in, Dallas and Trace following as the circle closes.

"Damn, I'm . . ." Macon shakes his head, and I watch as his guys slowly shift around the room, taking up position behind each Saint.

I blink long and hard. *Shit.*

"I'm really at a loss for words," Macon says. "What do you say, men? Five hundred years of keeping this land from them, and now, here, today, is finally the day they call our number and take us down?"

Laughter fills the room, and I curl my toes in my boots, my muscles burning ready.

Macon smiles at Clay. "All at the hands of Baby Collins and the Preppy Posse."

"I'm shitting my pants," Trace says.

"Shakin' in my boots," Dallas coos, eyeing Callum.

Macon moves in front of Clay, hovering over her, and Callum leaps, ready to grab her, but Santos grabs him instead.

"What the fuck?" Callum growls.

All hell breaks loose. Swamps grabbing Saints, holding them in locks, and I watch as Clay's pieces fall around her, leaving the queen unprotected.

I look to Macon, opening my mouth, but I clamp it shut again. She asked for this, didn't she? Let her find out how false her security was with me. How much I let her get away with when it could've been so much worse.

"Can I show you something?" Macon asks her, not breaking a sweat. He grabs her by the back of the neck, and she screams as he drags her over to a motorbike on cinder blocks; someone has already started the engine, the tires spinning wildly.

I squeeze my eyes shut for a split second. *Goddammit. Goddamn her.*

She just had to open her big mouth.

"Clay!" Krisjen screams, but she can't move. Trace is holding her.

"Get off her!" Callum bellows.

I hear Amy yell, "Liv! What the hell? Do something!"

But I don't budge.

Opening my eyes, I watch Macon push Clay to her knees and

squat down next to her, pushing her fucking face and a fistful of her hair within inches of the spinning spokes. "See that?" Macon asks her.

Someone's dried blood coats the chrome spokes, and I can't see Clay's face, but she doesn't fight or speak. Shoulders squared, she won't give him that satisfaction.

"You're right," he tells her. "All we have is anger. And it is not without its uses."

He pushes her nose closer, and Krisjen cries out.

I watch, my chest rising and falling, and my stomach roiling. I force away the feelings I remember from the locker room when I let myself think for a minute that her desire was real. She deserves this.

I still haven't gotten all the Sharpie off my body, and I will never be free of that video of Megan and me. Clay has terrorized me for years. She brought this on herself.

"You won't do it," I hear her say.

"The question is . . ." He looks at her. "Do I have to? Does Liv have to deal with you when she knows your grandmother and the old sheriff had a hideaway out at Two Locks, where they would meet for long afternoon hours?"

Clay remains silent, and I want to move closer to see her face. Did she know that? I know things about her family that could have shut her fucking face up years ago.

"When Garrett Ames was found with his sixteen-year-old stepdaughter in a hotel room last May and quietly paid for it all to go away?" Macon continues. "Or when your mother had a little procedure done before Christmas to take care of an unwanted pregnancy?"

I can see Clay breathing harder.

"You're right," he tells her. "Money is power. But do you know what's more valuable? Secrets." He jostles her. "Secrets are power, honey. There's a reason we've survived here, keeping the wolves at bay as long as we have." He gets in her face. "We may be your maids and your dishwashers and your pool boys, but we're always there. For smart, you're really good at stupid."

Her shoulders shake, and I don't know why, but it's killing me inside. I'd rather suffer a million of Clay's snakebites than see her shrink.

"Do it, then." She remains still, offering herself up. "Be like us. Hurt me."

Do what? What is she doing?

"Do it!" she yells at him.

"Clay, knock it off," Callum barks.

Apparently, she doesn't speak for all of them.

"Come on, badass," she sneers. "Go for it."

I step forward. "They want Bellona," I tell him, shutting her up.

Bellona is the Seminole flag, shredded and faded but still flying at the lighthouse a mile up the dunes. It's on her scavenger hunt.

Macon glances at me, still fisting her hair. I know he doesn't want to hurt her. She's not worth the jail time.

It takes him a moment, but he exhales and releases her, a half smile on his lips. "Of course, they do."

It would be the ultimate "fuck you" from St. Carmen.

He rises and pulls Clay to her feet, but she shoves him away, scowling. Macon shuts off the bike.

"Can they take it?" Army taunts.

Macon tsks. "Doubtful."

"Come on, Macon . . ." Trace bounces up and down on the balls of his feet. "I want to stretch my legs. Let's play."

My brothers, their friends, and their girlfriends—their faces filled with excitement—look to my brother for his permission.

He casts me a glance. "Oh, what the hell . . . ?"

And then he turns to Clay and her posse. "Go capture your flag. If you can."

"Whoop!" our guys cry out.

Clay, looking uncertain after almost losing her nose to my brother's bike, flashes her gaze to me, and I can tell she's not done for the night.

I grin, shouting to my brothers. "Move!" I yell.

Whoever gets it first wins.

Everyone runs, scattering out into the night, but Macon grabs me as I try to leave.

He yanks me into his face. "You lose my flag, you lose Dartmouth. Deal?"

My chest caves. "Macon . . . ?"

"Nuh-uh." He shakes his head. "You're grown up enough to invite them here without asking me first, it should be no problem to make sure you don't lose that flag to a country club princess, no matter how pretty her ass is. Put your money where your mouth is, Livvy."

Fucking prick.

"Fine," I grit out, pushing away from him. "Fucking fine."

And I run, because there's everything to lose now, especially time I don't have.

10

Clay

"Clay, let's go!" Krisjen pulls me toward Callum's car.

But I dig in my heels, everyone scattering around us and engines firing up. Guests at Mariette's turn their heads to see what's happening, and Trace hangs out the window, howling as Dallas speeds them away.

Saber Point Lighthouse is a short mile up the coast, and they'll kill us on the road trying to get there first. What a perfect cover-up for our murder. *No, thank you.*

Callum grabs my arm and twists me around. "Are you okay?" He takes hold of my face, as if the motorcycle spokes got me.

"I'm fine." I push his hands down. "It was fun."

He chuckles, hooking an arm around me.

"What a fucking asshole," Amy bites out.

"Not at all." I smooth out my clothes and check my handbag to make sure nothing spilled out when that ass threw me over his shoulder. "I would've done no differently in his shoes."

Macon is smart. Liv was holding out on me. Playing a lot nicer than she had to. She had options for retaliation. Why didn't she use them?

Amy pulls me. "Let's get out of here."

"We're not going anywhere."

My friends gape at me, and I'm not sure if they just want to go home or still get the flag, but they definitely don't want to stay here.

Liv runs out of the auto body shop, slowing when she sees us *not* running. Suspicion etched on her face, she hops into the cab of a truck, the guy in the passenger's seat getting out and giving it to her and jumping into the bed himself. Army drives off, Liv next to him, but her eyes remain on me until she passes.

"Are we going for the flag or what?" Milo snaps. "They're going to beat us."

I slowly back away, eyeing my friends. "I have another idea."

Spinning around, I bolt down the road, past shacks and run-down lawns, houses barely held together with spit and glue and chipped blue paint.

"Where are we going?" Krisjen calls as we leave the lights of the main village.

"There's another flag," I tell her.

"Where?"

I twist around, running backward with a smirk pulling at my lips. "Their house."

Her mouth falls open, and Callum laughs, everyone picking up their feet and running faster, excited. Their house isn't on the way to Mariette's—the only reason anyone from across the tracks comes over here—but I've driven past a time or two.

We race up to the house, an old Spanish-style pigsty that must've been great in its heyday, but lack of funds and the deterioration of the property values around it makes it look abandoned. The porch light glows bright, but no windows are lit up and no cars line the dirt road in front. I tip my head back, taking in the broken clay shingles and dead ivy scaling up the pink stucco walls to the second floor.

It was probably a very beautiful place once. The Seminole flag hangs above the detached garage, the bottom blowing in the light breeze.

"What a dump," Amy grumbles. "If I lived here, I'd want to kill myself, too."

Liv's mother comes to mind, all of us knowing she died in this house. The story was she hung herself in the shower. Was Liv in the house at the time?

"I'm sure it's tolerable when you don't know anything else," I reply.

Callum jumps up and rips the flag off the garage, and I step up to the door, touching my fingertips to the heavy, dark wood. Hundreds of years of rain weigh on it, and I run my hand up the surface, my body humming.

It feels like her. Cracks and splinters and sun and thunder, but she's still here. I inhale a deep breath, gripping the door handle.

"Want a beer from their fridge?" I ask my friends.

I open the door, my heart skipping when it gives way. How did I know they would think they were safe enough to never lock their door? No one steals from Macon Jaeger, right?

"Clay!" Amy shouts.

I walk in, my friends following, all of us tracking mud into the terra-cotta foyer. Stairs sit right in front of us, and I look left and right, finding a living room—if you can call it that—and a pool table in what should probably be the dining room.

The chandelier suddenly illuminates, lighting up the whole space, and I hit the switch, shutting it off again. "Flush the bong water out of your head," I growl at Milo.

Dumbass.

We filter out around the house, Milo and Krisjen heading for the kitchen and the beer, while Amy stays with me, and Callum inspects a tarnished silver candlestick before dropping it to the ground.

The crystal candy dish goes next, crashing into a hundred pieces on the tile, and I hear a commotion in the kitchen, knowing Milo is trashing the place. I pause, but then I realize Macon Jaeger almost killed me tonight, so fuck him.

"Don't do that!" Krisjen yells to her boyfriend right before I hear something shatter.

"Shut up," Milo tells her.

"God, you're an asshole."

"What are you gonna do about it?"

I round the railing to the stairs, their voices disappearing as I ascend, remembering Liv in the locker room this week. *Come to my shitty house tonight. Sweat with me between the sheets.*

Climbing the stairs, I draw in the scent of her that fills this house, hating how cold it is and how you can smell the mildew in the wood, but . . . While my house is clean, always tidy, and bright, it doesn't have something hers does.

Gliding my hand up the railing, I take in the pictures on the wall on my way up, seeing some missing as well, by the looks of the outlines where portraits once hung. Mismatched frames and some with broken glass feature black-and-whites and some from a hundred years ago, probably great-grandparents and other ancestors.

There's one of their whole family, including Liv's dad, crowded into an airboat, and one with Iron holding up a baby alligator and looking happy.

There aren't many of Liv. I'm guessing picture-taking hasn't been a priority since her mom and dad died, and she was so young.

I wander through the bedrooms, dipping back out as soon as I go in, because the smell of boy makes me want to throw up, but when I open the door to the last bedroom on the right, it's different. It's not hers, though. I know that instantly.

The bed is made, the floor is tidy, and it smells like furniture polish.

Macon. I guess military habits are hard to break.

I step in, seeing his room has a bathroom. Callum trails me, and I grab the flag out of his hand and run to the bed, crashing on top of it.

"Get this," I tell him, spreading the flag out above my head as I lie on my back on Macon's bed.

Callum grins wide, snapping a picture. "Goddamn."

Before I can get up, he comes down on top of me. I freeze and his mouth is on mine before I know what to do.

"We have to get out of here," I tell him, squirming.

"No, you gotta say yes," he tells me. "I have a picture of you on a much older man's bed now. What will your parents think?"

Is that blackmail? He pushes my shirt up and sucks on my breast through my bra so hard that my spine steels, my alarm raising.

No.

"Callum," I warn, pushing at him.

But instead of getting off me, he licks the skin on top of the bra, trailing kisses all over my chest.

I bare my teeth, fisting his shirt. "What will my parents think of doing business with Garrett Ames once they find out he's raping his teenage daughter?"

Callum halts, and I almost smile, despite the shudder in my body.

Did he really think he could pull this shit with me? Who else has he victimized?

He pushes off, rises from the bed, and looks down at me like I'm now the enemy.

"Well, well, well," he muses. "You just got interesting."

To be honest, his sister probably thinks she's a willing participant, but the man is in his early fifties, and we all have skeletons. I can throw a punch same as Callum.

"I will have you, Clay." His tone has an air of finality to it and an edge of a threat he's never spoken to me with before.

Yeah, you just got interesting, too.

I hear Krisjen yell outside—Milo is probably doing something stupid again—and Callum turns and leaves.

I sit up on the bed, watching the door to see if he comes back, an unease I'm not used to feeling settling in my gut. First with Liv and her brothers tonight, and now with Callum. I'd told Macon his power was an illusion, but it was becoming clearer that mine was, too.

Shit.

I fist the flag, grinding my teeth together as I toss it over my shoulder. I rise and walk out.

But I notice the door across the hall next to the bathroom, and I know it's Liv's. Stickers plaster the door, some rainbow flag ones peeking out. I grip the handle, but I don't go in.

It's so stupid, but if I ever find myself here again, I don't want to have to tell her I snooped in her room uninvited.

I drop my eyes and my hand from the knob.

A knock lands on the door downstairs, and I twist my head, my heart skipping a beat.

It's not the Jaegers. They wouldn't have knocked.

I jog down the stairs, keeping my steps light, and see Amy come around the stairs from the kitchen. Her eyes are wide as we both look to the door, and I try to decide if we should make a run out the back door.

But then we hear her voice. "Liv?" a woman's voice calls. "Anyone home?"

I go still, recognizing the voice. *Megan.*

"What the hell is she doing here?" Amy whispers.

"Liv?" She knocks again.

I ball my fists, jerking my head at Amy and sending her to the kitchen. I follow, moving backward down the hall and keeping my eyes on the door.

Son of a bitch. No wonder Liv hasn't tried for more with me in the days since the locker room. No wonder. She and this bitch are going at it, happy as clams.

I shake my head. *That bitch.*

Shielded in the shadows of the stairs, I only hold back a moment before I say, "Come in!" And hope she doesn't recognize my voice.

I slip into the kitchen; Amy lurks on the other side of the fridge, hiding herself as I keep the lights off.

I don't know what I'm going to do, but Megan Martelle sure as shit won't be here when Liv gets home.

The door opens.

"Liv?" she calls out again. "Hello?"

I kick one of the chairs at the table, hoping she'll follow the noise, and then I park half my ass on the table, waiting for her.

She rounds the corner, coming into view, and I let my eyes trail down her skirt and legs and wonder if she's wearing any underwear. She's dressed to get laid, and my anger rises. What did they have planned tonight?

She sees me and stops. She takes a step back.

"Team meeting?" I ask. "It's kind of late."

Amy steps away from the refrigerator, and I see Megan's back go straight, her guard up.

It fucking should be.

"Go get Krisjen," I tell Amy.

She leaves, and Megan searches the wall for a light, asking, "What's going on?"

But I speak up before she can find it. "You tell me." Tears burn my eyes. "What are you doing to her? Am I next? Do you watch us in the showers?"

"What?"

Vomit rises up my throat. I hate all the shit coming out of my damn mouth. Megan isn't bad. She's weak and a little annoying, but she isn't hurting Liv. If anything, Liv was in control in that video.

And that's why I took it down. I couldn't stand it. Liv was into it in the car with her. So into it, and it hurt.

She raises her chin. "I'm going to Father McNealty tomorrow and reporting you."

I laugh, the bitterness choked through the tears that she can't see in the dark. "Please do."

I hop off the table and approach her. "You'll have to tell him why I'm so angry with you and what you're doing at a student's house, late on a Saturday night. Then he's going to find out it was you in the sex tape with her, and you will never get another job again."

"Screw you, Clay!" she yells. "I have family, too, and they're not the Jaegers who you think you can bully."

"Stay away from her or else."

"Or else what?" she fires back. "You going to take another video of us? Well, enjoy yourself, because when she graduates, and I go to college in New York in the fall—oh, did she tell you about Dartmouth? As luck would have it, we'll be that close to each other . . ." And she gets in my face, taunting me. "And then I can fuck her every weekend where you can't get a hold of her."

My eyes go wide, burning.

"We'll be gone, and we'll laugh about how sad you were." She laughs. "Or are."

I grit my teeth together.

"You don't deserve her attention," she says, "and pretty soon she won't think of you at all!"

"Ugh!" I slam my hands into her chest, and she crashes into the wall next to the doorway. She cries out, falling to the ground, and I spot the garbage can next to her and grab it.

I hesitate a moment, a sob stretching my throat so tightly it hurts. *Fuck it.* I lift it high and dump everything on her head, and she screams as remnants of gumbo and chicken noodle soup smear all over her.

"Clay!" she cries.

I drop the can and clutch her jaw in one hand and the back of her neck in another, bringing her face up to mine. "Look at me," I grit out. "Look at me!"

She raises her eyes, whimpering. "Stop."

"Shut up," I say, tears welling in my eyes, because I know I'm losing. I'm going to lose her forever. "Her team spots her. Do you understand?" And then I lower my voice, pressing my forehead into her hard. "*I* spot her. If I have to repeat myself again, I will do damage you can't come back from. She is seventeen, a minor, and . . ."

Mine.

Megan coughs, and needles prick my throat, because she doesn't deserve this, but it can't happen. Megan doesn't deserve her. And Liv doesn't get to have someone. She doesn't get to forget about me.

She stares at me, clearing her throat as something crosses her eyes. "You want her," she pants. "That's what this is about. Oh my God."

Tears spill.

"You're a . . . a . . ."

And I throw her down, ready to hit her until she can't say the words loud enough for anyone to ever hear.

"What the hell?" someone bellows.

I look up, seeing Liv standing in the doorway as I hover over Megan on the floor.

Liv runs up, flipping on the light. She takes in Megan and me and dives down to pick up her friend, Megan shivering like a scared rabbit as she grapples onto Liv.

Liv turns to me. "What the hell is the matter with you?"

Her brothers spill into the house behind her, and I grab the flag from the table and bolt out the back door and into the yard.

Patting my hand over my mouth and singing, I dance into the forest. "I got the flaaaaag," I call out. "Come and get it!"

I dart back toward the village and Callum's car, but in moments, Liv is on my tail. I feel something muddy hit the back of my knee, and I'm on the ground, flipping onto my back and looking up at her.

She comes down, pinning my wrists to the ground.

"Get me off the ground," I order.

"In the dirt is where you belong!" she spits out. "You've never been uglier to me. How could you do that to her? What the fuck is wrong with you?"

I don't answer, clenching my teeth so my chin doesn't quiver.

I know she's right. The walls close in, and sometimes I feel like I want to die.

"That money and that house don't make you clean," she says. "They just provide a shield of defenders who are only there because they hope to get something out of you. They don't love you. No one loves you!"

She rises, and I pause, her words sinking so deep I can't breathe. In a fog, I climb to my feet.

"What, am I supposed to treat you like glass because you have a dead brother?" she bites out. "I'm supposed to make an exception for your behavior, even though a toddler has better fucking manners than you do?"

I clutch the flag in my fist as she advances on me and backs me into a tree.

"I swallow your shit," she growls, her cheeks flushed, "because you're not important enough to spare an effort, but I've reached my limit. I'm tired of hearing that I'm not good enough. That I deserve to be treated like garbage because of who I am or where I come from or who I want to be with."

I blink away the tears, steeling my jaw.

"That I can't have *that*. Or *that's* not for me, or I'll never have *that* life," she continues. "A lifetime of being told I'm wrong for your world. Of not seeing myself in your school hallways and represented in your town."

"You won't find what you're looking for in the back seat of your car, either!" I grit out.

She nods, looking like she has more to say, but deciding that it's not worth it. She looks at me, several breaths passing before she drops her gaze and murmurs, "Or at Marymount, I guess."

I narrow my eyes. "What does that mean?"

She's been there almost four years. She's all of a sudden realizing she doesn't fit?

She meets my eyes again, swallowing and sounding calm, her anger suddenly gone. "It means I don't have anything to prove. I don't know why I ever thought I did. Especially to you."

Because . . . because what happened in the locker room wasn't one-sided. She felt it, too. "Because you want to touch me," I tell her.

She scoffs, tears glistening in her eyes. "Is that what this is about?" she inquires. "Don't think what happened in the locker room was real just because I kissed you back. I was angry and full of a lot of steam to blow off, and pretty much in fucking shock, too, but I don't want you, Clay."

No?

"You're like vanilla," she says. "I mean, yeah, it's ice cream, but it's not really an option when there are other choices that taste better."

She turns away, and I grab her, but instead of yanking away from me, she grabs me back and presses me into the tree, its bark digging into my back.

She glares.

"Don't say that," I whisper.

"Why?"

"Because I can't . . ." I don't know how to explain. "I can't . . . I can't . . ."

I don't want you. I can't want you. It's just . . .

So I say the only thing that I do know for sure. "I can't leave you alone," I tell her.

That's all I know. I need to feel it again.

My hair falls in my face, but I can smell the remnants of her watermelon lip gloss. "Ask me to touch you."

Please. I want her to want me to touch her. I won't force her like last time. *Ask me.*

But she just shakes her head slowly, and I don't know what it means.

I place my hands on her waist. "Ask me."

But just then, a low hiss pierces the air somewhere behind her, and we both freeze.

My pulse echoes in my ears, and I peer over her shoulder as she turns her head, both of us spotting a glowing pair of eyes low to the ground about ten yards away.

"Liv."

"Shhh."

She still holds me pressed to the tree, but both of us are too afraid to move. I resist the urge to push her behind me. Alligators can't hear outside of water, but they have great night vision. I might not be Swamp, but any Floridian over three years of age knows the basics.

"Don't leave me," I beg.

She grew up out here. I don't know what to do.

"When I say," she tells me in a hushed tone, "run back to the path and follow it as fast as you can. They don't move quickly outside of water, but there could be more. *Don't* zigzag."

"Huh?" Why?

But she doesn't wait another second. "Run."

"Liv!" I gasp, not ready.

She grabs my hand and we pound the mud, the reptile slithering into view, growling and hissing, and I can't not look back. I scream, and Liv crashes into me, falling.

It advances, moving right for her, and she scurries back, trying to get up until it's damn near snapping at her feet.

"Ah!" My lungs drop to my feet, and I cry out, grabbing her and hauling her up. "Oh my God."

We run, stomping through the mud and jumping over fallen logs, and I take her hand, not letting her go until we reach the paved road, the streetlights shining overhead. I dart my eyes all around us, making sure we're safe.

"Did it hurt you?" I ask.

But she just stares at me, breathing hard and sweat glistening on her brow.

I don't know what I want to say. *Thank you? Are you okay?*

I'm sorry, maybe? I want to say I'm sorry for so many things, because I look like shit in her eyes.

"Touch me," she says.

And my heart leaps into my throat. I hesitate because I'm afraid she's fucking with me, but then I seize the chance offered and take her face in my hands.

She doesn't pull away as I hover over her mouth, every inch of me warm under my skin. She covers my hands with hers and whispers, "Take care of yourself, Clay."

"What?"

But I don't have time to figure out what she means when she pulls away and casts one last, long look before spinning around and running back into the forest toward her house.

I take a step. The alligator is in there.

But coming just around the corner is Callum's car, and I only consider running after her for another second before he's on me, Amy and Krisjen calling out and opening the back door for me to climb in.

Take care of yourself, Clay.

What does that mean?

11

Clay

I scroll through Liv's Twitter and TikTok, not seeing any new posts since the day of Night Tide. Nothing since our showdown. Nothing about the flag or the picture of me on Macon's bed that had made the rounds in our friends' text messages.

I draw in a deep breath, uneasy. Something's up. I mean, it's totally like her to refuse to acknowledge me, but she hasn't posted anything. Not even trading a barb with a politician or calling out injustice in the Sudan.

Nothing. Not even a response to anyone posting for her birthday today.

It is today. She's eighteen now, still off-limits as a student but otherwise perfectly legal for Martelle.

I grab the flag out from under my bed and stuff it in my backpack. Leaving my bedroom, I head down the hallway, touch Henry's door as I go, and race down the stairs.

I pass a long table with three small glass vases of calla lilies and take the bunch out of one, swiping the water off the stems.

But then I hear my mom. "Clay?"

I pause, hear the elliptical going from our home gym beyond the kitchen, and sigh.

I head over and peek my head inside, seeing the sun barely up out of the window behind her. It's Monday, and we have team workouts this morning. Olivia should be there. I tuck the flowers behind my back.

"We'll be coming to your game this weekend," she says, sweat glistening across her chest in her pink sports bra.

"Both of you?"

She smiles. "You don't have to be nervous."

I cock an eyebrow, looking away. It's an away game about an hour from here. I'm surprised he'll be home.

"You used to like us coming to your games," she tells me.

"A lot of things were different then." I shift on my feet. "Now I'd just like you both to stop pretending you're married for the cameras."

I might like it if they pretended for me a little bit, but hey.

She stops moving, the elliptical sinking to a resting position and her body along with it as she looks at me.

I keep going. "I think we can agree the façade is downright painful anymore, isn't it?"

The pain in her eyes feels good, and I hate that it feels good. I used to love my mom.

I know she's alone. She's suffered, and this week is especially hard, but no one is safe from me, I guess. I've started bullying my parents now.

How could my father not be here for us? After all we've lost? And did she really get an abortion like Macon said? How did he know that? Was it my father's baby? I don't know how it could've been. He's never home.

My parents have even less figured out about life than I do, it seems, and I can't trust anyone. Even my grandmother. What pieces of work they all are.

My mom says nothing, and I turn and walk out before she has a chance to. Squeezing the stems in my hand, I climb into my

Bronco and drive to school with them in my fist the whole time, racing toward the one thing I don't want to hurt anymore.

The hallways are empty, only a few cars in the parking lot yet, and I look around me, making sure no one is here. A pencil hangs off a string of yarn next to the car pool sign-up on the bulletin board, and I snatch it off its staple, keeping the pencil on one end as I tie the other around the flower stems.

I stick the pencil through a slit in the vent of Liv's locker, the yellow paint on the wood scraping off as I shove it through. Hanging from the inside, the little bouquet dangles down the outside of her locker, a few of the pretty white petals floating to the ground.

She probably doesn't like flowers. She'll probably think it's a prank and rip them off and throw them away, but maybe she'll think they're nice, whoever they're from.

Something for her birthday, because she didn't get flowers or cards or candygrams like the rest of us on Valentine's Day, and I'd hated seeing that.

I walk away, looking back at the bouquet, a flutter in my chest. Everyone likes flowers. Even girls in motorcycle jackets.

She should be here soon.

Heading into the locker room, I open my locker and hang up my backpack. I dig my AirPods out of the pocket and take my phone. The Seminole flag peeks out. Liv will be working in the theater after school today. Maybe she'll be alone. Maybe I could take it to her.

I pluck out my pill bottle and open it, wanting to calm myself down a little, but I stop, staring at the container for a second. I didn't take any all weekend. Not once. Since Henry's death, I certainly haven't needed it every day, but it didn't even occur to me. That's weird.

"You okay?" Amy asks at my side.

I recap the bottle and stuff it in my backpack, quickly zipping it up. "Of course." I close my locker. "You?"

"Still a little nervous."

And I know what she's talking about. She texted fifteen times yesterday. My grandmother gave me a stern look in church, so I muted it.

"They won't report it," I tell her. "And who knows? They might cross the tracks for a little more fun."

"I'm not worried about them reporting it," she retorts.

I know. The Jaegers would exact their own justice before going to the police. I still feel shitty about Callum and Milo trashing their house.

"Hey!" Krisjen chirps. She heads to her locker, rubbing a hand on my back. "How are you doing, babe?"

"Fine," I blurt out. "What is it with you guys?"

Why do they keep asking that?

Amy and Krisjen exchange glances, and Krisjen broaches softly, "It's just . . . I know this week is hard . . . on your family."

I turn away, slipping my phone into the side pocket on my leggings. It's been four years since Henry died, and I wait for the sting in my eyes to come like it always does the moment my mind wanders to him, but it's not coming.

I'm distracted. It's not . . . I don't know. I miss him. I miss him so badly I'd give up my hands to have him back, but it's not the only loss I'm feeling right now.

I glance around again, keeping an eye out for Liv, but she's nowhere to be seen.

And as we all head into the gym and I jump on the treadmill, she still doesn't show. Where is she? Maybe she skipped for her birthday, but I feel uneasy.

I fit my earbuds in and pretend to start music as I stalk her social media, looking for a reason why she isn't here. A dentist appointment. Suddenly sick. Self-care day.

Sudden death?

But nothing. She hasn't posted all morning.

"Conroy?" Coach calls, walking into the weight room with a tablet. "Your time has come. I need you to take Jaeger's position at midfield."

Krisjen's mouth falls open as she stops the treadmill. "You're not serious."

That's Liv's position.

I step forward. "What's going on? Where is Jaeger playing now?"

Coomer turns her eyes on me, looking almost hesitant. "She's . . . withdrawn from the team."

"What?"

"Nothing's wrong," Coach assures. "Don't worry."

She starts to leave, but I jump off the treadmill, stopping her. "Hey, wait a minute. She just . . . she just quit? You're joking."

Coach turns and looks around at the three of us, other girls faltering in their workout to listen.

"She's finishing the school year from home," Coach announces.

My stomach drops. "What?" *Like hell.*

But Coach just looks at me, replying calmly, "Well, what did you expect, Clay?"

And I fall silent, because my behavior hasn't escaped anyone's notice, it seems. Coach looks like she's surprised Olivia Jaeger lasted as long as she did under the circumstances.

Coach leaves, her question hanging in the air, and Amy rushes to my side. "Oh my God."

"She actually left school?" Krisjen joins in.

Amy's eyes smile and a lump swells in my throat. I turn away, pretending to look at my phone. The world spins in front of me, static in my vision, and I'm going to scream if I don't get out of here.

I don't have anything to prove. I don't know why I ever thought I did. Especially to you. This is what she meant when she told me to take care of myself. If it weren't for me, she'd be here. She'd be happy.

So she left. She let me win.

She just let me win. Just like that.

Amy and Krisjen talk, and I just stare at my phone, my thumb hovering over the screen and my head spinning in a million different directions, so much so that I don't know what I'm doing.

The allure of her will be gone now. That's good. Whatever my obsession was, she did me a favor. I can concentrate on other things: boys, friends, getting ready for the ball and prom and college . . .

It's over.

"You get to play now!" Amy argues, and I snap my attention back to my friends. "Why are you whining?"

"I like my minimal position, thank you," Krisjen says. "I can't play Jaeger's. Especially against Gibbon's Cross."

"Yeah," Amy sighs, agreeing. "Jaeger was good for something, I guess."

I squeeze my eyes shut, my chest tightening painfully. I can't . . . I can't.

I leave, whipping open the door and heading back into the locker room.

"Clay!" Amy shouts after me.

But I keep going.

I don't have to get angry about this. I'm not a toddler. She's leaving the team high and dry, but other than that, it's no loss. I drove her out. I did what I set out to do. I win.

So why do I want to kick every door I see? I pass Megan in the locker room, expecting a dirty look, but once she sees my face, a slight smile graces hers.

She gets to have her now. No one will know.

Stripping off my clothes, I wrap a towel around myself and carry my caddie into a shower stall. Closing the curtain, I turn on the water, breathing in and out as I wet my hair and let the hot water soothe me. I close my eyes, my shoulders heavy and my head feeling like it weighs a hundred pounds. I just want to sit down.

I just want to—

But all of a sudden, the rings on the shower rod slide together again. I pop my eyes open, spin around, and see Liv stepping into the private stall with me. My heart leaps as she closes the curtain behind her and approaches me, holding her towel to her body.

For a moment, I'm flooded with relief. *She's here.* She didn't leave.

I find my voice, confident again and refusing to smile, even though I want to. "What the hell are you doing?" I whisper. "Get out. Now."

I reach for my towel to cover myself, but in one swift movement, she pulls hers off her body and knocks my hand away all in the same shot. I stare down at her naked body, and the wind leaves my lungs. My chest caves, and I barely notice her backing me into the wall as she tips her head back and wets her hair. Streams of water cascade down her golden skin, and I can't breathe as it spills over her breasts and drips off the hard little points. My clit pulses as I hate her all over again.

She meets my eyes, smoothing back her hair, and approaches me until her nipples brush mine. I can't think, and I can't swallow.

"Maybe these separate shower stalls your bigot mother had put in weren't such a bad idea, after all," she says.

I watch as she tips her head back, opens her mouth, and places it under the stream, filling it with water. The pulse between my legs pounds so hard, I almost groan.

She kisses me, opening her mouth, the warm water spilling inside and down my chin and neck, and I lick my lips, thirsty for more, because tasting what she tasted makes me go mad. I throb down low, my body beating like a drum. I whimper, about to fucking come when she pulls away.

My lip quivers, and I can't find my words for a minute. "G-get out," I tell her.

But she doesn't. Grabbing the showerhead off the hook, she sticks it between my legs, and I gasp, stopping just short of crying out.

"Ah," I moan. I cup her face and hold her to me, almost in tears it feels so good. "Liv . . ."

The spray pulsates over me, and I'm already too close to stop it. I hold on to her, her forehead pressed into mine as she watches what she does to me, and my orgasm crests, so wound up it takes no time for her to get me there. Heat floods my stomach, my thighs shake, my knees go weak, and I hear voices and lockers slamming shut just as I cover my mouth with my hand and scream.

Fuck. I shake, and I don't know if I'm crying or what, because it feels so good.

"You don't feel with him what you feel with me," she whispers. "Do you?"

I shudder and grip her, every muscle clenched, and I can't stand it. Nothing feels like this. Nothing. "I hate you," I murmur in her ear.

But still, I don't let her go, grazing her skin with my lips.

Oh God. She lets the orgasm run through me before placing the showerhead back on the hook, and then she leans into my ear, the showers around us filling with people. "It's a shame you'll be wasted on him," she whispers, steam billowing around us. "We would've had so much fun."

Would've.

I don't look up as she takes her towel and leaves. I sink to the floor, unable to move another inch for minutes as everyone showers and dresses and the first bell rings for class.

Would've had so much fun, she'd said. *Would've.*

When I finally come out, her locker hangs open and empty.

O ver the next couple days, word spreads that Olivia Jaeger is finishing the school year from home—some story about her family needing her, but almost everyone knows it's because of me. Sideways glances greet me when I pass students in the hall or cafeteria, some with smiles of approval and some with hints of fear.

Speculation is abundant on what I supposedly did to scare her off, but no one knows for sure.

On Wednesday, I pass her main locker, noticing that the flowers are still there, dried and yellowed. Did she see them before she left? She would've taken them if she'd wanted them.

I have to hand it to her. She wasn't bluffing. She hadn't come back to school. She was serious.

I sit in Calculus, our fifth-period class we share—or used to share—her desk to my left and at the very front still sitting empty. It's nice not to have her here anymore. She always had to look so different. All that silver in her ears, glinting with the sunlight streaming through the windows, hugely distracting.

The slutwear, the short skirts and the fire engine red lipstick that no one understood the point of. I mean, was she trying to get the boys' attention? Because she did, which seemed opposite of what you'd think she'd want.

Still, though. The lipstick really was perfect for her skin tone. The little braids pecking out of her ponytails looked like they grew that way, and it was hard not to look at her.

It was hard for anyone not to look at her.

I draw in a deep breath and exhale. The school is more peaceful now. I'm better. Clearer.

The shower comes back to me, and fuck, it felt good, but if anyone found out, I'd be ruined. My friends might understand, but their parents wouldn't. My grandmother would send me to therapy, and my parents would break, thinking they'd failed after so much loss already.

"Yes," I hear Ms. Kirkpatrick say. "Come in, come in."

I look up, the rest of the students filling their seats as a young woman holds the strap of her backpack over her shoulder and hands the teacher her schedule.

Ms. Kirkpatrick leads her to a seat—Liv's empty desk—and smiles, handing her paper back to her.

"Class?" she says loudly. "This is Chloe Harper. She's joining us from Austin."

The girl turns her head, offering everyone a smile with her shade of pink gloss that could easily be mine. Her eyes land on me, and she hesitates on my gaze, nodding once in hello, a beautiful small smile grazing her lips.

She turns back around, and I shake my head, looking away. That's Liv's seat. So quickly filled like she was never here at all. Everyone has already moved on.

The talk has even started to die down. Most people have stopped mentioning her.

She's not in the locker room. The weight room. The lunchroom. Her desks don't exist anymore. She was never here.

Classes end, and I head to practice, passing her locker, and see something drawn on it in red nail polish. I stop, reading *Dyke* written vertically down the long locker.

And I straighten, glaring. *Who did this?* How dare they?

Even though I know I'm one of the culprits who's been calling her that name for years.

People wrote things on Alli's locker, too, I'd heard. I'm sure it was hard to have someone be cruel—I can certainly dish it but can't take it—but I finally realize it was probably more painful to see the taunts in full view of everyone who passed by. Hundreds of people are invited into your suffering.

I blink, charging off to the locker room to change into my gear. I throw on my clothes, grab my equipment, and head out to the field with my friends, needing to run to get rid of the urge to scrub the front of her locker with nail polish remover. The janitors will take care of it tonight.

My head overflows with lava, and it just keeps coming and coming, the fact that she's not here. And she won't be here tomorrow.

Krisjen takes up Liv's place on the field, Amy and Ruby laughing and joking around, everyone carrying on their conversations like she's not gone. Like she wasn't important.

She's smart. She works hard. She's in that theater every night, without pay, no one more devoted to earning everything she deserves. She comes from nothing, works her ass off, is honest and a good person. She's the muscle on the team, and they're all just acting like we actually have a shot without her. Like she isn't irreplaceable.

But to them, she's nothing. She's just the dyke who once went here.

"Come on!" I yell when Krisjen misses the goal again.

"I can't . . ." she gasps. "Clay, I can't. It's too fast."

"Too fast?" I bark, getting in her face, the numbness of the last few days gone. "Are you kidding?"

Krisjen backs away from me, scared.

"Gibbon's Cross is gonna be a lot harder on you. Stop pussing out!" I yell.

Everyone stops; sweat is coating my back and no one's fucking laughing now.

"I'm not losing the biggest game of my senior year because everyone wants to get lazy all of a sudden!"

The game is in two days, for Christ's sake!

"Collins . . ." Coach warns.

But I throw down my stick and my eyewear, sprinkles of rain hitting my arms. "God, you guys suck!"

I stomp off toward the locker room. Coach grabs my arm, but I yank it away.

"Coach, it's okay," I hear Krisjen tell her as I keep walking. "We'll go."

I leave, heading for the locker room without looking up.

It's fine. Everything is fine.

I yank my locker door open, but I haven't had enough, and I do it again and again, tears spilling down my face as I dig in my backpack for the pill bottle.

I fumble with the cap, finally giving up and resting my head on the locker next to mine, the cool metal feeling like heaven after the heat of the blood rushing under my skin.

"It's fine," I sob.

Someone comes up and hugs my back, and I crumble to the floor, Krisjen hanging on and falling with me.

"Clay, it's okay," she whispers, and I hear the tears in her throat. "I know you miss him. It's okay. You can cry."

Yeah.

Henry. Right.

I let her hold me, giving in to it as Amy kneels down beside us, and probably only there because she thinks she should be, but I'll take it, because the world feels empty enough. There's nothing. I'm nothing.

I wish tomorrow would never come.

It's fine. Everything is fine.

She's the one who loses. Not me. Everything is as it should be now.

Out of sight, out of mind.

Just leave her alone. Forget about her.

She's gone.

12

Olivia

"Did you think I wasn't going to find out?"

I swallow the small bite of chili and tap the wooden spoon on the edge of the pot before setting it down. I look over at Macon's hand, watching the screen of the phone that he holds in my face. The video of Megan and me plays, and Iron, Army, and Dallas crowd around him to see.

Aracely sits in the stool, leaning back against the wall with her arms crossed, and very interested in what the guys are talking about, because she's relishing it. She brought it to their attention, I'm sure.

I turn off the burner and grab a bowl for myself. "What were you going to do about it?"

It's not like I was trying to hide it. I reposted it, didn't I? I just didn't make him aware of it. There's a lot I don't make him aware of.

"Is this why you left school?" Army chimes in.

"I'm still a student."

I scoop up a bowlful and place the lid on the pot. Adding some oyster crackers, I pick a spoon out of the drawer and walk into the living room.

"You let them get away with everything," Macon barks. "And now you let them drive you away."

"You saw what they did to the house," Aracely chimes in, swinging her arm around as if I've yet to notice the destruction that took place when the Saints snuck in Saturday night. They all blame me, because I'd invited them over the tracks.

"Good thing it's not your house," I reply.

She casts a glare to Macon as if he's going to make me respect her.

I sit down on the couch and prop my elbows on my knees as I lean over my bowl on the coffee table. "And I didn't let them get away with anything." I look up at Macon. "I took away their entertainment. I won."

"That's not how they see it."

He steps into the living room, approaching me, and I look away, scooping up some chili. *So this is about his pride.* Got it.

"We're not letting it go this time," Dallas tells me.

"And you're going back to school," Macon adds.

"Not likely." I blow on my food.

Macon advances, tossing his phone to a chair on my right, but Trace inches in. "Just leave her alone."

"You shut up," Macon growls.

I put the spoon into my mouth, ignoring the fire in my brothers' eyes. Except Trace's, because he always takes my side, and Iron's, because he doesn't ever get mad at me.

Army picks up Macon's phone again, studying the screen. "Is this that assistant coach?" he asks, peering over at me.

I eat another bite, everyone's eyes and ears trained on me, and I'm so damn tired of putting out fires that I didn't start. *Damn her.*

"Is it?" Macon asks when I don't answer.

I shake my head, smashing the beans as I mix up the chili and crackers. "Don't."

"Livvy . . ."

"Just let me be!" I shout, glaring up at them. *Jesus! This doesn't have to be a family fucking meeting, Macon.* I shoot daggers at him, tired of everyone on my back. Even at home, I'm not safe.

They have no idea what it's been like for me. What every day is like for me in this town. I made a decision. *Just support me. Please!*

Macon blinks, hesitating. The last time I'd yelled at him I was ten, in tears, and thrashing. He'd hugged me until I couldn't hurt myself anymore.

When he speaks, his tone is gentler. "You are the only one ever getting out of here," he tells me. "Don't you think I've always known that? You have three months left. If you let them win now, it will follow you forever."

I scoop up more chili. "Clay Collins won't feel like she's won anything six months from now."

"Clay Collins," he says. "That's who did this."

He holds up his phone, smart enough to know that someone had to take the video of the assistant coach and me.

I ignore the question. "I'm a fighter," I inform him. "But that is something you never understood. Not everything is worth a fight. What do I care what they think about me in twenty years? I won't be thinking about them at all."

"Well, that's just great," he says, tossing his phone back down. "Because as usual, everything is all about you."

"On the contrary, finally something is." I stare hard at him. "I don't have to stay in a community that hates me. I don't have to put up with anything."

"Then bite back!"

I shake my head. I bit back in that shower with her, and I loved seeing how much she wanted it. I loved it too much. That was the problem.

Biting back could hurt me more than her. I can't.

So fuck it. I'm out. I'm eighteen. I got into Dartmouth. All I have to do now is graduate high school, and it really doesn't matter how or from where. If Marymount decided to send me packing when I withdrew this week, I could go to the public high school to finish my credits, and I'd still be going to Dartmouth in the fall. Living my life. Free. Happy. I win.

The doorbell rings, and I see Trace head for it as Macon's and my gazes stay locked on each other. I eat another bite, finally looking away, rather than play his infantile game of "Who's Going to Blink First?"

I know what he's saying. And part of me agrees. Part of me is consumed by pride, and I hate that Clay Collins and her friends will get even a moment's satisfaction by running me off, but it's not my responsibility to educate them. It's not my lot in life to survive them. *Fuck them.*

"What the hell?" I hear Trace gripe.

We all turn our heads as he opens the door wide, and I watch as Krisjen steps into the house, her lacrosse uniform on and her hair in French braids.

My brothers stare at her, knowing exactly who she is. Her grandfather is the judge Iron always gets every time he's in trouble, and the judge who would just love to be there when my brother gets his third strike.

"Really brave or really stupid," Trace says, sounding amused. He turns his head to me. "Any idea, Liv?"

"She's not brave," I tell him, scooping up more food and pinning Krisjen with a stare. "Or smart."

Just stupid.

"You have twenty seconds," I tell her.

She casts a nervous glance around the room, looking apprehensive to say whatever she has to say in front of my whole family, but whatever.

"The game is today," she says.

"And?"

"The car is running." She tips her chin up, bracing herself. "I have your uniform. Please."

I laugh under my breath. "Get out."

I take a bite, everyone else remaining silent.

But Krisjen doesn't back down. "Gibbon's Cross, Jaeger! I can't beat them."

"I'm no longer on the team."

"You're still a student," she retorts. "You could be back on the team with the snap of a finger."

I shake my head. "I said get out."

"Just this game." She moves in, hovering over me. "This is your team, too. You worked for months for this."

And for what? I stir the food, refusing to look up. Gibbon's Cross is the team to beat, and I wanted to be there, because winning would feel great, but I could only hold on for so long. Joining that team was never about lacrosse. It was me stupidly thinking that people would like me when they got to know me. I'd bond with the girls on the team. I'd be respected by classmates, be part of their world. The administration would value me and treat me as worthy of what I deserved if I was a team player in that *one* aspect.

And all I got was shit for my trouble. Let them learn the hard way how fucking valuable I am.

"Why should she lift a finger to help all of you?" Dallas says. "It's not like you won't go back to treating her like shit the moment you have the win off her."

"Fuck 'em." Army folds his arms across his chest. "Let them lose."

A car horn honks outside, and I don't know if it's her mom, or maybe it's Clay, sending her in here to do her dirty work.

I meet Krisjen's eyes. "Tell Clay she can go fuck herself."

"Clay's not even playing," she tells me.

I stop and look up at her.

"She's benched," Krisjen goes on.

I drop my gaze, staring at my bowl, absently stirring as thoughts whirl in my head. Clay's not playing. Will she even be there? What the hell happened?

I'll admit, the prospect of not having to deal with her bullshit on the field is enticing. But if I play today, they'll just try to coerce me into playing again, and eventually she will be back.

I'm done with Marymount.

Krisjen stands there waiting for me to say something, but when I don't, she sighs and walks for the door, giving up.

"I'm sorry about it, you know?" She pauses with her hand on the knob. "There's no excuse for our behavior."

I drop my eyes to my bowl again, steeling my jaw.

"But there is a reason," she says. "There is always a reason why people are the way they are. Even Clay."

My throat tightens, and I listen as she opens the door, walks out, and closes it behind her.

"That took nerve," I hear Army say.

"Or stupidity," Dallas adds.

Maybe both. Or maybe it's just humility. Krisjen is a follower, but I always knew she wouldn't be the way she is without Clay and Amy and their pressure. She might be a nice person otherwise.

Iron speaks up. "I'm not playing nice if those little pricks cross the tracks again, Macon. Without Liv at Marymount anymore, there's no reason for us to keep the peace."

"You'll do and not do what I tell you to," Macon fires back.

"Like Liv." Trace laughs. "You get her to do what you want so well."

"What . . . ?" Macon says. "I'm glad she refused her. I always hated that she was on that team anyway. It was a waste of time."

Aracely laughs from her stool against the wall, I hear the engine outside rev, and I drop the spoon back into the bowl, clenching my fists.

Only one person I want to piss off more than Clay Collins, and that's the people who love me, waiting for me to fail. In four years, Macon has been to one of my games. *One.* At least I have no expectations of Clay. All he cares about is my future. Never my happiness. He never listens.

Pushing off the couch, I slip on my leather jacket, grab my keys and shoes, and slip my purse over my body.

"Liv!" Macon yells.

But I don't look back. Racing out the front door, I see Krisjen's mom's Range Rover pulling down the dirt road, and I run after it, pounding on the rear window.

They stop, and I hear the door unlock.

I swing open the back door and climb in.

"I've got a spare toothbrush," Krisjen says from the driver's seat as she looks at me in her rearview mirror, smiling.

I sit down next to Ruby, Amy in the front passenger seat, and slam the door. "I'm not staying the night."

Just for the game.

The stadium in Gibbon's Cross is like walking into a lobster tank surrounded by butchers looking for the perfect specimen for tonight's special. It's small—smaller than ours—so no matter if it's a football game or peewee soccer, the stands always seem filled with home field advantage. Not a single empty spot on the bleachers remains, the benches overflowing with cheering parents and students, not because anyone here particularly gives a shit about girls' lacrosse, but they do like to win against St. Carmen. Private schools brim with people used to getting what they want for a certain price, so when anything is left to chance, it's stressful. And exciting. They show up for it.

We jog to the sidelines, everyone on the field stretching and warming up.

"You're late!" Coach yells at Krisjen, panicked. "I'd bench you right now if I didn't need you."

We stop in front of Coomer, and I see Clay in uniform on the bench off to the left as Coomer's eyes flash to me.

"She's still a student," Krisjen tells her. "I can't keep up with this team. Please."

Coach studies me, probably wondering about the change of heart after I'd stalked into her office Monday morning, told her I was out, and promptly left without a conversation. I hop on the balls of my feet, stretching my arms over my head, because we have no time for warm-ups before play starts.

"I'm not going to force you, Jaeger," Coach tells me. "Do you want to be here?"

"No."

Krisjen levels a glare at me.

"I want you to pay for victory pizza," I say instead.

Coach smiles despite herself and turns back to the field. "Get your gear on."

Coomer always takes us out to dinner when we win, but I never go. I go home.

But I'm going tonight, and I don't give a shit who doesn't want me there. We're going to win because of me.

Getting my shit on, I dart onto the field, Krisjen joining and taking up her position, protecting our goal. I look left and right, between the other two midfielders. "Stay sharp," I tell them. "Watch for me!"

They nod, sticks up, and I press mine to the grass, eye to eye with the other team.

"Oh, yay," Elle Costa from the other team snickers. "I was almost disappointed this was going to be too easy."

"I couldn't let you down, baby."

"No Clay today?" she cracks, her eyes flashing to the bench.

"Don't worry." I smile. "You'll still have your hands full."

The ref drops the ball, and I slam into her, my legs charged with some kind of juice, and I don't know where it comes from, but I have to admit I've missed this.

Completing schoolwork at home is lonely, and the last thing I needed this week is more quality time with Macon, but I've kept busy even though Macon was right. In some ways, my decision to withdraw and retreat had made perfect sense, but I also felt like I'd missed an opportunity.

Marymount isn't the only challenge I'll have in life. What happens next time? *Most people*, he'd once told me, *don't do great things, because great things don't feel great when you're doing them.* I shouldn't have run from them. I should've learned from them.

I snap the ball to Rodriguez, who passes it to Sinclair, and I race ahead, covering her as she passes it to Amy, who leaps, catches the ball and swings, hitting the post, and the ball bounces out.

"It's okay!" I shout, taking the lead, since our captain is busy warming her ass.

Play continues, Clay's presence heavy on my right, but I refuse to look. I'm surprised she even showed up, but I suppose she had to in case someone gets injured. What the hell got her benched?

Dinah Leister from Gibbon's Cross catches the ball and races toward our goal, but I dive in and snatch it, firing it over to Amy, running ahead just in time for her to shoot it back, and I snap it, holding my breath and watching as it rolls right into their goal.

"Yeah!" Krisjen shouts, our team celebrating.

Amy flips her stick around like a baton, all smiles, and I spare two seconds to feel the glow before I run back to get in play again.

Time moves fast, Gibbon's Cross scoring one, and us scoring two more in the second.

I bang my stick on the ground. "Amy!" I shout.

She flashes her eyes to me, hits the ball just as someone knocks her to the ground, elbowing her head. I grab the ball, shooting it into the net, and more boos erupt from the stands.

I smile, but I don't celebrate, running over and not thinking. I slam Costa in the shoulder while everyone is distracted, watching her land on the ground next to Amy and getting her comeuppance. This is the third time she's done that to one of us, and the refs aren't seeing it. Or pretending they're not seeing it.

I pull Amy back to her feet. "Thanks," she says.

I jog back down the field, throwing out my hands at the ref. "You gonna call something at some point?" I yell.

"Jaeger!" Coach yells, because I'm getting smart with the ref.

Fuck it. They're throwing cheap shots. We win nothing taking the high road.

I look over, seeing Clay standing now, her arms folded over her chest, concern or tension etched across her brow.

I get back in the game, Ruby passing the ball to Krisjen and Krisjen passing it back quickly. "Liv!" she shouts, shooting it to me.

Second and third periods pass, and I wipe the sweat off my forehead, hair loose from my ponytail tickling my neck. We're up two goals, but everyone is exhausted and Gibbon's Cross doesn't always play their best players first. They're about to get a second wind.

I debate for a moment and then walk over to Coach. "Bring Clay in," I tell her. "Ruby's exhausted."

But Coach shakes her head. "I'll make the decisions. Get back in the game."

I hesitate, ready to argue, but they're teeing off.

Running backward onto the field again, I growl at Clay, "So you just gonna sit there the whole night?"

Make her put you in the game. You can make anyone do anything, right?

But Clay just sits, her elbows on her knees, watching me. Making no move, like she's given up.

Cross scores again, and we're almost tied, all of us digging in our heels. I breathe hard, wanting this win so badly. I don't want them to say I came back and they still lost. I'd have swallowed my pride for nothing.

Ang shoots the ball. I catch it, a Cross player on my hide, and I let out a yell, shooting the ball and watching it get past the goalie and into the net.

"Yeah!"

"Woo-hoo!"

Someone grabs onto my shoulder and about five people hug me. We're back up two goals, and I glance at the clock, nine minutes left.

I run back to position, looking over at Clay. "That's okay," I taunt. "We're doing fine. Never needed you."

I smile, turn my eyes away, and resume play, but a minute later, I hear the whistle blow. Coach calls Ruby off the field, and I see Clay putting on her gear.

She heads right for me, brushing my shoulder as she passes. "*Teammates* doesn't mean *team*."

"*Friendly* ain't *friends*," I say.

"Just so we're clear."

Fuck yeah. We're clear. Help me score, and you're useful. Otherwise, you're not.

We play, the ebb and flow of our game settling back into familiar territory as I look over and see Clay always there when I need her. She anticipates me, and I guess it's from playing together so long, but I don't have that dynamic with all the girls. I pass, she catches, she runs, and I cover her.

"Here!" I call.

She doesn't hesitate. She passes me the ball, and I shoot it to Amy, Clay running ahead, taking the ball back and scoring.

Everyone cheers while the people in the stands boo, and Clay smiles, her friends jumping on her.

I pass her.

"Good job," she tells me.

I blow spit out, it landing an inch from her shoe.

She looks down and then at me, her smile gone.

"You trashed my house," I say as everyone moves into position around us. "You desecrated our flag."

She doesn't try to defend herself, and I don't want her to. I'm just reminding her that we're not a team.

"Liv!" someone yells.

Clay and I turn our heads, seeing Megan next to the coach, her blond hair spilling out of her baseball cap and a look in her eyes that warns me not to get myself in trouble.

Clay waves at someone, and I follow her gaze, seeing Callum and his friends sitting on the hood of his car on the other side of the chain-link fence in the parking lot. He watches us with that look in his eyes that reminds me of what my lactose intolerance feels like when it kicks in.

"You didn't feel like he does," Clay whispers, moving in close as play starts around us. "You didn't feel powerful."

He felt powerful? He's had her? I pause, staring at her. I guess I shouldn't be surprised that she's fucked him already. I don't know why I thought she hadn't gone that far. Maybe because Clay Collins is such a priss, she wouldn't want to get dirty.

She looks at me. "You can't do to me what he can do."

"I can do *anything* he can do," I grit out. "You want me inside of you?"

I watch her eyes fall to my mouth, a hint of my tongue showing itself.

"You want to ride me?" I offer. "I can do anything you want."

I can do anything to her a man can do.

"But I will never touch you," I tell her, casting a glance to the sidelines and Megan. "I like her. She's so ready."

Clay's eyes narrow, a fire lighting inside.

"You're bland and repressed, boring and bitchy." I grin. "Good thing is, rich or not, those things can be fixed."

Her own words thrown back at her from when she wrote on me in Sharpie and the knowledge that I'll have a good fucking time with anyone but her makes her eyes turn red. She growls, shoving me in the chest, and I laugh, fisting her shirt and dragging her down to the grass with me.

We roll, whistles sound, and the crowd goes wild, the showdown they expected by two rival teams taking a twist they didn't expect.

"Oh, you wanna be on top, huh?" I tease, Clay straddling me.

She screams, more pissed off, and I just laugh, barely noticing all the arms trying to pull us apart.

13

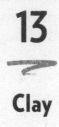

Clay

I yank my rubber band out, letting my hair loose as I rub my scalp where she tried to pull my hair.

"Krisjen?" Coach yells. "Amy?"

Both of my friends stand in the hotel room, muddy cleats in hand and their ponytails hanging by a prayer.

I glare at Liv, watching her stand there all calm, relaxed, and bored across the room, like this is all just a waste of her time. Like she barely knows I exist. *Bitch.*

I fold my arms over my chest, the tension like an electrical current. I'm going to kill her. Thank God my parents decided to not come tonight.

Coomer's eyes dart between Liv and me as she speaks to Amy and Krisjen. "Shower in Audrey's room and take everything you need," she orders them. "You won't be back for a while."

Amy hesitates for a moment, pressed into a quick decision at a moment's notice about what outfit to grab, or all the makeup she'll need tonight, but then she sees Krisjen just grab her whole overnight bag and backpack, and she does the same. Taking all their gear, hands full, they leave the room, their shit banging against the door as they go.

This is bullshit. I glare at Jaeger. She did this on purpose. Must've been a hoot when she'd found out the coach benched me. She just had to come back to see that, didn't she? And what did it get us? A forfeited game for unsportsmanlike conduct. She fucked us and got the last laugh.

But just as the door closes behind Krisjen and Amy, and I brace myself for some useless lecture, Coach turns and immediately follows the girls, leaving Liv and me.

"Wait!" I step toward her. "What are you doing?"

Liv stays rooted by the window.

Coomer turns her head over her shoulder, pulling open the door. "Sort it out," she tells us. "I don't care how you do it or if it takes all night, but you're roomies now, so take all the time you need."

"Are you kidding?" I burst out.

No fucking way. I can't . . .

Not all night. The team is supposed to go out.

My stomach drops, and I barely hear the coach tell us, "You're both eighteen now. Don't test me on how much worse the consequences get from here on out regarding assault. Do not leave this room." And then she points to Liv. "You're still a student."

Which means she can still tell Liv what to do, considering this is a school-sanctioned trip, and her family would assume she was in a teacher's care. Legal adult or not, Coomer's responsible for us.

Coach slams the door, and I watch Liv swipe her cell phone from the bed. She dials, holding the phone to her ear as she digs in a bag Krisjen left, taking out a change of clothes.

I hear someone talk in Liv's ear, and then she says. "Come to Cross and get me." She snatches jeans, a bra, and a tank top from the bag. "I'm at the Marriott."

I shake my head. "Yeah, by all means," I tell her. "Get expelled and solve all our problems."

I mean, technically, a whole stadium saw me attack her, so no one would fault her for refusing to stay locked in this room with me. She has every right to leave.

She almost looks at me but casts her eyes back to her task. "Trace?" she says, trying to get her brother's attention.

"She's not joking, Liv!" I yell. "She'll expel us for that stunt on the field just now! We can't leave!"

Her eyes finally flash to mine, but only for a second. Her brother says something.

"You just want to see me suffer," she tells him.

"No, I want you to get our fucking flag back!" he shouts.

And she pulls the phone away from her ear and stares at it for a second before tossing it on the bed. He hung up on her.

I almost smile. In her rush to leave Marymount and prove something to us, she'd forgotten about that.

"I doubt you can hide an expulsion from Dartmouth," I remind her, content that no one is coming to pick her up.

She brushes past me, carrying her clothes. "What do you care?"

"I don't," I fire back. "I care about the team, and as much as it pisses me off, you're the only one who can seem to perform up to a standard, so let's get each other past this so you can come back to school, back to the team, and we can finish the year out amicably before we *never* have to see each other again."

"I'm not going back to that school."

And then she disappears into the bathroom, slamming and locking the door.

I stand there, still in my uniform, cold and covered in dirt and grass from the fight.

I reach out, putting my palm on the door. "And the play?" I ask, knowing that graduating from a top-notch prep school wasn't the only thing keeping her at Marymount. We have the funds for the arts, unlike a lot of the public schools. "I hear you're Callum's understudy. The possibility of a major role? What you've been waiting for? Is she really more important than all the things you used to want?"

She's silent for a moment, and then I hear, "Who?"

I pull my head up, staring through the door. "Don't waste my time. I'm smarter than you think."

It takes a few seconds, but the door swings open and Liv stands there in some faded black skinny jeans, white top, and her hair loose and looking like it hasn't been combed in days.

"Martelle?" she asks, looking almost amused.

I back up a little, thankful for her calm tone for once. "It makes it easier, not being at school, doesn't it?" I point out. "You both won't be tempted to meet. You can keep your hookups secret. She can keep her job."

Liv blinks, and then something crosses her eyes.

Laughter.

"Um, yeah." She nods. "You nailed it." She steps into the room, walking to the bed and putting her dirty clothes in the duffel bag. "She thought it would be best. It was just too hard, not wanting each other all the time, you know?"

I lean against the door to the room, watching her. "You're still a student."

"As everyone likes to remind me."

"And I can still have her fired."

She laughs under her breath, still tending to her bag and not sparing me eye contact. "Well, that would be one way to ensure I never return to Marymount, Clay."

Son of a bitch. I shoot out my leg and kick the lamp on the little table next to the couch. It crashes to the ground, the shade popping off, the bulb shattering, and the room dims. "Well, go, then!" I growl, blinking through the tears in my eyes. "Just go! I didn't ask you to come back for this game!"

"Yeah, benched." She moves toward me like a snake. "Doing so well on your own, weren't you?"

"Of course I was," I grit out. "I'm me. Oh, the arrogance to believe this has anything to do with you."

"Oh, I think something does." She advances on me until I hit the wall, pressing her palms on either side of my head. "There's a reason you hate me so much. Why? Let's finally fucking have it out. Why have you always hated me?"

"Because you're nasty!" I blurt out, smelling the shampoo in her hair. "It's simple. The most basic human function is to reproduce, and you don't do that with another girl. You're fucked in the head. It's not what we're built for."

"Wanna see what I was built for?"

And she moves in, but I push her back. "You're disgusting."

"And you're miserable." She slams her hand against the wall near my head again. "You're a miserable human being, Clay."

"At least I don't fuck anything that comes along." I glare into her eyes, two inches from her nose. "You really think you're happy? Throwing yourself at anyone just to pass the time? You hate me, too. You know why? Because I don't need anyone. I may be pissy and spoiled and mean, but I don't need anyone!"

"You need this," she retorts.

This? The fighting or . . . ? "No, I don't."

"Oh, yes you do," she whispers, but her tone is hard. "You need this so fucking bad you fell apart when I left school, didn't you? Nothing to play with anymore, which is exactly why I did it!"

I shake my head. No, I . . .

"I didn't let you win," she tells me. "I simply removed myself from an environment that I hated. That didn't deserve me. That offered me nothing."

Tears well in my eyes, and I see her chin tremble.

"I got my credits," she continues, holding back tears. "I got into Dartmouth, and I didn't need any of that shit anymore. You weren't worth the fight." She grabs my collar. "You were worth nothing!"

I shove at her, but she keeps hold and so do I. "None of us are, right? Jaeger for herself, right? Go, then. Get the fuck out of here! Go!"

"I will!" she cries. "I'm leaving, Clay. And I'm not coming back!"

I gasp, nearly choking on my breath as my knees give out and I slide down the wall.

She follows. "I'm leaving."

No. A sob lodges in my throat.

"I'm going," she says.

I shake my head. No . . .

"And I'm never coming back!" Her shout rings in my ears, and in a moment, she's going to rise, walk out the door, and she'll never come back, because Liv doesn't lie. She's stubborn and strong and a survivor, and she never lies.

Knots twist so hard, they snap in my gut, vomit rises up my throat, and I squeeze my eyes shut, tears spilling down. I push her away and rush into the bathroom, dropping to my knees and heaving over the toilet. I cough, sputter, and choke, feeling it coming up, but the only thing that does is a cry too agonizing to hear.

Oh, God.

She can't go. She can't. I can't . . .

Resting my elbows on the seat, I hold my head in my hands as lumps of something fill my throat and my stomach quivers.

And then . . . I feel something warm cover my back, arms wrap around my body, and hands tip my chin back and wipe the hair away from my face.

I tense, instinct telling me to push her away, but all I want is her. She holds me to her, and I fall back, collapsing in her arms, crying. "You weren't supposed to leave," I murmur. "You weren't supposed to give up on me."

"Shhhh . . ." She smooths my hair back.

I keep my eyes closed, the tension easing from my face, my head swimming as the warmth and gentleness of her touch lulls me.

"You were the one who wasn't supposed to leave."

Everyone else gave up.

She holds me for a while, and I don't know if it's her or me, but the hold gets tighter. And tighter.

"What are you doing?" she whispers in my ear, and I feel the tears on her cheeks. "What are you doing to me, Clay?"

And I realize she's not holding me. She's holding on to me, because I'm not the only one alone.

"What do you need?" she asks. "Tell me what you need."

"Just this," I tell her. "Just don't move, Liv. Please don't leave."

My parents give me whatever I want because they don't want the fight. My mother doesn't have it in her to raise me anymore, and my father finds that his time is better spent elsewhere. Liv was all I had left. I wanted to hurt her so I could matter.

I live for her, an enemy I never wanted to defeat. A fight I never wanted to end.

But, God, her arms. The feel of her. Her voice.

More.

Opening my eyes, I look up at her, wiping my tears. "I changed my mind," I tell her as she looks down at me. "I think I need carbs."

14

Olivia

I chew the pizza, glancing up at her as she sits showered, hair wet, and dressed in sleep shorts with blue octopi on them and a white Henley on top. Despite the small, round table and two chairs behind me, we sit on the carpet, under the window of our sixth-floor hotel room, with the open pizza box between us.

Our eyes meet, but we haven't said much since she broke down in the bathroom an hour ago.

For now, we enjoy an awkward silence, but it's not fighting, and that's something.

Maybe this is a play. A way to reel me in so she doesn't lose her favorite chew toy.

But I think what happened in the bathroom was real. It's just hard to trust anything genuine from her. As much as I want to.

And whyyyyyy do I want to? I keep looking for the good in her. Why?

"I'm sorry about your dad," she says in a quiet voice.

I look over, seeing her pick at her slice and put it in her mouth.

I shrug. "It was eight years ago."

I take another bite, almost ready for my second. She ordered old-world pepperoni. My favorite.

She nods. "I know. At least he went quickly, though."

Her brother didn't. The Collinses could afford to put up a fight with leukemia, but it just prolonged his suffering. I guess they had to try, though.

"I'm sorry about Henry." It comes out as a rasp, and I don't know why. "I saw you with him sometimes. You were a good sister."

My dad died long before Clay and I knew each other, but Henry was only a few years ago.

She still doesn't look at me, just nods, and I watch the ball in her throat move up and down.

She picks off a piece of pepperoni. What's going on in her head?

"Do you like it?" I ask her.

She pops her eyes up, still bloodshot from the crying. "Yeah, why?"

"You usually like all the fixings." Olives, peppers, onions, sausage . . . She likes her pizza loaded. After years of playing lacrosse together, I know her pizza order by now.

She lifts the slice to her mouth. "It's good."

I smile to myself. I appreciate the sacrifice. Old-world pep is *my* thing.

"Why do you hate me?" I ask after a moment. I don't know why I want to know. Maybe I'm taking advantage of the opportunity to finally talk to her. "Why do you *act* like you hate me, I mean?"

She looks at me, holding my eyes, but when her mouth opens, nothing comes out. Her lids fall, her gaze drops, and I can see the tears pool again.

But she blinks them away, clearing her throat. "You don't have to come back to school."

She changes the subject, and I let her. "I know."

"But I'll miss you," she adds, and her voice is as small as a needle, and seeps right into my skin just as easily.

I'm dying for air. She's fixated on me, right? Because she has nothing else? That's all this is, right? She couldn't control me anymore because I'd started to react. She's starved for attention, and if that means going to bed with me, she'll do it. That's what she's doing, right?

You weren't supposed to leave.

"No one has left you, Clay," I tell her. "Your brother was taken. He didn't make a choice."

She's not alone.

"And your parents . . ." I go on. "They may be going through stuff, but they're there. They love you."

Demand their attention like you do mine. Why not?

"Did you feel like your mom loved you?" she asks. "Do you remember her?"

I stuff a bite of pizza into my mouth, hating how she's so savvy at deflecting. "I remember her. And, no, I don't think she loved her kids."

My mom had mental problems her whole life, but my dad was gifted in helping her handle it. After he was gone, she just couldn't hold on.

"You don't miss her?" she presses.

"No."

She raises her eyebrows, a challenging look in her eyes that says I'm a liar.

"I wish she was different," I clarify. "But I don't want her back the way she was. No mother is better than a bad mother."

Guilt curls its way through me. Maybe that was harsh. My mother's problems weren't her fault. I know that, it's just hard to truly believe it. It's hard to feel that neglecting us wasn't something she had control of. Everywhere else in life, we're taught our behavior is one hundred percent up to us.

"'If I could go back and do it again, I'm not sure I would've had any kids,'" I recite to Clay. "That's what she said in her letter."

I toss the pizza back into the box and dust off my hands before hugging my knees to my chest.

"It sounds awful now, but at the time it didn't really hurt." I look at her. "Everything was shit all the time anyway, I didn't expect more. My brothers were in trouble, causing my father stress during his illness like they didn't have a brain in their heads, but I was actually a lot happier than I am now. Behind my closed door, with my music and my books and my room, it was a perfect world. I didn't have to deal with anyone. They just let me be."

"Life is small when you're a kid." She stares at her pizza. "We get attached to what we can control and resist what we can't."

"Yeah." *Exactly*. I'm kind of surprised she put it into words so easily.

My little room was my domain, and I sought refuge there. From my father's failing health, my mother's . . . failing health, how no one in my house understood me, and the money we always seemed to need and never had. I shut myself away from it, resisting everything I couldn't control, just like my mother with her dark bedroom and the movies she watched all day taking her to any world but her own.

Macon won't let me do that anymore. He doesn't let me hide because he doesn't want any of us to end up like her. In our heads too much.

Unfortunately for him, it's too late. Our mother had already taught me how to leave.

I run my hands up and down my face, so confused about what I'm doing, what I want, and what's right. What am I searching for?

"I don't want to be like her," I whisper.

"I don't think she wanted to be like her, either."

I close my eyes. *I know*. I know children weren't her problem. Her husband dying wasn't her problem. Her problems were always there.

And she hated it as much as we did.

Maybe killing herself was mercy for our family. To not put us through more. To not give my brother another mouth to feed.

Or maybe she did what she'd wanted to do all along. She left.

I want to leave. But I don't want to leave them behind. I want the people who love me to miss me when I'm gone.

"I don't hate you." Her murmur is barely audible.

I look up, listening.

"I think about you all the time," she almost mouths.

I swallow the lump in my throat.

She holds the pizza, all of her hair loose and spilling over her shoulder, and she's so still, her gaze fixed on the food in her hands. "Was there ever anything you liked about me?"

The tips of my fingers hum, and I can't help my eyes trailing over her mouth. She was warm when I kissed her. Like how good coffee tastes on a rainy morning.

I'd like to pull her into the bathroom and into my arms, and kiss her in the shower. I'd like to see her smile.

Her eyes meet mine, her fingers move, and I stop breathing, wanting to hold her hand.

I inch closer, and she rises to her knees and leans over, her hand snaking inside my thigh and her mouth coming in.

But then the door bursts open and someone singsongs, "Hey!"

Clay rears back, looking away as Krisjen and Amy saunter into the room, and I ball my fists, slamming my back into the wall.

Goddammit.

"You're alive!" Amy giggles, carrying containers of food Coach probably got for us, not thinking we'd order room service. "That's a relief." Then she looks around, frowning. "Only one broken lamp? Y'all are disappointing."

"I thought you guys were gone all night," Clay questions.

I hold back my smile at the annoyance in her voice. *Just get them out of here, Clay. Please.*

But the door slams shut, and Amy and Krisjen set down their stuff and take off their shoes. "We weren't going to leave you alone," Amy tells her.

Her eyes dart to me and then back to Clay, and I tense at what she's leaving unsaid. *We weren't going to leave you alone with her*, she meant.

Krisjen presses something icy to my arm, and I look, seeing her hand me a soda. "Thanks for coming to the game, by the way."

"Yeah, fat lotta good it did us," Amy grumbles.

Krisjen rolls her eyes, throwing her friend a look, and I yank the can out of her hand, giving her a tight smile as thanks.

Yeah, like they would've won without me anyway. And definitely not without Clay and me.

"I'll take you home in the morning, okay?" Krisjen says.

I nod.

"Jaeger, you take that bed." Amy points to the one on the left. "We'll take the other one."

I raise my eyes and my chin, glaring at her. The three of them. In one bed. So the lesbian doesn't molest one of them in their sleep, right? Jesus Christ.

"Amy!" Krisjen barks. "What, did you suck down some bitch juice before we walked in? Shut up."

Amy lets out a bitter laugh, and I wait for Clay to step in, but she just sits there, avoiding my gaze and completely quiet.

"So, if a guy had to crash in here with us, our parents would be fine with one of us sharing a bed with him?" Amy retorts. "It's the same difference."

I glance at Clay, seeing her eyes downcast, and I know she has things to say. I know she wants them gone, but of course, nothing surprises me with Marymount girls. Once upon a time, I'd hoped I'd have some friends here, and if I didn't, then maybe one person who thought I was worth the sacrifice if she could just be close to me. But none of them want to stand up for themselves. They either need me or tolerate me.

"I'll share a bed with you," Krisjen says.

And I shake my head, surging to my feet. "Eat me," I say. "I don't need any favors."

Rain falls, thunder cracking across the sky, and I flash my gaze to the window, seeing the drops pummel the panes. Shadows dance across the ceiling, and I lie in bed, phone in hand, and contemplate dragging Trace's ass out of bed to pick me up.

Tears hang at the corners of my eyes. *It shouldn't hurt.* I'm used to being seen differently, aren't I? I close my eyes, my chin trembling.

The girls fell asleep easily, but I haven't slept all night. I'm ready to go home. I draw in a breath, my chest shaking, struggling to stay quiet.

But then the bed dips behind me, the sheet moves, and a body presses into my back, arms slipping around my waist.

Clay's scent surrounds me, and I open my eyes, seeing she's no longer in the other bed with Krisjen and Amy. She holds me tightly.

"Just let me go," I barely whisper.

"I can't."

Her breath caresses my ear, and I have no energy to fight her. The tears fall, and I just lie there, letting her mold her body to mine, holding me tighter as she buries her nose in my hair.

"Do you think I want it to be this hard?" I murmur in the quiet so Krisjen and Amy don't hear. "It's not a choice, you know?"

She's silent, and I stare over at the other two sleeping.

"Sometimes I tried not to feel it," I say. "Tried to force myself to get excited around a boy and to ignore the way my heart beat faster around . . ."

But I trail off, knowing she gets the idea.

I don't know why I'm telling her this. It's not that I need her to understand, because there are so many others in the world who will.

But for some reason, I can't stop talking. "But it wasn't who I was," I tell her. "I saw women everywhere. They were all I saw. I didn't notice men the same way. How they walked or laughed or danced. I could never picture myself in a guy's arms." I turn over in her arms and look at her in the dark. "All I dreamed about was someone wanting me. I wanted to look over in class and see a girl looking at me the way I looked at her. Having someone touch my fingers and hold my hand or pass me notes in class. I wanted someone to have a crush on me—someone with a soft body and soft hair. Everyone else got to have that. All the fucking movies and love songs, and . . ." I choke on a sob, forcing it back down. "It just got so lonely, and after a while, I just got angry."

There were other gays at Marymount. The odds were in my favor that I wasn't alone, but no one would out themselves in such a small town.

Except me. I was already an outsider because of where I come from, so why hide anything else, as if that would help?

"I sneak into Wind House sometimes," she whispers.

I blink. The funeral home?

"Why?" I ask.

She's quiet for a moment and then says, "To watch, at first."

Thunder rolls overhead, the rain growing harder on the windows, and we both lie on our sides, eye to eye.

"When Henry . . ." She swallows. "When he died, my parents called the funeral director and let them know which hospital to pick him up at," she tells me, keeping her voice just between us. "My mother was shattered, and Mrs. Gates held her hand and said, 'I will be very careful with him.'"

Mrs. Gates is the funeral director. It's a hard enough job, I can't imagine having to prepare children for burial.

"She puts people back together," Clay tells me. "She's started to teach me how to put people back together."

I stare at her, barely able to see her face in the darkness, but I keep listening, because I don't think anyone else knows this.

"I needed to know what happens when we're gone," she says. "That night, I just couldn't get it out of my head. How he was alone."

The kid was only ten.

"They wouldn't think that he was cold or scared," she continued, "so I went to him. Broke the basement window and climbed through and stayed with him."

I tuck my hands under my cheek, and she does the same, taking her time.

"Mrs. Gates found me the next morning." I watch her. "Asleep against the wall outside his locker. She tried to send me home. Almost called my parents, but I refused to leave. I wanted to see. I needed to see what happens after we die. Where my brother went."

I'll bet she put up a fight. No one says no to Clay. I almost smile, imagining the tantrum she probably threw. She was only fourteen.

"She was so frantic." I hear the amusement in Clay's voice. "She didn't know what to do. My parents would've killed her if they'd ever found out that she let me watch." She paused and then continued. "Johnny Caesar came in that morning. You remember him?"

A local rock star about seven or eight years older than us. Made a couple of albums with a small label who screwed him out of rights and royalties, but he got out from under it. Got a big record deal and was about to hit it big. Become a worldwide superstar.

"She didn't want to get in trouble, but I needed to know and she understood," Clay says. "I stood back, way back, and watched her embalm him. Wash him. Patch up the gashes from his car wreck. The track marks on his arms and how gaunt his face had become. She cut his hair. Put makeup on him. Dressed him."

I was at that funeral. He was a friend of Army's.

"He looked alive again," she goes on, lightning flashing across her skin. "She put him back together so he could be remembered how I'm sure he wanted to be. He looked nineteen again, with his whole life ahead of him. Before the world tore him apart."

My mom probably wishes she was remembered differently. Or better. I'm not sure it would've been a comfort, seeing her dressed in her best at a funeral, even if we could've afforded one, but people don't deserve to be remembered for how they died.

"She wouldn't let me watch her prepare my brother, of course, but after Henry was buried, I . . ." She hesitated. "I started coming back. I've gone back again and again—helping, learning—because every time her phone rings, someone needs her. Someone is looking for guidance and comfort, and I need to be reminded that life is short. I don't know what happens when we die . . ." Her breathing shakes, and I inch in closer. "But I do know life is too short. There is no tomorrow. This is all there is."

"This is all there is," I repeat.

And I reach out and touch her face. *Clay.* I smooth out the lines of worry and anger. The fighting and the hurt. I wipe away her tears with my thumb, feeling her warm skin and how she's the softest thing I've ever touched.

"Livvy," she whimpers, squirming against me.

"Clay."

She leans into it and exhales, her warm breath wafting over my mouth, and slowly slides her arm around my waist, pulling me in close.

"I'm scared," she murmurs.

"Me, too."

I still don't trust her. I know this is a mistake.

But fuck, I need to feel her once. All of her. Just once. *Fuck it.*

I want to feel her come undone.

She bites my bottom lip between her teeth, and I gasp, feeling it all over my body, and I slip my hand down inside her sleep shorts and inside her panties, shivering when I feel the bare skin between her legs.

She sucks in a breath, her mouth hovering over mine, and I smile as she squirms.

This is all there is. This could be it.

"I wasn't built for what they taught us we were built for," I whisper, running my fingers so softly over her pussy. "I was built to feel this."

Her smooth skin is like a feast, but all I can think about is what it will feel like on my mouth.

She holds on to me. "Don't take off my clothes, okay?" she says. "I don't want them to see."

"I'm taking off your clothes."

And she whimpers, looking like she's in pain.

But she doesn't fight me.

"I'm not stopping this for a hurricane," I tell her. I slip my arm between her and the bed, and I pull her body tight against mine, stroking her cunt.

I kiss her, slow and soft, gliding my tongue up her neck and rubbing my body up on hers. I suck her lip, going back for more and more. She tastes like a drug that if I go too fast, I'll go out of my mind and lose control. I need to slow down.

Rolling her nub underneath my finger, I feel the pulse in her clit throbbing as she starts to pump her hips into it, seeking me out.

She looks over my shoulder, breathing hard. "They're gonna see us."

"Do you want me to stop?"

Tell me to touch you. Tell me you want to touch me.

She pulls her arms away, and a shot of agony hits me that she's pulling away until . . . her hands dip between us, and she unbuttons her shirt. My thighs warm, my clit throbbing, and lightning flashes through the room again, illuminating her beautiful body as she opens her shirt for me.

I dip my hand inside, cupping a breast, and her hard nipple makes my palm tingle.

She shivers, grappling for me like she's dying, and I roll over on top of her, both of us glancing over to the other bed for a quick check. Krisjen is nearest, curled in the fetal position facing away from us, and Amy is on her stomach, her head facing the other wall.

I look back down at Clay, her soft, smooth flesh filling my hand, and I come down, kissing her hard.

She pulls up my top, her hands roaming up my back and over my hips, still too timid to go for what she wants. I peel open her shirt again, reveling in her naked skin, and then I sit up, carefully and quietly pulling my top off over my head.

I drop my shirt, watching Clay watch me, her eyes trailing over my body. I know she's seen me naked, and I've seen her, but not like this. This is for us.

Sitting up, she holds my waist and looks up into my eyes, the heat of her breath falling on my chest.

"I'm still scared," she whispers.

I stroke her hair. "Me, too."

I peel off her shirt, both of us glancing at Krisjen and Amy again.

Still no movement.

We should go into the bathroom. We should just wait until I have her in my room or me in hers, and there's no risk.

"It's okay," I say. "I'll stop whenever you want. We don't have to do anything."

"I'm afraid I'll feel different," she tells me as I run my hand up and down her stomach, squeezing her breast gently.

She means she's worried she'll feel bad about it afterward.

It's easy for women to feel shame about sex. We're good at feeling dirty for things that should be natural. She's afraid she'll feel wrong. That something will change and the knowledge of who she was will be lost. It hurts a little.

"You don't have to do anything you don't want to do." I gaze down at her. "Sex is a big deal."

"I didn't think it would be."

"Why?"

"With you, I mean," she says. "I thought . . ."

"You thought it wouldn't be real."

Because I'm a fetish.

She gazes up at me, and I move to climb off her, but she grabs my thighs, keeping me there.

"I thought it wouldn't matter," she murmurs. "It does. I want you so badly, and I'm scared it won't stop, Liv."

My insides flip, and I push her back down to the bed, her skin on mine as I cup her face.

She stares into my eyes, and then . . . her legs fall open, and I nestle between them. Our warmth seeps through the thin fabric of our shorts, and I'm dizzy at the feel of her underneath me . . . God.

I squeeze her jaw. "Keep talking, Collins," I growl in a low voice over her lips. "Tell me more. You fucking owe me."

She pants under my body, squirming and dying for it, and I love having her in my hands and so pliant. I roll my hips, grinding into her as I come in for kiss after kiss.

"I love the way you laugh," she says, quivering. "I never make you laugh, and I hate it when I see you from a distance and someone else did. But I love it, too."

A smile pulls at my lips. "You think about me?"

She nods. "I wonder how these little braids happen." She touches my hair. "If it's a nervous habit, you do them on purpose, or maybe a little girl you babysit plays with your hair . . ." I hover so close to her mouth I can feel its heat. "I stare at them in math class," she whispers.

It feels like bubbles popping under my skin, thinking about her longing for me. Wanting me. I want her fucking spread wide on my desk while Callum Ames loiters in the hall, oblivious to what she really likes to do.

"I think about you in the mornings," she goes on. "Right after I wake up. I can't wait to see you."

I take her hands, pinning them over her head as I roll my hips and rub on her, faster and faster. She turns her head to check her friends, and I trail kisses over her jaw and down her neck.

"I wanted to be in that car with you," she murmurs.

You were.

She arches her back, sucking in air through her teeth. "I want to eat you up so badly," she groans, "I can feel your body between my teeth."

Lightning flashes, her hot little mouth hanging open an inch from mine as I thrust. Thunder cracks, covering her groan, and the sheet falls down my back as I move, dry fucking her and grinding my pussy into hers.

Releasing her wrists, I trail down her body, squeezing her breast as I cover her nipple with my mouth. The little point is so hard on my tongue, and my eyes roll into the back of my head. *Fuck.* My clit throbs—everything so hot. So soft. *God, she's soft.*

She starts to cry out, and I clamp my hand over her mouth, not breaking stride for one second as I kiss and suck, nibble and tug. Her body is a goddamn feast. She's so perfect. The arches, the curves, the beautiful hair and mouth and . . . cunt.

God, I want to taste her. The pulse between my legs beats like a drum, my thighs on fire.

I dart my gaze over to see Krisjen turn onto her stomach, feeling Clay's body tense underneath mine. Krisjen's mouth falls open a little, and I hear the steady rhythm of her breathing continue.

I take a mouthful of Clay, fisting her other breast and trying to keep my nails out of her flesh. I switch sides, eating up the other one as my palm glides up and down her body, touching, grabbing, savoring . . .

"How do we do it?" she asks. "I need more. How . . . ?"

I lick her stomach, inching farther and farther down, my heart jackhammering like I'm having a heart attack at the thought of licking her for the first time. I don't know if I can keep her quiet for that. I don't know if I want to.

Moving back up her body, I press my breasts into hers, holding her head in my hands as I grind between her legs. I don't know why, but I like that she's worried about them waking up. It's not that Clay thinks she's doing something bad that turns me on. It's that she can't stop herself. "We can do to each other anything a guy can do to us," I whisper, repeating the same thing I said on the field. "I can be inside you." I flick her ear with my tongue as I slide my hand down between our legs. "You can ride me."

And I find the little dip through the fabric of her shorts, pressing my fingers into her.

"I can do anything you want me to," I whisper.

She stares up at me, the dim light piercing the clouds outside lighting up her face a little more, and then . . . she brushes her fingers down my body and holds my eyes as she pushes my shorts down, panties and all.

"Don't leave my body," she says. "That's all I want."

She closes her eyes, fists my hair, and pulls my head back down, kissing my neck as she yanks off my clothes with her other hand.

Yes.

I kiss her deep, dipping my tongue inside and tasting hers as I gently palm her breast. I slide off the rest of my clothes, leaving breathy little kisses on her mouth, and keeping my body on hers just like she wants before I peel her shorts down.

Her skin sticks to mine, everything already so hot.

I slide my fingers between us, down inside her panties and inside her, and she gasps, her hands immediately diving down to cover herself.

I hide my smile in her neck as I leave little kisses. I like that she's shy. Like she would be with anyone.

This is real for her.

Gently, I pry her hands off as I nibble her ear. "Let go, Clay."

Her chest shakes, her breathing ragged. "I don't want them to see."

"They won't, baby."

It takes a moment, but she lets go, her hands falling away, and I slide down her body, her naked tits round and full, nipples pointing toward the ceiling.

I stroke her first—the soft skin between her legs, the inside of her thighs, the nub inside.

She whimpers, grabs onto me, and moves to close her legs, but I wrap my hand around her thigh, pressing my lips to her pussy.

"Open your legs, Clay," I whisper against her heat.

She shudders, my breath tickling, and I watch her back arch again, so naked and beautiful and in plain sight if they wake up.

"What do you want me to do?" I ask.

I don't want to take her. I want her to want it.

I feel her fingers thread through my hair, fisting at my scalp. "Lick me," she begs.

She holds me tight, my scalp burning a little, but I don't care.

I slide my other hand under her ass, holding her in place, and pull her panties to the side, diving in for a kiss. My lips are on fire as I suck her into my mouth, sampling, tasting . . .

And suddenly, I'm so hungry. Sweet and warm on my tongue, she moans as her body shakes. Her fists tighten and her breasts bob like Jell-O, and I can't go slow anymore.

Easing her into it, I kiss, nibble, and lick her skin, tugging it gently with my teeth. She relaxes, starts pressing me to her and rolling herself into my mouth, getting demanding like Clay is so good at doing when there's something she wants.

That's my girl.

She spreads her legs wider, opening up for me, her body rolling on the bed like a wave, and I can't take my eyes off her. Dragging my tongue, I bring it up and down in smooth, long strokes, back and forth, again and again. Her body tenses, demanding more, and I pick up the pace before diving down onto her clit and sucking it so hard her head shoots off the pillow. She stares in fright at the other bed, convulsing as I suck, rub, circle, and tongue her clit, tugging it between my teeth every so often.

Then, with my eyes cast up and savoring the euphoria of the expressions on her face, I slide my tongue into her cunt.

She goes rigid, losing her fucking mind as she releases my hair and throws her arms above her head, gasping and arching.

"Livvy . . ." She whimpers, and I move my tongue inside her, rubbing her clit in circles with my thumb.

I know, baby. I know.

I flick my tongue over her clit. "I know you like it."

"Yes," she cries, sounding so vulnerable.

"You want me to keep going?"

She nods. "Don't stop."

"How long have you wanted your hands underneath my skirt, Collins? Tell me."

She grips my hair again, and I can tell by her breathing she's about to come. "So long," she pants. "I want to press you against the wall in every empty classroom and pull down your panties."

Heat pools in my belly, and I'm about to come, too. *Shit.*

But just then, an alarm sings from the bedside table, and my heart leaps into my throat.

What?

Clay freezes as a bright light suddenly flashes.

15

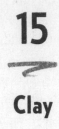

Clay

We jerk our heads, seeing someone's cell light up and play a standard jingle.

Shit.

Amy whines, Krisjen yawns, and I see movement under the sheet. *Oh, God.* I flail, shoving her off me, and Krisjen sits up in bed, grabbing her phone as Liv and I pull the covers up over us. Her tank top lies between us, and I grab it, stuffing it under the covers.

My blood still rushes hot, the pulse between my thighs hammering, and a cool sweat covers my body.

Fuck. What time is it? I glance at the window, seeing light stream through, although the rain and thunder haven't let up. Coach usually has us out of here by seven or eight. Is it time to get up already?

Krisjen rises from the bed in the dark, and Amy stretches, kicking the covers down off her body.

My mind races. What if they heard something? What if they saw?

What if they plop on the bed and notice I'm fucking naked? Where are my clothes?

I put my hand over my mouth, afraid they can hear my breathing, and I'm not sure if I'm scared or about to lose my mind at how good she felt.

I just couldn't stop.

Krisjen looks down at us in the darkness, yawning. "Hey, you switch beds? Sorry, I'm a worm when I sleep."

I clear my throat, my mouth like sandpaper as I look over my shoulder at her. "Yeah, it's okay," I choke out, feigning grogginess. "Your alarm sucks, though. I think you woke up the entire Eastern Seaboard."

Amy snorts, and Krisjen makes some mocking sound, grabbing her hoodie off the bottom of the bed and pulling it on. "I'm a deep sleeper, too."

"So, we all have to suffer?" I grumble.

Fingers find me under the covers, caressing me between my legs, and I suck in a breath, slapping Liv's hand away and glaring at her.

She grins that grin that always reminds me I'm not the one in control. Not really.

"You're so wet." Her self-satisfied whisper is barely audible.

I can feel it. God, I'm far from satisfied. Now I'm pissed.

Krisjen sticks her feet into her Vans, loose hair frizzing around the messy bun on top of her head as she takes her phone and wallet. She crosses her arms over her chest and yawns again. "Going down to the Starbucks," she says, making her way to the door. "I want the shower when I get back."

Liv slips her finger into her mouth, and I watch her as she wets it and slides it back down under the covers, fingering my cunt.

I grab her hand, wanting to stop her, but she holds my eyes, and all I want in the world is to climb on and finish her.

I hug the covers to my neck, my legs intertwining with hers in the dark room, and I ball my fists to keep from reaching for her.

"You're not getting away from me," she mouths so softly only I can hear. "Because as soon as the lights come on, you'll be Bitchie

Cunterson again and clutch your pearls like I'm the one who's corrupting you, and then you'll go sleep with the dick just to prove you don't like this."

I lick my lips, tasting the beads of sweat as she swirls circles, rubbing so soft and gentle between my legs. My eyelids flutter.

"Cinnamon soy latte," I gasp out to Krisjen. "Liv wants black."

"Affirmative."

Maybe if we give her a big enough order, she'll take Amy with her.

But then Amy shouts out, "And a chai tea latte! One pump of vanilla, one pump of hazelnut! And a croissant!"

"Jesus Christ," Krisjen barks. "I'm not y'all's damn waitress."

The door slams shut as she leaves without Amy. I'm about to scream, but then Amy hops out of bed. "I'm taking the shower first," she says.

She walks past the bed, the lights still off, and disappears into the bathroom. The light pops on and dims again when she closes the door.

I exhale. "That was close."

And without a moment to lose, Liv dives in and I grab her, taking her in my arms. "You should come over to the swamp tonight," she whispers. "No one will stop us."

"I can't wait until then." I'm in pain. I push her over, climb on top of her, and throw her hands up over her head, pinning them to the bed. "You're mine, Jaeger." I kiss her, sinking my mouth into hers, strong and hard, her hot tongue sliding into my mouth. "Mine."

Releasing her hands, I slip down, cupping both of her breasts and move my mouth from one to the other, the feel of her flesh lighting a fire under my skin. *Fuck yes.*

She fists my hair, holding me to her, and as soon as we hear the shower turn on, she pushes me up, fists my panties, and rips them off my body. The fabric screams, and I barely have time to appreciate how her eyes heat up, taking in my body until I can't take it anymore.

I come down on top of her. "What do I do?" I ask.

"You know what to do."

I know what feels good. The warmth between her legs hits my groin, her thin strip of hair electrifying every nerve between my thighs. I'm bare, but I love that she's not. It feels so fucking good.

I bend my left knee at her side and slip my right one under her leg, opening her up. She reaches down, gripping my ass and nestling her center to mine. I close my eyes, tip my head back, and moan, hesitating all of half a second before I growl and press my chest to hers, grinding.

I roll my hips, thrusting myself into her again and again, faster and faster, our clits rolling over each other in agonizing, sweet little circles as sweat covers my back. A groan fills my body, the friction so fucking good.

"Clay . . ."

But I grab her jaw, pinching it tight as I whisper against her cheek. "Shhh." I watch the ecstasy on her face. "You're mine. You've always been mine. Whenever I want. You're my fucking girl."

Rolling my ass, I fuck her, her tits sticking to mine as the sweat from her stomach warms me, and my hips piston faster, needing more.

Our wet heat mixes, and static fills my head. I can't think. We grind, fucking and speeding up the pace, her clit rubbing mine.

"Ugh," I pant, kissing her hard as the sheet falls down, baring us to anyone who walks in.

My orgasm builds as I thrust harder and faster in her hands, her hands gripping my ass and pulling me into her. I lean back, sitting up, and she rises, sinking her mouth in to suck on one of my tits.

I grip her neck. "I like playing with you."

She kisses and nibbles my breast, tugging my nipple with her teeth. "I know you do." She flicks me with her tongue. "Anytime you want."

I want it all the time.

Pushing her back down, I hover over her mouth. "I want you inside me," I whisper.

She whimpers, her mouth falling open, and I can tell she's about to come.

"You still got your cherry?" she gasps.

I caress her hair, nodding.

Her eyes narrow, and she bares her teeth, trying to not come yet. "He's never been . . . ?"

"Between my legs?" I finish for her. "Just you."

She holds my face, her nose an inch from mine as she stares into my eyes looking like she wants to eat me.

"I want you to lose it in my bed," she whispers.

Her bed.

"Anytime I want," I demand.

She nods. "In my bed."

Okay, yes.

"I promise," I tell her, kissing her deep.

My place is in her bed.

Heat swarms my belly, tingles spread between my thighs, and I lean to the left, chasing the angle to grind on her better. With my hand on her throat and her hand squeezing my breast, I cry out.

"That's it, Collins," she breathes out. "Fuck me."

The shower shuts off, my heart stops, but I can't. "I'm coming."

She grips my hair, holding me to her. "Faster."

I grind faster, loving the feel of being on top of her.

"Come on, come on, come on . . ." she pants, chasing it, too. Her breath stalls, she gasps, and then she bites my lips, fucking me from the bottom as her orgasm explodes.

"Oh, Liv," I cry. "Fuck!"

I pump, so wet and slick, going, going, going until . . .

I arch my back, throwing my head back, and I thrust into her one final, hard time—blood boiling, sweat cooling my pores, and my insides free-falling.

I collapse on top of her, looking up into her eyes as I try to catch my breath.

She kisses my forehead, breathing hard. "God, you have a beautiful body."

All I can manage is a half smile, too exhausted to tell her I love touching hers.

I love kissing it and smelling it and tasting it.

I want more of it.

But before I can cop another feel or two, we hear the bathroom door unlock.

Liv's eyes flash to mine, and I hop off her, pulling the covers up over us and looking for any clothes.

Shit.

I find my shorts and top under the covers and pull them on, the door opening just before I can button my shirt.

I hold it closed, swinging my legs over the side of the bed and pretending to be looking for something between the bed and the wall.

"You okay?" Amy asks, walking out of the bathroom.

I glance up, my heart still pounding. "Have . . . have you seen my yellow Chucks?" I ask, trying to hide my nerves and steel my voice.

I see Liv's shorts on the floor and slide them under the bed with my foot.

A shoe lands on the bed. "There's one," Amy says.

"Thanks."

I'm afraid to look at Liv. Knowing her, she's probably smiling.

"Give me five minutes." Amy holds the towel wrapped around her head, clasping her clothes to her towel-wrapped body. "I need to rinse out this hair mask, and then you can have the shower."

"No rush," I chirp.

Amy shuts herself in the bathroom again, and I swipe Liv's shorts out from under the bed and walk around to the other side, tossing them to her and buttoning my shirt. I catch sight of myself in the mirror, locks of my hair in spirals like a bird's nest that's been through a tornado.

I pull the covers off her, avoiding looking at her body. "Get dressed."

I'm not satisfied. Not nearly, and everything aches. I don't want to leave her. I don't want to leave her arms.

She sighs, rising from the bed, and I see her black panties on the sheets and pick them up.

I stare at them, thinking about her other pair that I have.

"I want more," I whisper, sitting on the bed. "I want to make noise."

She stands in front of me, and I raise my eyes, taking in her smooth stomach, and how I want my turn to taste her under the sheets.

I wince, something inside me hurting, just looking at her.

Opening her underwear, I lean down, waiting as she steps into them.

"Sleep over at my house tonight," she tells me.

I pull her panties up her legs as I hear the shower come on. Liv pulls on her tank top. "Your whole family will know," I say.

She falls silent, and I know I've said something wrong.

I meet her eyes, seeing a question in hers. "Don't look at me like that." I pick up her shorts off the bed and help her into them, and I'm not sure why I'm dressing her. "I'm still trying to figure out what's happening. Just let me enjoy this before the whole world has an opinion about it."

"Relax, Clay." She brushes my hair out of my eye. "I'm not going to out you. You want to keep it quiet, that suits me, too."

Why?

I cock my head at her.

She just shrugs. "I mean, it's not like this is a relationship, right?"

Well . . . I open my mouth but nothing comes out. *I guess not.* I hadn't thought that far ahead.

Just that she's the only option for me. She's the only thing I want in the world.

"In a few months, you'll be going to one college," she says, "and I'll be going to another. And I'm still not entirely sure I like you, so . . ."

At that, I smile. "You like me." I glide my fingers up her legs, teasing her. "And you are coming back to school."

She cocks a brow.

"I'll be *so* pleasant," I tease.

Like soooooo pleasant.

"So, a piece of ass is enough to get me back to that shithole?"

"Not just any piece of ass," I remind her. "And I'll get even better with practice."

I know it was my first time, and I know she'll probably lose patience, having to teach me everything, but I'm a fast learner.

She tips my chin up, no longer smiling. "Don't change a thing," she orders.

A shiver runs through me, and I hold her waist, staring up at her.

I don't want people's reactions to this. I just want her. That's it. Why can't I have what I want?

I just don't want to have those conversations with people like this is any of their business.

But I'm not ready to stop. We've already gotten it on, and whether my friends find out I fucked her once or twenty times, it's still something I can't undo. So why not a couple more times?

I don't want to sleep tonight. I don't need sleep.

"Don't call anyone to pick you up when we get to school," I tell her. "Walk around the back. I'll swing past and pick you up." A grin pulls at my lips. "Sleepover at my house."

My parents probably won't be around, and if they are, they won't bother us. Just a friend and me—talking about guys, eating junk food, and doing whatever we want in the dark. All night.

"Okay," she says.

I smile, and we finish getting dressed, my head going crazy with the idea of having all night with her. Just us.

Maybe I'll make her something to eat. I don't want to just see her in my room. I want to see her in the kitchen, in my bathroom, in my shower . . .

Krisjen brings us coffee, and within an hour we're all showered up and packed, a whole weekend ahead where, if I'm clever, I can spend it sneaking around with Liv.

The whole way back to school is torture. Krisjen offers to drive Liv home since she picked her up, but thankfully Liv declines, opting to ride the bus with me instead.

She slips into a seat to the right, and I pause, nearly sitting down with her, but Amy is behind me, and I panic, moving on a couple more rows and sliding into a seat on the left.

Liv catches my eyes, leaning against the window, and props her leg up on the seat, winking at me.

I breathe easier, still feeling like shit, but she knows what this is. She'll have all my attention soon.

We glance at each other from time to time, spells where I find myself staring at her as she leans back, eyes closed, and her earbuds playing music. A blush warms my cheeks, thinking about everything that just happened between us and how I can still smell her on me. In my hair.

I had sex. With someone else. I've made myself come before, but does this mean I'm not a virgin now? I still have my hymen, but that can't be the gauge, right? Guys don't have one, and they still refer to themselves as virgins if they've never had sex.

I'm not a virgin anymore. And I fold my lips between my teeth to hide my smile. *Liv was my first.*

I look over at her again, watching her listening to her music and feeling different all over. I guess it's kind of a cliché to think sex changes you. The old "Do I look different?" joke and all.

But I feel different. Krisjen and Amy each had lost their virginity a while ago, but I know they didn't enjoy their first times.

Mine couldn't have been any better. Except maybe for privacy and the opportunity to keep her in my arms awhile longer.

How is she going to break my hymen? And what about protection? Were we supposed to use something? *Shit.* I need to google some stuff.

But first, my house.

I nearly cut my lip biting it so hard to keep from smiling as I saunter off the bus and feel her behind me. I dig out my keys, trying to stay calm, but I can't stop the somersaults in my stomach.

I'm not going to be a breath apart from her for the next twenty-four hours. God, I'm addicted.

But someone wraps their arms around me and lifts me up, swinging me around. I startle.

"That fight made YouTube, babe," Callum exclaims, kissing me. "That's my girl!"

I struggle in his arms, trying to pry free. *What? Fight?*

Why is he here? I glance around, seeing my team head to cars and parents picking them up. I don't see Liv.

I press my hands to his shoulders. "Let me go, Callum."

Where is Liv?

"Don't worry," he says. "She came at you in the cafeteria. She deserved that."

He's talking about the fight on the field last night. That seems like ages ago now.

He takes me hand. "Come on. Let's grab some food, and I'll take you home." My head spins with what I have to say to send him away, but he looks over his shoulder. "Amy! Call Kris and Milo to meet us at Coco's."

No. I pull my hand out of his, digging in my heels. "I have my car."

"Good." He takes my keys. "Because I don't. I'm driving."

Drops of rain start spilling down, and I look around as he heads for my truck. Liv stands at the open gate, watching me, the rain coming down harder as she blurs beyond the downpour.

"Clay!" Callum yells. "Come on!"

"We're riding with you!" Amy skips past me, bringing a guy I don't know, and I stand there, seeing Liv shift on her feet, the rain spilling down her legs. She looks at me, I look at her, and in a moment, she inches away, taking a left down the sidewalk. She disappears around the side of the school, hidden under a canopy of trees like I told her to.

So I can pick her up.

Goddammit. I jog for my car, ready to tell them all to take a hike. I have shit to do. *I have to meet my mom for a fitting, or visit Mimi, or I'm grounded for the fight, or something, but . . .*

Callum will still want a fucking ride home.

"Let's go!" all of my friends call from the back seat.

"Just . . ." I grit my teeth, ready to scream.

They'll know. They'll know something is up. They'll come over to my house. They'll talk. Maybe Amy or Krisjen knows something already. We weren't careful this morning.

"I'm not going to breakfast," I tell them. "You didn't even ask. I have things to do."

"Like what?" Amy pries.

Bitch. "I'm going into Miami shopping with my mother. What business is it of yours?"

"Does your mother know that?" Amy spits out. "Because she's already with my mom today, meeting with the caterers for Easter brunch. In Miami."

Fuck. I forgot.

Callum chuckles and gives me a condescending grin. "You got another guy on the side, Clay?"

I sneer back, but the walls close in, and . . . I can't think. I don't want them to know.

I snatch my keys, pushing Callum out of the way. "No one drives my car."

And I climb in the driver's side as he runs around to the passenger side.

I'll text Liv. I'll get away and meet her later. We have all day. All weekend.

I'll get out of this.

But as I pull out of the lot, take a left, and see her form walking in the downpour, I know I've fucked up. I lighten my foot on the pedal, seeing her drenched already, and wanting to stop so badly. I told her I would be there.

But I don't stop. I pass, leaving her behind in my rearview mirror, closing my eyes and wanting to cry.

I can't, Liv. I'm sorry.

This isn't a relationship. In the fall, she'll go to one school and I'll go to another. She'll get over it.

16

Clay

She doesn't get over it.

I called. I texted. I even DM'd her on social media. I almost crossed the tracks yesterday, but I didn't care to have her slam the door in my face in front of her whole family.

I walk through school Monday morning, keeping my eyes peeled but already knowing she's not here. She didn't show up to work out, she wasn't in the locker room, and if she didn't want to talk to me all weekend, she definitely won't come back to school like I want her to.

My mom had asked about the dress yesterday, finally realizing she hadn't seen it in the house yet, but I'd forgotten about what Liv did to it. I told her they had to take it in a little more. *I lost weight*, I lied.

I slide my school jacket off, my arms heavy and my head detached. The last two days passed in a fog, and I'm going a little crazy. Even spending all afternoon with Mrs. Gates yesterday didn't help.

And holding off Callum is starting to become a problem. I know he's getting it somewhere else, and I couldn't care less. I don't love him, but what if that's not the reason I don't care. What if I don't care because he's not my type.

What if no guy is my type?

I drift my eyes around me, stealing quick glances at the students loitering in the hall. Seeing his smile. Her eyes. The way he wears his clothes. Her legs. The way he fills out his shirt. What she looks like underneath hers.

And I stop, my gaze lingering on Ava Young. *What she looks like when she moves.*

Her hair down her back. The softness of her lips. The way she fits her clothes.

My stomach roils, and I feel the tears burn the backs of my eyes. I look away.

I shake my head, clearing my throat and stuffing my shit in my locker. *No.* It's just something about Liv. I'm obsessed with her. I'm unhappy and latching on. That's all she is. Someone to get off on who will keep her mouth shut in an arrangement where I call the shots.

I pull out my forensics book for class; my requirements for science were fulfilled last year, but the elective sounded fun, and I knew Liv was taking it. Or had been.

But actually, I kind of like it. Maybe I want to study forensics in college.

Or maybe I thought it would be useful when helping Mrs. Gates. Some of the bodies that come in are pretty interesting.

I walk to class, entering the lab, but as soon as I enter, I see Liv immediately. I stop, my heart leaping.

She reaches up to the blinds on her tiptoes, her black Polo and skirt creeping up, and her shiny black hair spills down her back in waves. I ache.

She closes the blinds, blocking out the sun, and turns around, red lipstick beautiful and lips looking like they were never swollen from my kisses. Her skin perfect, like it was never hot underneath me.

There's no evidence of me on her at all anymore.

I stand there, waiting for her to look up, but she doesn't.

Strolling up to her, I drop my book on the lab table next to hers and reach around her still body, taking one of the tests McCreedy put on our tables.

"This isn't over," I say in her ear.

She doesn't turn around or respond. Her head bowed, she puts her name on the packet and slides a stool across the floor, sitting down.

Students mill around us, entering and finding their seats.

"You came back to school," I point out, labeling my packet, too.

She must want more if she came back. And looking her best today, too.

I look over my shoulder, her back still to me as she begins.

"Say something," I growl in a low voice.

But she doesn't. It's like I'm not even here.

I mean, what did she think was going to happen? I was ambushed, and we're not dating. That pizza was the first time we'd spent any time together amicably.

I grab my test and pencil and swing around to her table, taking the seat across from her. This isn't my lab table, but oh well. "I don't apologize," I tell her. "So you may as well exhale, because it's not happening. We're both leaving, there's no commitment, and you knew the score."

She stares at her test, writing and checking boxes as if I'm not talking.

I narrow my eyes. What the hell does she want from me? *Fight with me. Do something!*

But I don't know how to battle this Olivia. She won't talk.

I stare at my test, the teacher starting the timer on the projector and flashing the screen on the whiteboard.

"I gave you my virginity," I whisper.

Her pencil pauses.

"I've had opportunities, Liv." I swallow, coming as close to an apology as I can manage. "I didn't hesitate with you."

I search for her eyes, but she still won't look at me.

"I never wanted you to stop," I tell her.

I want more. I want it again.

I want more right now.

My head spins with all the secluded spots we could find in this school, but I know she won't forgive me that quickly.

Ronald Baxter takes the seat next to me, and Liv finally looks up, meeting my eyes. Her gaze falls to my mouth, and I think she might brush her foot over mine under the table or something, but she takes my test, turns on the Bunsen burner, and I watch wide-eyed as she lights the corner, the papers going up in smoke.

I see Ronald freeze out of the corner of my eye, watching.

"You left me in the rain," she says quietly, the white papers turning black, curling and peeling. "You left me behind in the rain while you drove off with that prick."

I stare wide-eyed as my test turns to ash.

"No commitment works for me, but you damn well better be where you say you're going to be," she bites out.

And before I can even worry about what Ronald is making of what she's saying, she dumps my test into the sink and walks away, taking her papers with her.

Shit.

I flex my jaw, watching as she says something to the teacher and then leaves the room. I flip on the faucet, putting out the fire, and snarl at Ronald to mind his own business.

Okay. So she's not going to forgive me quickly.

Fine.

But she will forgive me. She just really won't like how far I'm willing to go to force it.

I swipe Ronald's test, ignoring his look, and erase his name, writing my own. The first four questions are already done. *Thanks, Ronny.*

Callum stares into my eyes, swinging me around the dance floor and moving like water. He's perfect. His dark blond hair is swept up, off his forehead, and hugs his ears. His flawless skin and bright smile. His blue eyes and how he rises several inches above me—in control, dominant, my protector. Everything my family wants for me, but nothing about it feels right. If he were Liv, I'd be pulling him in close. Wrapping my arms around him like a steel band and reveling in the promise of his mouth.

I catch sight of us in the mirrors that cover three of the four walls, windows covering the last one. We're both still in our uniforms, his white button-down untucked and his tie loose, while my saddle shoes lie underneath the row of chairs against the wall of the studio, the heels on my feet required for our lesson.

"Bigger steps!" Ms. Broderick, the instructor, chants. "Keep your head up!"

She walks around as the couples move. We've practiced the waltz for the ball so much that there's no way we can get it wrong now, and she should just let us leave. I hate how he's looking at me. Not leering so much as challenging me. He knows something, and I'm waiting for the shoe to drop.

"I think you'd get tired of my shit," I say as we spin.

"Keep your head left!" Broderick shouts for the millionth time.

I face left. "You can get from anyone what you're hoping to get from me."

"Getting it isn't the challenge," he replies. "Getting it from *you* will be so much sweeter."

A spark lights up his eyes, the words coming off as more of a promise. Like it's inevitable, because he always wins, and he's not afraid of a little hard work.

Honestly, he is pretty perfect. Direct, and he doesn't treat me like a delicate flower. I've always appreciated that. Most women would find him overwhelming. Brusque, even. They need to be seduced. They need to be romanced.

They need to be lied to.

He doesn't do that.

"Why not tell me to take a hike?" he asks. "Anyone could escort you to the ball, and you couldn't care less if it were me."

No, but . . . It's not like I have anyone else in mind, either. I want to go to the ball. It's a family tradition, and it's my night. I want it.

I can't walk out on that stage alone, can I?

"I'm worried there's something in you that I don't yet see," I tell him plainly. "Maybe I'll still see it."

A smile grazes his lips. He appreciates my candor, too.

"Feel the music!" the teacher calls out, stopping Amy and her escort and straightening their shoulders.

The chandeliers sparkle above us, and I look away, facing left again as we twirl. The last of the sun glows against the orange wall, the light slowly moving down, down, down as the clouds roll in and thunder cracks.

But instead of staying at home as recommended tonight because of the storm coming, there's a party at the lighthouse. I'm supposed to meet my mother as soon as dance class is over, but the lighthouse is across the tracks, and it's been a long week, busy ignoring Liv as much as she's been ignoring me.

And stupidly thinking she'd give up and come chasing me when she wanted more.

But she didn't, and I've let her stew long enough. She's going to look at me tonight.

"My father sleeps with his stepdaughter," Callum says in a low voice.

I meet his eyes.

"What do you think of that?" he asks.

My pulse quickens. Macon had outed the Ameses and my family at Night Tide, and while anyone who'd heard had apparently done us the service of not bringing that shit up again, Callum is clearly still thinking about it.

What do I think of that? Honestly, I wasn't surprised. About any of it.

"I think we're dogs," I tell him. "And I think perfectly tailored suits and European cars hide it really well."

St. Carmen looks good. I look good. And people judge you differently when your lawn is manicured. When you shop at the best stores. When you're picked up in Town Cars.

"But we're still dogs," I murmur.

He moves his hand on my waist, circling his arm around me, and pulls me into him. I stop breathing. He holds me tight against his chest, his breath on my forehead. "That's why I don't get tired of your shit," he whispers down on me. "Or of never getting any reciprocation from you."

I grip his shoulders, about to push away as we stop dancing.

"You're afraid of the dirt, but you know it's there." His mouth trails a line across my temple. "And when you get it all over you, Clay, I want to be there."

I gaze into his eyes, finally seeing something in him I didn't before. I haven't been in as much control as I thought.

And I'm not completely unexcited by that prospect.

He picks me up, cocking his head and surveying me like a snake. "Who's giving it to you?" he asks. "I know you're not a virgin anymore, and I know it was recently."

Instead of getting nervous, though, I smile. It's nice not to have the hard discussions. I'm glad he knows.

"I won't tell," he whispers. "I just want to hear about it. Where does he do it to you at?"

She does it to me in secret.

"In a car?" he presses. "In a cheap motel? One of the Jaeger boys, maybe?"

I warm between my thighs, thinking about the Jaeger girl and how much more I want to touch her. He's got the wrong details, but he's on the right path.

"I'm not jealous," he assures me before a gleam hits his eyes. "I'm hard."

I don't feel it, but I take his word for it. I try to push out of his hold, not liking the weight of hanging from his arms. A reminder that he can always overpower me.

"I'll keep your secrets," he says. "You keep mine, and what a team we'll be."

I study him, kind of hating him for trying to make this so easy on me. Like my grandmother, he's absolutely fine with me having everything I want as long I shut up about it.

Maybe this is my future. The one way I get to keep Liv. How many husbands will be as understanding?

"That's enough, you two," Broderick snaps.

Thunder rolls across the sky, and I swear I can feel it vibrate through the room as Callum drops me to my feet. He laughs, because everyone's heads are twisting around, trying to see what the hell we're doing.

"All right!" the dance teacher claps. "That's enough for today! Practice at home this weekend. Chin up." She tilts her chin up, demonstrating. "Watch your footwork and feel free to join my group class this Sunday afternoon for a little extra practice!"

Everyone heads for their gear and to change back into their shoes, and Callum pulls me back into him, hugging my back. "I want to see you really dance now."

I shove his hands away, spinning around and walking backward for the chairs. "All you do is talk."

His eyebrow arches up, and I catch a smile before I spin around and get my gear.

I don't change my clothes, simply slipping on my shoes and taking my bag before we jet down the stairs and out the door. We step onto the deserted sidewalk, wind kicking up debris and the palms on the trees flapping. My hair flies around me, and he tosses me a look over the hood of his car. I should take my own ride, but . . . It doesn't get old. Fucking with her head. Forcing her hand. I climb in, tossing my duffel onto the floor.

Amy and a couple other girls pile into the back, giggling as the wind whips under their skirts, and Callum fires up the engine as Amy passes me a flask from the back seat.

I hesitate, feeling Callum's eyes on me. Alcohol has a way of making you do shit you wouldn't normally do, and I should keep a clear head around him.

But my head has never been clear. Ever. Screw it. I close my eyes, tears I didn't realize were there gathering at the corners as I tip the flask back and swallow a mouthful. Then another. And one more.

"Hey!" Amy laughs, tapping my shoulder. "Save some for me."

"Let's go!" Callum calls out, shifting the car into gear, and laughter fills the back seat as he speeds off.

Where the hell is Krisjen? Meet you at lighthouse? I text her. I should give her a verbal kick in the ass for doing my job and bringing Liv to the away game without speaking to her captain, but I can't be mad about how that night turned out. Despite the fact that we still lost.

I reach over the seat, snatching the flask out of Amy's hand as I take another drink, finishing off the last of it. Already, the warmth of it starts to coat my veins like a nice thick syrup, and I relax a little.

I don't give a shit that Krisjen went over my head or that Callum wants to watch me roll around in the mud like a pig for his entertainment.

I don't care that I had sex for the first time last week and it was with a girl, and I don't care that it keeps hurting every moment I realize that some part of me isn't touching some part of her.

I toss the flask back into Amy's lap as we cruise across the tracks, "Cool Girl" playing on the stereo and the sky darkening to a steel gray. Clouds overlap clouds as the sea in the distance fills the air with its scent, nice and thick so that when you inhale, it's almost like you're eating.

I lie my head back, enjoying it while I can. I'll miss this weather. I hate the cold, and while North Carolina isn't the North, it's north. Florida is south, but it's not the South in the same way other states are.

It's Miami and Cuban sandwiches. Music and history. Explorers and conquerors. Tacky-ass mailboxes and flip-flops all year long.

It's how we're vampires who love the night, because the sun's not beating down on us. It's the swamps—the mangroves, the shade and the hidden spaces underneath the Spanish moss, the tall birds with their long legs quiet and still in the calm waters . . .

It's the summer monsoons and the reptiles that keep you sweating and your heart jumping out of your chest. It's laughing at the "Florida Man" jokes right alongside the Yankees, knowing full well come retirement, they'll be jetting down here to play golf, eat seafood, and stay warm, because nothing beats the subtropics.

I know college isn't forever. I can always come home. And until recently, I wasn't really dreading leaving.

But now, I'm counting the days like an inmate on death row. Before I know it, a week will have passed. Then a month. Soon it'll be summer, and I'll be leaving a part of my heart behind. Everything feels wrong.

"Hell yeah!" Callum howls out the window to Milo as he swings into a spot on the side of the dirt road.

"Yay!" Amy squeals. Everyone in the back seat scrambles to get out, and I exit the car, pulling my Polo over my head and tossing it into the vehicle.

The lighthouse rises above us, a coral pink barely discernible against the black sky, and I dig my crossbody bag out of my duffel and slip it over my head before slamming the door. Everyone else runs ahead, while Callum falls in at my side, scanning down my tank top and taking my hand. "Let's go do some stupid shit," he says.

I close my eyes, inhaling the air charged with whatever's brewing tonight, smelling more than just fucking rain. Storms carry promise. Something—anything—is about to happen, and people are always on the verge. Ready to run. Ready to be surprised.

"Fall" by The Bug spills out of the lighthouse, the steps leading up the foundation to the open door already filled with people standing around or coming and going. We walk into the structure, the sounds of the waves outside crashing onto the beach, but you can barely hear it as we enter a cave of darkness and smoke, the air thin with so many bodies crowded into such a small space. Speakers hang over the sides of the spiral staircase, and bodies I can't identify loiter on the steps as far up as I can see.

"The Jaegers are here," Amy shouts in my ear.

"Oh?"

I stop myself from looking to see which Jaegers she's talking about, but when Callum slides an arm around my waist from behind and holds me like I'm his, I let him. Even going so far as to caress his hand over my stomach.

"Probably keeping an eye on their flag," I tell her.

She shoots me a wicked look, and I think we're both wondering how much trouble we're in for tonight, especially since we're on their turf.

I turn my head over my shoulder, inviting Callum closer and snuggling into his body. "I'm gonna dance."

"I'm gonna watch."

His mouth comes down, and I come in, but before he kisses me, I dive into his ear instead. "I hope you like it," I say, talking loud over the music. "You're gonna watch me a lot."

And I pull away, biting my bottom lip and teasing him with my eyes all the way to the dance floor with Amy.

She's here. Liv sees me. I know she does.

And if she won't let me have her, then I want her pissed. She thinks she's punishing me, but she's going to learn the meaning of the word tonight.

The music pumps, rain hangs in the air, and I tip my head back as the energy rocks my body. Everyone jumps to the music, and I smile.

Letting my eyes drift around the room, I flash my gaze here and there—feeling her—but before I can find her, I spot Krisjen. I pause, watching her dance with Trace Jaeger, half hidden behind the stairs with her back into his body.

He glides his hands all over her, and my first thought isn't her boyfriend who's here and about to catch them. It's how lucky she is that she can let her Jaeger paw her in public, but she still won't suffer half as much as I would if mine were doing that.

I roll my hips, moving my arms and bouncing on my feet, and as I twist my head side to side with the beat, I see her.

I think I see her.

I keep going, back and forth, blood rushing to my head as I take more of her in every time I turn right. It's her. Sitting on a pile of crates and leaning against the wall, her head tipped back, one arm hanging over her bent knee, and the other leg dangling over the side.

Dressed in black jeans with holes in the knees and a white tank top, a flannel tied around her waist.

She watches me. Her eyes are shrouded, but under the cover of shadow, I know she's watching me.

And immediately I know that I can't even fool myself. I'm not in control.

She has my heart in her fist.

I dance for her, my hand grazing between my legs and across

the sliver of visible bare skin between my shirt and my skirt. Reminding her of what I felt like. Of who loves her good.

Arms slide around me, lazy but invasive, his finger slipping under the waist of my skirt and touching my skin. Callum presses himself into my back, and I watch Liv, knowing she's watching me. Watching us. Under the shadow of the speaker above her. Under her black lashes and dark eyes that could've been closed, but I know they're open. I know she's watching. Her hand hangs over her knee, her thumb calmly and steadily grinding back and forth in her fist.

And I don't stop him.

Callum moves, bringing me with him as his hand creeps up my torso. His lips graze a line up my neck, and Liv still doesn't move, digging her thumb into her fist back and forth, over and over, her gaze still hidden under the cover of darkness.

Krisjen spills out of the crowd, laughing with her drink sloshing and spilling over the rim of her cup. I reach out to grab her, Callum's hands falling away, and I break into a smile as I steady her. She looks like she's having fun. More fun than I've seen her have in a long time.

She shoves the drink in my hand and wraps her arms around me. "I love you!"

I shake with a laugh. "I'll bet you even love Amy right now, don't you?"

"Huh?" she shouts over the music.

Whatever. "Nothing!" I shout, drinking down a couple gulps of her beer as "Fuqboi" comes over the speakers.

Krisjen gasps, excited, and starts bouncing, because right now she loves this song, too. Belting out the lyrics, she takes my hand as I turn, tossing the cup into the trash, and she pulls me to the center of the room, everyone dancing around us. The chorus starts, Callum is forgotten, and Krisjen grabs hold of me, her arms hanging over my shoulders as she starts to dance. She rolls her hips, slow at first and then faster, and I only hesitate a moment, thankful that someone saved me from him. Even though I think it was working at making Liv jealous.

I join in, both of us swaying and dancing, smiling and laughing as the music belts out, filling up the room. We move into each other, and I can only imagine Callum is somewhere off to the side, enjoying the view. Krisjen puts her hands on my waist, the lyrics making us laugh, but she sings with it, almost shouting in anger.

She rocks her arms behind her, back and forth, and I don't know if it's intentional, but she brushes up on me. Again and again, her chest meets mine. I let my eyes fall, her breasts like half peaches, poking through her thin top. The dark outline of her small nipples shows through as her hair brushes my lips.

I dart my eyes to Liv.

Her thumb has stopped grinding.

She doesn't move.

She sits there, and I grab onto Krisjen, our legs threaded as we dance. The heat of Liv's eyes travels over the band of bare skin between my tank top and skirt, watching me move, and maybe she's remembering exactly what I feel like under these clothes.

And that maybe Callum isn't a threat. Another girl will eventually want me.

But when I look back, Liv is gone. Krisjen moves into me as sweat trickles down my back. I twist my neck left and right. Where is she?

Where did she go?

And then I tip my head up, seeing her climb the spiral staircase. A girl holds her hand, pulling Liv after her, but it's not Martelle.

What the fuck? I stop. Who is that now?

They disappear around the curve of the stairs until I can't see them anymore, and my stomach sinks.

"Whoo!" Krisjen squeals, oblivious.

But I fall away from her, stepping back and watching the stairs. How many girls does she have? She thinks she can just move on? She thinks I'm disposable? Replaceable?

Some cute brunette shakes her skirt at you, and you think you can have her? I clench my jaw.

I'm sick of chasing her. She said she wouldn't put pressure on me. She said we could keep this quiet. I know what she must've felt, me leaving her on the street like that, but what was I supposed to do? What would she have done? Let's not pretend that after years of me treating her like shit, she's prepared to be seen with me, either. How would that look?

We're not a couple. That's not what this is.

But we're also not done. I charge after her. She doesn't get the last word. I do.

I step up the stairs, the grates vibrating under my shoes, the whole staircase shaking a little with the weight of all the people standing on it. I push past bodies, looking up as I climb and squeeze through the crowd. Windows stacked about five feet from each other, one on top of another, letting in what little moonlight seeps through the clouds.

The lantern at the top stopped functioning decades ago; Saber Point Lighthouse was falling into ruin like so many lighthouses now obsolete with the invention of computers and radar. The last lightkeeper died the year my mother was born; some of his furniture was still sitting in the living quarters that he had shared with a corgi named Archie. Rumor has it he also shared the living quarters with a woman about thirty years younger than him, but no one ever saw her, so I don't know how the rumor started. Some say she was here illegally and hiding. Some say he rescued her as a girl and she refused to leave him when he tried to send her on her way. All versions of a truth no one would ever know because he died, and as far as I know, the place was empty when they found him.

Except for Archie.

Old places have a way of growing more alive the longer they stand. The stories they house, the memories they facilitate . . . We can't meet Elvis, but thousands of people visit his home every year, because to be where he was is like seeing his ghost.

Saber Point erodes more every year, and eventually they'll tear it down when it becomes a hazard, taking its century-long history with it, like the lightkeeper and Archie (and the girl) were never here at all.

Like I was never here at all and about to kill Olivia Jaeger.

The crowd falls away as I climb and climb, and I hear a door slam above me. The service room and watch room are before the catwalk at the top, and I launch up the rest of the stairs, drops of rain pummeling the windows like darts as the music fades to a low beat below me. I jump up to the landing, grab the handle, but then I pause, my heart beating so hard it hurts my chest.

Pressing my other hand to the door, I lean my ear in, listening. But I Prevail's rendition of "Blank Space" drowns out everything. Even the sound of my breathing.

I should leave. What will I accomplish by ripping their hair out? I'm better than that. I can have anyone. She should beg for me.

But my gut twists into knots, and I can't ignore it. I've lost everything that's important. I'm not losing the only other thing that matters anymore.

Twisting the handle, I inhale and hold it, bracing myself as I open the door and enter the room.

Moonlight casts a dim glow through the fifteen or so small, circular windows spread out around the room that lightkeepers used to watch the weather, the walls paneled with wood, unlike the brick of the rest of the structure.

A blackboard sits on the wall to my right, remnants of chalk still dusting its surface, and a square wooden table fills the center of the small room alongside a large canister. The old gears and axles inside the glass windows that once operated the lens are now still and quiet.

Another narrow spiral staircase leads up through the ceiling, but the small hatch door to the lantern is closed.

No Liv.

I spin around, heading for the service room, but she's there, stepping around the corner and into the doorway.

I halt. The other girl isn't with her.

"You dance nice," she says.

She leans into the doorframe, pulling her gum out of her mouth and sticking it in a piece of foil.

I steel my spine. "None of that was for you."

"*All* of that was for me."

She finally looks up, cocking her head, and even though I can't see her eyes, I feel the self-satisfaction rolling off her.

Bitch.

"How much have you had to drink, Clay?"

Not nearly enough. The slight buzz in my head is probably from the hundred bodies downstairs, sucking up the oxygen, rather than the shots I did in the car.

"Where is she?" I demand.

"Who?"

"You know who."

A flash of white and I know she's smiling. I glance above me and then back to Liv, knowing her slut is waiting either in the service room or up at the lantern. I wouldn't have missed them if they'd come back down.

She sticks the foil back into her pocket and steps farther into the room. "About that dress, Clay," she says. "You're losing weight. I need to measure you again."

The dress? She's making it after all?

I don't give a shit about the dress.

She closes the door behind her, and the music fades a little more, my hands shaking the closer she gets. *I hear my breathing now.*

"Hold out your arms," she says in barely a whisper.

But I don't. "How do you know I'm losing weight?"

She approaches, taking out her phone and opening an app. Her eyes meet mine, and while she doesn't reply out loud, I read it in her eyes. *She knows my body.*

A thrill courses through me, and I dip my head a little, wanting her mouth only a few inches away. But I hold back.

I hadn't been trying to lose weight. I'd just . . . forgotten to eat. I'd spent more time at the gym the past week. I was waking earlier and staying up later, my head preoccupied.

She forces my arms wide, ready to use her phone and some kind of measuring app, I guess, but I push her hand away. "Who is she?"

"A friend."

"Someone you've been with before?"

"Yes."

My chest caves, and my stomach knots. Tears burn my eyes. *Fuck.* I don't know what's worse—Martelle or someone she has a history with.

Definitely someone she has a history with. It's a reminder that she had a life before me. That there are other people who can make her happy.

What the hell's happening? I see Callum talking to girls. Girls looking at him. I don't give a shit. In fact, it relieves me a little to see him preoccupied, his attention off me.

With Liv, I could stab someone, because there's nothing I can do to stop the past. That girl above us has kissed Liv. Touched her. Liv was alone with her, doing things and tasting and biting and not thinking about me at all. Ugh . . .

I grab her waist and yank her in. She shoves me off, growling, but I grab her again. "I'm sorry I drove past you last weekend," I whisper over her lips.

I'm sorry, okay?

She stills, her hands paused, about to push me off, but she doesn't.

"You didn't deserve that," I tell her. "I wanted you there more than anything."

"Would you have done anything differently?" she asks.

I stare into her eyes, her nose an inch from mine. The lie sits on the tip of my tongue. *Yes. I would've told them I'm tired, and I'm going home and to find their own rides. Then I'd swing around the corner, risk being seen, and pick you up.* How easy would that have been?

But I know I'd be scared. They were right there, watching me.

She takes my face in her hands, not blinking once. "You know what I want?" She hardens her voice. "For you to stop lying to me."

She backs me into the table, and I reach back, gripping it with my hands to steady myself.

"I don't need you to be soft," she says. "And I don't need to be seduced. You wanna fuck because it feels good, right?"

No, I . . .

But she shakes me. "Right?"

"Yes," I gasp. "Yes, it felt good."

"Because I get you off."

"N—"

"Right?" she grits out.

I nod. "Yes."

She leans into me, pushing me onto the tabletop. The pulse in my clit thrums like a jackhammer as she positions herself between my thighs and sets her palms on the table at my sides, looking down at me.

"Liv . . ."

"Because I'm safe, right?" Her tone is an icy bite. "The dirty Catholic girl cliché you'll tell your husband about someday?"

I can't swallow. I touch her neck, holding it in both hands and caressing her jaw and throat with my thumbs.

"Right?" she asks.

Tears sting my eyes, and I hate this. I hate that I did this to her.

"Right," I whisper, but the sob in my throat says the opposite, and I know she hears it. "Like I would ever love you."

"You would never."

I shake my head.

"I'm convenient and quiet," she tells me, "because you're not a slut or a whore if you're doing it with a girl one night during a naughty sleepover, right?"

I want to tell her she means so much more to me, but she and I both know whatever happens between us won't last.

So I play along. "No one will ever know I've been touched," I tell her.

My future husband will never know what really turns me on.

But for now, I'm hers. "Open your camera," I say.

She stares at me.

I take her phone out of her hand, still unlocked, and open her camera app. Turning it to selfie mode, I switch it to video and put it out to the side, fitting us both in the frame. She looks into the camera and I meet her eyes before hitting *Record*. Slowly, I dip my head into her neck.

I leave little pecks at first. Soft kisses on her warm skin, my gaze flickering to the camera every once in a while. She watches me on the screen, and it only takes a moment before her chest starts rising and falling faster and harder and she tips her head back.

My kisses grow stronger—taking in more of her skin, using my teeth, sucking . . . I glide my tongue up the nape to her ear, seeing her watching the screen out of the corner of her eye.

I trail wet kisses up her neck, over her jaw, and then take her mouth in a few short nibbles. "I liked it when you fucked me," I gasp loud enough for the video. "I want to do it again."

She shudders, and I take her hand, sucking one of her fingers into my mouth.

She turns her head, forgetting the camera, and watches me blow her. In and out, I suck, flicking and swirling my tongue and showing her what I want to do. "I want to bury my head between your legs under the sheets," I tell her.

Her mouth falls open like she can't breathe, and she reaches up, taking my face again, forehead to forehead as she stares at my mouth like it's a meal.

I stop recording, smelling the spearmint on her breath from her gum. Reaching around, I slip the phone into her back pocket and hold her tight to me. "I'm in your hands now," I whisper. "That's how much I trust you."

She can shatter my world anytime she wants with that video. I will happily give her that power to prove that I'm willing to risk almost anything for a few more months with her.

I wrap my arms around her, burying my face in her neck and holding her close. "We always think that if we can have the one thing we want, we'll be happy, but the wanting never ends, does it?" I say, muffled in her neck. "There were things I wanted before all I wanted was my brother back."

I've wanted her longer.

She clasps my chin in the crook between her thumb and index finger, nudging my eyes up to her. "What are you doing to me?" she murmurs.

But I get smart. "Nothing yet," I whisper. "But I'd really like to do that bury-my-head-between-your-legs-under-the-sheets bit."

And she loses it. She moans, slides her fingers underneath my tank top, and pulls it up and over my head. It falls off my body, but before I have time to feel the chill on my breasts, she yanks my body in, grips the back of my neck, and fuses her mouth to mine, kissing so hard a roller coaster does a barrel roll between my thighs. I suck in a breath between kisses, pressing my breasts into her, and squirming as my hands roam, because I can't get close enough or feel enough to be satisfied.

Liv's hands slide under my skirt, and I smile through the kisses, unable to contain my excitement. Christmas never felt this good.

She leans into me, and I fall back onto my hands, her standing over me as she runs her hand up and down my torso. She cups my breast and meets my eyes before she pinches my little pink nipple. An electrical current shoots through me, and I clench my thighs, moaning.

Yes.

"Liv, did I see you come up here?" someone calls out.

I pop my eyes open, hearing the wooden door hinges creak, and I dart up, ducking into Liv's chest before I can see who's behind her.

"Liv?" a man's voice says again.

"Get out," she tells him.

One of her brothers?

There's nothing for a moment, and then I hear him again, his tone amused this time. "Damn, who you got there?"

"Trace, seriously," she barks over her shoulder. She holds my naked shoulders as I cover my breasts and huddle into her body. "Get out!"

But he doesn't. He steps up behind her and meets my eyes.

"All right," he says, smiling. "Way to go."

"Fuck off," she blurts out next.

"Okay, okay." He shrugs and leaves, the door shutting after a moment.

"He won't say anything," she tells me. "I'll make sure of it."

I put my arms around her again. *I don't care about that right now.*

I hop off the table, pushing her back until she falls into an old wooden chair in the corner. Pushing my panties down my legs, I step out of them, climb on top and straddle her, and see her eyes fall to my breasts.

I love watching her watch me.

She slouches down a little in the chair, gripping my hips, and I don't need instruction. I start to roll my hips, grinding on her through her jeans, rubbing my pussy up on her fly. Heat floods me, and I know I'm wet as the rough fabric of her clothes feels so good against my bare skin.

I glide my fingers over her hands and up her arms, but I feel the bracelet she always wears and trace the snake wrapped around the hourglass. I can almost make out its fangs as I hold her eyes.

"I like it when you bite me," I tell her. "With your teeth . . . and your words."

"I couldn't stop myself anymore."

"Why?"

She leans up and takes my face in one hand, nearly grazing my lips with hers. "Because sometimes two wrongs make a right, Clay." She breathes hard. "Because venom works slowly but surely, and I was so tired of not fighting for my life. And because one of the ingredients in antivenin is venom, and sometimes you need poison to counteract the poison."

"And if the antivenin doesn't work?" I tease.

She plays with my skirt. "Isn't it?"

I smile. *Oh, yes, it is.* She pushes back, and I'm not at all unhappy about where she pushed me to.

She drops back again, her eyes zoning in on me bare and open as I dry fuck her, and I thrust my hips, still slow but deeper and deeper. Her hands trail over my ass and up my skirt to my stomach before steeling on the joint between my hip and thigh. Her thumb rubs circles on my clit as she bends her knees just slightly and stretches her legs behind me.

Can she feel it? Even with her clothes on? I want to get the hell out of here, but I don't want to stop.

I roll and roll, battering my hips into her until her nails pierce my skin, and I wince at the pain but love it, too.

She grabs the back of my neck and pulls me in, growling in a whisper over my mouth, "It's not over between us until I'm wearing something you can really ride."

A shiver shoots down my spine, and she doesn't have to elaborate.

"After that, you can go fuck a guy," she taunts. "But you and I will know nothing is better than this."

I kiss her, her confidence tasting possessive, and I like it.

Nothing is better than this.

I groan. "I . . . Oh, God, I . . . Liv—"

But a blaring sound hits my ears, and I startle. Liv sits up, hands still on my hips as tingles and heat rock through me.

What? I wince at the sound.

It's a horn. Outside. It goes and goes. Blaring. Constant. What is that?

"Liv?" I ask.

But worry hits her eyes. "Shit." She doesn't look at me. "Baby, get dressed."

17

Olivia

I almost reach for Clay's hand, but I stop myself. Swinging the door open, I bolt out of the room, making sure she's behind me, and we run down the staircase, hearing a commotion of chatter, laughing, and squealing as the horn screams into the night outside.

Clay straightens her clothes and fixes her hair. "What is that?"

"It's the old storm siren."

"It's still operating?"

Obviously. I peer out the window as we descend, seeing waves rising high and crashing onto the beach. Darts of rain spear the windows, the staircase now empty as everyone evacuates, not so much because people are scared, but because rain means the canal floods and *a lot* of rain means the tracks close in case a train needs to break schedule to get out of Dodge.

Anyone from St. Carmen needs to get home now or they're here all night.

Bodies pour out of the lighthouse, running to cars, and Clay and I stop, looking around. Dallas, Trace, and Iron came with me, and I look past the lightkeeper's house, down the dirt road running parallel to the beach, seeing my brother's truck.

"Oh my God," Clay breathes out, covering her head, rain plastering our clothes to us.

I turn to her, wondering if we're saying goodbye now, but then I decide for her. "Get in my brother's truck."

She's staying.

I walk and she better fucking follow.

We both run and then stop, cut off by the crowd scrambling in every direction as they bump into each other and slip on the ground. Headlights light up the night, engines peel off, kicking up the inch of rain that's accumulated already, and I see Dallas and Iron making their way for the truck.

But then I hear someone scream "I don't care!"

Krisjen stands opposite her shitty boyfriend, throwing her phone and then her arms, getting in his face and challenging him.

"I couldn't care less!" she goes on.

He advances on her, the back door of his car open and a couple of guys from our school inside.

"Post them!" Krisjen tells him, the rain making her white crop top see-through as her hair hangs in her face. "Post the videos and my texts and everything! Fuck it all! I don't care!"

He grabs her hair, and I jerk to attention. *What the hell?*

"Liv, come on!" I hear Iron at my side.

But I ignore him, seeing Clay move over to her friend ahead of me. "Milo!" she warns.

But he pays Clay no mind. "You don't care, huh?" Milo growls in Krisjen's face.

"What's he talking about?" Clay yells at Krisjen.

"He took a video of me ages ago," she chokes out as he yanks her in by the hair. "The little bitch didn't like me dancing with another man tonight, so he posted it online."

"He did what?" Clay barks, kind of forgetting she did the same thing to me, but whatever.

"And she doesn't care." Milo repeats her words. "Doesn't care at all."

"Nope, post them all!" she growls, defiant. "It'll be the best way to get rid of you!"

And it happens before I can leap—his hand whips across her face, sending her spinning and falling into the car. She catches herself, I jump into action, but then I feel Iron advance first.

No. I stop and push him back, knowing one more arrest will be his last. "I will handle it," I bite out, shoving him away.

"Fuck that." He pushes, trying to get past me to slice Milo up.

"No!" I yell.

I spin around to help Krisjen, but she's already recovered. Launching back around, she slams a fist across Milo's face, and he grabs his jaw, hunching over a little. I barely have time to be impressed before the back of his hand sends her flying to the ground.

My brother grabs my shoulders, trying to throw me out of the way, but I dig in my heels, wanting to jump on Milo's back and bring him down, but Iron is about to end his life, and my brother is more important right now.

Clay runs over to Krisjen, but Milo reaches down and grabs his girlfriend. He shoves her into the back seat. "Meet some of my friends," he says, spitting blood onto the ground. "You wanna fuck other guys? You can fuck them."

The guy in the passenger seat looks over his shoulder at the dazed Krisjen, while the guy next to her takes hold of her and Milo slams the door.

I launch myself toward the car, yanking on the handle and hitting the glass.

"Milo!" Clay screams. "No!"

"Fucking Saints pieces of shit!" Iron growls, trying to kick the windows in.

But Milo speeds off, all four men taking Krisjen with them.

"Liv," Clay cries.

"Car now!" Iron yells over my head, and I turn, seeing Dallas and Trace jumping into the truck.

Jesus Christ. Iron's going to jail tonight.

He runs, meeting the truck as Dallas pulls it around, and I push Clay toward the back door. "Get in."

I can't let my brothers do this alone. Usually, it's their own damn fault, but Krisjen needs help. I opened up the Bay to the Saints. This is my fault.

We climb in, Dallas kicks it into gear, and we speed off after Milo's douchey BMW.

"Guys, don't, okay?" I tell them. "Please. We'll get her and then we're gone."

But no one hears me. "Where's he going?" Dallas glances over his shoulder at Clay.

"How would I know?" She meets his eyes and then mine, suddenly defensive. "Back over the tracks where there's more cops to stop you guys, probably."

"His house, Fox Hill, somewhere else? Where?" I question her.

"I don't know!" she insists. "There's no clubhouse where our men take women to commit felonies, Liv! What do you want from me?"

Clubhouse . . .

"Fox Hill!" I shout to my brothers as I grab the dog tags and key hanging from the chain around my neck. *We'll try there first.*

Clay takes out her phone, probably calling Krisjen. "Pick up, pick up . . ." But after a moment, she grits out a "Dammit" and hangs up, dialing someone else. "Milo, you asshole." And then she hangs up again, Milo not answering, either. "I'm calling the police," she says. "I don't care."

But I push her phone down. "Don't."

She stares at me. "He's going to hurt her."

"They can hurt *us.*"

"Which is exactly what they want," Dallas shouts from the

front, eyeing Clay in the rearview mirror. "You all live for this, don't you? Are you that bored? Need to slum to feel a little excitement once in a while? Huh?"

She narrows her eyes to slits, glaring back at him.

"You got this bitch messing around with Trace to make her boyfriend jealous," Dallas gripes, "and you're doing the same thing, flashing your fucking little ass around here and screwing with Liv's head."

I lock my jaw. *Great. Thanks, Dallas.*

But instead of yelling back at him, Clay jerks her head toward me. "I'm not trying to make Callum jealous."

"You came with him, didn't you?" I look at her. "Tryst Six are just toys to you."

"That's not true."

"Shut up."

I stare out the window, avoiding her eyes. I know I'm being unfair, but Dallas is right. The shit is hitting the fan, and it's all the Saints' fault. If Iron gets busted, we're the ones who pay. Not Clay. She goes off to college in the fall, her little dalliance in girl snatch a nice memory for her. What the hell am I doing?

"You know," she starts, her tone low and hard, "let's stop pretending that I am making you do anything you don't want to do. If you were so angry with me, you wouldn't have come back to school. You wouldn't have come back to me."

"I didn't come back to you."

She falls silent for a moment, and as we bounce over the tracks, I hear her start to moan.

I turn toward her again.

"'God, you have a beautiful body.'" She whimpers my words. "'I want you to lose it in my bed.'"

You've got to be kidding me.

"'I can do anything you want me to,'" she whispers, breathing heavy and dragging her hand up and down her body. "'That's it, Collins. Fuck me.'"

Trace snorts in the front seat, while Iron has turned and is watching her.

I see Dallas shake his head.

I swallow. "Yeah, you liked that, didn't you?" I reply curtly. "You like me inside you. And you want more of it. Not of him. You know why?"

She arches a brow.

"Because you're gay," I tell her. "You're queer, Clay. Just like me."

The corners of her mouth tighten. "I am not."

So it's just me, then? Just something about me? Bullshit. She was checking Krisjen out on the dance floor tonight. Well, not really checking her out, but she was definitely noticing her.

"And if I said I was in love with you?" I ask her. "What would you feel?"

She stares at me, her wet blond hair sticking to her amazing body, and those big blue eyes losing their defiance for a fraction of a second. Her chest caves a little, breathing hard.

"I'm in love with you, Clay," I tell her.

The car falls silent, like my brothers are afraid to breathe because they might miss something. Her lips open a little, and God, the softness that hits her eyes makes her look like she'd blow over in a light breeze. I swear I see a smile desperate to get out, and I want to say it again.

"Just kidding." I force a scoff. "Just wanted you to see how fucking gay you are."

She jerks her gaze away, focusing out the window, and I stare at the reflection of her in mine. I can almost see her little snarl as she stares at my reflection, too.

I'm not in love with her. I'm leaving.

Rain swipes across the windows, the wind blowing the drops

into lines streaking over the glass, and the next thing I know, Dallas is jerking the wheel to the left and stabbing the brakes.

The car stops, and Dallas shifts it into park. "Get those motherfuckers," Iron growls, grabbing a tire iron off the dash.

"Stop!" I yell, seeing we're on Main Street. We've caught up to them before they were able to get to Fox Hill. This is too public.

But no one listens to me.

The boys open the doors, racing out of the cab as the storm rages and gusts of wind bend the palm trees. I jump out and run, seeing Clay and Trace run around the other side of the car.

I grab Iron by the belt and haul him back with everything I have. "Stop!"

He's just looking for a fight. Damn him. He's the most violent nice guy I know.

Milo's BMW sits stalled, his right front tire up on the sidewalk outside Enchantment, a boutique soap and shampoo shop. The traffic light above bounces on its wiring as it hangs over the middle of the thoroughfare, and the streets are empty, everyone taking cover in their homes.

Another car skids to a halt behind Dallas's truck; Aracely and Santos jump out with other friends of my brothers—Carissa, Benny, and Tomb. I spot headlights over the roof of Milo's car, and Callum Ames drives up in his Mustang, hurrying to his friend's aid.

Shiiiiit.

"Krisjen!" Clay calls.

She swings open the back door and pulls her friend out. Krisjen stumbles, holding her head, but her eyes are open and alert.

She sees Milo climb out of the car and run around the hood, the tire probably inoperable, the axle most likely broken.

My hair sticks to my body, a lock draped across my nose, and I grab Krisjen and shove her and Clay toward my brothers' truck. "Get in."

I turn, pushing Iron back. "Leave it," I grit out, but his eyes bore into Milo. Iron doesn't give a shit about him hitting Krisjen. I mean, he doesn't like it, but this is an excuse for a fight, and men are fucking stupid.

He advances, and I push him back again. "No!" Then I look around. "Trace! Dallas! Get in the car! Everyone, now!"

But Krisjen pulls her hand away from her face, seeing blood smeared on her fingers, and glares at Milo. "You son of a bitch!"

And she launches for him, her arms swinging and giving Iron the only invitation he needs.

He dives in, wraps an arm around her, and hauls her away, pushing her toward me before he lunges for Milo himself.

And the next thing I know, everyone is diving into the fray. "No!" I yell.

Iron grabs Milo's collar and throws him onto the hood of his car, pinning him with the tire iron, and Dallas crashes to the ground, one of Milo's friends slamming into him and falling with him.

I twist. "Clay!" I bark, seeing her hold Krisjen's hand, looking left to right and backing up as their wet hair flies side to side. Why the hell isn't she in the car?

She meets my eyes, and I start off, but something grips my hair, my scalp screaming. "Ahhh!" I cry out.

I hit the ground, my wrist twisting and hitting the pavement, and I flip around, blinking up at Aracely through the rain.

"Let them play, Liv," she snarls. "Go take your little white-bread pussy and get out of here."

I growl and shoot out my foot, slamming her in the knee. She flinches and hunches over, but before she can fall, Clay barrels in and shoves her to the ground.

I suck in a breath, watching Aracely crash to the sidewalk, falling into the curb and crying out.

I shoot my eyes to Clay. *Dammit.*

Milo charges Iron, throwing his shoulder into his gut; Santos and Trace punch a preppy, taking him to the ground; and Dallas has Callum in a choke hold, but Callum heaves forward and throws Dallas over his shoulder and onto the sidewalk. My brother howls as he hits the ground.

"Clay!" I rush over, grabbing her arm. "Stop!" I yell.

She pinches her brows together.

"Take Krisjen and walk home!" I shout over the storm, glowering at them both. "This is all your fault anyway. Just leave!"

I don't need her help. That's the last thing I need. Aracely isn't my friend, but she's practically a sister. I can hit her. Clay can't hit her.

"Just go home!" I yell at Clay and Krisjen.

I pull Aracely to her feet. Dallas is right. None of them will pay for this. Swamp doesn't get away with shit. We'll pay for everything, and tomorrow my brothers will be in front of a judge.

As soon as Aracely rises, she shoves me off and runs back into the fray, reaching down and yanking Amy by the hair, dragging her off Carissa.

I turn back to Clay, who stands in the street, chaos swirling around her, making her look like the eye of a storm. The rain pouring down her face looks like tears, her eyes glistening, too.

"We'll always be this," I tell her loudly, but there's too much going on for anyone to hear us. "Do you see that? Me loyal to my family, and you afraid of yours and your friends. This is all we'll ever be!"

Why did she have to come tonight? She should've just left me alone.

"No one is worth this much trouble," I tell her. "Not even you."

Her eyes fall, and for the first time, I see her speechless. She knows it's true. We're never going to hold hands, and I will always choose my family over her.

Amy crashes to the ground at Clay's feet, crying out as she lands on her elbow. Red instantly starts staining the rainy street.

Clay barely notices, looking down and blinking as if she were beamed into this brawl and is trying to figure out what's going on.

Aracely grabs her hair and yanks her head down. Clay's face contorts in pain, but she doesn't make a sound as Ara shoves her with her foot and she lands in a puddle, breaking her fall with her hands.

Aracely advances, and I dive in to stop her, but she takes hold of Clay again, fisting her hair at the scalp and dragging her.

"Ara!" I bark.

But no one hears me. I glance up, searching for my brothers, the rain shrouding everything. Dallas holds his hand over his eye, probably to keep it from bleeding as he swings his foot back and kicks something on the other side of Milo's car. I can't see whoever he's finally subdued.

Trace is on the ground underneath Luke Houseman, choking him from the bottom, while Milo tries to get his legs under him and shake his head clear.

Aracely releases Clay, but only for a moment. Fisting Clay's tank top, Ara pulls, ripping the back of the fabric, and I can hear it scream from here. Clay hugs herself with her arm, holding it to her body as everything seems to happen in slow motion.

Ara lets her go, takes out her knife, swings out the blade, gathers a handful of Clay's hair, and . . .

I suck in a breath. Breaking into a run, I pull my own blade out of my back pocket, unsheathe the knife, and reach out, yanking one of Aracely's braids. She growls but releases Clay just in time, and I put myself between the two women, glaring at Ara.

"She's mine," I bite out. "Mine! Get the fuck away from her or she'll be Army's tonight, too."

Aracely pins me with fire in her eyes, and I know that nothing makes her crazier than Army with another woman. Because he's what she really wants. Even though he has no interest in her.

She rises, glaring at me. "She won't always have you around, you know?"

And she walks off, the threat hanging in the air.

I peer down at Clay, her arm still holding her shirt to her body, no bra underneath the camisole. I untie the wet shirt around my waist, throwing it around her.

"Are you hurt?" I ask.

She shakes her head as she lets her tank top fall away and slips her arms into my shirt. She stares off, not focusing on anything. Does she even realize Aracely was about to chop off her hair?

"I'm not gay," she says quietly, and I have to strain to hear her over the rain. "I'm just in love with you."

My mouth goes dry. What?

Tears pool in her eyes. "I can't apologize for everything I do to hurt you, Liv." She finally looks up, blinking against the rain. "Because I can't promise I'll stop."

I watch her.

"But I promise," she goes on, "I hurt every time you do."

My chin trembles.

My instinct is to push back. *What does that mean? You think that justifies the last three and a half years?*

But the pain in her eyes splits my heart down the middle, and in that moment, I don't care what else she has planned for me, because I can push back, too. *Just don't stop.*

Sirens pierce the air, and we both twist our heads, seeing blue and red lights flash through the rain, making their way down the street. Some of the girls scatter, running to cars, while others race in between buildings, disappearing.

I shoot to my feet, pulling Clay to hers.

"My brothers," I gasp.

They scatter, Dallas racing away in the truck, and I can't tell if he has everyone with him, but the streets empty quickly, and I am not going to be taken in for this.

I grip Clay's hand. "Come on."

I run, pulling her behind me, but it only takes a moment for her legs to catch up, and before I know it, we're around the corner. I slam into the boutique door, the neon sign reading LAVINIA'S dark. I look around, noticing the streetlights off, as well. The power is out.

Pulling my keys from the breast pocket on Clay's shirt—my shirt—I open the shop door and wait for Clay to dip in before I follow her.

Lightning flashes, thunder roars, and my heart almost stops, the mannequins inside looking like people. I pull the door closed, locking it from the inside.

I move to the window and peer through the blinds. "See anything?" I call.

I should be with my brothers, but everything happened so fast. The last thing Dartmouth needs to hear is that I was arrested for brawling.

But Clay doesn't answer me.

Stepping away from the window, I walk into the main room, drapes hanging to my left and sectioning off three dressing rooms. A riser sits in the center, an armchair on each side, and mirrors spread out around the walls. Clay stands at the windows to my right, next to the tiara and jewelry displays.

But she's not looking out the window. She's staring at me.

"Clay?" I prompt.

Is she okay?

My flannel hangs on her, water dripping from the unbuttoned sleeves, and I see the upside-down V patch of skin starting underneath her breasts and falling below her belly button. She didn't have a chance to finish buttoning the shirt.

Her hair is darkened with rain, drops shimmering across her face, while her skirt sticks to her thighs.

Red and blue lights flash beyond the curtains, and I jerk my attention to the window, it only taking a moment for them to pass and fade away down the street.

Clay moves, pulling her little handbag over her head and reaching inside for her phone before she tosses the purse down.

I should check my phone for water damage. The video she took on it pops into my head, filling me with excitement. I don't have any pictures of us together, except for team photos.

She moves closer, inching forward and dragging her finger over the glass tables along the wall. I know what she wants. Her nipples look like berries poking through my shirt, and my eyes fall to her legs again, the water bringing out the tone of her thighs and her tan. I want to lick my lips, but I don't.

"I want you to leave me alone," I tell her quietly.

She walks her fingers—index and middle—playfully across the table, seemingly satisfied now to have me all to herself. "You know what I want?" she questions. "I want you to stop lying to me."

Those are my words.

She taps her phone, taking her eyes off me for only a moment before a song starts playing. "Dirty Mind" begins, and Clay walks toward me, matching her steps to the tune, almost like a dance. Like she's hunting.

"Because I know exactly what pleases you." She meets my gaze. "Despite what comes out of your stupid mouth."

Excuse me?

She grabs my wrists and pins them behind my back as she presses her chest to mine, taking *my* control for once. I don't have time to draw in a breath before she releases me, throws me down into the cushioned chair behind me, and the chorus starts, her body coming down on top of mine in time with the music.

What the fuck? My eyes go wide, heat spreading between my legs as all of a sudden the music fills the room, and Clay hovers over my mouth, stares into my eyes, and rolls her hips into me.

Liquid fire spreads through my stomach, and I suddenly can't catch my breath, breathing hard.

Oh my God.

Cocking her head, she plays with me, arching her back, closing her eyes, and bending her neck back as her body moves, fucking me with a dance. I scale my gaze down, unable to relax but unwilling to stop her. I can't.

I slide my hands along her waist, but she plucks them off and pins them to the arms of the chair, pushing herself off me.

She backs up, moving slowly—so slowly—with the music, stretching her back long and graceful, and I don't know when she lost her shoes, but her pretty toenails are painted so light a pink that I can barely see it.

She hoods her eyes, and they never leave mine as she looks down at me and runs her hand down her body, unbuttoning her shirt. The shirt opens, falling off one shoulder, and I lean forward, resting my elbows on my knees, barely able to feel my limbs. She unzips her skirt, her hips rolling with the tempo.

I want to get up. Honestly, I do. I need to leave.

But Iron's right. Everyone is our type when they're naked. She lets everything fall, and her ass juts out, swaying in a circle before she turns and faces forward, giving me her whole body, naked except for her thong.

I can't take my eyes off her, pain racking through my body as I ball my fists.

Hanging an elbow over her head, she runs the other hand up her body, grazing her perfect breast. Her hands come down her face, her torso, and stop at her panties, her fingers threading through the white ribbon straps around her hips, a small triangle of white lace covering her in front.

What the hell was she doing wearing that with a skirt? And dancing with Callum with that on?

My eyes dart up to hers. She's still watching me, barely moving anymore and looking down on me. Sticking three fingers in her mouth, she wets them and runs the hand back down her body, slowly driving for that little triangle between her legs. Her chest rises and falls hard, and I'm throbbing. God, look at her . . .

Threading her fingers underneath the strap with one hand, she plays with herself over her panties with the wet ones while slowly tugging at the ribbon and teasing me. Taunting me. The promise in her eyes that she's going to pull it down farther and farther each time.

Falling back into me, she pushes me back, hovers over my mouth, and I want to touch her so badly. But I grip the armrests instead.

"I can't leave you alone," she whispers.

My fingers hum.

Don't leave me alone. I'm an idiot.

"Sometimes my feelings for you are good and sometimes they're bad," she tells me, "but they're always strong, Liv. Like no one else."

Twisting around, she faces the mirrors and lowers herself onto my lap. Threading her fingers through mine, she keeps my hands at bay as she leans back into me, her head on my shoulder. Rolling her hips with the music, she looks up into my eyes as she rubs her ass into my crotch, and even though my clothes are wet and cold, I'm sweating.

I find her in the mirror ahead, a groan escaping as soon as I see the picture of her body writhing on top of me. Her nipples are dark and hard, her stomach like an hourglass, and I can't take it anymore. My hands start to shake, and I fight free, taking hold of her, one arm around her waist as the other reaches up to thread fingers through her hair. Holding her in place, I sink my mouth into hers, finding her tongue and so fucking hungry I want to swallow her whole.

Her wet mouth brushes mine, and I slide my other hand down into her panties, finding her nub and caressing it oh so gently.

She moans, and I can feel her smile through the kiss. "I want to taste you," she begs. "It's my turn."

But I can't let go of this view right now. "You will," I say. "Pay attention to what I do to you. What you like. So you know what to do to me, okay?"

She nods.

I continue to tease her clit, slow and gentle, drawing her out, caressing her pussy.

"You like that?" I ask.

She nods. "Yeah."

I pull my fingers off her, bring them to my mouth and suck on one. She watches me wet it and slide it back down into her panties. Her nipples pebble, the skin shrinking, and I smile.

I rub her just a little faster.

"Did you like *that*?" I ask.

She swallows. "Yeah," she whispers.

I watch her in the mirror, her legs between my spread jeans-clad ones, and she kisses my jaw as I play inside her panties.

"I'm going to put a finger inside you," I tell her.

She searches my eyes, a hint of fear there.

"I'll go slow."

Her jaw flexes, but she doesn't respond, and I take that as my go-ahead.

Sliding my hand down a little farther, I feel her legs stiffen.

"Open," I whisper over her mouth. "Open your legs, baby."

She hesitates, and I don't think she's breathing, but after a moment, she relaxes and slides a leg over mine, opening for me.

I find her entrance and rub the outside, not going in yet. "God." I kiss her cheek, lightly taking a chunk between my teeth. "You're so tight. I can already tell you're going to be so fucking warm."

She whimpers, shuddering under my touch, and I feel it. Her slick heat coating my fingertip. She's ready.

I take it a centimeter at a time, working my middle finger just past her opening, little by little, kissing and licking her skin as I move my other hand from her hair to her breast. I knead the handful, distracting her.

Her warmth travels up my arm, and I groan, feeling it between my legs, too. "So fucking tight," I murmur in her ear. "I want to go deeper, Clay."

She reaches back and threads her fingers through my hair, turned on.

I push my finger a little more, her body clenching and tightening around me, its natural resistance kicking in. She squirms in my arms, and I wanna fucking die, my arms so charged with how good this feels.

I massage her clit again. "Open your cunt," I whisper. "Open."

She sucks in a breath but finally nods like a good girl. "Okay."

She spreads wider, and I finally have my finger buried to the knuckle, enough that I don't have to go any farther. I crook it, slowly and gently, moving, massaging, and testing over and over until I feel her jerk and hear her gasp.

I smile, closing my eyes for a moment as I kiss her temple.

There it is.

She stops breathing for a moment, and I continue, bending my fingers into her belly, hitting the same spot over and over again.

Finally, she exhales, relaxes into me, and spreads her thighs wider, giving me all of the room I need to finger her.

"Don't stop," she moans, searching for my mouth.

Jesus Christ, this is better than me coming.

"Pull your panties down," I tell her. "Let me see."

She slips her thong down to her thighs, and I look in the mirror. She slides a hand around the back of my neck and starts relaxing more, moving into my finger and searching for it. Her breasts bounce with the thrusts, and she arches her back so her tits pop up. The room sways in front of me.

"I wanted to be the first girl to kiss you," she says.

I look down at her in my arms. *I wanted you to be the only one to kiss me.*

My heart would pump so hard. So fucking hard, and she never saw it, did she? And then everything started to feel cold—years of cold—and I didn't even notice how cold everything was, and nothing feels like this. Nothing.

I hold her tighter, burying my nose in her hair and hating her for so much, but most of all, hating her for denying us this for so long.

"I know I'm not your first," she says. "But you're mine. I want to be sacred to you."

Tears fills my eyes. She's such a cunt, but then she says things like that and I just want to give her everything she wants. I want her to know that I wish to God this didn't feel so good and that she didn't feel so good.

The rain rages outside, the streets deserted, and it feels like we're the only two people on the planet. And if that's the case, all would be right with the world, because no one would be in our way. "Baby," I mouth against her skin, "you make me melt."

She climbs off me, turns around, and straddles me, and I slide the same finger back in, hearing that sweet, little whimper of pain as I fill her again.

With my fingers tangled in the strap of her thong, I grip her ass as she fucks my hand. I want to lean up and suck on her breast, but I love the view too much as she rocks on me and I rub her with my thumb.

A ringing pierces the air, and we both blink but don't stop.

One hand in her pussy and the other on her ass, I keep her going as she digs on the side of the chair for her phone.

Pulling it out, she pants. "My mom."

"Answer it," I tell her. "If you don't, she'll worry, and then she'll track it."

Her mouth falls open, caught up in the pleasure.

"Hurry," I tell her.

I'm about to come with her writhing on top of me like this. Shit.

She answers it, holding it to her ear. "Mom," she says, breathless.

I laugh quietly, hearing her mother on the other end.

Clay rolls her hips, biting her bottom lip as she stares down at me. "I'm okay," she pants, and then clamps a hand over her mouth. "I'm, um . . . I'm with Callum."

I lean up, flicking her nipple with my tongue and smiling. "Yeah, Mom. She's with Callum."

I suck hard, and she moans. "Uh-huh," she says to whatever Gigi is telling her. "I'm safe. I'll be home as soon as the rain lets up."

"You'll be home when I'm done," I correct her, jerking her harder into my hand.

Clay comes down, covering my mouth with hers, a smile peeking out. "Shhhh . . ."

My clit throbs, and I'm so wet. I push up into her as I bury my finger inside her, feeling all the warmth pool at my center and my orgasm almost there.

God, fuck, Clay . . . She grinds harder.

She mewls, and I bite my bottom lip again to stifle my own orgasm as I clamp a hand over her mouth, watching her getting ready to come.

"I'll just sleep at Krisjen's, actually," she spits out really quickly. "It's already so late. I'll be home first thing in the morning, okay?"

A pause, Clay jerks, her face twists in pain, and I stick two fingers inside, breathing hard as she loses her mind.

"Mom, I have to go," she gasps. "Krisjen's leaving. I'll call you in the morning!"

Ending the call, she throws the phone somewhere, and her pussy clenches around my fingers as she cries out.

I shake, my body exploding as she rides it out, and I arch as she comes down and kisses me. Her cry disappears down my throat, and I feel the sweat trickle down my back.

"Fuck," I gasp.

I can't believe I came. I'm still fully dressed. I groan, keeping my fingers inside her for another minute as she lies down on top of me.

I wrap my arms around her, feeling warm and wet, surrounded by her heavenly skin.

"Is there blood?" she asks, her voice sounding weak and so sweet.

I hold back my laugh. I slide my hand out from between us and take a quick glance at my glistening fingers, a shot of pride that I got her so wet.

"No."

It's going to take something bigger and wider than my finger. Contrary to popular belief, a hymen isn't really something you break. It's stretched, flexed, strained . . . It's not a barrier the way most people think.

She sits up, and I wipe my finger on my jeans.

"Look at me," I tell her.

She does.

"Virginity is a concept invented by people to make women feel worthless for having sex." I raise my eyebrows matter-of-factly. "You want to worry about protecting something, protect your credit score. That'll come in a lot handier someday."

She breaks into a laugh, and my face falls a little, her smile leveling me. I don't make her laugh much. Of course, she doesn't give me much reason to, but how wonderfully we might get along if we could stop fighting. I'd love to find out who she really is.

She leans down, kissing my forehead. "Hot shower," she says against my skin. "Take me home with you. Now."

18

Olivia

Her eyes almost glow in the dark.

We rest on our sides in my bed, facing each other with my hands tucked under my cheek. We can't sleep, though, and I haven't been able to give her the shower she wanted. With my brothers being home, she preferred to stay in my room.

She scoots in, and I can feel her breath. "Tell me about your first time."

I shift, a little uneasy. "It was in a car."

My late father's old Chevelle that Macon sold a year later to help pay for my junior year at Marymount.

I stare at her, drawing in a breath. "The carnival had come through the day before, and we'd spent all afternoon on the rides," I tell her, "laughing and eating junk food and getting sun-scorched." I can still feel the hot plastic of the sticky seats as my mind drifts to the memory. "I remember being so sweaty with my hair plastered to my back, but I'd never felt so alive. It was like everything vibrated off my skin. The wind in my hair as the Spider whipped us around. The dizziness in my head, the tingles on my skin when she touched me, the cotton candy on her mouth . . . It heightened everything, and I didn't care about the heat, because I was throbbing."

I pull out my hand, sliding it down between her legs.

"I was throbbing here," I clarified, starting to feel my pulse beat again at the curve of her through her panties. "She took me and laid me down on the back seat in the parking lot." I licked my dry lips. "It was midday, the sun still bright overhead. I didn't . . . I didn't come. I was just too nervous, but I liked it. I wanted it again." I laugh at myself, sounding bitter. "I thought I was in love. Jesus."

Clay stays silent, and I'm grateful. I don't want to talk about it, but I feel the tears spring up despite how many years it's been and how I barely remember what she looked like.

I swallow. "She slept with Iron that night."

Clay's head shifts just a hair, but she still doesn't say anything.

"Turns out she was just looking for a way in the door," I murmur, dropping my eyes and remembering that slice of pain like it was yesterday. Her attention was an instant addiction, and for just a little while I felt like I wanted to die. She wanted someone else. She wasn't thinking of me every second like I was of her. "He never found out."

It isn't uncommon for things like that to happen. Thinking back now, I remember how girls would move from one bed to another in my house, using Trace to get to Dallas or using Army to get to Macon. Sanoa Bay is a small community. There aren't many women at least one of your buddies or brothers hasn't slept with. It never struck me as anything other than normal. Until I was the idiot who got played.

"How old were you?" Clay asked.

My eyes strain, aching. I close them. "Fifteen."

Tears spill out, and I turn my head into my pillow to cover my face. Why am I crying? My body shakes, and I don't know if I'm laughing at how ridiculous I am or trying to hide a sob.

I tilt my face to her again. "Why do people think sex doesn't mean anything to us?" I ask, but don't wait for an answer. "I was alone, and it felt good to have someone, but sex wasn't all I wanted. I'd had nothing of my own, and maybe she was an escape for me that afternoon, but in hours it went from feeling like I finally had something to look forward to, to feeling like nothing. Used. Degraded. Trash. Like it meant everything to me and nothing to her."

Even my own family. Not one of my brothers gives a shit about who I sleep with because they think pregnancy is the only way I can be hurt. They don't ask about girlfriends. They don't think this is anything more than fun.

But Clay dives in, pressing her body flush with mine as she lays a hand on my cheek. "Stop crying," she whispers, pressing her forehead to mine. "Please stop."

I go to grab hold of her, slip my hand around her waist, but I hold back. I already told her too much.

But the tears keep coming, no matter how I try to hold my breath to stifle the crying.

"All right, I'm gonna shave her head," she says. "Where can I find her?"

I break into a laugh through the sobs, wiping my eyes. But when I look at her, she's lifted her head off the pillow, and while I can't make out her whole expression, she's not joking.

"Seriously," she says, pushing me onto my back and climbing on top of me. "You're under my protection now and I get shit done. Want her fired? Arrested? Her car repossessed?"

I smile, no more tears stinging as I slip my hands under her shirt—my T-shirt—and caress the fucking amazing skin on her smooth stomach.

"Porta-potty shit dumped on her lawn, maybe?" she goes on. "I know a guy."

I snort, almost able to see her waggling her eyebrows with mischief. She wears my black **Headlines don't sell papes. Newsies sell papes.** theater T-shirt, the sleeves cut off and the sides cut out. I pull my hands out from under and slip them under the arms, her bare breasts so easily accessible.

It takes no time at all for my body to stir.

"Tell me about your first time," I tease, breathless, as her nipples turn rock hard under my fingers.

I'm not sure if the locker room, the shower, or the hotel constitutes our first time, but I damn well know it was me.

She pulls my black top hat, a relic from the discard pile when we sorted old costumes last year for donations, from my bedpost and fits it on top of her head. Underwear, T-shirt, freshly fucked hair falling down her body . . . God, she's hot.

She drags her fingertips down my body, playing. "Well, I always thought it would be a huge endeavor," she sighs. "I'd know exactly when it was going to happen. I'd be in total control, planning out every detail." And she lists on her fingers. "The location. The music. Protection. Looking my best. I'd do everything I could to make it perfect."

I can imagine she even had an outfit picked out. Clay's a micromanager.

"But the perfect moment found me instead." Her voice softens, serious. "And I couldn't stop it."

I scale my hands underneath her arms, and we meet, her coming down and me rising up until her arms are wrapped around me and we crash to the bed. The hat tumbles off her head.

"She was better than I'd dreamed," she tells me against my cheek. "Nothing could tear me away from her."

Nothing. How hard it would've been to stop if she'd asked me to in the hotel room. I would've, but it would've been painful. There was no music. We weren't alone. We didn't plan it, and we were both disheveled. Nothing went according to her idea of perfection, because you realize everything you end up wanting is the last thing you expected.

But it was perfect. God, it was good.

"I'd dreamed of her a lot before we did it," she says. "Sometimes I'd lock my door at night and take off my clothes."

A jolt hits me down low. While she was busy hating me, she was fantasizing about me, too.

She settles her head on my shoulder, her lips tickling my neck. "I wanted to feel my sheets on my skin like I would if I were in bed with her."

Like now. My brothers' laughter carries up the stairs, and I wish I were alone in the house with her, because I'm tired of worrying about being interrupted or caught.

But I can already feel her growing heavy on me, her speech getting sleepy.

"Did you dream about me holding you like this?" I ask her.

She nods. "Except in the dream, you're the boss, and I'm your assistant and we're going to New York on a business trip for the weekend. It was kind of hot for you to abuse your authority on me in bed when I simply bring you papers to sign to your room that night, but then . . ."

"Yes?"

She holds her breath for a moment and then sighs heavily. "I was in a turtleneck on the plane."

I raise my eyebrows.

"A black one," she spits out. "Me. In a black turtleneck. And you made me style my hair in a ponytail like Ariana Grande, and you know I don't look good with my hair pulled away from my face. It was awful."

I laugh, holding her close and shaking. I feel her smile on my neck.

Threading my fingers through her hair, I pull her lips up to mine. "I like ponytails," I tell her, layering our lips. "I need a good handle on you."

She shivers, and we kiss, going in for more and more. Visions

of wrapping her hair around my fist, her on her hands and knees . . .
My stomach swims.

"How about I dream of you tonight, instead?" I ask her. "I'll be
thinking about that dance for the rest of my life."

She nods once, sounding pleased with herself. "Good."

I don't think my brothers ever got lap dances they didn't pay for.
I'm loving my sex life lately.

Gently, I slide out from underneath her. "I'll be back, okay?" I
leave a kiss on her cheekbone. "Get some sleep."

"'Kay."

She tucks a pillow under her head, remaining on her stomach
on top of the covers. I pull on some black cotton shorts, my loose
white tank top a little see-through with my purple bra, but they'll
live with it. I need water.

We need water.

I walk for my door.

"Liv?" she calls.

I stop and turn my head, my hand on the knob.

"I'm sorry," she says.

I shake my head, amused. "Is this becoming a habit for you?
What are you sorry for now?"

"You said you were fifteen," she says. "We knew each other by
then. I wanted you by then."

When I lost my virginity in the back of a car.

"You should've been at that carnival with me," she tells me.

A knot tightens in my throat. I would've loved that. For her to
realize sooner that this was going to be good. We might've been
happier years ago.

But Clay has hurt me as much as anyone else, if not more, so
who's to say anything would've been different. She might've broken
my heart back then, too. It was always a risk.

"Go to sleep," I tell her. "I'll be back."

I leave, closing the door quietly and heading down the stairs, my bare feet picking up the dirt my brothers tracked in. I growl under my breath, knowing who's going to have to clean it up.

"Did you see him limping away?" I hear Trace shout. "I was like bam! I almost broke his damn neck."

I pass them in the living room, grab a cup, and pour some water from the Brita pitcher into the glass.

"I'm glad you didn't," Dallas replied. "We're not done with them."

"You got that right," Iron adds. "And I hope they fucking come over here. God, please."

I step back into the living room, the TV playing *Castlevania* on low volume, while Trace throws up his booted legs onto the coffee table, knocking over empty beer bottles.

They're drunk. But at least they're safe. I walk over and swipe up three bottles by the neck with one hand and dump them in the trash. I plop down on the couch, next to Trace, Iron on his other side and Dallas in the chair.

Where the hell were Macon and Army? Did they know about the fight?

"Where'd you disappear to?" Dallas asks me, picking up his bottle off the end table.

I sip my water. "Were you looking for me?"

He makes a face, and I breathe out a laugh. Of course he wasn't. Probably didn't realize I was gone until just now.

Trace belches and scoffs at the same time. "Just have her out of here before Macon sees her," he says.

I look away, not sure how he knows I have Clay in the bedroom. But before I can respond, headlights flash through the front windows, and we all turn our heads.

In less than five seconds, Macon is barreling through the front door, and my heart leaps into my throat, seeing the rage all over his face.

His eyes dart over the room, his jaw set, and he lands on Iron, rushing over with his arms flying. He swings at Iron, and I drop the glass to the rug, curling into a ball and turning away.

"Macon!" Army shouts, coming through the front door next.

But no one moves.

"You fucking fought?" Macon bellows at him.

I steal a peek, nausea rolling through me as he slaps Iron again and again, and even though Iron is nearly as big, he doesn't dare fight back. He just holds his arms over his head, trying to protect himself.

"You goddamn motherfucker!" Macon growls, and then launches over and swings at Dallas. He shields himself as best he can in the chair.

"Macon!" Trace yells.

"Goddammit!" Macon fires back, slamming Iron over the head again. "Goddammit, you lousy sons of bitches!"

"We had to, Macon," Trace tells him.

"Shut up!" And Macon slaps Trace twice over the skull, as well.

He rises, breathing hard and fists balled as he glares down at his brothers. I look away, my whole body in a knot.

Then Macon kicks the coffee table, sending it toppling over to its side and everything onto the floor.

"You think those fucking little shits will spend a single night in jail with their connected mommies and daddies?" he shouts. "Do you? Huh?"

"Macon . . ." Trace tries, but my brother isn't listening.

"Goddammit," he growls, and storms out of the room, shoving a small table in the foyer to the floor as he passes.

Doors slam, and I look over, seeing Dallas beet red and sweating, but sitting in the chair quiet and frozen. Iron has a cut on his cheek, a thin line of red glimmering in the light. Trace leans his elbows onto his knees, the laughter and pride they felt five minutes ago all gone now.

Dex cries upstairs, and Army turns to go, but he stops and faces us. "You guys got any goddamn idea how much pressure he's under?" He only pauses a moment before he slams his hand into the wall, shouting, "Do you?"

He steps up to Iron, who can't face him eye to eye. He stares at the floor.

"What's he going to have to give them to keep your ass out of jail?" Army grits out. "You ever think of that? You're tying his hands, Iron!"

I blink, reminded that our situation in Sanoa Bay is growing precarious. Or more precarious than I let myself believe.

And Macon hasn't told us.

But he's scared. Very scared. That's very obvious now.

I still sit with my knees up to my chest, but my muscles have relaxed a little as Dex cries.

I almost rise to get him, but Army turns to leave.

He stops once more at the entryway. "You know, we were supposed to grow up someday," he says over his shoulder. "Eventually, we were supposed to grow up, and he wasn't going to have to do everything alone anymore."

I bite the corner of my mouth to stifle the sudden guilt. I want to leave. Dallas has zero attachment here. Trace and Iron are constantly fucking up and putting themselves at risk. Army has a kid who takes precedence.

"He wasn't always going to be the only one to care about this family," Army says, something strangled in his voice. "That's what he thought anyway."

And he leaves, heading up the stairs to his son.

It was a helluva thing, to put this burden on people. To stay someplace you weren't happy. To support people who expect rather than appreciate. To know that a richer life is out there and not have the freedom to seize it.

For a long time, I've known that Macon is just as trapped as I am, but for the first time, I pity him, because he must know this is all for nothing. Even now, he must feel it. Are we worth saving?

I trail back up the stairs, hearing Army in his room playing Van Morrison for Dex, and spare a glance across the hall to Macon's closed door. There's no light coming from underneath, and for the first time, I realize he sleeps in the room where my mother killed herself. Every night he sleeps in there.

I enter my room, my gaze lingering on Clay sleeping soundly on the bed, but I don't go to her. Heading to my desk, I pull open a drawer and take out the chain I wore tonight, slipping the key off it. I turn around and lean back against the chair, watching her again. My insides cripple with the same fear as I look at her. *This will all be for nothing.*

But I'm going to have her for as long as I can.

I stare at it in my palm, the sharp copper glinting in the twinkle lights wrapped around my wrought-iron headboard.

When you're in the eye of the storm, the only way out is through.

You win, Macon. I'll protect the family.

19

Clay

M y hands tremble, a light sweat covering my forehead as my heart thuds.

Just one more time . . .

I can't stop hearing her whisper or feeling her mouth since I left her Saturday morning. God, I'm exhausted. A fog sits in my head, but I'm floating. Blissfully floating.

As soon as I'd woken up, I'd rolled over and needed her. I didn't want to leave Liv's bed until I'd tasted every inch of her, and I couldn't believe I'd had any energy left to go yet again after that, or that I'd gotten laid twice that morning and immediately wanted more. But I had to get home and she had work yesterday, and I almost showed up at Lavinia's just to see her, but I knew I wouldn't be content with just that.

I'm on fire, and I can't wait to see her.

I dig my books out of my locker, taking deep breaths to calm myself down, but it's not working.

"Clay," someone says.

I turn my head, a couple guys shouting down the hall.

The new girl from my math class stands next to me, holding a folder and a book. Her blond hair ends just above the shoulders, straightened with layers. She carries a Hermès backpack that even my mom probably wouldn't treat herself to.

"Sorry, I don't mean to ambush you," she says, smiling, and I notice the subtle pink gloss that plumps her lips. "My name's Chloe. We have Calculus together."

She holds out her hand, and she stands so close the hair on my arm touches the hair on hers. Awareness rises.

"Right." I put my practice clothes in my duffel bag to take home and wash. "You're from Texas. How are you liking it here?"

She shrugs, her navy blue Marymount sweater vest not something we really wear anymore, but I like her retro style. "Still getting used to it."

"Yeah, I know people in Texas are maniacal."

"Maniacal?" she broaches. "About what?"

I pull out my pencil bag. "About being Texan."

She smiles big and nods. "Can't argue there. Texan first. American second."

She doesn't sound southern, though, so she's definitely from the city. A bigger city than St. Carmen probably.

I close my locker and finally meet her eyes, seeing her watch me. I straighten, not sure if I'm imagining a signal or not. I look around for Liv.

"Anyway," she finally goes on, "I just wanted to introduce myself. And see if you need a study partner? Maybe some help with derivatives and integration?"

A study partner? Are those still a thing since Google?

She laughs. "Okay, I need help with derivatives and integration."

Ah. "Well, I'm no genius," I add, "but two heads are better than one, I guess."

But time with a new friend means time I won't have with Liv, and I can't do that right now.

I search my brain for an excuse to get out of it, but then I catch sight of Liv approaching behind Chloe.

She stops at my side, her hair in the two French braids I did. She leans her shoulder into the lockers and pins Chloe with a look. "Excuse us."

Her words are flat, commanding, and void of patience, and I bite back my smile even as a flush rises up to my cheeks.

Chloe's eyes flash to me and then to Liv again, and I turn, spinning the dial on my locker. *Awkward.*

"See you around," I hear her say, and when I turn around again, she's gone.

Facing Liv, I give her a scolding look, but I'm sure she can see my amusement. "She was just saying hi."

"She can wave."

And that look and tone—possessive and jealous and all for me—sets me on fire again.

"Get in the bathroom, Clay," she mumbles as she rubs an imaginary itch on her chin, trying to look covert in the school hallway.

Butterflies swarm my stomach, and slowly, I make my way past the special committees bulletin board and the couple making out. I push through the locker room door and head for the restroom.

I think Liv likes our secret, and although I'm grateful, because I just want her to myself, I have to wonder why she's not putting up more of a fight to go public. I know she said in the hotel that this probably wouldn't turn into a relationship, given that we're both leaving for college in a few months, but something is eating at me. I told her I loved her. I don't know if she forgot, is ignoring it, or she thinks I was lying, but when she said it back, she said she was kidding, so that doesn't count.

She hasn't said it back yet—not really—and I don't know why it hurts a little.

Part of me wants her to fight me on this. To demand we walk down the school hallway hand in hand.

Liv checks the stalls to make sure we're alone and then follows me into one, the door locking and my books dropping to the floor in a flurry right before she grabs me into her arms.

Slipping my hand under her skirt, I press my body into her as she holds my face, and we kiss. I moan, taking advantage of however many seconds we have alone to let her know how good she feels.

Her tongue caresses mine, and I inhale her scent and the taste of her watermelon-flavored lip tint.

"Mine." She pants, rubbing her thumb across my lips. "Until graduation. Okay?"

"Yeah."

She tips my chin back and kisses slowly down my neck. "No one has to know, but you better."

"I know." I nod. "Don't worry, I know."

I'm yours. Just don't stop.

We grind on each other, but whenever I try to go faster, she slows us down, and I'm going insane, because it'll be hours before we can be alone again.

I lift my leg, setting my foot on the toilet seat, and she slips a hand inside her black bandana that she tied around my thigh. Hidden underneath my skirt and from everyone except her who tied it there this morning.

I look down, lifting her wrist and turning it over to see the octopus I drew on the inside, hidden from everyone but me. I drew it there this morning.

We weren't going to get to talk much at school, but we wanted a constant reminder of each other.

"I know why you like octopi," she teases.

"Octopuses," I correct her, moving in for her mouth again. "And there are so many reasons to love them." We nibble and bite. "You know they can detach limbs at will? Like not rip it off but detach it when they're in danger?" I keep kissing her, her warm body making chills spread across my arms. "They all have venom, even just a little, and they have nine brains—each arm can act independently from the others. Isn't that wild?"

"Mm-hmm."

"And they use tools," I tell her. "They have three hearts. They eat their arms when they're bored."

"They can slap eight people at the same time," she adds, and then cuts off my laugh with a kiss that grows deeper and deeper until I'm breathless.

And I can't take it anymore. I wrap my arms around her and bury my face in her neck, just holding her.

Just hugging her.

She stills, and I know she's probably wondering what I'm doing, but I just need to memorize this. I don't know if I really love her, but it's going to hurt to lose her. I know that.

Finally, I pull away and kiss her again, knowing we're pressing our luck.

"Let's go," I tell her.

I pick up my stuff, and we head into the locker room, clearing out our gear for the day. Only a few people remain, and I'm due at my grandmother's in the next fifteen minutes.

I really should put in an appearance at Wind House soon, too. I've only been doing what I absolutely have to if it doesn't involve Liv. But . . . I don't want to lose Mrs. Gates, either. I know I help her, and it feels good.

"What time are you home tonight?" I ask quietly, keeping my eyes peeled despite our row being empty.

She passes me, tosses something into the trash can, then grazes her hand under my skirt as she comes back.

"I'll be in the theater until at least seven," she whispers. "You?"

"I'm free by then," I tell her. "Can I come over?"

She tosses discarded towels into the laundry basket and walks over, stopping behind me and pretending to be interested in something in my locker.

"Or my house?" I ask instead.

My mom knows the Jaegers and she might know about Liv, but she'd never suspect.

"You need sleep," she murmurs. "I need sleep."

"We don't have to do *that*," I clarify, even though she's pressing her body into mine and sending me completely different signals. "We can sleep. We can do anything. I don't care. I just want to be somewhere where I can touch you."

We both look around, seeing the coast is clear, and her nose brushes my cheek, her warm, fantastic breath sending chills down my spine.

"Pick me up from here at seven thirty," she says.

"I'll be here."

Her eyes meet mine as her hand slips under my shirt, caressing my stomach. I can see the war going on in her head. The hesitation.

"I'll be here," I say again.

I won't let her down again.

She dives in again, inhales me, and then kisses my temple. "Okay."

Something moves behind us, and we both jerk our heads, seeing Coomer frozen midstep between the rows of lockers, her clipboard about to spill out of her hand.

Her mouth hangs open, gaping at us, and Liv backs up, heat seeping out of every pore on my body. How long has she been standing there?

But our coach just blinks, clears her throat, and purses her lips to hide her smile. "Well, that makes a lot more sense now," she mumbles, and keeps walking.

I close my eyes, mortified, not so much out of fear, but because she's well aware I've acted like I hated Liv for nearly the past four years.

Jesus.

"She won't say anything," Liv tells me.

"I know."

But that was close. It could've easily been another student.

Liv takes her things and walks past me. "See you later. And if you stand me up again, I'm going to kill you, okay?"

"Understood."

She leaves, and I bite my bottom lip, because there's just something about how even her threats are a turn-on.

I shake my head clear. *But yeah, I won't stand her up. She'd really kill me.*

C lay?"

I twist my head, seeing my mom through the open passenger side window of her white Rover. Her huge cat-eye sunglasses make her look like a movie star sunbathing on a yacht in Monaco.

Or a big bug. I'm still not sure.

I move toward her, away from my car. "What are you doing here?" I ask. "I have my car."

School let out eight minutes ago, and the parking lot swarms with students trying to make their getaway.

But my mother tells me, "I'll bring you back for it."

I shift on my feet, releasing a sigh. I want my car, because I want to leave Mimi's when I'm ready.

Mom cocks her head. "I've barely seen you in days. Get in."

I click the key fob, locking my car again as I walk to the Rover. Opening the door, I climb in and drop my bag to the floor. We'll be back way before seven thirty. My mom will probably be ready to escape Mimi long before I am.

She pulls out of the parking lot, taking a left onto the quiet street, and I take out my sunglasses, shielding myself against the afternoon sun.

The silence consumes the car, and I can almost hear her breathing it's so quiet. I glance at the radio, wishing she'd turn it on, but I know if I turn it on it will be playing the audiobook of *The Giver* that she and my brother were listening to before he died. My mother can't bear to hear it, but she won't listen to anything else. That would be like moving on.

"So, I spoke to Cara," she finally says. "She's quite concerned because Krisjen didn't come home Friday night."

I turn my eyes out the window. *The night of the fight* . . . And I don't think she was with Milo.

"She probably wasn't worried," my mom adds, "just that Krisjen wasn't there to make breakfast for Marshall and Paisleigh this morning."

Krisjen's dad left them for another woman about a year ago, and her mom is in a rut she can't seem to pull herself out of. Not that the marriage had been faithful on either side, but Cara enjoyed her position through the marriage and maintained it for appearances. Without her husband and being Mrs. Lachlan Conroy III anymore, she's now stuck with a family she no longer wants.

Krisjen is the oldest, and while she never talks about it, I know she's raising her siblings while her mother tries to chase down another husband.

"I was also concerned," my mother says, "considering you were supposed to be sleeping over at her house that night."

I don't reply.

The silence stretches, and I hear my mother exhale. "You know, you scare me, Clay."

Her tone is soft. She's not yelling.

"I admire how you don't rush to cover your tracks when caught," she tells me, "and I appreciate you not wasting my time with another lie, but it's also off-putting." She hesitates. "It means you don't care if I find out."

I am scared, and I do care if she finds out. I won't tell her the truth, though. I just won't say anything.

"It's frightening when you realize you've lost control of your child."

But it's not like that. If I tell her about Liv, she'll ruin it. I just want to enjoy it for a while before the stress.

"Some days I still feel your age," she tells me. "And I know even less about what I'm doing than I did the day before. You think you'll reach an age where you finally know your place in the world, but nothing ever gets easier."

I look at her out of the corner of my eye, her lips pursed as she stares at the road, her beautiful clothes and jewelry the image of perfection. Not a blemish. Barely a wrinkle. Not a single dry patch on her hands or a pore on her face visible from where I sit. I want to ask her about the pregnancy. I want to know if it was my father's. I want the stalemate in our lives to end.

But I don't want the unknown, either. Not all change is good.

So I stay quiet.

She clears her throat. "You're being safe, right?" she asks, seemingly resolved to the fact that I'm sleeping with someone and now wants to make sure I'm not an embarrassment. "We've had this talk. I'm not raising any more babies. Don't be careless."

"I know."

I don't know if I'm relieved that she hasn't caught my scent yet or disappointed. She thinks I'm sleeping with Callum. I wish I could tell her the truth. I want to tell someone about this excitement I feel every time I look at Liv. I want to share it with someone.

"Do you want to talk about it?" she broaches all of a sudden.

I squeeze my eyes shut behind my glasses, almost breaking into a laugh because the words are on the tip of my tongue.

When I don't respond, she slows the car, and I turn, watching her pull over to the curb on quiet Levinson Lane, under the canopy of some Spanish moss.

God, just go. Please.

She puts the car in park, and I feel her twist her body toward me to speak. "Sex is a big deal," she says, "no matter all the images you see on TV and in movies that try to prove otherwise."

Yes, yes. We've had this talk. Years ago. *Just go.*

"Sex isn't just two people being physical, Clay. Young women, especially, can get attached and emotionally invested very quickly. It's important we feel connected to the people we're physical with."

Mm-hmm. I nod.

"And it's very easy to be hurt when we believe they feel the same and we find out they don't," she continues.

"You don't need to worry," I tell her, gesturing to the road ahead. "Can we go now?"

I don't look at her, but I can tell she's studying me. "I want to know things, okay? If you're excited and falling in love, I want you to know you can talk to me and share it with me."

My jaw flexes, my throat swelling.

"Is he making you happy?" she asks.

I draw in a breath. *Jesus.*

"Is he gentle? Does he make it special?"

I bite the corner of my mouth. I want to tell her how good Olivia Jaeger feels. *Yes, Mom. She's gentle. And I love it when she's not gentle, too. She makes it special. I don't want to be anywhere else when I'm with her.*

She threads a lock of my hair through her fingers. "You're stunning, you know? Anyone would be lucky to have you."

As long as it's a young man, right?

I open my mouth to say it. To tell her it's a girl and not a boy, and maybe I'll lie and tell her I'm just experimenting. I mean, maybe I am.

I could tell her Liv means nothing and we don't date, but I like what she does to my body and it's nothing to worry about. But I catch sight of my brother's picture hanging on the rearview mirror, and I close my mouth again.

One kid dead. Another who's . . . not normal.

Yeah, her whole world will fall apart. She's hanging on by a thread as it is. My family is hanging on by a thread. I don't want to put something out there that I can't take back.

"It's okay, Mom," I whisper. "Just go."

She stares at me.

"I'm not going to get pregnant," I blurt out. "I promise."

I know she's hurt I won't talk to her, but if she knew, she'd wish she didn't.

After a moment, she sits back in her seat and pulls away from the curb, driving us to my grandmother's.

My mother won't eat after five o'clock, so these dinners with my grandmother happen early in the afternoon and every week now, given that I'm so close to the ball and getting my ducks in a row for college. Mimi likes to be kept abreast of *everything*.

Tucker opens the front door before my mother has a chance to and steps aside for us to enter. I swipe my phone from my school bag before he has a chance to take it from me, and then I follow my mom into the foyer.

"Good afternoon," I hear Mimi say.

My mom embraces her, their lips not quite touching each other's skin as I shiver in the cold marble room. I look around, inhaling the scent of talcum powder and lavender that always pervades this house, like my grandmother is ninety when she's only sixty-five.

The white walls are only discernible from the white floors by the streaks of gray in the stone under my feet. I like white, but this house is like 1980s white—white wood with gold fixtures, splashes of yellow, and beveled mirrors where the frames are also mirrors. I'm pretty sure it's supposed to look Art Deco, but it just looks stupid.

"Hi, Mimi." I smile, mimicking my mother and embracing her with a kissing sound.

"Oh, you're getting so pretty," she coos.

She says that every time. *Getting* pretty. Not quite there, but *getting* there.

We walk toward the dining room, down a long hallway, interrupted sporadically with doors on one side and a wall of photos on the other. Black-and-white portraits from years ago, childhood photos, some of my brother and me, my cousins, Easter Sundays, family picnics on the lawn, and my mother—at sixteen at her ball, on the arm of my father as he stands next to her in a tux, his chin high and a loaded smile on his lips. I pause as my mom and grandmother head in to supper.

My parents looked so young.

They *were* young, I guess. I can't help but wonder what was going through their heads back then. How ready they were to live. How excited they were to dream about the future—vacations, their home, laughing, family, holding each other . . . The years spread out before them, and it was only going to be gold, right?

Did they know they were going to do bad things to each other?

Would they go back and do it again?

I walk into the dining room, Tucker holding my chair out for me.

"Thank you." I sit down.

Taking my napkin, I pull it off the ring, but my mother stops me. "Clay."

I stop, realizing myself. I set my napkin down and look to my grandmother. She gives me a look, but it has a hint of a smile. *Rookie mistake, Clay.* When a guest at dinner, take your cues from your host. I wasn't supposed to lay my napkin in my lap until she'd done it.

She holds out her hand, and I know what she wants. I set my phone in her palm, and she places it on the small tray Tucker holds out next to her.

We start with salad, a citrusy vinaigrette dressing gleaming over the arugula.

"The senior sleepover is happening soon, right?" Mimi asks. "Have you RSVP'd with Omega Chi at Wake Forest?"

I sip my water, setting it back down. "Mm, yes."

I feel my mom's eyes, and I look at her, getting the signal. I straighten and smile, giving Mimi my full attention.

"Yes, Mimi," I say more clearly. "Dues are paid, and I've already reached out to some of the other attendees via social media to get a rapport going."

"Social media . . ."

"It's the standard of the times," I tease, finishing up the small serving of greens.

But she waves me off, picking up her glass. "Oh, I know. I just lament the days of privacy and being able to make mistakes without an audience."

I hold back my eye roll and smile wider. Old people say things like that a lot, as if the downfall of society started with Facebook.

"That reminds me," Mimi pipes up again, eyeing my mother, "she needs to delete her social media history, and I want access to any other secret accounts, Clay." She pins me with a look. "Don't think we're not aware they exist."

My shoulders slump, but I put them back again, recovering. I'm not giving her my hidden profiles. She's the one who told me I could have secrets.

"I've been reading articles," she tells my mom as Tucker brings the next course. "And the experts suggest deleting your history every once in a while to spare any embarrassment down the road. People get fired over a bad post from eight years ago."

I groan inwardly. I wish my grandmother wasn't so proactive.

"You need to think of your future," she points out to me. "Your husband and children who could be caught in the crossfire of something stupid you said at this age."

My mother nods, but Mimi cuts her off. "I would suggest it for you, as well."

My mom stills, swallowing her retort with her glass of water. I almost snort. One of the reasons I love coming to these dinners is just to see my mom still under her own mother's thumb just like I'm under hers.

But then I see myself twenty years from now in my mom's seat and her in her mother's, my daughter sitting where I am. Every woman at this table is carrying a secret. What will my daughter be hiding?

"The foie gras," my mom says to Tucker. "Amazing."

"I'll tell Peggy."

His wife is the chef, but I haven't eaten a bite. This dish is inhumane, and I know my grandmother is challenging me on purpose.

"I have dresses in the den for you to try on for the ball," she says, cutting into the duck.

My mom coughs, swallowing a sip of water to clear her throat. "Mama, we have her dress."

But Mimi just looks at me.

Fuuuuuuuuuck.

My mom sighs. "What did you do to it, Clay?"

How did my grandmother find out? I'm tempted to throw Liv under the bus here, but I'm filled with a sudden desire to protect her at all costs.

I simply remain silent, knowing there's nothing my mother will do to hold me accountable.

A smirk curls Mimi's mouth as she lifts her glass to her lips and locks eyes with my mother again. "I never would've guessed one child would be harder than four," she taunts.

My mother's jaw flexes, she and her three siblings far less trouble than one little ol' me, and I can feel every muscle in her body tighten from here.

Reaching my hand under the table, I slide it under my skirt and wrap my fist around the bandana, exhaling.

Three hours and fourteen minutes later, I grab my phone off the tray in the dining room and pull my saddle shoes back on as I hop out the front door. My shoelaces drag on the ground, and I open up the Uber app to escape here while they think I'm off getting something from my mom's car. The dinner lasted a full hour more with the dessert and the practice interview questions for Omega Chi. Then we tried on dresses, and I just let my mother—through the approval of Mimi, of course—choose the strapless A-line charmeuse with the chiffon draping. Actually, quite pretty, but I still felt like a moron in it.

Spotting Mimi's rosebushes, I quickly bend a stem back and forth, breaking it off as I avoid the thorns.

"Young man?" I hear Peggy call out.

I lift my head, realizing the cook is on the balcony over top of me. I slink back so she can't see and look out into the driveway, where Trace Jaeger loads up a rusty Ford truck. He's in jeans and covered in sweat.

"Put your shirt on!" she scolds him.

"Aw, baby," he whines, and my eyes go wide.

"Now, I said!"

"But you're so hot, it's making me hot." He holds out his hands, looking like Romeo serenading Juliet. "Look at this, I'm drenched!"

I cover my mouth to quiet my laugh. The butler's wife not only cooks, but she practically raised my mom, aunts, and uncles. She also served as a nurse in the Navy for five years. She isn't about the bullshit.

"You rascal!" she chides.

"Sugar plum," he coos, feigning a condescending tone but smiling as he does it.

"Caveman!"

"Love bug!"

"Ape!"

"Sweetie, honey pie!"

I snort, nearly dying.

"Shameless hooligan!" she cries.

"Buttercup."

"Ugh!"

Then I hear a door slam, and I let a laugh escape. I've never seen anyone handle her like that.

"You know . . ." I head out from under the balcony and across the driveway toward him. "One of these days she's going to decide your hedge sculptures aren't worth it and have you fired."

"And quickly realize her mistake." He pulls out his shirt but uses it to wipe his back dry. "She loves me."

Sure. I look over the load of tools in his truck bed, everything he needed for landscaping today. The rest of the crew is already gone.

"Can you give me a ride back to school?" I ask, glancing over my shoulder at the house. "Like quickly?"

Before I'm caught and before I'm late. It's after seven already.

He opens the door for me, and I hop in, the smell of rust and dirt immediately hitting me.

But I pull the door closed and wait for him to round the truck to the driver's side.

The ripped imitation leather pinches the backs of my thighs, and I find some footing through the takeout bags and empty soda cans on the floor.

Trace gets in, starts the truck, and turns up the radio, peeling out of the driveway like he's unaware he has to stop and wait for the gate to open.

As soon as we're through, he rolls down the window, and I do the same, the wind blowing through the cab.

"So you want me to put my shirt on, too?" he asks.

I turn my eyes on him, not seeing a shirt in sight, so I don't know how he's going to do that.

"Didn't even notice, did you?" he teases, lighting a cigarette. "I guess I don't have to worry that you're faking it with my sister."

Smoke puffs up as the end burns orange, and I kind of want to ask him for one.

"I notice men." I wave the air, clearing the smoke. "Your sweat and stench, however, outweigh any attraction."

"I can shower." He eyes me. "Wanna help?"

Help him shower? "What are you doing?" I ask. My ire perks up that he'd make a pass when he knows I'm seeing Liv. I didn't peg him for a shitty brother.

"I don't trust you," he tells me, turning down the music and speeding down the road. "I think you'll hurt her. I think you'll get her into a situation that will devastate her."

He thinks he knows me.

"She acts tough, but everyone's the same," he goes on. "They just want someone to love, and when a Jaeger gets attached, it's as quick as flipping a switch, Clay. It'll be sudden, and she won't be able to turn it off."

A flutter hits my heart, and I'm surprised at myself. I don't feel that from Liv, but the way he describes it, I really want to.

"I don't want to hurt her," I say.

"But you hide her."

I frown. Everyone gets hurt by love at some point. It's not my intention, but who knows where the next few weeks will take us. I just want to be here. Today. Now. With her. The future is uncertain. Why worry about it?

"We're none of your business," I tell him.

"If I decide it's my business, it's my business." His tone is deep and suddenly biting. "And I'm the nice one, so it would be wise to have this conversation with me and not one of the others."

"We're keeping it quiet," I explain as if he's entitled to that. "We're going off to different schools in the fall, and we don't want others distracting us from what time we have together. Liv agreed."

"Well, what was she supposed to say? The alternative was

demanding you out yourself, which you never would have agreed to, so she took the scraps she could get." He takes a drag of his cigarette. "She's used to that."

That's not true. Why would he say that? When the choice was either being with someone else—Megan or that ex at the lighthouse—she chose to be with me, knowing I could be using her and I might end up hurting her? It doesn't make sense.

"Liv is very outspoken," I point out. "She would've raised her concerns. She wouldn't have sacrificed her pride to be a booty call, if it was a problem."

"A booty call is better than a long time of nothing," he fires back. "You get tired of being alone."

So he's saying she chose sneaking around with me over a solid relationship because . . .

Because she likes me. A lot.

That's what he's worried about. How much she's going to tolerate from me just to have a piece.

Liv . . . While guilt tugs at me that I'm not broadcasting her to the world, I'm a little happy. She really likes me.

"You should take her on a date," Trace adds. "You should hold her hand."

I'd love to go anywhere with her. Go everywhere.

But when Callum touches me in public, no one bats an eye. We could be standing on the sidewalk in front of the movie theater, but I can't stand on the sidewalk in front of the movie theater with my hands on Liv's waist or my body pressed to hers. It would be a scene. A statement.

And every minute I was out with her, I'd be worrying about everyone looking at us, judging us, talking about us, and I wouldn't be thinking about her or us. I would only be thinking about that.

"I hate the way things are," I tell him, "but I'm afraid everything will change. I can't tell my parents I'm bi . . . bisexual. I can barely even say the word. And what if I'm not? What if it's just Liv? There would be no going back. What if I'm confused? What if I'm wrong? I . . ."

I trail off, my panic evident, but it feels kind of good to let it out. To talk to someone about it other than Liv.

Trace nods. "You shouldn't tell them you're bisexual, Clay," he says. "You're not."

Huh?

"I mean, some people are," he assures me. "But I've also learned that some people will simply *say* they're bisexual rather than gay because they feel it's easier on their families."

I stare at him, his words tumbling around in my head.

"It softens the blow," he explains. "'Look, Mom and Dad. Part of me is still normal. I might still marry a guy, have babies, and not completely fucking embarrass you someday.'" He turns to me. "You strike me as the type of person who would give up as little as possible about herself to maintain the status quo," he says. "The one who will sacrifice the bare minimum to get what she wants but nothing more."

I open my mouth to retort, but I clamp it shut again and turn my eyes out the window.

We don't speak again, and he drops me off at the school a little after seven thirty. I see my truck still in the parking lot, and I head up the stairs in a kind of daze, my head still back in the cab of the truck with him.

He's wrong. I'll sacrifice what I have to in order to keep her mouth on mine. The alternative is too hard to consider.

I run my fingers through my hair, untangling what the wind did to it, and dig in my bag for some lip gloss. Smoothing out my hair and brushing my hands down my clothes, I enter the theater, hearing voices immediately.

"Let me be taken, let me be put to death!" someone cries.

I stand at the back of the theater in the dark, and I can't help but smile at the scene on the stage. The set looks like a wintery New York evening if New York had royalty and a strictly black option for clothing. Cathedral arches adorn the backdrop along with silver skyscrapers reaching up into the night. Clouds float past the full moon, and a stone mansion in ruins sits in the middle.

Liv is dressed in a long, black coat, fitted at the waist, her face chalk white and her hair in a wild ponytail. Smoky black surrounds her eyes, and I grip the back of a chair, because she's so beautiful my knees feel weak.

"I am content, so thou wilt have it so, I'll say yon gray is not the morning's eye; 'tis but the pale reflex of Cynthia's brow," Romeo drones on, played by Clarke Tillerson in a way that I know I'd be asleep if I didn't have Liv to look at.

Snow falls from above, and this must be one of the final dress rehearsals. Or they're working on a scene that needs extra time, because I'm pretty sure Mercutio's understudy isn't in the bedroom scene.

"Nor that is not the lark, whose notes do beat."

"Stop!"

Lambert comes up, the actors turning to receive direction, and Liv turns my way. I raise my hand to wave, but she keeps turning, not seeing me.

I put my hand down as she crosses her arms, and I don't like the tension I see in her body. What's wrong?

Ms. Lambert speaks quietly and closely to Clarke as Juliet sits on the bed, hugging her knees to her body and inspecting her fingernails. Everyone looks worn out. Some pace, some look bored as hell, and some are slouched in the theater seats, passed out.

Voices rise between Lambert and Romeo, and they're starting to talk with their hands, their body language aggravated.

"Let me be taken," someone calls out.

I find Liv as everyone turns toward her voice, and I see her stare at Juliet.

She runs and jumps up on the bed, Juliet falling back onto her hands, a shocked smile on her face.

"Let me be put to death!" Liv shouts, standing over her. "I am content, so thou wilt have it so."

My heart creeps up my throat, and slowly, I move down the aisle, taking her in.

Liv crouches down, one black boot over Juliet's body, her black coat spilling around them as she holds her beloved's face. For once, Lizbeth Mercier, who plays Juliet, looks actually speechless as she's carried away in Liv's gaze.

"I'll say yon gray is not the morning's eye," Liv tells her, caressing the girl's cheeks, her words so gentle and her eyes searching her love's. "'Tis but the pale reflex of Cynthia's brow."

She doesn't take her eyes off Juliet, so close, and I feel like she's holding me. Everyone watches. "Nor that is not the lark, whose notes do beat, the vaulty heaven so high above our heads."

Liv whispers into her temple, her microphone brushing the girl's skin, "I have more care to stay than will to go."

And my heart shudders, feeling the words, because I know what her breath feels like.

And her mouth dips close, taunting the corner of Lizbeth's. I don't think the girl breathes.

In one fell swoop, Romeo comes down on top of the girl, sending them both to the bed, and Lizbeth yelps, letting out an excited laugh, while Romeo smiles devilishly. "Come, death, and welcome!" Liv taunts playfully. "Juliet wills it so. How is't, my soul?" She presses their foreheads together. "Let's talk; it is not day."

And the girl smiles, captivated and wanting to be nowhere but with her Romeo.

Olivia's perfect. Why have they not given her the lead in anything all these years?

Everyone stands quiet, and after a moment, the curtain over

Liv's mind seems to close again, and she sits up, her demeanor serious once again.

"See, Clarke?" Lizbeth props herself up on her elbows, looking around Liv. "Just like that."

I laugh to myself, seeing him shifting uneasily.

Lambert claps. "Okay, everyone! Tomorrow. Be here at three!"

Everyone starts to gather their things, chatter filling the room, and I watch as Liv doesn't come down to me but disappears backstage.

She had to have seen me. I check my phone, seeing I'm twenty minutes late.

I carry the rose, climbing the stairs, and veer behind the curtain and down another small set of stairs. I find Liv in a dressing room with the door open as she sits on a stool.

I hover at the door. "I brought you something to remind you of me."

I hold the rose, and she doesn't look right away, but after a moment, she glances up.

She eyes the rose, looking sad, and my heart pounds. "Pink?" she asks.

I step into the room, closing the door and stopping in front of her. I lower myself to the floor and to my knees. "Thorns."

I set the flower on her dressing table and lay my head on her lap, hoping she forgives me. I'm late, and I promised her I wouldn't be.

"I'm full of thorns," I say softly. "But there are things about me that I hope are worth it."

After a few seconds, I feel her hand in my hair. "I hate Romeo," she says, stroking my scalp. "But I'm starting to understand him. Fuck you for that, Clay."

I half smile, because I know she's bitter, because she's cracking, and I want that. I want what Trace promised. That the switch would flip, and she'd be mine.

I peel up her sleeve and gaze at the octopus on the inside of her wrist. "This is mine." I smooth my thumb over the ink. "Forever mine. My piece of you." And then in a murmur, "'Within this inch . . . I'm free.'"

This patch of skin won't be anyone else's ever. It'll be mine when she marries someone else. When she's eighty. It's all I really have of her.

I kiss her wrist and tip my head up as she puts one of the costume hats on my head, a top hat like the one in her room.

She regards me, the wheels turning in her head, but before I can ask what she's thinking, she pinches my chin and leans down.

Her breath brushes my lips, and I can almost taste her.

"Let's go get you naked," she whispers.

20

Olivia

Can't we just go park somewhere? Or go to my house like she suggested?

What was I thinking?

I gaze out the passenger side window, concentrating on keeping my hands on my lap instead of fidgeting, because all of these houses remind me of that feeling I've been fighting since I was a kid. That there are places I don't belong.

Smooth roads void of any puddles or potholes. Gates and trimmed hedges.

White houses.

White Rovers.

Lots of white people who will take one look at my last name and think I'm here to clean, cook, or rob something.

I look over at Clay, wishing she would've let me drive so I wouldn't feel so vulnerable right now with nothing to do, but then I catch sight of her toned, tanned thighs peeking out of her skirt, and I exhale, remembering. *Yeah, that's what I was thinking.* I shake my head at myself.

She pulls into her driveway, and I look out at the oaks lining the circle, a fountain spilling water in the center. I scan the windows for lights.

Everything appears dark, except for the gaslit lanterns—one on each side of the front door and two more posted farther down the exterior to the left and right. I can't see the third floor from inside the car, though.

Clay parks and climbs out.

"Are your parents home?" I ask, leaving my school bag in the car and following her.

"My dad, probably not." She carries her bag, with her keys out as we head for the front door. "My mom won't bother us."

She unlocks the door and steps inside, lights immediately illuminating without Clay doing anything. I hesitate a moment as she heads for the small entryway table and drops her keys into a blue glass bowl.

"It doesn't look like she's home yet," Clay says. "Her keys aren't here."

The hair on my arms rises, feeling the air-conditioning escaping as I inhale the scent of new things.

Or really the scent of almost nothing. Like how a furniture store smells. Or a library or a car dealership. Like places where people don't live.

My house smells like wet wood, the spiced rum Trace spilled all over the floor last week, and last night's spaghetti.

I step inside, closing the door behind me, and hit the sensor on the wall, the lights dimming again. I feel a little safer in the dark. Just like Clay.

She spins around, dropping her bag to the floor, and I approach her, the only warm thing in this house.

"Are you hungry?" she asks.

The crystals of the chandelier clink overhead as the air circulates, and the stairwell looms behind her, both rooms on either side of the center hall dark, except for the moonlight streaming through the sheer curtains.

She drops her eyes, and I swear I see a blush.

"My mom always keeps so much food in the fridge," she laughs, sounding nervous, "I don't know why. She barely eats, and my dad's hardly here."

I don't want food.

"I want to see your room," I tell her.

I'm pretty sure she saw mine even before I invited her in. I can't imagine she resisted the urge at Night Tide.

I'll feel safer behind a closed door. Hopefully she doesn't have a chandelier in there, too, and I can forget that I'm in the house of one of St. Carmen's most influential families.

I cock my head, watching her. *But then* . . . I kind of like that I'm here. In the house of one of St. Carmen's most influential families.

About to fuck their daughter.

I keep my smile to myself, loving that she's suddenly nervous like it's our first time.

Turning, she rounds the table and heads up the stairs, my eyes memorizing her body as I follow. When we reach the top, she veers left, and we head down a hallway, over hardwood floors decorated with white Persian runners and portraits on the walls in silver frames. Two blond kids on a beach, building a sandcastle. A little boy on her dad's shoulder as Clay and her mom cheer next to him at a Florida State game. The two kids making faces for the camera under the water in a pool.

Clay stops at the first door on the right, but I'm already staring ahead at the first door on the left, several feet farther down the hall. Dark blue, wooden letters that read HENRY hang on the door above a tin sign warning of GAMER AT PLAY—DO NOT DISTURB, NO GIRLS ALLOWED (EXCEPT MOM).

She opens her door, but I tip my head toward her brother's room. "Show me."

She shifts, looking uneasy, but doesn't budge.

I study her. "When's the last time you were in there?"

"I don't go in there."

I know I shouldn't press it. What happened to Clay is devastating and personal, but something pushes me toward her brother's room, because I want more between us.

"No, just . . ." She calls, running up to catch me. "Another time, okay? Don't ruin this. Don't ruin tonight."

"You were in *my* brother's room," I point out.

I saw the video. Everyone saw it. Macon wasn't as livid as the rest of my brothers, though, because Macon doesn't look for fights with frilly teenage girls who are just trying to get famous.

"Open the door, Clay."

What happened to her brother had a profound impact on her. And on me, as it would turn out. I need this piece of her.

She opens the door, probably because she knows I'll leave if she doesn't.

I step inside, the room dim but the curtains open and shining moonlight on the floor. I walk into the room, keeping the lamps off and my feet gentle, as if too hard a step will be disrespectful.

His twin bed sits made without a single wrinkle on the blue duvet cover, the carpet beige, but everything else matches the bedspread. Light blue walls with white trim. Blue curtains. Bookshelves, posters, a desk with art supplies, and model cars and planes sit on shelves. A PS4 sits on a table under a flatscreen on the wall, and a gumball machine sits on top of his dresser, still half full. A picture of him and some friends, or cousins maybe, stands next to it, all of them holding a papier-mâché planet they made in class or in summer camp. I lean in close, seeing the same smile on him that I see on Clay sometimes.

"He looked like he was going to be Jensen Ackles someday," she says, sadness in her voice.

I look over, see that she's still hovering in the doorway, leaning against the frame.

"He was a cute kid," I tell her.

"Dynamite personality, too." She sighs, smiling and crossing her arms. "He would draw spiders on the toilet paper and replace my yogurt with mayo."

I walk over toward the window, checking out his view. "And what did you do to deserve that?" I tease.

As if he was the instigator. If I know Clay at all, he was simply retaliating.

"I may have replaced the filling in his Oreos with toothpaste," she says.

I grin.

The room is spotless. Tidy, clean, not a speck of dust. Someone cleans in here regularly, and I'm guessing it's the one room Clay's mom doesn't let anyone touch but herself.

"You loved him a lot."

"I didn't realize how much." She nods. "He was annoying and we fought a lot, but when he got sick, I almost couldn't breathe." I hear the tears thicken her voice. "It wasn't fair for him to go through that. I just wanted it to stop."

There's no sign of his illness in this room. No medical equipment. No prescriptions. I have no idea if he died at home or passed in the hospital, but I can bet the family was with him every hour.

Clay's breathing shakes, and I see her trying to hold back the tears. I walk over, taking her face in my hands.

"Why were you so patient with me?" she whispers. "So tolerant? I didn't deserve it."

I lean in, her silky hair brushing the backs of my hands. "Happy people don't fixate on things they hate," I explain. "They move on. I knew it was coming from somewhere, Clay." I glide my hands down her body and circle her waist as we hold each other, and I stare into her eyes. "It doesn't matter how much money we have or don't have or how stable our home is. Anyone can have problems."

I never thought Clay's life was gold just because she's rich and beautiful. Happy people don't act how she did.

She kept up the façade for a long time, though. Resisting me.

"Why did you finally let it happen?" I ask, nearly brushing her nose and gazing at her mouth, which I want so badly.

She kisses me softly. "Because for four years, if I wasn't sleeping, I was thinking of you," she murmurs. "And even then sometimes in my dreams."

Her mouth lingers on my cheek, and I know now what the tattoo means. The one on the inside of her finger and what she meant at the theater earlier when she didn't think I heard her. *Within this inch, I'm free.*

It's a paraphrase of a quote from *V for Vendetta*. A part of us that we'll never sell—a small piece we keep to ourselves and covet and hold tightly for dear life, because it's the only place inside us we truly live.

Just an inch. But it's ours.

"I wanted to be alone with you and touch you and smell you and talk to you with every part of my body, except my voice," she says.

My eyelids flutter closed, and I understand. After years of her treatment, my pride is dented, because I should've told her to go to hell, but . . . There was always more. Almost as if I knew we'd be here eventually.

She bites my jaw gently, the heat and wet of her mouth sending tingles spiraling down to my stomach.

"Do you hear that?" she asks. And then kisses me where she bit. "And that?"

I nod. *I hear you.*

"Take me to your room," I tell her.

"You should call home." She continues to peck on my jaw. "Tell them you won't be home tonight."

"Later."

Macon tracks my phone, so he never really worries.

She pulls me, backing up toward her bedroom as I pull the door closed behind me and follow. Her mouth covers mine, her moans sinking down my throat as we nearly trip over our feet.

I work my ponytail out, my long locks falling down around me, and Clay pushes me up against her desk, closing her door and locking it.

"You're so beautiful." She kisses me again and again, lifting my shirt over my head. "Especially onstage. God, you blew my mind tonight. I loved watching you."

We keep the lights off, and I forget to even look around to see if my predictions of either a white or pink color scheme are correct.

"I know someday everyone will be watching you," she says, biting my ear. "As you play . . ." She pauses, thinking. "Mad Max surrendering to the animal inside you as you navigate the barren wasteland of Earth to avenge the death of your wife and child."

I laugh, but she's kissing and biting everything—my ear, my neck—and my head drops back, my eyes closing.

"Or maybe you'll be her love interest," Clay teases. "A damsel in distress?"

Never. I'm always in charge.

But then I hear a click and feel something cold and sharp between my legs.

I go still, a jolt of surprise hitting me. *Maybe I'm not always in charge, after all.* "Clay?"

And just then, I register my blade missing from where it was hooked onto my skirt.

She holds it drawn, between my legs, as she glides her mouth up my neck and paws my breast with her other hand.

"You're so pretty, Liv," she breathes out. "You know you're never getting away from me, right?"

Clay Collins presses her body into mine, kneading me—squeezing what's hers—and inhaling my scent as she nibbles my neck.

"Say, 'Yes, I know,'" she orders me.

"Yes."

Holding the knife, she peels down my underwear. "You know you're mine. Say yes."

"Yes."

My knees quiver, and I'm turned on but a little scared, too, because her voice is more of a warning than a comfort. Like no matter how much I think I'll stand up for myself and fight back, she'll always have power over me.

Like she knows that she'll be Mrs. Ames someday, and I'll be working for her, part of my job taking place in her bed when her husband's not around.

"Clay . . ."

But she releases my breast and grips my neck, instead. I gasp. "You're never getting away from me, Jaeger," she whispers, and drags her tongue across my collarbone to my shoulder where she bites my bra strap. "Take it off."

And at the moment, I want nothing more than to do everything she tells me to. I reach behind me and unhook my bra, the cool air caressing my nipples, and Clay's warm hand covering one.

But before I know what's happening, she's swiping her arm across her desktop, sending everything crashing to the floor and bending me over the top of it.

I plant my hands on the desk on both sides of my head, sucking in air like I can't catch my breath. She yanks my underwear, tearing them from my body, and then she lifts my skirt and spreads my legs.

"Clay . . ." I moan.

But her fist is in my hair, her hand palms my breast, and her mouth trails up and down my back, sucking, kissing, and biting like she's starved.

I feel a flood of warmth between my legs as she presses into my ass.

"God, what are you doing?" The world tips sideways, and I close my eyes. "I'm so wet for you."

"You're never getting away from me," she says again.

I know, baby. I know. God, what is she doing to me? Just when I think I'm in control and I have a handle on her, she sweeps me away.

She rises, pulling me up with her, and whispers in my ear. "I love these." She squeezes my breast, moving from one to the other as she kisses my shoulder. "They feel so good."

I kiss her, tasting her with my tongue again and again.

But then I spot something on the floor, something she'd pushed off her desk. "You got film in that camera?" I ask.

She follows my gaze, seeing her vintage Edixa 35mm on the floor.

I got a video of her. Fair is fair, I guess.

"Take my picture," I tell her.

A gleam hits her eyes, and she walks over and picks it up, blowing on the lens before adjusting the settings.

I lean over the desk again, propping myself up with my hands and leaving my skirt hiked up in the back where she left it. I push up on my tiptoes and let a little hair fall in my eyes as she starts some music: "Take Me to the River." When she looks up again, her chest caves and she almost drops the camera.

"You okay?" I tease.

A lump moves up and down her throat as she takes in the sight of me, but slowly she raises the camera to her face.

The camera clicks, and I almost smile at the thrill that runs through me. It feels like a touch, having your picture taken.

Tipping my chin down, I look at her as she snaps shot after shot, moving around my body and getting different angles. She gets a shot or two in the front and then moves behind me, diving in for a really naughty one I certainly hope she knows how to develop herself, because Walmart won't touch these photos.

I peer at her over my shoulder as she snaps more shots, and then I turn around, scooting up onto the desktop and slowly dragging my skirt up my thighs. I tease her as she watches and waits, knowing I don't have anything on underneath as the camera falls away from her face and she's captivated.

I don't go all the way. I smile, pulling my skirt back down, but she drops the camera onto the carpet and rushes me all of a sudden. Gripping me under my arms and pulling me into her body, she kisses me hard. Her mouth moves over mine, and I hook an arm around her neck, pulling up her shirt with my other hand.

"Not yet," she pants.

I kick off my shoes as she slips her hands underneath my skirt, locking her eyes onto mine as she touches me with her fingers.

"I'm dying to kiss it," she murmurs, stroking me.

My eyelids flutter at her soft touch, loving how she touches. How she explores, because everything is new to her and with every touch, she learns who she is.

I love that I'm here for it.

The tips of her fingers play just inside me, teasing but not taking, and she pulls her hand back out, her fingertips glistening.

Her mouth falls open a little, watching herself rub her fingers together and rub me over her fingers, and I think she'll lick it off, but she doesn't. Instead, she slips it under her skirt and into her own underwear, rubbing me on herself. All over her.

"Clay . . ." My body shakes.

Pulling out her hand, she rolls her desk chair behind her and sits down, looking up at me. Spreading my legs, she hooks her arms around my thighs and yanks me down to her.

I whimper, startled as she pushes up my skirt and sinks her mouth between my legs.

"Don't talk." She bites my lip down there. "Just listen."

I tip my head back. *Oh, fuck.*

My heart hammers, her tongue gliding up and down my pussy

in slow, long strokes—taunting me, priming me—and I'm already so turned on, sitting here like her fucking meal.

Like her fingers, her tongue learns my body. Feeling its way over my flesh, stopping and playing when she feels my body respond, and it isn't so much what she does but how she does it. The little moans that escape her when she covers my clit with her lips and sucks, patting it with her tongue to taste. How slowly she moves, taking her time and savoring. Mixing it up with light biting before she dips her tongue inside me, the tip making my blood turn to fire and my lungs shrink so small I can't breathe.

She takes her time. She wants to know me.

She wants to please me.

"Clay . . ." I moan.

I thread my fingers through her hair and tip my head forward, loving to watch her go to town on me, her mouth moving more frenzied and faster, because she's wet, too. Her fingers dig into my ass, hauling me harder onto her mouth. I grunt as she jerks me again and again until I take the hint and roll my hips, fucking her lips and tongue.

"Come on, Jaeger," she breathes out, grinning up at me. "Let me hear you. Make some noise."

We have the whole house to ourselves. Why not?

She tongues me, I grip her hair, and we move in sync, my pussy grinding into her mouth.

I moan.

"Louder."

My breasts shake as her tongue flicks over me, sending shivers down my spine.

"Fuck, Clay."

"Louder, Jaeger," she orders, using my last name again to remind me she's my team captain and our soon-to-be prom queen, and she really likes slumming with the bad girl.

And I like it, too. Right now, her double life is such a turn-on.

She rolls her tongue over me, groaning louder and louder, and I start letting my moans loose, and I don't give a shit if anyone hears us in here.

She slips a finger just inside my opening, and I whimper again, watching her rise and press her forehead into mine.

"Liv," she whispers, working it in farther inch by inch. "God, you make me crazy."

"Fuck me," I beg.

She squeezes my ass in one hand and rubs my clit with the other while the middle finger sinks inside me. "Right there?" she asks.

Her fingertip slips up low in my belly, and there's an itch she almost reaches.

"A little . . . farther," I gasp. "Curl your finger into me a little."

She presses against me from the inside, burying herself to her knuckle, and I have to force my toes not to curl as pressure hits the spot.

"Oh, God, that's it," I tell her.

Yes. And in a moment, we're kissing, panting, and she's rolling her hips into me in time with her finger sliding in and out, caressing my G-spot.

She kisses me hard, bites my neck, licks my lips as her hips piston harder and faster, pushing her finger inside me with each thrust.

Where the fuck . . . ?

I narrow my eyes, even as my orgasm starts to tease. "Where the hell did you learn all this?" I growl.

That fucking new girl Chloe wants her bad. I saw that with just one look.

I don't think Clay would do that to me while we're . . .

But she's fucking good. How did she get so good? We've only done it a few times.

When she doesn't answer, I grab her jaw. "Where the fuck, Clay?"

She startles. "I . . . I watched a . . . a movie."

"A movie?"

She breathes over my mouth, thrusting into me and groaning herself, because everything is turning her on, too, and she's liking this.

"Porn, okay? I watched a couple of porn videos."

I cock an eyebrow. She'll have to show me those. Most lesbian porn is made by men who do what they think looks good on camera instead of what actually feels good to women.

"Two fingers," she says. "I'm going to put two in."

"Clay . . ." But I don't have time to brace myself before she enters me again, this time thicker.

"Oh, God," I moan.

She grinds into me, sliding in and back out and then in again, kissing and biting until the room is spinning.

"God, you're so wet," she whispers. "So hot."

I yank her shirt up over her head, peeling it off before I pull down her lacy, pink bra.

I caress her breasts as she fucks me and leans down to suck on mine.

Her thumb rubs my nub, and I move into it, our rhythm growing faster.

A phone ring pierces the air, but neither of us stops. Her mouth on my nipple, I thread my fingers up the back of her scalp, under her hair, and kiss the top of her head.

"Would that be your boyfriend?" I whisper, teasing. "Hmm?"

God, what I wouldn't give for Callum Ames to see his prom queen between my legs.

She thrusts, her tongue licking my hard nipple, and I hold her close. "Fuck me, Clay."

The ringing keeps going, the pulse in my clit hammers, and heat pools in my belly as my orgasm crests. I brush my lips gently over hers. "He doesn't need to know," I tell her. "Just fuck me, Clay. Fuck me harder."

I'll still be sneaking off to screw her ten years from now, because that's how much I love this with her. It's perfect, and I hate how much I'll sacrifice to keep it, but I know I won't be able to stop.

She shakes, and I burst, crying out in the dark house, my orgasm exploding as her hips jolt into me like a car crash.

I press my mouth down on hers, her own cry filling me as she comes, and I taste the sweat on her lips.

I kiss her for a long time, her soft, wet skin feeding me food and water and air, and I don't need anything else.

I caress her face, my muscles burning and my skin overheating.

When her phone rings again, she pulls it out of her skirt and hurls it at the wall. I smile as she lays her head on my chest, and even though my arm is spaghetti and barely holding us up, I would never ask her to move. Not in a million years.

She breathes into my neck. "I don't want to ever stop this," she says.

I hold her to me and kiss her head again, my damp skin sticking to hers.

Whether it ends badly or it ends at all, I'm not sure I would do anything differently if I could. This feels too good to not have ever had it.

I wake with a start, blinking my eyes open in the dark.

It only takes a few seconds, but I register the sheer white canopy overhead, the frigid air-conditioning, and the scent of Clay everywhere.

Her bedroom. Clay lies plastered to my body, more on top of me than off, our naked skin pressing together and her head resting on my shoulder. Our legs are entwined, and I look down at her face, feeling her breath on my chin.

I kind of have to go to the bathroom, but I don't want to move her. My arms tighten around her, and I lightly brush my fingers down her smooth back.

God, her bed feels like a cloud. I could get used to this.

"You're drunk!" a man yells somewhere down the hall.

I freeze, training my ears. Did Clay lock her door?

"Keep your voice down," a woman snaps.

I glance over at the clock, reading 1:08 a.m., and try to be as still as possible. I should get out of here before her parents find me.

"Is she even home?" the man—Clay's dad, I assume—asks. "Are you sure? I don't think you know anything that's going on with anyone but yourself!"

"How dare you!" Gigi yells. "How dare you! I'm the one here. You're gone! You're always gone!"

I hold Clay, wondering how often they don't guard their volume to save her from hearing them.

"Grow up, Regina!" Mr. Collins growls. "I support you. I pay for that closet full of handbags and shoes. Now I gotta dry your tears because you need attention like a five-year-old?"

"I hate you!" she sobs.

I stop breathing for a second, hearing the tears and agony in her voice. Like she wishes he were dead.

"You don't hate me," he replies. "You hate that I finally decided not to let you drag me down with you."

I swallow, but my mouth is dry. Clay's breathing has changed, and I look down at her, just making out her eyes staring up at me.

"I'm sorry," she whispers, hearing everything I just heard.

"Don't apologize, baby." I hold her face and tuck her in close. "We all got our shit."

"I finally gave up on you, because you know why?" her dad fires back. "We lost a son. We lost a son, and I needed you, and you know what you did? You went to a spa! You got a prescription! You spent Henry's college fund redecorating this house and buying Clay a car! You wouldn't come to me. You wouldn't talk to me. You wouldn't go to therapy with me. You've barely let me touch you in four years, Gigi, and when I did, you aborted the only chance we had to be a family again! I needed you! I needed that baby! I lost Henry, same as you!"

I hear her sob, and I try to picture it, but Clay's mom has always seemed like an icicle, and I can't.

"I run to her bed," Mr. Collins continues, "because if I didn't have that to look forward to, I wouldn't be able to stick this out with you until Clay graduates."

A slap reverberates through the door, and Clay buries her face in my neck, breathing hard.

A door slams and then moments later, another farther away, and a beam of headlights flashes out the window before disappearing.

"Clay." I nudge her chin. "Look at me."

But she shakes her head, her face still pressed into my skin as she shivers with tears.

"Clay," I urge her, trying to tip her chin up. "Don't hide from me. Not in here."

I hold her for a moment and then look down at her, touching her face. "This could be it."

She sniffles and lifts her eyes. "What?"

"The last time we see each other."

She looks at me, and I don't know if she understands, but I know she's like glass right now. One crack will splinter off into a dozen, and I can't lose her yet.

"Stay with me now," I whisper. "Tonight is mine."

She touches her lips to mine, and in a way that's so soft it tingles over my entire body, she says, "Okay."

We kiss, her fingers tracing the symbol on my bracelet, and I love being wrapped around her to the point where I don't know my limbs from hers.

How am I ever going to leave her for school?

"Don't sneak out before I wake up, okay?" she tells me. "We'll go to school together."

I hesitate, knowing her mother knows me. She's on the school board. She would be aware of me since they voted on renovating the showers because of me.

But Clay doesn't want me to sneak out like I'd planned. "Promise?" I touch her face again. "I'm not going to leave."

21

Clay

"God, I need a shower," Liv whispers, trying to slip a pair of my black leggings on as she hops on one foot.

I pull my sports bra over my head, tucking my breasts inside. "I know." I lean down and give her a peck on the lips. "I'd like to do that with you right now, actually, but we're just going to get sweaty again in class."

Coach Coomer added another workout today, since the basketball team is done for the year and the baseball team is spending more time on the field. We're going to be late if we don't jam. I slip a rubber band around my wrist, grab my duffel, and shove a clean uniform inside, tossing Liv a skirt and a Polo, as well.

"Thanks."

She doesn't have time to run home before school, especially since we woke up late and then proceeded to just stay in bed even longer, not wanting to leave. After my father left last night, I just buried my face in her neck, lying awake for a long time before I was able to fall asleep again.

And I love that she just held me tighter, despite my embarrassment.

Nuzzling into me, stroking my back, and kissing my hair . . . After a while, the shame dissipated, and all I felt was safe.

"I'm just going to make sure . . ." I gesture toward the door, but she just nods, pulling on one of my sports bras before I find the words.

I step into the hallway, close the door behind me, and pad in my bare feet down the hall to see if my mom is up.

Was my father telling the truth last night? Are they just holding it together until I leave for college?

And the pregnancy . . . It was my dad's baby, after all. How in the hell could she do that? Is she trying to destroy what little we have left?

I sweep my hair back into a ponytail, but as I pass the bathroom, my mom calls my name.

"Clay," she says. "Come here."

I look inside, seeing her press buttons on the treadmill and come to a stop.

I remain at the door.

"Come here," she says again.

I shift on my feet, seeing the red rings around her eyes, telling me that she probably cried more than slept last night.

"Just cut me a break, will you?" she says, stepping off the machine. "Come here for a minute?"

She doesn't snap. She just sounds . . . tired. I glance down the hall—Liv's waiting for me—but I walk into the room.

She sits down on an exercise ball, breathing hard. "I'm sorry about last night," she tells me. "I know we were loud, and I'm sorry. I just . . ." She stops, thinking. "I'm just sorry."

Water bottles sit on the glass table next to me, along with some towels and a prescription bottle.

"I'm almost happy you're going off to North Carolina soon," she says. "Your dad and I will fix this. I promise."

She can't promise that. She's saying that so I'll concentrate on my senior year and being young and all that.

I look over at her, seeing the sixteen-year-old from the picture at Mimi's house yesterday. She had no idea then that this was where she'd end up. She thought she knew everything, probably.

North Carolina is hundreds of miles from where Liv will be. Hundreds.

"Maybe you should go away," I tell her, my voice soft. "Take Dad and just get away for a while."

We lost Henry, but for some reason, I don't want to lose everything else. Even if it's broken, it's all I know.

"You should leave and take him," I whisper. "Get out of this town, somewhere where you both can see something new, away from distractions."

Her head falls, and I see a tear spill.

"I abandoned him," she finally says, shocking me. "He's right. I couldn't think about anything else other than my pain, and I couldn't muster a care for my daughter or my husband."

I listen, having wanted to see her façade crack for so long, but I'm not sure I like it now that it is.

"He's going to leave me, Clay," she says matter-of-factly. "And part of me understands why. And the other part can't forgive him." She looks up at me. "How could he think about anything else? How could he want a woman when our son is underground?"

Because it's not about the sex.

Liv feels good to me. Everything feels good with her, and I crave her every moment, but it's not about the sex. It's about everything that comes with it. Talking to her. Touching her. Her scent and the promise of more. The feel of how she loves my body, and how being with her and doing things that make her breathless reminds me that I feel just a little bit lonely with everyone else in my life, except her.

It's about having someone to look forward to who wants your love.

She approaches me and takes my face in her hands. I blink away my tears, coming back to the present.

"Fuck the dress," she tells me. "And fuck Mimi."

I have to hold back my laugh. *Excuse me?*

"Wear what you want to the ball, okay?"

I nod, not really caring about the ball anymore, but I like this side of her, so I keep my mouth shut.

She kisses my cheek and starts to move around me, but then she stops, like she's listening for something.

That's when I notice the sound of running water.

Oh, shit. Liv's washing up in my bathroom.

She steps back, eyeing me. "Did you have someone over last night, Clay?"

I guess I hesitate too long, because she gives me a look.

"Clay . . ." she chides.

"It's Krisjen," I blurt out. "Don't worry."

But she cocks her head, and I know it was stupid to say Krisjen, because all she has to do is call her mom and I'm caught.

"It's Liv Jaeger," I finally tell her.

Her brow narrows. "Olivia Jaeger? The . . ."

The . . . the what, Mom?

"The motorcycle girl from school?" she finally asks.

Yeah, Mom. The *motorcycle girl.*

My mom stares at me. "You're not going over to their house, right?"

I raise my eyebrows. "Am I not supposed to hang with the help in Sanoa Bay, snobby?"

"I'm just saying my plate is full at the moment. No trouble, Clay," she warns. "Can I ask that of you? Please?"

Yessssss. Even though it's usually the Saints who cause the trouble over there, but okay. "No trouble," I tell her.

"All right, have a good day," she says, kissing me again and leaving the room.

I blow out a breath, thankful she doesn't press that more. Which is kind of weird. I thought for sure she'd be like "I don't

want you hanging around her and absorbing her gayness," but she
was actually cool about it.

Minutes later, Liv and I are out the door, carrying our bags and
her wearing my clothes and shoes as I toss her the keys.

She gets in the driver's side, and for the first time ever, I'm a
passenger in my own car. Callum can't drive my car. Liv can.

"Are you okay?" she asks as we near school.

The streets are still quiet, classes not starting for over an hour,
and I check my neck in the mirror, dabbing on some foundation to
cover the hickeys. She went to town on me again after we got into
bed last night, and I pull up my bra a little more, hiding the little
one on my breast.

"Just park over here," I reply, instead, gesturing to the curb.

I run my hand down her thigh, smooth in my leggings, giving
myself one last moment of contact before I have to be close to her
and not able to touch her for the next hour.

"And yeah, I'm okay," I say.

My parents are splitting up. I don't want to go to Wake Forest.
I'm infatuated with someone that everyone else will make their
business if it ever gets out.

But I'm okay, because I have her.

We head into the locker room, already empty, and drop off our
bags before jogging into the gym.

Weights clank, machines run, and giggles fill the air as our
teammates chat, Coomer giving us the eye as we run in.

I almost turn to check with Liv before I leave her, but I stop
myself. We arrived together. People already noticed that.

I walk away without a word, jumping on the treadmill next to
Krisjen, Amy on her other side.

"Hey," Amy chirps.

"Morning," I say, realizing I forgot water bottles. "You, uh, made
the appointments for mani-pedis next Friday, right?"

I look to Amy before she has a chance to ask about why I'm late and why I walked in with Olivia Jaeger.

"Yeah, I took care of it," she replies. "Then we'll be at your place for hair and makeup. I'm going to have my dress delivered the night before and steamed again."

"Good idea." I look to Krisjen, seeing Liv out of the corner of my eye start on the shoulder press. "And your parents got the limo, right?"

Krisjen's mouth opens and closes, and it takes a moment, but she finally nods. "Yes." Like she's not sure.

"It should've been done months ago," I point out. "You're scaring me."

We're all handling our share to do this together. I've got hair and makeup. Amy is paying for mani-pedis. Krisjen has transportation.

The boys will pay for prom, but the debutantes' families handle the ball.

"It'll be there," Krisjen assures. "I said I got it. Don't worry."

Now I'm worried.

Amy takes something out of her pocket and reaches over Krisjen, setting it on the dash of my treadmill.

"What's this?" I ask. But my heart thumps in my throat, and I know what it is. I quickly pick it up and hide it in my hand, checking for the coach. The square foil packet crinkles in my fist.

"You won't buy them yourself, and you can't rely on the guy," Amy says quietly. "You're welcome."

Krisjen laughs and pulls another one out of Amy's pocket.

"You are not sleeping with that dickhead again," I whisper, scolding her.

"You're right," she teases. "I'm not."

"Then who do you need one for?"

She shrugs. "I don't know what you're talking about."

Yeah, right. Please don't let it be Trace Jaeger. They looked pretty hot and heavy at the lighthouse, and the last thing I need is to run into her as I come out of Liv's bedroom one morning.

But before I can worry about Krisjen, Amy starts instructing me. "You should just get it over with, Clay," she tells me. "The first time will suck, but it gets better, and then it gets really good." She checks for anyone listening. "The secret is priming yourself. Blow him while you finger yourself, and by the time he's hard, you'll be wet . . ."

Ew, what?

"Ugh, stop it," I tell her.

Way too much information. I think I actually almost gag.

"You're such a prude, Clay." She snickers at me. "When you get good, it gets amazing, but you need to get good first. Just get it over with."

Images of Liv coming on my desk last night drift through my head, and I smile to myself. *I* am *good.*

I slide the condom into the secret pocket inside the back of my leggings and start running. Liv completes her set and sits up, stretching her arms over her head.

She looked so beautiful last night. She looks so beautiful all the time. What would she look like in a gown? With her hair on point and her makeup done?

She sits alone, no friends around, without me next to her like I should be, and I'm getting sick of it. She shouldn't have to be alone.

Megan approaches her, the new girl Chloe at her side, and they talk to Liv, and while Martelle pisses me off, I'm a little grateful. She introduces Liv to the new girl, and Liv smiles, very different from the curtness she had toward her when she caught us talking yesterday morning.

And the walls close in a little, watching them. Liv is going to realize she deserves more, and she'll have no trouble getting it.

Megan wants her, and I'm pretty sure Chloe isn't straight, either. Liv could pursue her. She'll meet other women at college, too.

Part of me wonders if Amy is right. *Just get it over with.* Maybe I need to know for sure. Maybe I should just screw Callum so I know for sure.

But I know I only want to do it in the hopes that I see something in him that will save me from having to take the step I'm so afraid to take. In hopes that I'm not in love with her, I don't need to face anything, and I don't need to suffer when it's time to leave her.

I don't want him to touch me. My skin crawls just thinking about it.

Liv looks over, meeting my eyes, and with a glance to my friends, she comes back to me and winks just covertly enough that only I notice.

I can't hide my smile as a blush crosses my cheeks. I feel right again. The weight of Amy's awful words and the rubber in my back pocket are suddenly forgotten.

"Liv's leggings look just like the Michi ones you have," I hear Krisjen say.

I blink. Huh?

Liv walks to the stationary bike, and I notice the clothes I gave her to wear. I turn to Krisjen.

"But it can't be," she says as she runs. "There's no way she has two hundred dollars for yoga pants, right?"

And then she winks at me, just like Liv just did, with a smile. *Fuck!*

M y knee bobs as I wait for the bell to ring, my fingers hovering over the keys of my laptop.

Krisjen doesn't know anything, right? And even if she did, she's not a gossiper.

Well, she joins in when we gossip, but she doesn't perpetuate it. She wouldn't say anything she wasn't sure about, right?

The bell goes off, and I glance over at Krisjen as she gathers up her materials and packs up her bag. I couldn't get her alone at lunch, and Spanish is the only class we have together, so I stuff my things into my satchel and push through the others to join her at her side.

"Look, don't tell Amy that Jaeger and I are kind of friends," I tell her as everyone filters out of the classroom. "I'm trying to grow up a little. She was late this morning. Forgot her gear. I let her borrow some clothes from my locker."

Krisjen doesn't look at me.

Sweat dampens my back. "Maybe I'm hoping she invites me over to where her hot brothers live," I tease.

But Krisjen continues to exit the classroom and then stops outside the door, stepping right to let the other students out.

"Clay . . ." She holds a book to her chest and gives me a placating smile. "I may have let my piece-of-shit ex-boyfriend get away with so much because I lack self-confidence and sometimes it was either him or home, and I didn't want to go home," she explains. "But it's not because I'm a moron, so please, I'd rather you not explain at all than insult me with a lie."

My face falls.

She pats my arm. "I'm here when you're ready. See you in the gym."

She walks off, her brown ponytail swaying as she disappears into the crowd.

Ugh, great. She knows. She totally knows.

I push through the crowd, heading downstairs and into the hallway that's flooded with more students. Eighth period has been cancelled for a pep rally, and locker doors slam, everyone trying to put away their materials so they don't have to take them into the gym.

Some of us skip the rally, though, and duck out early for the day.

I don't want to risk being caught with her out in the parking lot by the administration, but we can certainly hide out in the locker room until school is over.

But as soon as I get closer to her locker, the crowd thins, and I see her. A few yards away, staring at something.

I slow my steps, following her gaze.

A noose hangs on her locker door as people pass by, some whispering, some oblivious, and some snickering.

A noose. Like Alli Carpenter.

Liv's hand hangs from the strap of her bag, limp like she's been deflated, and I look at her face, seeing shock turn to defiance as she closes her mouth and flexes her jaw.

I just want to wrap my arms around her. *I'm here. Baby, I'm here.*

She heads to her locker, dials in the combination, and opens it, the noose dangling against the metal.

Without a look to the bystanders drifting back and forth with their eyes on her, I charge over and grab the noose, ready to yank it free of the tape.

But Liv stops me. "Leave it," she says.

"Liv—"

"Leave it, Clay."

I stare at her, the bite in her tone making it seem like she's mad at me.

"Why?" I ask, trying to keep my expression even.

"Because it checks my reality," she replies stiffly, stuffing her bag into her locker. "This isn't the first time. It's a little late to care now."

And she slams the door, heading straight for the gym. I watch her for a moment, alone in a sea of people, and it shouldn't be that way.

Part of me can't wait until she leaves, because she'll find a bigger world. But once she knows how much better the world is outside St. Carmen, she'll never come back.

I drift into the gym, barely noticing the band pounding out a fight song to commemorate the spring sports lineup as I find her standing back next to the bleachers.

The drumline beat fills the air, vibrating under my shoes, and I walk up behind her, leaning in close and whispering. "I do care."

Slipping my hand between her and the bleachers, I take hold of her fingers. I half expect her to pull away, but she curls hers around mine, the silent despair peeking through.

I don't want to do this anymore. I thought it would be easy to hide. A long-distance relationship wasn't going to happen anyway, so there was no need to go public.

Just physical. Just fun. That's all this is.

But I'm sick of her being alone and excluded. How happy would it make her to not stand alone for once?

"I want you to make me show it," I say. "Why don't you make me show it? Why do you let me act like a coward?"

She stands there, her back to me, but after a moment, she turns her head, saying in a low voice, "Because I'll never do anything to bring you more pain. What we're doing has a shelf life anyway. It's not worth it. It's just fucking, Clay."

I falter, the words cutting deeper than I expect. I don't want her to look back on us and think that's all this was.

But she's not wrong, either. If I can do anything to make her happy for a little while, I know what I'm good at. Digging my phone out of my bag, I text a picture to her. "Good," I whisper. "Check your messages."

She lifts up her phone, the cheer team flipping into the air and chanting as I watch her shoulders rise with a sudden intake of breath.

"Clay," she almost pants, tucking her phone away quickly before anyone sees the picture of the toy I ordered.

I lean in, keeping my eyes focused over her head and pretending

I'm watching as I whisper, "Can we do that?" I ask her. "I want to ride that in your bed."

"Jesus, fuck . . ." She laughs nervously, and I pull my hand out of hers and slip it under her skirt.

She breathes hard, and I hide my smile, thankful I could take her mind off this bullshit for a little.

"I'll have it by tomorrow," I tell her.

Reaching around her front, I rub her through her panties. Her hand covers mine through her skirt as the scent of her hair makes chills spread up my arms.

I want her so bad, I can't breathe.

I pull away from her, almost in pain, and step quietly through the crowd to the doors. I leave the gym, heading to my locker, because Liv has rehearsal and then work tonight, and I have etiquette class as well as some final prep for the ball.

The wait to see her will be worth it, though.

I round the corner, but I spot Callum, and I stop dead. He has a junior girl pressed into the lockers, and he holds her face, his tongue halfway down her throat.

I tense, my eyes scanning down her knobby knees and turquoise flats that don't even match our uniforms.

But her brow work is nice, I guess.

They both look over at me, a slow grin curling Callum's mouth and a startled look in her eyes. He leans into her ear, whispering, and she looks at me again before ducking out and leaving us. She heads down the hall in the opposite direction, but she needn't have bothered. I don't need to talk to him.

I walk, passing him, but he grabs my arm. "You know why you don't tell me to take a hike?" he asks as I pry myself out of his hold. "Because I'm an investment. You know I need you."

I narrow my eyes, and he falls into me, my back hitting the lockers as he plants his hands on both sides of my head.

"You know that I know that I'm nothing, and you know the life I promise," he continues.

I tip up my chin. Is that what he thinks? That I keep him around because I'm just too excited to assume the same role my mother has with my father? A trophy wife to take care of the kids and represent the charities?

"I'm not like my father, Clay." He stares down at me, and I can smell the girl's perfume on him. "A powerful man needs a powerful woman, not a weak one. And you will have power." He pushes off the locker and stands up straight. "You'll have your lovers in college, and I'll have mine, and after it's all done, we'll come home and build a fucking city. We'll be quite a team."

I want to laugh. Like I need him to do any of that.

He takes my face, and I flinch, shoving his hand away. But he comes back in and pulls me into him just as Liv appears around the corner.

I turn to her, my heart stopping as she halts, and the look in her eyes hits me like a ton of bricks. I go weak in Callum's arms for only a split second, gazing at her and seeing myself in my head, hurling my body into her arms and assuring her that I'm hers.

Callum stills, his eyes darting from me to her and back again. "Oh, I see." He beams. "Well, my perception sucks. Damn."

I shove out of his arms, growling. "What are you talking about? Just—"

"Clay, I'm into it." He cuts me off. "I'm *really* into it." He smiles, coming in again, and I see Liv walk past him, toward the front doors. "You can have as many women as you like as long as I get to watch."

My stomach roils. *Oh, God . . .*

"And as long as you're only mine after the ball," he says. And then he takes my hand and places a small vial with white tablets inside in my palm. "These will help your legs fall apart."

What?

He leaves, and I look back toward the direction Liv walked, but she's already gone. Opening my fist, I see the pills, and have to swallow to keep the bile from rising.

Molly. I feel sick.

For Christ's sake. At least he's not planning to slip this shit into my drink without me knowing, I guess. He wants me comfortable and willing. He wants me to drug myself.

And I would have to. It would take a lot more than Valium to get me into bed with him.

To get me to want him.

To get me to forget about her.

I dump the pills in the trash can on the way out of school.

22

Olivia

I slide the scissors up the fabric, cutting in short snips, but the day has taken its toll, and I jerk the tool, sliding the blade until there's a huge slice right through the middle.

"Son of a bitch," I bite out, rising off the floor and wiping the sweat off my forehead.

Dammit.

I grab the bolt of fabric off the table and start unraveling, measuring more.

Clay's never going to stand out by choice. She was always going to wind up with Callum or someone of the like, because that's what perfect looks like.

I know that. I've always known that. But God, it sucked to see her in someone else's arms. I didn't expect it to suck that much.

I'm pretty sure she didn't invite it, but she will choose him. Ultimately. That soulless, arrogant prick who hires people to do all his thinking for him. He doesn't know what she likes.

But then I falter. *Does he?*

Clay is really hot in bed, and my ego didn't even take into account that she would ever be that good with anyone else. I thought it was just us together.

Not likely. Someone else will be holding her in a few months.

She knows what she likes now, and when we're off to college, she'll find someone else to pass the time.

"Miss Jaeger?" Lavinia calls.

Shit. I dive over to the cabinet and grab the container of pins. "Got it!" I call, jogging out of the workroom and into the dressing room. I hand Lavinia the container I'd forgotten minutes ago. "Here you go."

I hand it to her, and she takes a few out, sticking them to the magnet on her wrist. Amy stands on the riser, her debutante dress a strapless A-line with a simple belt around the waist tied with a bow. She pulls on her long white gloves as Lavinia walks over to grab her matching shoes.

Amy meets my eyes in the mirror, her black eye from the fight the other night just about gone. "You can tell that bitch I always have the last word," she says.

I pick up a couple of discarded tiaras and the flowers Amy probably ordered Lavinia to cut off the dress. "Too bad for you Aracely isn't interested in talk," I tell her, knowing the only way Amy can win anything is because of her daddy. And I back away. "You should also be wearing champagne. You look like death."

Her red hair looks horrible against the dress, and I know there are rules about the colors they're allowed to wear, but progress, people. Come on.

As I head back to the workroom, my phone buzzes with a notification.

I lift it up, seeing a missed text from Clay. That's two in the past hour. At least she waited until I was out of rehearsal before she started blowing up my phone to do damage control about Callum.

I turn off the screen and go to set it down, but it buzzes again.

I can't stop myself. I glance over. I don't want him, the text reads.

Yeah, but you'll choose him. I toss the phone down. I'm not mad. I just don't want to act like it's okay, because it's not. While she's mine, she's mine and no one else's, and that's it.

The phone buzzes again, and every muscle tightens. *I have work to do, Clay.*

But then it vibrates again, and I can't resist.

You don't care, right? She challenges me. We're both leaving? This is just fun, right?

My eyes burn. *Yeah, it's just fun, and . . .*

I want you to care, she types. I want you to come and get me and take me anywhere or just come inside my house.

I stare at the words, my longing for her twisting unbearably in my stomach.

I love that my bed smells like you, she writes. I love it when I smell like you.

I smile softly, my anger fading.

Do you ever think about doing what Alli did? she asks. We want out until we remember why we want to live. If only she had hung on. If only she'd felt this.

I grip the phone. But when I don't respond to her texts, she sends another.

Hey, quick—what can jellybeans do that we can't?

I narrow my eyes.

Come in different colors! she replies. Hardy-har *tap-step-hand clap*

I snort, more at the fact that she's trying so hard to get my attention than the actual joke.

Please.

I'm sorry, she texts. I just . . . I wish I was looking at you right now.

God, she's killing me. Why is she doing this? It's not forever, right? We can keep this up for fun, but she needs to know she's not the only one moving on to a different life when this is over.

I'm not waiting for her.

Megan asked me to go to prom, I type. With that new girl, Chloe. As friends.

I wait, seeing the **Read** receipt, but seconds turn into a minute, and she's not replying. She's not even typing.

If none of us have dates, we'll go together. I hesitate, my mouth dry as my fingers hover over the screen. I'm going to say yes.

She sees the text but still nothing. That's good, I guess. This is the reality. If I'm not going with her, I'll go with someone.

I wait another few moments, and I text again. We're meeting up this weekend to dress shop.

I toss the phone down, but it immediately rings. I stare at it, the pulse in my neck kicking into gear.

Great. I answer, no time to say hello before she speaks. "That girl doesn't take a hint, does she?"

"This isn't about her, and you know it."

I know very well that the shit she pulled with Megan was to scare her away from me, and while I kind of like Clay's jealous side, Megan's not the issue.

"You don't even want to go to prom," she says.

"When did I say that?" I lower my voice so Lavinia doesn't hear. "I'd actually like to go. You'll be with Callum anyway, so why shouldn't I? You thought I'd stay home, waiting for your call afterward when you're ready to have sex? When I'm good enough for that?"

But not good enough to be seen with? We don't have to go together, but that doesn't mean I shouldn't get to go at all.

Clay is silent for a few seconds, and when she speaks again, her tone is quiet. "Please don't go with them."

"But you can go with Callum?"

"I don't want to fuck Callum!" she shouts.

"And I don't want to fuck Megan!" I fire back. "I never did!"

I breathe hard, wishing she were here, so I could fucking grab her and kiss her crazy. Is she stupid? Does she not feel everything that happens between us when I'm on top of her?

That it hurts to worry that she might go looking in Callum for what she might not find in me?

I dip my head into the bulletin board on the wall, tears filling my eyes as I hold the phone to my ear. "Do you have any idea . . ."

But I can't say the rest. I pull my head up, blinking away the tears. It hurts. It fucking hurts to see her touching him, and I'm sick of tap-dancing around her bullshit. Does she have any idea how much that cut today, to see her in his arms?

"You've been the best I've had," I tell her. "It's like nothing else, Clay. Honestly. But I don't want to ruin this. Maybe we should stop before—"

"Baby . . ." she bites out, interrupting me. "If I think you're not mine, I might make a scene. Be very careful what you say next."

Her hard voice cuts into my ear, the sudden threat a surprise.

And I smile, despite myself. I do like Clay's jealousy.

"Are you threatening me?" I gibe. "You haven't seen what I can do yet."

"Oh, I know what you can do."

And my phone buzzes with a text. I look at the screen, click on the photo, and see Clay on her stomach. She peeks over her arm, locks of hair in her face and her naked back visible just before her naked ass.

Heat pools between my thighs, and I gaze at her skin and mussed hair, like she always looks after I'm done with her.

I groan louder than I expect before putting the phone back to my ear.

"You can do anything you want to me, that's what," she says. "And I want to take you on a date tomorrow night, to Mariette's."

I listen. A date?

"You ever eat raw oysters?" she goes on. "I want to watch you eat and get you drunk and hot on tequila and sweat with you and fuck you in the back seat of my car. And I want to do that as many times as I can before we have to leave each other in August, because nothing feels better than you, Jaeger. Nothing."

I lick my lips, my whole body wired and hot, and she's fucking right. She's the only thing I look forward to.

"Turn over," I tell her. "I want a topless one."

She's got pictures of me. It's my turn now.

A moment later, my phone vibrates, and I see her sitting on the edge of the bed, the phone up high with a view of everything from her little smirk down to her stomach. I strain my eyes, trying to see farther down than where the picture cuts off, but I'll have to wait to see her in person, I guess.

"I'll meet you there at eight," I say.

"I'll bring the booze."

And we hang up, an excited smile that I don't release warming my blood.

"God, I think I like you a little," I whisper.

She gets me going, and while I may not be holding her hand in public, I own her body. She loves it with me.

My face heats up, thinking about tomorrow, and I look in the mirror, seeing a blush on my cheeks.

I pat my face, shaking my head clear. "Snap out of it."

But I don't stop smiling the rest of the night.

23

Clay

"You have to stop," I pant as Liv sucks on my neck. "I want to be crazy for you tonight."

I want to be starving for her.

But she slides her hands up my skirt as I straddle her on the desk, her fingers digging into my ass. "I can't help it. Those pictures drove me insane."

I dive into her lips again, unable to fathom wanting to ever be anywhere else.

The abandoned woodshop classroom at the end of the second floor sits far away from any remaining students in the school. Most have gone home for the day, but Athletics is still going on and I'm late to meet my friends, but I don't care.

The desktop cuts into my back, but I thread my hand through her hair, gripping it at the base of her skull, and pull her head back. I stare down at her, keeping my eyes open as I come in for kiss after kiss after kiss. She's so soft. I grind back and forth, loving the feel of her slender body between my legs.

"It's just fucking, right?" I whisper.

She gazes up at me as I roll my hips, her hands pulling me in harder but nice and slow. "I just wish time would stop," she tells me.

I kiss her mouth. Her face. Her cheekbone. Her mouth again. *Four hours.* I'll see her in four hours.

The final bell rings, signaling the end of the teachers' workday, and I growl, knowing we have to go.

"I have to get to the theater," she says, but makes no move to stop caressing me through my underwear.

I kiss her one last time. "And I have to meet Amy and Krisjen." I whimper, breaking into a sweat as I climb off her. "I'll see you at eight, okay?"

She rises, and we kiss, grab our bags, and head for the door, stopping periodically to paw each other, giggle, and kiss some more.

"Do you have it?" she asks.

I smile, knowing what's on her mind. Digging in my bag, I pull out the toy—a long, black, vibrating, strapless gadget that filled me with equal parts dread and excitement when I took it out of the package.

"Whoa." She pushes my hand down, trying to hide it from the window in the door. "You brought it to school?"

I press the button, the vibrations humming through our hands.

"Is it okay?" I ask, looking at her hesitantly. "It looked like something we both could, you know . . ." *Get off on.* "And the reviews were good."

We can both use it at the same time, the ends positioned perpendicular from each other, so one end goes inside her, and the other inside me as I straddle her. There's a ribbed section that presses into her clit, so hopefully we can both come.

But she stares at it, not answering, and I tense a little.

Maybe this is too much. Or wrong, I don't know. I want to lose my virginity to her. This is all I could think of.

I lick my lips and stuff it back into the bag. "I guess I should've just let you pick it out." I laugh nervously, shaking my head. "I'm not sure what you've used before, so I don't know. Maybe—"

"It'll be amazing," she says, taking me by the back of my neck and kissing me softly. "Bring it tonight."

I kiss her back, murmuring, "Okay."

My pulse races, and I'm not sure if it's her or because I'm nervous, but these toys are a thing, so there must be something to them. I guess we'll see.

I wrap an arm around her waist, pulling her in while I cover her breast with my hand.

She moans, and I smother it with my mouth. "Shhh . . ." I laugh.

It takes another twenty seconds, but I pull away from her and shove her toward the door. "Ugh, okay, we gotta go." I kiss her again. "Go, go. Please."

She rights her clothes and opens the door. "Bye."

I follow her and pull her back, kissing her one last time. "Bye," I whisper.

She jogs down the hall, looking back once to flash me a smile, and I watch her disappear down the stairs.

I let the door close, and then I twist my skirt right again and tighten my ponytail.

"I was looking for you."

I jump. *What?* I follow the voice and see Amy step out from the other side of the lockers across the hall. My chest caves.

How long has she been there?

I swallow a couple of times, blink, and tamp down my rapid breathing. "Yeah, I know, I'm late."

I walk down the hall, hearing her footsteps fall in behind me.

"What are you doing, Clay?"

"Leaving."

I close my eyes, dread twisting my gut. *That damn app.* I completely forgot we all downloaded it years ago to locate each other. I've never used it to find my friends, so it didn't occur to me that they would.

She grabs my arm and swings me around. "What the hell is going on?" she barks.

It takes a moment, but I recover. "Um . . . lots." I step over to my locker and dial in the combo. "The House passed a cyber-safety bill this morning, although it will probably die in the Senate. The president ordered air strikes on Syria. There's a storm advisory for this weekend, and I scuffed my vintage saddle shoes at lunch."

I pull out my handbag, empty my satchel, and refill it with what I need for homework.

"Clay, I'm your best friend." She steps to my side. "Or one of them anyway. What the hell were you two doing in there?"

The shade was down on the door. Could she have opened it and peeked inside without us hearing?

But I guess she wouldn't have needed to. We kissed right outside the door like idiots.

"We were knitting sweaters," I mock.

"Bullshit." Her voice sounds like she's spitting out a bug. "God, Clay. Seriously? I've been naked in front of you! Slept in your bed. Are you serious?"

I slam the locker door and keep walking. She follows.

"I'll tell your parents," she says behind me. "I'll have to."

I stop. *Excuse me?* I turn, glaring at her so hard my eyes feel like they're on fire.

"I don't give a shit about what those 'woke' assholes try to tell us," she spits out. "There's something mentally wrong with people like Olivia Jaeger."

I reach out, grab her by the collar, and haul her ass into an empty classroom. She stumbles, and I let go, yanking the door closed behind me.

"It's not natural, Clay," she argues. "Just stop. Right now. I'm not letting you throw your whole life away."

I advance on her, and she backs up.

"Clay, you're not gay," she tells me. "She's confusing you. You've been through shit, and you're an easy target."

"Shut up."

I drop my bag to the ground, and she bumps into a desk, quickly stepping away.

"So, you're telling me we're going to raise our kids next door to each other someday? You, a man-hating dyke with a shitty haircut and your sperm donor offspring, and me with my kids asking why Auntie Clay is groping the babysitter?"

I grab her by the collar with both fists and slam her up against the wall.

She whimpers and tries to push me off, but I grip her hair at the scalp with one hand and dig my fingers into her stomach, pinching the skin there with the other.

She cries out. "Clay!"

"Shhhh . . ." I whisper over her lips.

She squirms, but her hair is wrapped around my fingers, and she's trapped.

"Stop," she snivels.

But I'm not listening. "If you ever speak to me this way again, I will knock your teeth out." I stare down into her eyes, a new energy filling me that kind of scares me, but I won't fucking stop. Nothing comes between Liv and me. "Do you understand?"

Fear fills her blue eyes, and I squeeze harder as she tries to shift out of my grasp.

"Do you understand?" I bellow.

"Clay—"

But I'm doing the talking now.

"Now, Amy, I realize your sister is a Jesus freak who mainlines coke to cope with her minister husband getting another woman pregnant," I say calmly but firmly. "And your father likes to court teenage boys for two weeks every summer in Thailand, so you're just projecting your demons onto an easy target, but if you're not my friend anymore"—I bite out my words and dig my fingers in harder—"I just don't know how I'll survive."

She groans.

"Everyone will believe *you* and not *me*," I tell her, both of us knowing that's not true at all. "Because *your* word means so much more than mine, right?"

Wrong.

I continue, the sudden rush of power emboldening me. "I'll lose all my friends," I say. "The rest of the school year will suck. No parties. No prom. Can you imagine the TikToks and Snaps? I mean, is it me who has several gay-bashing posts for people to find on my feed? Is there a picture of me in blackface at a Halloween party from a few years ago?"

No.

That's all her, and my threat hangs in the air, her eyes widening as she remembers who's really in fucking control here.

"Clay . . ."

"Those have been screenshotted already," I say. "Won't look good when you apply to Omega Chi or go for a fucking job interview in five years. Hatred for you will go viral." I gasp.

"I was Beyoncé . . ." she whimpers, trying to explain her Halloween costume, but I push her into the wall again before I let go.

I swipe my bag off the ground and hook it over my shoulder as she stands frozen against the wall.

If she talks, I will end her.

"And don't worry," I say, casting her a glance up and down like I'm checking her out. Like I ever checked her out when she was sleeping over at my house or naked in a dressing room with me. "I was never tempted. You ain't got what Liv's got."

And I stroll out of the classroom—and the school—quickly bringing up all of her different accounts and screenshotting all the shit I just bluffed I had on her before she deletes it.

I check my face in my side mirror, feeling a little weird, less dressed up than when I go to school.

But Liv isn't into frills, and I don't want to be beautiful or manicured or make her afraid to mess me up.

Holding my phone, I walk toward Mariette's, a little early, so I can pick the table. Saints don't usually come here in the middle of the week, but I don't want to take the chance. I want her to myself.

The warm air caresses my bare arms, my stomach, and my chest, everything that's not covered by my tank top as I walk inside in my jeans and flip-flops. I put some waves in my hair with the curling iron and minimal makeup, hoping I look so positively kissable that she can't wait to touch me.

"Sit anywhere," the server with the ponytail and black bandana tells me as I walk in. "Can I bring you something to drink?"

She grabs a tray of crawfish and carries it to a table. "Two Diet Cokes?" I ask. "And a dozen on the half shell to start. With condiments, please."

She nods once, and I make my way through the diner to the courtyard in the back, the scent of flowers hitting me as I veer through the sparse diners to a table situated on the other side of a tree.

I drop my bag to the ground and sit down at the white wrought-iron garden table, my chair scraping against the brick floor. The white tent walls billow with the breeze, the plastic windows fogged with the humidity, and I look up as the tree next to me reaches beyond where the roof should be, the sky overhead filled with stars.

The server sets down two drinks and then returns with a tray of oysters on ice. I pull my water bottle out of my bag and uncap it, the scent of Patrón overpowering the scent of the buffet along the wall.

"Don't get started without me," I hear someone say.

I smile and look up, seeing Liv head for the table.

But my heart nearly stops, seeing her short black skirt, long golden legs, and black studded heels with a band secured around her ankles, making her look like she's cuffed to a bed. Her ankles are definitely a feature I missed. One of her best. Fantastic ankles. And calves. And thighs.

Heels. I've never seen her in heels. Her faded black band T-shirt is twisted tight around her body and tied at the back, baring her stomach, and I have no idea who Black Flag is, but I kind of love them now.

She wears faint red lip tint, and her hair is straightened and spilling around her.

She stands there, and after a moment she laughs a little. I realize my mouth is hanging open. I close it, my eyes trailing down her legs again.

I rise and kiss her, lingering close and smelling her soap, perfume, and lotion that all mixes to have this wonderful effect inside my belly.

"Nervous?" I ask.

She smiles. "In a good way."

"You look amazing."

She pulls away and sits, and I do, too, a blush crossing my cheeks as I meet her eyes. All I want to do is touch her, and she knows. Now it's just a matter of going through the motions until my bright idea of having a date ends, and we can get out of here.

We sit there for a few moments; the awkwardness of "what to do now" when we're used to either making out, having sex, or fighting leaves us at a loss for words.

"I own one non-school skirt," she says, breaking the silence and unwrapping her straw. "And this is it."

I like it. I slide my legs out a little more, hugging one of hers between mine. She leans her head on her hand, playing with her straw as her eyes fall to the little tears in my white top, the skin peeking through.

"What?" I ask.

"You look amazing, too."

I feel underdressed now, but . . . her eyes don't lie as they continue to linger on me.

She clears her throat as the server moves around the courtyard, music drifting through the entrance from the diner. "I haven't been on many dates, to be honest," she tells me. "Not sure how this is supposed to go."

"We eat." I unwrap my straw. "That usually takes the pressure off."

I take a sip and stretch my arms over my head, taking some deep breaths to get those heels off my mind, but then her skirt reminds me of something, and I smile.

"I've seen you in that skirt before," I tell her. "You wore it to a furniture store a couple years ago."

She cocks her head, not seeming to remember.

"I was there with my mom." I hold up the Tabasco sauce and the lemons, giving her a choice. She points to the Tabasco. "I think Army was working there, loading a piece onto a truck, and you were tagging along, I guess," I tell her as I season two oysters. "My mom spoke to the salesman about our new dining room table she had ordered from their gallery in New York. You were moving around the store. Playing around. Plopping onto beds and couches and faking passing out when your brothers would try to lift things with you on top of them."

She smiles, her head still leaning into her hand.

"The bay doors were open," I go on. "Blowing loose locks from your ponytail into your face, your white smile so big even from yards away. I remember I couldn't hear your laughter, but I could like . . ." My voice drops to a whisper, remembering the moment I knew I was in love with her. "I could feel it inside me."

Her smile starts to fall as her breathing quickens.

"A bee caught scent of you and put you into a panic," I tease.

"Which was funny, because you don't panic. Army put you in a headlock, trapping you and making you squeal."

"I think I remember that."

It was a while ago. We knew each other by then, but I made sure she didn't see me. I didn't want her to stop playing.

I stare off into the tray of oysters. "You all seemed so happy." And then I gaze across the table at her. "You were so pretty. I was dying for you even then."

It's actually amazing the skirt still fits her.

I stare at her, both of us suffering a lot of loss in the past few years, and both of us with our own hang-ups—me with my family and she with hers. She might not want to carry this relationship to college, and I might not want to go public and invite criticism for something that's a fling, but I know without a doubt that I will never hurt her again.

I jerk my chin at the oysters. "Eat one," I tell her.

She picks a shell up, and I watch as she opens her mouth, tips her head back, and swallows the mollusk, hot sauce running down the corner of her mouth. She dips out her tongue and swipes it up, tossing the shell down and licking her lips as she meets my eyes.

I groan inside, looking at her supple, soft lips.

I set the bottle in front of her, and she struggles to hold back her smile.

Uncapping the bottle, she tips it up and swallows, the plastic container crinkling in her hand.

"Mmmm . . ." She wipes her mouth with the back of her hand, the breeze blowing her hair into her face as she caps the bottle again.

I nod at the shells. "Again."

She gives me a look that tells me she knows what I'm doing, and she likes it.

Swallowing another oyster, she chases it with a shot, her eyes closing and a light sheen gathering at that little dip in her collarbone.

My thighs warm, watching her mouth move and swallows go down her throat. Everything is warm.

"These are good," she says, seasoning the rest of the oysters for us. "Almost like we shouldn't tear this place down to build a golf course."

I give her a knowing look. "No, we shouldn't."

Mariette's and Sanoa Bay are Florida, and I'd rather have this particular Floridian in front of me here than a sea of tourists making my father richer.

We eat, and I take a couple of shots, hiding the bottle when the server comes by. My stomach growls, realizing I haven't eaten today besides the oysters, and I kind of want to order a meal, but she's too far away, and I don't know if I want to stay here longer.

"I hate this table between us," I grumble under my breath.

She suddenly stands up, moves her chair next to mine, and sits down, her arm around the back of my chair, and her beautiful leg draped over my lap.

My hand immediately slides up the inside of her thigh as my lips find her neck. "I really like your outfit," I whisper.

When school uniforms are a thing of the past, it'll be fun to wear whatever I want and let her taunt me, doing the same.

She takes another shot, and I lick the tequila off her lips. She blinks, surprised as her eyes flit around us to who could be watching, but just this once, I don't care. "This could be it," I tell her, taking her again.

She feels too good to stop.

She kisses me, leaning into me and moaning, and I can't stop smiling.

"So, when is this part of the date over?" she asks.

"Are you ready for part two? A romantic walk on the beach?"

"Ugh."

I laugh. "A movie, then?"

She scowls.

"Mini golf?"

She shakes her head, staring at my mouth.

But I keep going. "Followed by an in-depth conversation about our sociological, political, and theistic values, in that order?"

She snatches up my lips, and I'm really glad her house isn't far away. We can still watch a movie or talk about theology, just in bed.

"Clayyyyy?" A voice booms in the distance.

I still, Liv stopping midkiss and hovering over my lips.

Was that . . . ?

"What the hell?" I gasp.

My nerves fire, and I sit up straight, pulling my hands off her body.

Callum. I peek through the tree, seeing him saunter into the courtyard with Milo, Amy, and a couple of his friends in tow.

"What are they doing here?" I whisper, scooting away on reflex with my stomach twisting. "I got rid of that app."

Shit. How did they find me?

Liv stares at me, but I don't look at her. I can't do this now. Not *right* now.

She waits a few seconds, the option to just take her back in my arms and own this hanging between us, but . . .

She rises. Scooting her chair back over to her side of the table, she takes out her phone and taps away, and I don't know what she's doing, but I just sit there, leaning back, and see them head our way.

"Hey, baby," Callum says, strolling over with a plate of key lime pie, Amy carrying a soda.

I glare at her. Did they follow me or something?

Callum slides a chair over and takes a seat at our table, his posse hovering behind him. He shifts his gaze to Liv. "Hey, baby."

She scoffs under her breath like her patience with both of us is about gone.

Callum grabs my fork. "Heard you were here without me," he says. "And here I thought you were with one of the Jaeger boys." He looks from me to her. "Team meeting, ladies?"

"Bored, Ames?" Liv fires back. "Money, sex, privilege, but you're still so bored, you gotta come all the way over here to look for entertainment, huh?"

I hold my glass, the icy condensation cooling my palm but not the rest of me.

"All the way over here," Liv taunts. "Because if I were Clay, I wouldn't want you." She glances at me. "If I were Clay, I would find you pretty pathetic, and that must piss you off."

His gaze sharpens on her, and I watch them, ready to mobilize if he moves.

She fixes her eyes back on him. "I'm even willing to bet you don't get her hot. Or any woman, for that matter. That's why you're sexually abusive, isn't it?"

Abusive . . . what?

"They don't get hot," Liv says again. "They smile. And they fawn. And they fake." And then she sits up, rolling her hips a little and moaning. "'Oh, oh, you're the best, Cal. The best.'" She follows with more whimpers and groans.

I bite back my smile.

"Maybe she is hooking up with one of my brothers." Liv shrugs. "Maybe more than one. I have five, after all. Sometimes they work as a team. I mean, how could you compete?"

I narrow my eyes, kicking her under the table. She laughs under her breath.

Callum cuts into the pie. "Your words hurt," he says, "but not as much as I will, and you know it. We could carry you and Clay out of here right now and get away with it."

"Could you?" she retorts.

His eyes gleam. "Five against two, Liv."

"Is it?"

Just then, howls fill the air. "Ow, ow, ow!" And goose bumps spread over my skin, knowing who just entered Mariette's.

That's who she was texting. Her brothers.

Callum straightens in his chair, his blue eyes alert as four out of the five Jaeger boys fill the entrance, looking for their sister. I do a double take, seeing Krisjen holding Trace's hand.

And Milo's here. *Awesome.*

In a moment, everyone surrounds the table where Liv and I sit, the other diners in the courtyard casting glances and noticing something is up, but no one moves.

I speak low to Krisjen. "What are you doing with Trace?"

"We hooked up the night of the brawl," she whispers over her hand.

I knew it.

I look left to right, the tension thick as the two groups stare at each other.

"So I hear there was a break-in at Fox Hill last night," Callum says, eyeing Liv's brothers. "Know anything about that?"

A break-in at the country club? I didn't hear about that.

"I don't know a thing," Dallas replies. "We'll keep an ear out, though. Anything stolen?"

"Nothing," Callum snaps back. "Strange, huh? Just the face of the founder's portrait scorched, even though there was a cash register and tons of liquor on the premises."

"Yeah, strange," Army tells him. "We'll keep our ears open."

"Sure, you will."

And I dart my eyes between the two groups of people, feeling like I'm missing something. The Jaegers don't keep the grounds at Fox Hill, nor do any of them work there in any other capacity. They wouldn't break in just to defile a painting.

I'm not sure who would. Callum seems to know something I don't, though.

Liv sits back in her chair. "So, um . . . Callum here thinks Clay is sleeping at our house tonight," she announces, the truth about to slip off her delighted little tongue as she beams. "He thinks she's in bed with a Jaeger."

Her brothers chuckle, and Trace approaches me, grabbing his crotch. "Oh, come on, baby," he coos down at me. "You know you own this."

Ugh.

The Jaegers laugh again, because they know exactly where I'm sleeping tonight, and I stare at Liv, shaking my head. "You're enjoying this."

"Oh, immensely." She grins, her face flush with enjoyment as she speaks to her brothers again. "I told him it was probably two of you."

"Aw, why'd you have to go and tell him that?" Dallas teases.

She shrugs. "Everyone knows you and Iron are a team."

"I guess our secret's out, Dally," Iron boasts, the brothers skimming their palms together and ending with a fist bump.

But Army speaks up. "Why doesn't anyone ever think it's me?"

Liv grumbles, "Because baby mamas are too much drama."

I laugh to myself. Army is good-looking, but yeah . . . No one wants to saddle that pony and be a stepmom.

"Maybe it's Macon," Iron adds.

I clench my teeth.

Liv nods. "Older man . . ."

"Experienced," Trace taunts.

But Dallas cuts them off. "Nah, Macon doesn't like rich princesses."

I ball my fists, losing my patience. I don't want the whole world to know my sex life, but I also don't much care that it's being insinuated that I'm sleeping with people I'm not.

"Well, it could be Macon," Army inserts. "Because . . ."

And all the Jaegers sing together, "Everyone is our type when they're naked!" Like it's some fucking family motto or something.

Liv laughs with her brothers, all of them amused at my expense, and I'm pretty much done.

I reach over, scoop up a glob of Callum's pie, and fling it right at Liv. It slaps into her damn chest, sticking and splattering on her chin, and she jerks, gasping.

Not so funny now, am I?

Everyone stills, barely breathing as they wait for Liv's reaction. I lick my fingers, waiting.

"Oh, shit," Milo whispers, covering his laugh with his hand.

Liv clears her throat and sits up. Iron moves forward, but she pushes him back as she rises. "It's okay," she chirps, looking between her brothers and the Saints. "No punching. No blood." She picks up the tequila and downs a shot. "No arrests tonight. Agreed?"

I nod once. It would suck for this to get out of hand and stop being fun.

And just as she sets the bottle down and picks up the Diet Coke, I suck in a breath before she leans over the table, raises it high, and tips it over, emptying it onto my head.

"Ohhhh!" someone laughs.

Callum snaps his fingers, smiling excitedly for Amy to start filming with her camera phone, but I'm inhaling short, shallow breaths as the icy drink mats my freshly washed hair and plasters my thin tank top to my fucking braless chest.

I'm gonna kill her.

I stand, grabbing a spoonful of whipped cream from the plate and hold it up, ready to launch it at her.

"Don't do it." She points her finger. "You got me. I got you. We're even."

Slowly, I shake my head, and I don't care who's checking me out in my indecent shirt right now. All I see is her.

"Uh-oh," Trace laughs, and everyone backs away, getting ready.

I whip the spoon, the glob slamming right into her neck, and howls fill the air.

"Food fight!" Trace bellows up to the sky.

And everyone scrambles.

"Woo-hoo!" someone screams, and laughter fills the air.

Liv kicks her chair back and launches herself around the table, and I yelp, running. Trace grabs a pan of key lime off a nearby table, joined by his brothers, and everyone starts slinging food. Nearby diners grab their plates and jam, diving into the dining room and out of the line of fire.

"Keep filming this," Callum shouts. "Hell yes!"

I grab someone's abandoned beer on a table and whip around to face Liv. "Insinuating that I'm sleeping with your brother, and more than one at that?" I shout.

I shake the beer, letting it rip all over her.

She screams but then breaks into laughter. "I'm sorry!"

You are not.

I pick up anything I can find, tossing it at her, and she inches closer, holding up her hands to protect herself.

Amy films as Callum, Milo, and the guys pitch fruit salad, cakes, and drinks into the air, Liv's family giving it back as good as they get, chasing the Saints around the patio.

It's lucky this hasn't evolved into a fistfight yet.

I leap over the buffet table, slipping and landing on my ass, but before I can climb to my feet, something warm and gooey spills over my head and down my arms.

I squeeze my eyes shut, the smell instantly hitting my nose.

Mashed potatoes? She's dumped an entire vat from the buffet on top of me. "Ew!" I cry, shooting to my feet and peeling the mush out of my eyes. "I'm going to kill you!"

Ew, ew, ew.

I shake, feeling nasty. I need a shower.

Liv laughs so hard that she throws her head back.

But before I can find food to hit her with, she slides over the table and grabs my hand. "Now I get to wash you." And she kisses me.

Hell yes. "Get me out of here."

Now. While everyone is distracted.

Food flies through the air, Dallas stalking Callum with a couple of eggs that look like they'll hurt if hit with them, but we don't stick around to worry if this escalates. Grabbing my bag at the table, we run, leaving the mess for tomorrow, which is, I hope, how long it takes Macon to realize we just destroyed the place.

Leaving my car behind, we run down the dark dirt road, Liv removing her heels to keep up in her bare feet.

We stop so she can unlock her front door.

"I need a bath, baby," I whisper in her ear from behind.

The tequila has kicked in, and my body stirs. She opens the door, and I head straight up the stairs ahead of her, seeing the house dark.

"Macon!" she calls out.

There's no answer.

The others are at Mariette's, and I know she has a nephew around here somewhere. Must be with a babysitter.

She tails me as I head to the bathroom, and we both step in, locking the door behind us.

I drop my bag to the chair next to the tub and kick off my sandals. "Good first date?" I ask.

"Not bad."

She starts the water, turning on the shower, and the room soon fills with steam. I sit on the edge, watching her bend over and check the water's temperature.

It hurts to look at her. The perpetual red tint of her lips that makes them look like she was born that way. The glow of her olive skin, the ever-so-subtle blush of her cheeks. Her long legs and long hair and the sweat on her body and my mouth on her tits that would make Father McNealty rain down fire and brimstone during Sunday Mass if he knew what we were doing.

Am I really letting Callum escort me to the ball? Am I really not taking her to prom?

I lower my eyes. I want everyone to know she's mine. She has my heart, and it scares me that she may not want it as much as I want her to have it.

She still hasn't acknowledged that I told her I loved her.

"I wanted to tell them so badly that it was your bed I was in," I say quietly.

She looks over at me, and I rise, leading her into the shower, both of us slowly peeling off each other's clothes and my eyes never leaving hers.

I unzip her skirt, letting it fall into the tub. The shower douses my back as she peels off my tank top and helps me strip off my jeans.

We dump our food-stained clothes into the sink to be washed out later, and she pushes me back under the spray, helping me clean my hair.

But I've barely tipped my head back, closing my eyes, before her mouth covers my nipple.

There's something mentally wrong with people like Olivia Jaeger.

I shake with a laugh at Amy's words today. Then there's something wrong with me, too. I'm so hard for her already.

"What are you laughing at?" Liv asks.

I grab her face and bring it up to me. "Nothing, baby. You just make me shiver." And I kiss her, swirling my tongue into her mouth and wrapping my arm around her, holding her tight against me as the warmth blankets us.

Spinning her around, I rinse her off, her hair and body, never taking my hands off her as her kisses on my neck seep down into my belly.

"You said you could do anything a man could do," I taunt. "Prove it."

"Or what?" She bites my lips. "You threatening to get from Callum what you can't get from me?"

She licks my mouth, and we grind on each other faster.

I groan. "Start getting more possessive, and I won't have to. Tell me I'm your girl."

Tell me.

"You trying to start shit right now?"

"Yes." And I kiss her deep and strong, covering her mouth like it's my last meal.

She slides down the wall, squatting between my legs, and yanks my hips toward her mouth. *Oh, Jesus.* Her tongue glides up my pussy over and over again, ending each time with a nibble or sucking.

Again and again.

My eyes roll into the back of my head, her lips tugging my clit and making me moan. I don't care who's here to hear. Let them hear.

I lift my leg, placing my foot on the edge of the tub behind her, fisting her hair with one hand and reaching up, gripping the windowsill with another.

"Fuck me, princess," she says.

She bites me, and I let my head fall back, overcome. I roll my hips, thrusting into her mouth against the wall, and I peer down, taking in the view.

She kisses and tugs, sucking on my inner thighs and swirling her tongue over my slit. "Fuck." I shake, grinding on her mouth faster. "More, Liv."

She takes my ass in both hands, diving inside me with her tongue, and I cry out. Heat fills my stomach, and I throb as she thrusts into me and rubs her own clit between her legs.

She licks and tastes. "You're so wet, baby." And then she meets my eyes again. "But I'm dying to stretch you."

I pause, my body aching to come and every inch of me hot. My pointed nipple hovers above her.

Before I can make sure I understand what she wants, she stands, turns the showerhead toward the wall and off us, and reaches outside the shower, digging out the toy.

Once I see it, my heart jackhammers. "I'm scared."

She meets my gaze. "Me, too."

She holds it under the water, rinsing it clean, and while I know she's just saying that to soothe me, I appreciate it. It feels, for a moment, like we're doing something together for the first time. Even though I know I'm not her first time. Or probably her fifth.

She kisses me again. "It's the anticipation that makes you worry," she says, pressing the button and finding a slow, steady rhythm.

She glides it between my legs, and I jerk, grabbing onto her.

"I can't wait till you fuck *me* with this," she whispers.

And I can't help but smile. I would do anything to bring her pleasure.

"Come here, baby." And she pulls me down on top of her as she sits on the bathtub floor, leaning back into a relaxed position. I straddle, following her lead, both of us rolling our hips and grinding on each other.

"You want to do it in here?" I ask.

She nods. "Yes. We're wet. If we leave here, you'll be cold. Stay with me."

Always.

She moves the toy between us, and I scoot down her legs a little, watching her fit the shorter end inside herself. It vibrates, I hear a sudden intake of breath, and my eyes dart up to hers, seeing a pained look on her face as she sinks it inside.

She whimpers, and my heart skips a beat, but . . . the pain fades out of her expression and she calms.

She rolls the toy a little, working the ribbed part over her clit until her breathing is no longer short and shallow but hard and deep.

Then she looks at me. "Come here."

God, she's beautiful.

Leaning down, I kiss and suck her stomach, nibble her breasts, and then I lower my mouth on the toy, taking it down my throat and giving her something to watch.

"Clay . . ." she murmurs.

I wet it, not sure if the fright has dried me out, but I'm doing this. I'm doing this with her. Bringing my leg over, I straddle her again and lower myself onto it, feeling the tip dip inside.

I immediately tense up.

"Is it too big?" she asks.

I want to say yes. I want to retreat. But people do this every day. *I can do this.*

I move my hips in a circle, brushing the vibrator over my clit and getting warmed up again, and then I sink it inside, just an inch at first, and then I stop. "Just give me a minute," I tell her.

I slide it out and back in, feeling the bulb of the shaft stretch me, and it hurts, but I sink farther down, the pain uncomfortable but bearable.

Liv thumbs my nipples, both of us silent and slow as I slide out and then back in again until I'm fully seated on her.

"Liv . . ."

"Just stay there," she whispers, holding me on her. "Stay there. Give it a minute."

I lean down, stretched, a little sore, and filled. It's inside me, all the way.

I kiss her, squeezing her breast, and I start moving, grinding on her.

"Ride me, Clay."

"Yeah," I moan.

I rub on her, letting the vibrations do their work, and in a moment, I'm so warm, I know I'm wet. I slide off and back on it, moving it in and out easily now, not feeling bad at all. Just . . . stretched.

I smile, lean back, and grip both sides of the tub, loving her eyes on my body as I move and put on a show for her.

"You want it, baby?" She grips my hips.

I grind faster, the thickness, the tip hitting me deep inside, and the little motor jackhammering on our clits, making a combination beat of the best fucking thing I think I've ever felt.

I groan, changing positions to bounce on top of her. "Oh, God," I cry, feeling it there now. Chasing it.

She squeezes my hips, baring her teeth and staring between us where our bodies meet. "Fuck, Clay. Harder, baby. Come on. Harder. It feels so good."

And I can't tell the difference between her moans and mine as we fuck in the bathtub.

I bring her hand up and suck on her finger, and she arches her back and digs her nails into my skin. "Jesus," she gasps.

And then throws her head back, every muscle tightening as she comes, and I thrust my pussy into hers, grinding her so hard I feel her clit throb against mine until I fucking come.

"God!" I cry. "Liv! Oh, it feels so good."

She grips my tits as I shudder and shake, my insides bursting with a wave of euphoria. My hips piston against her, jerking harder and faster until the orgasm starts to leave me, and I collapse on top of her, every part of me burning with exhaustion.

She holds me to her, and I think I register kisses on my hair, but the world spins too fast for me to be sure.

The vibrator still buzzes inside us.

"Again," she tells me, taking hold of my ass.

I look up, smiling before I kiss her lips.

"In the bed," I tell her. "You on top. Fucking me backward."

Her eyebrows shoot up.

I want to see her back move, her hair bouncing across her skin. And her ass.

I pull myself off the toy, wincing at the ache I didn't feel a moment ago. I stand up, my legs wobbly, and she pulls the other end out of her. I take her hand and help her up.

"You okay?" she asks.

I think so. "Yes."

Except none of this is leaving my system. I simply keep wanting more.

She holds one end of the toy under the spray, and I see the water turn a little pink from my blood.

I feel a blush cross my cheek and a smile begging to get out at the reminder of what she did to me.

How I can't go back now.

Then she turns it over and washes the other end.

Again, more blood.

I shoot my eyes up to her, but she's not looking at me.

Wait . . .

"You never did that with anyone before?" I gape at her.

"No," she says quietly, still not meeting my eyes.

But I thought that . . .

My mouth falls open, and I want to speak, but I don't know what to say. There are too many thoughts.

It was her first time, too.

I grab her by the arm, turn her to me, and I hear the toy drop to the floor as I cover her mouth with mine.

I can never go back now.

24

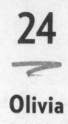

Olivia

"You can borrow something from me," I tell her.

Clay backs out of my room, the house still dark as only the faint hint of light pierces the clouds outside.

"I gotta brush my teeth and get my books." She kisses me, both of us walking and holding each other. "And charge my phone and do my math homework before class and . . ."

I cover her lips, silencing her. She pulls away, smiling and laughing and looking playful as we jog down the stairs, but I'm not smiling. Everything hurts, and I don't mean my body.

I'm falling. I hate seeing her leave, even though we'll see each other in a couple of hours.

But I hold back as we walk past the living room to the front door. I don't grab her again, even though my arms are screaming.

God, I got pathetic.

She stops, looking left, and I follow her gaze. Macon sits in the chair on the other side of the kitchen bar, his long legs in jeans, but he doesn't wear a shirt, and his hair is mussed. His head rests in his hand as a stream of smoke drifts to the ceiling from the cigarette between his fingers.

He stares at us.

"Good morning," she says.

I shoot a glance at her, seeing her approach him, and I try to stop her. "No, don't."

But she ignores me, and I wince like I'm bracing myself for a car wreck about to happen.

"I'm . . . uh," Clay stammers, breathing hard as she stares at my oldest brother. "Um . . . About the . . ."

He blows out smoke, his eyebrows narrowed, and I'm caught between being amused at seeing Clay nervous, and being scared because no conversation between these two will end well. Macon is an ass.

Her mouth opens and closes, Macon eating her for breakfast without moving a muscle, and then she exhales and turns to me.

"Yeah, fuck this," she says, kissing my lips once. "I'll see you later, okay?"

I smile tightly and nod. *Yeah, I tried to tell you.* "Bye."

Clay leaves, and I lock the door behind her, turning and meeting my brother's gaze. "She was just trying to apologize for being in your room during Night Tide."

He doesn't say anything, and I give up. There's no talking to him. I head for the stairs.

"Olivia?" he calls.

I stop, not in the mood.

I enter the living room again. "We're not supposed to smoke in the house."

His rule.

He drops the butt into a leftover beer bottle, the little sizzle of the embers extinguishing filling the silence.

He turns his eyes on me. "Finish with her."

My muscles tighten. "It's none of your business."

"She's using you."

My eyes immediately sting, and I shake my head.

"She will always think she can use you," he explains.

No. I can understand why he would think that, because I

thought it, too, but he doesn't see what goes on when it's just us. It's not like that.

"Because you're less to her," he says, rising from his chair. "And she's more."

He moves toward me, all the feelings and doubts and insecurities I had when I started this with her flooding back. I'm not attached. I like her. It feels good.

I'm not attached.

"She thinks she's more because she'll never want what you have," he continues. "Because she thinks you want what she has. Because she thinks everyone wants to be her."

No.

He advances on me slowly. "She has the power, Liv. This is how they think."

I swallow.

"You are giving her your power."

"What do you know?" I bite out.

"I know."

I shake my head absently, dropping my eyes to the floor. I'm in control. She's not running the show. Is that what he thinks? "I'm not in love with her," I tell him.

"Liv . . ."

I dart my eyes up, glaring at him. "You don't know anything."

"I know it will be over when she says, not you."

My lungs empty because I don't want to believe that's true, but I know it is. Everything relies on her. Where we show our faces. How we have to hide at school. The future. We get along in and out of the bedroom, and neither of us wants to be away from the other, but . . .

I'm out.

She's not.

Everything comes down to what she's going to do and how long it will take for her to own up.

But I don't care. I'm not taking this relationship to college. I don't know what Macon's worried about. Yeah, I like her.

I don't love her.

But my head swims the moment the words drift through my brain. *I don't love her.*

Macon leaves, his words hanging in the air as he heads up the stairs, and after a moment, I follow. He disappears into his room, and I grab my doorknob, ready to escape into mine, but Iron's bedroom door opens.

A redhead in ripped jeans and a pink cutoff T-shirt walks out, Dallas pulling on his jeans behind her, and Iron still passed out in the bed in the corner.

Amy pulls the door closed, but not before Dallas winks at me, a shit-eating grin on his face.

Ew, really? What the fuck? How did that happen? Goddammit. I guess things got more interesting after we left last night.

Amy adjusts her bra straps inside her shirt and looks up, freezing as she spots me.

Outstanding. This day started two minutes ago and sucks so badly already. Clay and I shouldn't have left the bed.

Amy sighs, a blush crossing her cheeks as she makes her way over to me. I'm pissed, but I'm not exactly sure why.

Maybe because my brothers are sleeping their way through my teammates all of a sudden? Because Amy got off in this house? Because the Saints might be treating this house like a brothel? Take your pick.

She stops in front of me. "Can I please ask you to keep this quiet?"

What? The threesome you just had with two older men?

"And I'll do the same about you and Clay?" she says matter-of-factly.

I narrow my eyes. She knows?

Fine, whatever. "Okay."

Not like I'd gossip anyway. Amy having sex with my family members isn't a bragging right for me.

But I hesitate. "Are you okay?" I ask, just making sure. They're experienced. She's not, and I don't want her suddenly feeling guilty about whatever happened in there.

Not that I think Dallas and Iron would coerce her into a situation she wasn't comfortable with, but it's a lot.

But she simply breaks into a smile, zero regret evident. "Is Clay okay?" she teases.

I open my door and enter my room. "Fuck off, Amy."

And I slam the door, happy to continue our silent hatred of each other.

D o you ever feel like you're living the same day over and over again?" Becks asks.

She tosses her carrot down on the lunch table, and I peel another string off my cheese stick, clicking out of the TikTok video.

"I used to," I say.

To be honest, I never really considered it a bad thing, though. Just the waiting period I needed to go through before I got to college and started my real life.

"What changed?" she asks as Chloe takes a seat beside me with her tray. "I need advice."

I smile to myself, but I keep Clay quiet. *She's what changed.* I'm not bored, that's for sure. I wish I could talk about her to someone.

"I'm getting out of here," I tell her instead. "That's what changed."

"Dartmouth." Chloe feigns a shiver. "It's going to be cold."

"Really?" I gasp. "Damn."

People keep saying that as if I'm unaware I'll see snow in New Hampshire.

"If you got into Dartmouth, you can get into Tulane," Becks points out. "Come on."

"Hmm . . ." I think, weighing the pros and cons in each hand. "Within driving distance to New York City, Boston, and Philadelphia, or more bugs the size of my fist and hundred-degree humidity. Tough decision."

Becks smiles, continuing to eat her carrot. I can always visit New Orleans. I've made my choice.

"I booked a limo for prom." Chloe elbows my arm. "My treat."

I glance at her, remembering. *Prom.* "Right." I hesitate, searching for words. "I mean, in case we don't have dates?"

In case I'm not going with Clay, and I know I'm not, because Macon is right, but it would be perfect to go with her. We still have a month. A lot can happen in a month.

"Absolutely," she says. "You should wear purple."

"I don't . . . wear purple."

"Red, then? With your black hair, it would look niiiiiiice."

"Black," I state.

But then she eyes me, her pink lips wet from licking the hummus off her cracker. "With red underneath?"

Her tone is soft and tantalizing, and awareness makes the hair on my arms rise. She's flirting.

"Maybe."

Chloe is pretty and she wouldn't hide me. She would be easier.

I look over my shoulder, seeing Clay surrounded by her friends at a table, hovering over an assignment she's trying to finish before class. Her eyes lift to mine, as if she already knew exactly where to find me, and all I can see anymore is her wet and on top of me in the shower. The perfect girl with her perfect hair, and her little secret.

Chloe would be much easier. But even if I'd met her before I started with Clay, I still wouldn't have been able to resist Clay as soon as I saw her. As soon as she spoke, I would've craved nothing more than to make her only see me.

"I love this bracelet." Chloe touches the metal symbol on my leather band. "An hourglass."

I pull my arm away. "Yeah, it's kind of a family thing." I stand up, grabbing my materials and garbage. "I gotta go," I tell her.

But as I drop everything into the trash bin, Chloe touches my arm, stopping me. I turn, seeing her standing in front of me. "Do you have a girlfriend?" she asks.

Huh?

Jesus. Almost four years at this school, and now people want to make me feel liked and accepted?

"Sorry, I asked Ms. Martelle," she says, "so I didn't embarrass myself before I asked you out, and she said she didn't think so. Will you go out with me sometime?"

I flash my eyes to Clay, seeing her watch us. The look in her eyes, like she's not breathing, owns me. She owns me.

It takes a moment, but I meet Chloe's gaze again. "I have a girlfriend," I tell her gently.

I belong to someone.

"But you're not going to prom with her?"

I fight not to look in Clay's direction again. "Maybe." *I hope.* "I'm sorry. It's . . ."

"Complicated," she finishes for me. "It's okay. I think I knew. I mean, how could you not be taken, right?"

Yeah, right.

"See you this weekend," I tell her.

I leave, heading to my locker and feeling a little bad. If Clay weren't in play, I would've accepted. How nice would it be to have someone anytime I want?

I stop at my locker and look down the hall, seeing Mark Calderon leaning into Sophia Herrera, the whispers between them and everything in his body language telling me they're getting it on.

How nice would it be to be as close to Clay as I want, anytime I want, and wherever I want, like them?

I could have that with someone like Chloe or Megan. I can have that when I leave for college.

But I really like my crazy-as-fuck Barbie doll with a mouth that pisses me off one minute and arms that hold me so tightly that I don't care if I can breathe the next.

I open my locker, and a paper drops onto the floor from inside.

Bending down, I pick it up and unfold the half sheet.

Fear grips me. It's probably a hate letter. A threat. It wouldn't be the first time.

I almost crumple it up, but I see the words and start reading.

It never looks like me, the person in the mirror, the black script reads.

She looks like everyone else.

I look around, not seeing anyone else in the hall, except for a few loiterers down by the doors to the lunchroom.

I keep reading.

She's like every woman on his arm—the same hair, the same clothes, the same smile, because to beat she has to compete, right?

I stood in front of the mirror this morning, a mouthful of toothpaste and my hair tangled by your fingers. You sucked my lips swollen last night, and I can still smell your kisses on my skin.

The world swims, how hard I'm used by you.

How all I have when you're done with me is my bones.

I don't care what I look like anymore as long as I look like yours.

Marked, raw, tangled, sore, and scented like you—I don't care.

As long as I look like yours.

My eyes burn, a baseball lodged in my throat as I read it again and again. *As long as I look like yours.*

A tear spills down my cheek, and I hear a locker open. I look over my shoulder, down the hall, and see Clay watching me as she pulls out a book.

Even from this distance, I can see her eyes pooling, too.

The hall floods with students, afternoon classes about to get under way, and I lose sight of her, but my body overheats under my skin, and I'm so hot.

I need her. I need her skin on mine like I need food. More than I need food.

I love Clay Collins.

A text rolls in, and I click it, seeing it's from her.

As long as I look like yours.

I hover my fingers over the screen; nothing I want to say is good enough. I just want to haul my ass over there and press my mouth to hers in front of this whole fucking hallway.

I can't breathe.

Clay, I'm dying, I type. You're killing me. Please stop.

A text rolls in a moment later. Can you?

25

Clay

I pull up in front of Mimi's house, parking right behind my mother's Rover. I check my phone before I get out of the car.

Liv never texted me back.

It was a rhetorical question anyway. I don't believe for one second that she wants me to stop. She's capable of walking away when she wants. She's proven it.

I want to give her everything she deserves, and I will. Prom is coming. Almost at the end of the school year. After the debutante ball. Near graduation.

I'll face everything then. I guess I just thought this would be easier. I thought it was just sex. I didn't expect . . . to never want to walk away.

I type out a text. Send me a pic.

I wait, a cool breeze sweeping through the trees as the sun starts to set. I'd stayed at school, knowing Liv had rehearsal today and then had to babysit her nephew, and did my homework in the library, killing time before my visit with Mimi.

Her reply rolls in, and I click on the image she sends.

A bowl of penne pasta with white sauce, artichokes, and chicken. I roll my eyes. Of your face, please?

A few seconds later, I see her beautiful lips, a faint blush red, puckered to the camera next to a forkful of penne.

I smile. She must be eating dinner. That mouth is mine in about thirteen hours, I say. I can't wait for school.

I'll be done with my pasta by then, she assures me. Because it and me are having a total relationship without you right now.

I send her a kiss emoji with a heart and then head into my grandmother's house.

"Mimi?" I call out, setting my bag down and straightening my sweater vest and Polo underneath. "I'm heeeeere."

No one answers, and I drift through the living room, den, and dining room, looking.

"Mom?" I say loudly.

I see movement outside, and I walk through the solarium toward the patio.

"That has never been an option," Mimi bites out.

I halt, moving to the side, behind a fern. My mom and grandmother sit at the patio table on the other side of the glass, the open door next to me allowing their voices to drift inside.

"My family is miserable," Mom tells her.

"Then fix it. For God's sake, I'm not against divorce when it improves a woman's situation," Mimi fires back, "but leaving Jefferson Collins and letting some other woman win . . . How could you live with yourself? What are you teaching Clay?"

"That perhaps she should know when to walk away?"

"A divorce is failing," Mimi says, "and you are both better than that. And don't act like you don't still love him."

A divorce? I stand there, unmoving. My mother's actually considering divorce. I thought maybe a trial separation after I graduated, but . . . Have they already started the process?

"And when my father cheated on you?" Mom asks her. "Do you still think you won anything?"

"Oh, honey." Mimi picks up her glass of lemonade, the pristine blue of the pool in the yard beyond. "I knew exactly what I was getting into. And I knew exactly what I would get in return." She takes a drink and sets the glass back down. "Some days were almost unbearable, but I'm still here and those women aren't."

My grandfather cheated on Mimi? I guess I'm not shocked. I didn't know the man well. He passed when I was seven. But Mimi wears it like a badge—the fact that she was his wife.

She goes on. "You will never regret keeping your chin up and making the sacrifices it takes to maintain the life you have spent years building. She will come into your home, not because he loves her, but because he misses you and can't be alone. Once a man becomes used to being taken care of, he can only live that way. He'll replace you out of necessity, not desire."

She. My father's mistress.

"She will come into your home," Mimi continues, "and parent your child and spend your money and drive your cars. Fix it."

My chest rises and falls with shallow breaths. *Everything's changing.*

I back away from the patio, heading back into the house, and ball my fists.

I knew about the other woman. I even thought there might be more than one. Who could blame him? My mother was a bitch and made the house unbearable, trying to control everyone and everything, and we were all suffocating under the clothes and the makeup and the standards, but . . .

Is he actually leaving her? Is he making a new life without us?

Is he leaving me *with* her?

Or is she leaving him? It sounded like my grandmother was trying to talk her out of something.

Where do I go when I come home for holidays? They don't know me anymore. Do they even want me around—my mother forced to keep up appearances, and my father forced to support a family he no longer wants?

Jesus, do they even know I'm still here?

I rub my hands up and down my face, drifting down the hallway, past all our photos that my grandmother will keep up because we look like a happy family, and my grandfather looks like a doting husband.

I drift until I find my way upstairs and in my grandmother's room, veering straight for the hidden cubby drawer in the mantel of her fireplace.

Reaching inside, I dig out the stack of letters I'd found there when I was eight that now make a lot more sense since Macon told me about Two Locks—the old, abandoned farm on Harley Creek my family owns where he said my grandmother hid her affair.

I stare at the stack—more than fifty letters probably—yellowed with age and secured with a white ribbon. At the time, I'd thought it was adult stuff. Letters were how old people communicated; I'd thought my grandmother was much older than she was and didn't have a phone or some shit.

I never thought they were romantic gestures.

I hold the tattered envelopes, sifting to the bottom of the stack and take note of the postmarks and dates.

They start in 1983. They end in 2017.

Thirty-four years.

Carefully, I set them back in the cubby as something I don't like winds through my stomach, making me feel like I'm in a place I don't recognize. Surrounded by strangers.

I don't want things to change. I won't recognize my life, and I'll be lost. Nausea rises up my throat, and I groan. I don't like this feeling.

I want my father back. I want my mother and Mimi to be proud of me.

I want our life back together.

Without telling them that I'm leaving, I jump back in my car and think about going home—or to Liv—but in minutes, I'm in front of Wind House instead. The parking lot is empty, and Mrs. Gates's car isn't in the driveway.

I park and drift past the door I usually come in during business hours, sneaking through my same window and down into the basement. I switch on the lights and look around, finding it empty and quiet, all the tables vacant and the tiny hum of the coolers making the only noise in the room.

Such a sharp place. Hard and cold, and I don't know why I find it comforting.

I walk over and put my hands on the sterilized steel table Alli lay on all those weeks ago, images running through my head that she's now ash. Gone.

Forever.

If she could go back, would she make the same choice? It makes sense to suffer for who you are rather than who you aren't, but ultimately, nothing is as bad as dead, right?

There's only so much a person can take. We all have a limit.

Without thinking, I hop up, sit on the table, and swing my legs over before laying my whole body down on the freezing metal table.

I settle my back in, molding myself to the surface, and rest my legs slightly apart with my hands at my sides.

Everyone who lies here is dead. They don't get to stare up at the stark fluorescent lights and let it sink in that their shot is over. That was it.

I'll be here someday. Done. Never to speak or love or kiss again.

What will I regret?

What if I'm alone?

26

Olivia

So, I was kind of thinking," I say quietly as students make their way into the women's locker room for field practice, "I could cancel shopping with Megan and Chloe and go shopping with you instead?"

Clay sits on the bench, pulling on her sneakers and tying the laces. Her beautiful hair is flipped to one side as she leans over in her black leggings and sports bra.

She doesn't answer.

"Clay?" I press.

"Shopping?" she repeats, not meeting my eyes.

I tighten my ponytail, looking around for eavesdroppers. "Dress shopping for prom?" I remind her. Did she even hear me?

She meets my eyes, looking like a deer caught in the headlights. "Oh, um . . ."

What the hell is wrong with her? I sent her a proper sexy pic of me last night, after the dumb one of me with my pasta, and she didn't answer, and she's barely made eye contact since we walked into school for our morning workout.

"Uh . . ." She swallows, standing up and avoiding my gaze. "I actually already have my dress."

She has a dress . . . Okay, so what does that mean? I stare at her,

her body language all wrong. What the hell happened between yesterday and today? She can't go shopping with me?

I fight to find my words, but she sees me staring and meets my eyes briefly. "I mean, we said we'd keep this casual, right?" she says, letting out a laugh. "The date on Wednesday was enough risk for a while, I think."

Enough risk . . .

Why won't she look at me? Maybe I can stand being a secret for a little while longer, but I don't like this distance that's there all of a sudden. I'm not just some fuck.

I turn and take my phone out of my locker, grabbing my earbuds, too. "I like spending time with you outside of bed, too, Clay."

But she doesn't want that. Or she's not ready to admit it.

She reaches for me. "Liv . . ."

"Just forget it." I move aside and close my locker. "Macon was right. He always is. I'm the stupid one."

She slams her locker and moves past me, murmuring, "Meet me in the shower, now."

"No," I tell her. "I'm over it."

I'm not doing this anymore. Shit's changed. I want to go to prom, and I want to go with my fucking girlfriend. That's it.

I walk the other direction, but someone slips in front of me, cutting me off. "Hi," Chloe chirps, carrying her bag and smiling as she looks me up and down. "You're right. Black is your color."

I force a tight smile as Clay tries to hide her snarl. "Thanks," I say to her.

She moves past us to the next row and Clay comes in close. "I don't want to lose you, okay?" she whispers. "Just give me a chance. I'm just not ready yet. I'm not sure. What if this isn't real? What if it's—"

I grab her by the arms and back her into the lockers, the metal clanking echoing throughout the room. She gasps as I glare at her, my teeth damn near bared.

Someone comes around the corner, and I look at Ruby. "Beat it."

She looks quickly between Clay and me, ultimately deciding to not get involved before she ducks back out of sight. I press my palm to Clay's chest, feeling the rapid beat inside. "When your heart beats too fast," I grit out, "it doesn't pump enough blood to the rest of your body. It starves your organs, making you light-headed, unable to breathe, dizzy, weak, you can't think . . ." I dive into her, pressing my forehead to hers. "I do that to you. Not him. *I'm* real."

I release her, backing away and waiting. Waiting for anything. Waiting for a yes. A no. Waiting for her to realize that she loves her life with me in it, and the fact that she's willing to sacrifice how good this feels breaks my heart.

She stands there, her chin trembling as she stares down at nothing, agony written all over her face. "I can't . . ." she mouths before finding her voice. "I can't tell my parents that I'm gay. I can't ever tell them that. They won't see me the same way anymore. I'll disappoint them."

Pain racks my body as she goes blurry in my vision. "You don't have to tell them you're gay," I whisper. "You just have to tell them that you're in love with me."

Please. I understand how scary it is to change things. To fear being seen differently in the eyes of the people you love.

But she will regret not taking this chance. She may lose me, but she will never stop who she really is, and someday it will be too much to hide anymore.

"Just take my hand," I murmur. "Please take my hand."

But slowly, she shakes her head, tears spilling down her face as she backs away.

I take a step. "Clay . . ."

She shakes her head, backing up more and more.

"Clay, don't do this."

"I'm sorry," she says, wiping her tears.

And I lose it. I slam my hand into the lockers, on fire. "Goddamn you," I growl. "Goddammit! I told you to stay away from me, didn't I? I told you to leave me alone!"

I knew this would happen. I always knew she was a cunt.

She sobs, and I get in her face. "Why didn't you just leave me alone, huh?"

But I don't give her a chance to answer. I step around her, exit the locker room, and run through the still-empty school until I'm out of the building and a mile away in minutes. My lungs give out, I pant, and halt, hunching over as I try to breathe and stop the tears.

H ours later, my eyes still burn.

But I've stopped crying. I can't believe I did at all.

"Heart Heart Head" plays as I dip one pearl after another into the glue and stick each to the bodice. Lavinia is running an errand in Miami today, so the shop is closed, the music's on low in the workroom, and I'm alone. And thankful for it. I didn't want to go home right after school, and I'm not in the mood to have to talk to customers. I hadn't turned on the lights when I came in. I still wear my sunglasses. I don't want to see too much.

I breathe in and out, gluing pearl after pearl, and still smell her with every breath. Why do I still smell her?

Why do I still feel her weight on me like I did the other night when we woke up to her parents fighting? She fit so perfectly in my arms, and I didn't want to move from that spot, even if a dozen tornadoes were headed our way or a bomb dropped. I would've died there.

Macon was right. I would never have been the one to stop it.

I hate this feeling. I hate that maybe I finally understand a little of what my mother felt. I don't want to understand. That kind of despair is pathetic.

I close my eyes, pushing away the tears again, but then I hear the back door slam shut, and I blink.

I lift my head from the worktable in time to see Callum Ames stroll into the room. My muscles tense; Milo and two others from our class—Bailey and Keagan—are following Callum in.

Everything inside me tightens, alert.

"What are you doing in here?" I demand. "Get out."

Callum approaches, and I twist in my stool, about to jump off, but he leans in as the others take up position around the table.

I glare at him. "Don't touch me."

"I will never touch you unless you want me to," he says in a low voice. "And you will want me to."

I look around at the boys, the sun low in the sky outside the windows, and I take my phone out of my jeans pocket, tapping away.

"I'm calling my brothers," I tell him.

"Do," he replies. "You're not in danger."

I meet his eyes.

"I guess I've never understood rapists and roofies." He laughs to his friends. "What fun is it to win something that you have to steal?" He lowers his voice, husky. "I want things you don't know you want to give me."

Oh, please.

"Kiss me," he says. "Kiss me and I'll go."

Is he high?

He pulls off my sunglasses, and I jerk away.

"Have you ever kissed a man?" he asks.

"Have you ever kissed a cow?"

He laughs under his breath as if I'm just so naïve. How many times have people asked me that same stupid question? As if I need to try everything to know for sure that I don't want it.

He inches closer, and I press my back into the table, still holding my phone.

"Did you know my father is appraising your land today?"

I stare at him.

"Did you know his plans include demolishing the old light-house?" he asks. "They're building cabanas in that spot."

His friends draw closer, ever so slowly, and he raises his eyes to meet mine.

"Did you know that they'll break ground by the end of the year?" Callum taunts.

The lump in my throat grows, but I don't falter.

He's lying. That's too soon.

"Did you know that a structure *can* be deemed a historical land-mark and cannot be destroyed after it reaches one hundred years old?" he tells me. "And while fucking *for* me will get you Mercutio, fucking me will get you a meeting with Raymond FitzHugh to push through your petition to protect the lighthouse. And, in ef-fect, your land." The corners of his eyes crinkle as he pins me with a look. "Fucking me *good* guarantees it, in fact."

I squeeze the phone in my fist.

"And did you know—"

"Shut up." I clench my teeth, steeling my spine.

He cocks his head.

"Just shut up."

And did you know . . . ? And did you know . . . ? I should keep my mouth shut, but the anger is spilling over the side. I'm full.

"Everything in the way you act tells me I'm supposed to be scared," I say. "Showing up here with your boys. Uninvited. When I'm alone." I gaze around the room at all of them. "What happens when you find out that the one thing you want is something you will never get? You will never feel like a man, Callum."

That's why he does this. Because hurt people hurt people. He doesn't want me. He doesn't want Clay.

I know what he wants.

"You'll never take enough from people to erase him and how he fucks your stepmom and fucks your stepsister and hates you."

His jaw flexes. "You think you know—"

"There's nothing else to know about you," I bite out. "You're not in control. You're a bottle of Jack Daniel's away from slitting your wrists."

The threat of four bodies surrounding me vibrates off my skin, and I don't want to antagonize him and risk myself, but I'm tired of them making me cower.

And cry. *Do your worst, you fucking asshole.* I don't think I can feel any more pain than I already do today.

I turn, slide my phone into my pocket, and start gluing again, feeling them all behind me.

I wait for the pushback. For the grab. The yank of my hair.

But it doesn't come. The bodies in the room start to filter out, the back door opens and closes, and I glue more pearls, still feeling him behind me.

"We still have a deal," he says. "And if you accept that role, I expect you to keep your end of it. Fox Hill. Be ready when I call. I'm dying to see you fuck."

I keep working, his words making my stomach roil.

"How is she, by the way?"

I pause for a moment.

"She's good, isn't she?" His voice is almost a whisper.

I swallow.

"A woman's body is made for men."

My heart punches against my chest, unbidden images of him with Clay . . .

"She will fuck me," he says. "You know she will."

I close my eyes, knowing without a doubt that he's right. She won't do it because she wants to. She'll do it because she's tired of fighting herself and she'll give up. She'll just let it happen, because it's easier to surrender.

I bite the corner of my mouth to stifle the tears, hearing him leave as the feel of her floods through me. My arms around her, my nose buried in her neck.

His mouth on her body, his fingers inside her.

I drop my tools, a sob lodged in my throat. *Fuck her.* How did I let her do this to me?

As if on autopilot, I take my bag, leave the store, and lock the doors.

She hasn't called. She didn't approach me the rest of the day.

She's going to fuck him this weekend, and there's nothing I can do about it.

I don't know when it starts to rain, but in the half hour it takes me to leave St. Carmen, cross the tracks, and walk home, I'm drenched. My hair sticks to my face, and I trudge through puddles without the energy to avoid them. I step into my house, hearing the TV going and a radio blasting upstairs.

"Liv?" Iron hops off the barstool. "Jesus, why didn't you call for a ride?"

Water spills down my legs and drips from my clothes. I walk for the stairs.

"Hey." He hurries over and grabs my arm. "Christ, what happened?"

He looks down at me, but I can't look up. "I'm fine."

I can't stop the tears welling; I only hope he can't tell the difference with the rain on my face.

"That fucking bitch," Dallas says, strolling over. "She break it off with you or you with her?"

I shake my head and climb up the stairs.

"Liv?" Iron calls.

But I keep walking.

"It's dinnertime," he says behind me. "Come and sit down. Please."

I hear the worry in his voice, and it reminds me of Mom. How we would watch her avoid us and disappear into her room.

But I just want to be alone.

"Liv!" Iron shouts as I reach the top of the stairs.

"That's what they do," Dallas bites out. "Use and abuse until they've had their fill. I told you! We all told you!"

I push open my door and slam it shut, dropping my bag to the floor.

"Macon!" I hear Iron shout downstairs.

I slide down the wall, sitting on the floor of my dark room, and lean back, my arm hanging over my bent knee.

I'm here. She's somewhere on the other side of the tracks—shopping or doing homework with her friends or meeting him or . . .

If she wanted to be here, she'd be here. She doesn't want to be here.

She doesn't want me. She's not thinking about me right now. She wants to be free of me.

Silent tears spill down my face, and I lean my head back, squeezing my fist as I hear paper crinkle.

I look at my hand, seeing a ball of paper inside that I didn't realize I'd grabbed hold of from my school bag.

I open my fist, recognizing the lined paper and black handwriting. It's her note. I don't remember reaching into my school bag for it on the way home.

She wants to be free of me. Yesterday, she was mine.

I bend the other knee up and rest my elbows on them, burying my head in my hands.

Fuck her.

Fuck Clay Collins, piece of shit Saint with her money and hair and . . .

But I can't stop sobbing, nearly choking.

My door swings open, and I smell the grease on Macon's hands as he squats down next to me.

"Please don't yell at me," I beg, not looking at him. "Just let me get past it, okay? I will. I'll get past it. I just need tonight."

My family is good about staying in their lane, but when one of us is upset, everyone goes on alert. With our mother being clinically depressed, it only makes sense that one or more of us will have inherited her problems.

I'm not depressed. I'm just . . . shredded.

"Look at me." He puts his hands on mine. "Livvy."

I shake my head. *Please go away.* A lump stretches in my throat so big it hurts. *Just let me get past it.*

"You're going to stand up," he says.

I shake, a cry in my throat. "I can't . . . stand up." I gasp, fighting for air. "I can't breathe."

He pulls my hands away, and I see him hover over me and take my face in his hands. "You're going to stand up," he tells me, "and you're gonna do your homework, and you're gonna go to prom." My stomach twists into knots, and I shake my head. *I can't.* "You're going to be in the same room with her, Monday through Friday for the rest of the school year, and you're not sacrificing yourself out of fear. You're going to do all of this, Liv."

I cry harder, squeezing my eyes shut. I'm not in love with her. She can't do this to me. This wasn't supposed to happen.

"You're going to go to Dartmouth." He dips his head down close to mine, holding my eyes. "And you're going to join a club and make some friends, and in a couple of months you're going to have a life."

How?

"You're going to leave," he grits out. "You're going to leave here and leave any hope of her. You're going to do the hardest thing you've ever had to do, because it'll save you, Liv. Because you're Trysta Jaeger's daughter, and we're going to do what she would've wanted us to do and didn't have the courage to do herself. We keep biting back. We survive, because sometimes that's the most violent thing we can do to other people. We stay alive."

My body shakes as the tears pour.

"And in a year, you won't even understand how you could have loved her this much," he tells me. "I promise you."

How can he promise that? He doesn't know. No one does. I don't think I can see tomorrow, much less months from now. God, how do I leave?

"I promise," he says again, his eyes hard. "I promise."

But I can't imagine not wanting her. I can't see not hating her with someone else and wanting anyone else as much as I want her. I cry, covering my face with my hands again so he doesn't see how fucking awful and pathetic I became because of her.

How did I let this happen to myself?

But for a moment, maybe I understand a fraction of what my mother felt all her life. The despair. God, I hate it. I hate it so much.

Macon doesn't say more. He scoops me up into his arms and carries me out of my room. Holding me tight, he carries me into his, where my father's old recliner still sits, and sits down, hugging me close.

"Old-world pepperoni," he orders as he tucks my head into his neck.

And faintly, I hear Trace's grumble. "I hate old-world pepperoni. It scratches the roof of my mouth."

But he leaves, following instructions, and after a moment, I let my arm circle my brother's neck as he holds me until the pizza comes.

27

Clay

"Y ou okay?" Krisjen asks.

I empty my books into my locker, pulling out my Spanish book and my copy of *Othello* for homework tonight. "I'm fine."

Liv stands across the hall chatting with Chloe, and I hear laughter. I glance over my shoulder, trying not to look like I know exactly where she is every moment. Chloe leans in and greets Jessa Washington and Erin Merluzzi, who approach. Girl certainly makes friends fast. They strike up a convo in their small group, Liv smiling and like . . . actively fucking participating.

"Are you sure?" Krisjen's voice is low. "You look like hangry, like you haven't eaten in days and you're going to morph into something outrageous if you don't get to dine on an unbaptized baby soon."

I shut my locker and close my bag, tearing my eyes away before Liv sees me looking.

"Clay . . ." She touches my arm.

But I pull away. "I'm fine."

"Did you tell her you loved her?"

I snap my eyes to Krisjen, who stares me in the eyes, dead-on.

"I don't." I drop my eyes, fiddling with my bag. "It just felt really good. I don't know, I'm . . ." More laughter echoes behind me, and I look over my shoulder, watching all four girls head down the hall away from me. Liv doesn't spare a glance my way, as if she actually never noticed that I'm right here. I swallow. "I'm just confused."

"Are you?"

Oh, shut up.

I walk away without saying goodbye and leave school with most of the other students; Liv is probably staying late for rehearsal again.

She didn't even look at me. She hasn't looked at me in days, as if she wasn't begging me not to leave her bed last week. Gone. Done. Over. She's surviving.

And from the looks of it, surviving well. For someone who had a chip on her shoulder about the new girl, she's making her a bestie awfully fast. She has people now.

And all I want is her. What the hell happened?

I drift to my car and drive home, my head racked with pain from holding back tears all day. But I finally let them go.

I've barely eaten anything in three days. I can't stop thinking about her. If she called right now, I would rush to her wherever she was for just a chance at one more night.

God, I miss her. Why can't she be more patient? Why can't she give me that? Why does anyone need to know? How was she so willing to give me up over me just wanting her to myself for a while longer? Was it too much to ask not to be rushed?

Just be understanding. Just love me. I loved her so good. It should've been enough.

Forgetting my bag in my car, I trudge through my front door, not noticing anyone or any sound as I traipse up the stairs with a weight almost too heavy to carry on my shoulders. I enter my room, close the door, and head over to the bed. I collapse and roll, pulling the comforter over me as I bury my head inside.

I'll get over it. First loves never last anyway. I knew it would hurt when it eventually happened.

It won't always feel like this.

But the idea of Liv getting over me makes the tears stream harder and faster. I hate this feeling in my stomach. I hate the thoughts whirling in my head like a tornado of someone else making love to her and dancing for her and waking up to her.

I hate it so much that my mind starts to tilt, and I'm angry. Even though I broke up with her, and this is all my fault, I'm angry with her so much that I want to fucking make sure no one compares to me. That she's miserable forever, unable to forget me. No one else will be able to make her happy. No one will feel like me. She should've waited for me.

I don't know when I fall asleep, but when I wake up, the sunlight streaming through my windows is gone, and the room is dark. I blink my eyes, my head still aching, but I register voices. The ones that woke me up.

"Get out, then!" my mom yells. "Get out! Run to her."

"It's not about her!"

I sit up, my eyelids heavy and tears dried on my face as I listen from inside my room.

"I'm not even in love with her," my dad says. "Goddammit, Regina!"

"Just leave!" Footfalls hit the stairs. "All you care about is yourself. You're always gone anyway."

"And you're here?" he retorts. "Is that what you think? I can't do this anymore! I'll be back for the rest of my stuff."

Something breaks, a door slams, and I hear a car start.

I throw off the covers, bolting from the room. "Dad . . ." I pull open my door and race down the stairs, seeing my mother standing in the foyer as headlights skim from one window to the other outside.

I run to the door, open it, and leap out into the driveway as his taillights speed farther and farther away.

"Dad!" I cry.

No! I hurry to my car, reach inside, and pull my phone out of my school bag, dialing his number.

"Baby, no!" Mom calls out.

But I shake my head, all the rage and despair and heartache pooling into a fucking boiler inside my gut, and I can't stop myself.

He left me. He didn't talk to me or say goodbye or . . .

I head back into the house, walking and not even paying attention to where I'm going, only that my mom stumbles after me in tears.

I hear the line pick up, and I'm speaking before he says a word. "Don't come back."

"Clay . . ." he whispers, and I can hear the tears in his throat. "Baby, I . . ."

"'Clay, baby,'" I mock. "'I . . . uh, uh, uh . . .' God, enough!" I roar. "Just say you found a new life, and you don't want us anymore! Just have a fucking backbone! I hate you! Say it so we can finally be free of you! Say you don't want us anymore!"

My eyes burn so hard I can barely keep them open, but I feel good for a hot minute, having someone to take this out on.

"Listen to me," he says.

But I don't. "Don't come back," I grit out. "We were always this weak, weren't we?" I head up the stairs. "Without him, we're nothing, and pretty soon, it will be as if he never existed!" I rip Henry's portrait off the wall in the hallway, my mother sobbing behind me. "As if we never were a family!"

I cry so hard, but I can't stop myself. I drop the phone, charging down the hallway and pulling all of our pictures off the wall, the glass in the frames crashing onto the floor.

"Clay, stop!" my mom begs.

"It was always a house of cards!" I hiss. "Because we're weak! We were always weak!"

I was always weak, and now I've lost everything. I wanted to be perfect and for what? For this?

I growl, taking our family portrait—the last one with Henry in it—and slam it onto the floor, the whole thing shattering.

My mother grabs me, but I flail, running away. "Leave me alone!"

I scurry down the stairs, out the door, and past my car, racing into the night. I don't know where I'm going. I have no money, no phone, but I don't care about anything anymore. I don't care if I never come back. I gave up the one thing that made me feel alive—made me excited for tomorrow—and with her I could've withstood anything.

But now, everything is foreign. School, my home, even my skin.

I run until the air in my lungs hurts, and I can't tell if it's sweat or tears on my face, but when I stop, I realize I'm in front of Wind House.

I head around the back, down the small incline at the side of the home, and up to the back door. The hall light glows inside, and I don't know what time it is, but maybe she's in there. I'd forgotten my keys and everything.

I knock hard, hoping there's work tonight, despite the fact that I'm actually wishing someone has died so I have something to do.

I knock again and again, ready to crumple onto the ground, because I can't keep my legs under me.

The door opens, and Mrs. Gates stands there in her scrubs. I gasp in relief and try to push past her.

But she stops me. "Clay, no."

I wipe the tears on my face. "I can handle it. I'm fine."

She doesn't know what's wrong, but she can see I'm upset.

I try to veer around her, but she fills the doorway. "Clay . . ."

"Please!" I plead, pushing past her. "I need to be here."

"Clay, it's a child," she rushes out as I pass.

I stop, staring at the floor but not seeing it.

Children don't come through often, but when they do, she makes sure I'm not present. Maybe it's because of Henry. Maybe it's because she knew my parents weren't aware that I come here, and the death of a child, even ones I don't know, will be hard.

I don't turn around to look at her, merely raising my gaze to the steel double doors ahead. It feels like my heart is floating in my chest as my stomach roils.

I keep walking, hearing her rush after me. "Clay, please."

But I ignore her. Pushing through the doors, I enter the room and see the boy, a small body outlined under a sheet.

He's uncovered down to his stomach, and something spills down the drain, but I don't look to see what.

I walk over.

"Clay . . ."

I know she's worried, but I don't know . . . Maybe I'm just too numb tonight to be scared anymore. I need to do this.

Approaching the boy's side, I see his wet brown hair slicked back, his jaw slack, and his eyes partially open, the brown pupils foggy.

She'd just washed him. Water still runs down the drain underneath the table, and his palms face up at his sides. There's dirt under his nails and scratches on his forearm, probably from playing with his cat or dog.

A lump grows in my throat, always finding this part hardest of all. The evidence of their lives. Bruises, skinned knees, old scars, chipped nail polish . . .

A tear spills over as I look down at his skinny arms. "He's, um . . ."

"Like Henry," she says, seeing what I see. The coloring is different, but they're about the same age. Ten or eleven.

"What happened to him?" I ask her, still letting my eyes roam for any evidence of violence.

"He drowned," she replies. "He was swimming at the Murtaugh Inlet. Got swept into the current."

It isn't unheard of. We swim a lot in Florida. Drownings happen.

The hard part is that it's not a quick death. He would've been aware with every second that passed that help wasn't coming.

Like Henry.

"His brother was making out with his girlfriend in his car and didn't notice for ten minutes," she whispers, her throat thick.

I almost feel sorry for him, too. A mistake that will haunt him forever.

And I'm here. Alive. Healthy. Continuously making problems worse because I act like I don't have a clue.

I smooth back his hair, everything at home forgotten for the moment, because somewhere out there in town is a devastated family who will never see their son smile again.

I draw in a deep breath and swallow the tears that want to come as I raise my eyes to Mrs. Gates. "Embalming?"

"Yes," she tells me. "There will be a viewing on Thursday followed by cremation."

I nod and pull the rubber band off my wrist, sweeping my hair up into a ponytail. "I'll take the lead."

We work for the next two hours, not talking other than her instruction here and there. I can't look him in the face when the needles go in, feeling the bile rise, because it's hard not to see Henry on the table. We prepare him to stay preserved until the funeral, and I'll come back in a couple of days to take care of the cosmetics and dress him, but the embalming process takes longer with me here now, because it's like the first time I'm doing it all over again. What mattered most to me with Henry was that Mrs. Gates was gentle with my brother. I take extra care with this one.

"Did I ever tell you that I lived in New York for a time?" Mrs. Gates says across the table.

I meet her eyes as we work.

"I loved it." She smiles a little. "Too cold, but it was a lot of fun. That's where I studied to become a funeral director."

I think I knew that, but I can't be sure.

She shuts off the machine. "It's one of the best schools in the country for mortuary science."

Mortuary science?

"I can get you in," she says. "If you want to go."

I stop, locking eyes with her. My first instinct is to laugh or scoff. I can't tell people I'm an undertaker. It's not romantic like an actor or an artist, or heroic like a lawyer or a doctor.

But then, most people haven't seen what I've seen here, either. Mrs. Gates is there during one of the most important times in a person's life.

"You have a strong stomach," she tells me. "You empathize. You care. I think the best people to help us say goodbye are the ones who've had to do it themselves."

I keep working, listening.

"You know what these families need." She drops tools to the tray, picking up another one. "Funerals aren't for the dead, after all."

They're for the survivors.

The idea is ridiculous. Everyone will laugh.

My grandmother would have a cow.

But then, I look down at the kid, Mitchell Higgins from the name on his file, and know that tomorrow I could be him.

If not tomorrow, next week. Next year. Five years from now, because no matter when, it is coming.

"I know your parents want you to go to Wake Forest," she says, "but if you decide your life should go a different path, I'll sponsor you."

Sponsor me?

"You work here on vacations and give me two years after you've gotten your degree," she tells me, "and I'll pay your tuition."

28

Clay

N ew York. Why does the idea of being that close to Liv make
me so happy? I can't follow her. I gave her up, and being that
close will only make it impossible to move on.

And worse. Being that close and knowing she's moving on will
be unbearable.

I can't go to New York. Wake Forest is perfect, actually. It's
halfway between home and her, not an easy distance to either. I
need to let her be. Just like she asked me to weeks ago.

I walk up my driveway, seeing lights glowing from inside my
house, and I know I'll find my mom sitting at the table, waiting
for me.

Not so much because she's worried, which any other parent
might be since I left my phone in my room hours ago and she
couldn't get hold of me, but because it would look bad to go to sleep
with an angry teenage daughter out this late.

I step inside the house, the clock chiming one in the morning
as I lock the door behind me.

But as I would normally stomp up the stairs and try to hide in
my room to avoid her, I find myself listening for her.

I hear nothing.

I drift from room to room, looking for her, a lot calmer than I was hours ago.

They weren't always like this. I keep forgetting that. When my brother was alive, we were pretty happy, actually. My parents are disappointing, but when I remember the parents Henry knew, I miss them.

A painting has been ripped off the wall and lies on the marble floor facedown, a vase with roses shattered next to it amid a puddle of the water that was inside.

I head up the stairs, seeing their wedding pictures broken on the floor of the hallway, as well as the destruction I wreaked before I ran out. I find my mother in her closet, gowns, shoes, and blouses strewn everywhere as she leans back against the dresser in the center of the room, holding a large bottle of Evian between her bent legs.

She meets my eyes, and I'm stricken for a moment.

She looks like me.

Uncertain. Deflated. Too many feelings and no way to put them into words.

Young.

She wears a pair of cream-colored silk boxers with a white cashmere sweater, her hair a mess and black around her eyes from crying.

Not the usual masterpiece she's been the past few years.

She holds up the nearly empty Evian bottle, and I notice another, drained and lying among the clothes. "I thought champagne would be the answer, but . . ."

"'Carbs are never the answer.'" I recite our motto.

I walk over and slide down to sit beside her, my back against the dresser.

"I'm still deciding," she sighs. "So stand by." And then she downs the rest of the bottle.

I stare at her, wondering if she ever had any idea this day was possible. When she bought her wedding dress, or when they bought this house, did she know there was no guarantee? That someday she'd end a pregnancy because she couldn't stand to raise another child and love something so hard and possibly lose it? That her husband would give up, his heartbreak making him hurt us when hers just made her hurt herself?

She gazes off. "I don't know how she did it, Clay," she tells me. "For years, I've been trying to crack your grandmother's secret."

I listen.

"I mean, I would wake up the day after Thanksgiving when I was little," she continues, "and the house would be completely decorated for Christmas already. I would go to sleep on New Year's Day and wake up with it all gone again." She smiles to herself. "It was like magic, how she got things done, as if she had a wand and never needed to sleep."

Does my mom know that's how I see her, too? Somehow, she handles everything.

"Perfect wife, perfect mother," she murmurs. "Perfect house, on time for every event, always looked impeccable, and that woman can schmooze a room full of Norwegian investors without speaking a single word of Norwegian, or a room full of good ol' boys who think America's decline started with a woman's right to vote." She pauses. "She could do all that, Clay. I can't do any of that." She turns her head toward me. "I mean, how could she do all that? She would never have let me see her like this. Like you're seeing me now. What was her secret?"

I feel my lips press together for a split second before they open. "Mimi was having an affair with the old sheriff."

Her eyes narrow on me, and she cocks her head ever so slightly as her chest caves. "What?"

I nod. "For thirty-four years," I say. "They used to meet out at Two Locks."

Her mouth falls open a little, and I can see the wheels turning

in her head as her eyes go from confusion and disbelief to realization.

"That's how she did it, Mom." I keep my tone gentle. "That's
how she put up with Grandpa and a life she didn't love."

She sits there, and I watch the news play out behind her eyes as
the dots connect. "How do you know this?"

"She has his letters hidden in the mantel in her room."

Looking back now, that's what Mimi was telling me at Fondue
with Father. How people like us, born with the duty to perpetuate
this "empire," have a responsibility to not follow our hearts. But
that doesn't mean we can't have what we want. We just need to
keep it a secret.

She knew that because that was her life. She considers herself
noble for denying herself a man she really loved, because let's be
honest: a thirty-four-year affair was love.

She raised her daughter to commit to unhappiness, and they
raised me to keep my chin up and my mouth closed, as well.

"Perfect doesn't exist." I can only manage a whisper. "It never
did."

My grandmother may or may not have had choices, but my
mom does.

And so do I.

In twenty years, I could be sitting here with my daughter, realizing I'd lived a lie for a life that made me miserable and given up
the one person who fed my every breath. I'll realize how I'd ruined
my life with such a massive mistake.

I stare at my mom, tears filling my eyes. "Mom?"

It takes her a moment, still lost in thought, but she looks over
at me.

"I have to talk to you," I tell her. "I don't want to trouble you
right now, but I need to say something. I need to say it now."

It's not the right time, but there will never be one. I clasp my
hands together, looking down as I try to find the words.

"What is it?" she asks when I don't say anything.

I open my mouth but close it again, not sure how to word it. I search my brain for the gentlest words—the easiest way—to explain it, but all I see is her losing her mind again and ready to hide in this closet the rest of the week because she'll feel like she failed. But I need to talk to someone. I need to say it out loud, and this is so hard because I need my mom, even if she's just going to make this about her. I'll be able to see the disappointment all over her face.

Tears stream down my face. "Clay, my God," she breathes out, her tone alert. "What is it?"

I open my mouth. *Just say it. Just say it and then it'll be out and over.*

I lick my lips, staring at my legs. "I'm in love with Olivia Jaeger," I say, just above a whisper.

I feel the walls crash in, and I close my eyes, waiting for it. Waiting for the meltdown.

She doesn't say anything, and I don't look up. I know she heard me.

"I'm in love with her a lot," I finish.

More silence.

I wait.

And then she falls back against the dresser again, exhaling a huge breath. "Oh, thank God," she gasps, breathing hard. "Oh my God, I thought you were pregnant. Jesus, Clay. You scared me."

I jerk my eyes over to her, seeing her with a hand to her chest as she tries to catch her breath. Huh?

She heard me, right? This isn't a joke.

She looks over at me again, concern still in her eyes. "That's all you were going to say?" she asks. "That's it? Nothing else?"

What?

"Are you serious?" I burst out, sitting up straight. "You're not surprised that I'm . . ."

"Well, honey, we kind of knew."

My eyes go wide, and now that the fear is gone, I glare. "What?" I screech. "How could you know?" *I didn't know!* "And what do you mean 'we'? You mean Dad knows, too?"

Are they serious?

She smiles softly. "Honey, you had pictures of Selena Gomez and Peyton List on your wall when you were twelve," she tells me. "Krisjen had Booboo Stewart and Harry Styles. Yeah, we . . . kind of had an idea."

"Why didn't you say anything?"

"Because you were twelve," she explains. "You're the only one who knows who you are. We didn't want to make assumptions. We just wanted to let you come to us when you were ready."

"But the showers at school," I say. "You changed the showers at school because of Liv Jaeger."

"I voted to change them because you asked me to."

"I did not."

She nods. "Yeah, the end of freshman year," she tells me. "You complained about Olivia constantly being late to class because she was waiting for everyone else to finish bathing before her and something about her not showering at all sometimes and just dousing herself in perfume and deodorant. People were being mean to her, making fun of her . . . I took that as a hint that you felt bad for her. You kind of just spit out that separate stalls would make your lives so much easier."

I pause, the vague memory playing out in my head. *Right.* I do remember that. I hated seeing her waiting around in her towel all alone.

"So you're just fine with it?" I sputter. "Seriously?"

"I am now," she replies.

I cock an eyebrow. *Now?*

"Well, at first," she says, "part of me kind of hoped it wasn't true."

Why?

"I'm sorry to admit that." She frowns. "But I want us to be honest with each other. It was my initial reaction. 'Oh my God, did I do something wrong? Is this my fault?'" She shakes her head. "I can't help where my mind went, but that's not where it is anymore, Clay. I'm glad I had time to prepare myself, because I would've been ashamed to have had that reaction in front of you."

Does she still feel that way, even a little?

"No one wants their kid's life to be harder," she goes on, "and then when we lost Henry, I thought I was losing control of everything. I'm glad I had time to figure myself out."

"And now?" I ask, waiting for the hard truth. "Do you still think you did something wrong?"

She smiles softly, her eyes pooling. "There's no feeling in the world like being in love," she says. "Are you in love?"

It doesn't take a moment for me to nod. "I think about her all the time," I tell her, my voice thick with all sorts of feelings. "I want to be with her all the time. Everything feels good when she looks at me and kisses me and breathes on my neck and . . ."

"Okay, okay . . ." She laughs under her breath. "You're still my child."

I lean my head on her shoulder as she reaches around and touches my cheek.

After a moment, she leans in, too. "I would never want you to not feel that," she finally whispers. "Henry will never feel that."

Needles prickle in my throat, the constant reminder behind the closed door of a little kid's room down the hall that this life is our only shot.

"I will always love you." She kisses my forehead. "No matter what."

I want to go to my room right now and check my phone, and if she hasn't called, then I want to, but I'm dreading it, too. I'm afraid she'll hang up on me. Or worse, scream and growl. Hearing her hatred would hurt worse.

"I'm starving." My mom sighs. "I've been hungry for twenty years, and I'm sick of it."

I laugh. "Popcorn and Milk Duds?"

Years ago, we'd pig out and watch *Burlesque* with Cher and Christina Aguilera—my favorite film—every few months, but we hadn't done that in a long time.

"You get the food," she tells me. "I'll load the movie."

29

Olivia

"You're not actually dating Trace Jaeger, are you?" Amy says to Krisjen somewhere off to my right.

Calculus fills up, students pouring through the doors, and I feel Clay somewhere behind me, but I don't turn to look.

"Of course not," Krisjen replies. "That would involve talking. And talking is the one thing we don't do."

I smile to myself. I like Krisjen, simply because most Saints wouldn't admit to the world that they sleep at my house. Or any house in the swamp.

She's proof that Clay's a fucking wimp.

My phone buzzes with another text, but I keep it facedown, underneath my palm on my desk. I don't care how much she wants me. I don't care if she "took the first step" and told her mom about us or how many times she's called in the last week.

And it's fine if she can't march her ass over here right now in front of everyone and pull me into her arms.

I just won't trust her again for anything less.

My chest aches, still feeling how much I'd wanted to sink into a hole forever when Macon picked me up the other night. I deserve better than her.

"Hey." Chloe smiles at me as she hugs her books and walks to the seat behind me.

"Hey."

My phone vibrates underneath my hand, and I press the power button, turning it off completely.

"I'm trying this on." And I feel my leather jacket that hangs on the back of my chair slide out from behind me. "It's the best jacket," Chloe says. "I want one. Can you buy them aged like this?"

I force a little laugh, like I've done all week, so Clay knows she didn't beat me. "Yeah, that one was brought to maturation in charred oak barrels."

She goes wide-eyed.

"I'm kidding."

I guess I'm the only one here who knows how to make bourbon, thanks to Army.

"It's actually just years of wear and tear," I tell her. "Gotta put in the work."

She hops up, standing next to me as she slips her arms into my jacket, and I don't even mind that she doesn't ask permission. I want Clay to see me have as many interactions that don't include her as possible.

I look up at Chloe, her blond hair just grazing the shoulders as she grips both sides of the zipper and models the distressed leather. Her skirt flares as she spins, and she could almost be Clay.

"It suits," I say.

"Definitely hot," Curtis Harbor coos to my left. "Even hotter if you didn't have anything on underneath."

"Ugh," Chloe gags.

But then her eyes turn on me, and something passes behind them, almost like she's wondering herself if I'd like how that would look.

But I picture Clay instead. Lying in my bed as I peel the jacket open and kiss her body underneath.

I clench my thighs.

"All right, point me to your supplier," Chloe tells me, slipping out of the jacket. "I'm getting one."

But I stop her. "Wear it," I say, hoping Clay hears every damn word, and I don't care how childish I seem. "You can wear it today, if you want."

I hear a crackle, a gasp, and then Amy's yelp, "Clay!"

"Shit," someone growls, and I can't hide my smile, recognizing Clay's voice.

Oops. Someone just spilled their Starbucks.

"Are you sure?" Chloe asks me.

"It looks good."

She puts the jacket back on and takes her seat, and it's funny that I was jealous of Clay talking to her, and now I'm using her to make Clay jealous.

I hate it. I hate acting like this.

It's over with Clay. Why do I want to make her suffer? Why does it feel so good for her to know that I could hook up with anyone today like she doesn't matter?

But as Ms. Kirkpatrick starts class and the hour goes on, I can't seem to forget she's in the room. Behind me.

I have no doubt she's been completely honest. I know her heart is mine.

But she ruined it. She made what happened between us dirty, and now, every memory of feeling her and holding her is covered in shit, because now I know I can't trust her. I'll always be waiting to be kicked to the curb again, because I'm only good enough when it's on her terms. After hours. When no one's around.

My mother let herself be slowly eaten alive by whatever went on in her head. The dark places. The despair. Clay hurt me hard. She won't get a chance to kill me.

I leave the room when class is over, every step away from her down the hall, to the next class, and all the way to the end of the day feeling harder than the last, but eventually, I make it home.

I make it home without letting her corner me and convince me that we're in love and she'll tell her friends soon. *Not today but soon.* No.

I turn my phone back on, a rolling storm of texts, missed calls, and voicemails buzzing and dinging, and I immediately go to Clay's number, my thumb hovering over the *Block* option.

I haven't read any of her texts today, but I'm dying to. I miss her. I want to know she's dying for me.

I drop to my bed and lean back against the wall, my finger shaking over the screen. Finally, I tap it, blocking any more calls, and I erase the text thread, so I don't look.

Forcing myself not to think, I cut us off from each other on every social media account I have. It's not like she won't see me or have opportunities, but maybe now realization will set in that I'm serious.

She's not good enough for me.

A knock hits my door, and before I can look over, Army peeks his head in. "Tickets?" he asks.

Tickets?

Oh, the play. Oh, shit. How did I forget that? I'm only an understudy, so I won't be performing, but I made the costumes, and Army and Iron like to be supportive. I quickly check my missed-call list to make sure there's nothing from Lambert.

"On the desk," I tell him.

He steps in and finds tickets for all my brothers. I get one for everyone, even though only two or three of them ever show up.

I don't see anything from the theater director about performing tonight. I would've loved it if Callum kept his word, but on the other hand, I'm kind of glad he'll now be off my back.

I look up to Army. "You don't have to come."

"We want to come."

I smile coyly. "Dallas doesn't want to come."

"Dallas will be a pain in the ass until the day he dies."

Yeah.

Army plops down next to me, a full head and a half higher than me, and I don't bother to strain my neck looking up.

Digging something out of his pocket, he hands me a key on an old ring.

I take it. "What's this?"

I examine the silver key that looks vaguely familiar.

"Call it Macon's belated birthday present," he says.

It takes me a minute, and then I remember. "The Ninja?"

The bike he bought when he was in the Marines and had only himself to support. He hasn't driven it in years, though. It's been in the garage under a tarp.

"I thought you'd be jumping up and down," Army says when I don't smile or do cartwheels over finally having my own transportation.

"When do I ever jump up and down?" But I smile. "Why didn't he give this to me himself?"

"Because you know why," he retorts. "And don't thank him. He'll just get pissy about it."

I chuckle as he slides off the bed. I'm pretty sure he's right.

So instead, I tell Army, "Thank you."

He winks at me and leaves, taking tonight's tickets with him.

I stare at the key—my key to my very own bike—remembering what Clay felt like hanging on to me that time she rode with me.

My phone rings, and for a split second I close my eyes, the urge to answer too much to deny.

But then I remember I blocked her number. It's not her.

And then it occurs to me . . . Ms. Lambert.

My heart kicking up speed, I answer the phone. "Hello?"

"Olivia?" Lambert says. "Hi, it's Jane. I need you to come in now."

My stomach sinks just as an electric charge warms my blood—dread and euphoria hitting me at the same time.

"On my way," I almost whisper, and then hang up.

He did it. I'm onstage tonight.

I'm playing Mercutio.

A text rolls in, and I look down, reading.

Congratulations. I can't wait to see your
performance.

And my mouth goes dry, Callum's double meaning of "performance" hitting me like a steel rod to the kneecaps.

I wanted to thank you," a voice says to my right.

I look up, seeing Lizbeth, our Juliet.

She steps forward. "I was so over the old costumes," she says.
"Every little girl wants to be Juliet with her romantic hairstyle and
princess dress, but . . . you know."

"Shit changes."

She breathes out a laugh. "Yeah, exactly."

We stand backstage, a whirl of activity up and down the hallway as people rush to get their makeup on, repair last-minute tears
or lost buttons, and pace back and forth, practicing their lines. I
lean against the wall, trying to get my head straight. Trying to
push Callum and Clay to the wayside for the next two hours, because this is my time. I've begged for this for four years, and I'm
not going to let them take it.

Lizbeth's gaze falls down my body, taking in my black Gothic
coat and black leather pants and boots. "Now I'm kind of wishing
I was Mercutio."

"Yeah, me, too." My heart won't stop racing, and I feel sick. I
can't seem to channel him all of a sudden. God, I'm nervous.

She smiles, much cooler than me, but she's been onstage several times before. I need to do this no matter how much I'm dreading it, though. How can I expect to do this for life?

"Well, break a leg," she tells me.

I smile tightly, too afraid I'll puke if I talk. She passes by in her black jeans and flowing white peasant's blouse, a black military jacket with gold buttons covering it, and her hair spilling down her back. I wish I could've rewritten the script like I rewrote the set and costuming, but that was a fight for another day.

I look down at my phone as if I'll see something from Clay, but I won't. I still have her blocked.

Walking back into the dressing room, I pass Juliet's nurse—Evie Leong, taking over my role—and tuck my phone away, heading out to the curtain. Lifting the flap, I peer through the peepholes, watching the house get seated as the lights dim.

The snow begins to fall, a perpetual night as the backdrop of the Kingdom of New York looms on the horizon, and the swords are changed out for bows and kung fu.

The audience quiets; the narrator enters from stage right, walking past the audience, finishing her monologue just as she disappears into stage left. The theater darkens, thunder cracks, and lightning glows behind the cathedral and skyscrapers as the houses of Montague and Capulet enter crowded Central Park.

Sampson and Gregory speak, bantering with each other. "Therefore, I will push Montague's men from the wall and thrust his maids to the wall!"

And then the other, "The quarrel is between our masters and us their men."

"'Tis all one," Sampson replies. "I will show myself a tyrant. When I have fought with the men, I will be civil with the maids; I will cut off their heads."

That line alone was what first got me thinking I wanted this role. I'd enjoy entering the stage and playing one of the production's most enigmatic male characters and showing them that the "weaker" sex would get a few cuts in herself.

But standing here, watching the story play out, and my entrance grow closer, it doesn't feel like I thought it would.

I'm not even nauseous anymore. I peek out to the audience once more, smiling when I see my brothers slouched and clearly bored, Army and Iron sitting quietly, and Trace already asleep. Army will wake him when I come on.

And then the door at the back opens, and I notice the large frame that fills the doorway before it closes.

My heart swells a little. *Macon.* I watch him hide back by the wall, standing quietly, because as hard as he acts and as worried about him as I sometimes am, I know he loves me.

But still, I can't help but scan the crowd again, searching for someone else.

The drums beat, Juliet and her mother talking about the party tonight, and I watch Lizbeth in the new costuming, wishing Clay were here. Hoping she's here, because I want her to see this. I want her to be proud of me.

Romeo and Benvolio enter stage left, and I draw in a deep breath, close my eyes for a moment, my heart suddenly pounding in my chest.

Clay.

My head swims, and somehow all the tears and anger and bitterness of years of hurt and a freshly axed heart swirl like a whirlwind, and for the first time I know that Mercutio isn't dynamic at all. He's lost. He's missing that one thing that being loved gives you, and that's why he needs Romeo. That's why he's protective of him. He lives through him.

Romeo must be protected at all costs.

And now, I get it.

"Nay, gentle Romeo," I call out, stepping onto the stage. "We must have you dance."

I hold my friend's eyes, the spotlight on me and following me to him, and the adrenaline burns down my arms, something inside showing me the way.

I pull off my friend's jacket, Benvolio and other maskers dancing around, and whip it off to the side, but Romeo resists me. "Not I, believe me," he says, continuing.

I attach myself to him, his sidekick, because Mercutio adores his best friend. Needs him.

The audience laughs as I joke and jump around, and I can feel her eyes, the sadness of loss so obvious as I dive into his Queen Mab monologue. How his humor and passion are just a shield for the pain.

And he gives you that tiny peek inside before . . . he closes it up again. The curtain falling once more.

Tears spilling down my cheeks, I breathe hard, and my friends pull me to the party. I clutch Romeo's hand, meeting his eyes so I never have to look in the mirror and see myself.

The scene concludes, we leave the stage, and I hear my brothers throw out whistles in the audience as people clap.

"You were great," Clarke says.

But I can't look at him. I swallow hard, something making my heart feel like it's getting too big for my chest.

I enter the stage again for the party, for the scene with the nurse, for my battle with Tybalt . . . My death.

I scream, tears streaming down my face as I fall to the ground and Mercutio realizes that this wasn't worth it. He'd tried to protect his friend's life, but he failed to protect his happiness. He made it worse. Just a domino in the tragedy who failed to see how short our time was.

How it wasn't going to end unless someone changed the game.

And how, for the first time, I realize that the glaring plot hole in this story was never a plot hole at all. Whether Juliet left her parents' home under her own two feet or in a casket, she still had the same endgame, so why fake her death at all? She just should've left when her father gave her the option.

But she didn't. Because she would've rather her parents see her dead than a Montague. Because she loved them and didn't want to disappoint them.

And now, maybe, I finally understand that Clay's fear isn't because she doesn't love me. It's because she loves them, too.

I don't want what happened to Alli to happen to her. I'd rather see her from a distance than never again.

30

Clay

"You girls look beautiful," my mom says, setting down a tray with nonalcoholic cocktails that she made herself. I know because the rims are splattered with orange juice pulp.

Eh, she tried.

"I'm excited," Amy squeals, taking a drink as my mom leaves the room again. "Transportation will be here at six. The guys better be dressed correctly when we get to the venue. Makes me nervous, them left to their own devices."

We sit in the living room, vanities set up and the stylists at work on my and Krisjen's hair. Amy sneaks a flask out of her bag and adds vodka to her drink.

"Want some?" she asks, pushing the glass in front of me and trying to act like we're still friends, but we've barely said two words to each other since I threatened her. I wish I didn't know why I don't tell her to take a hike, but I do, and I can't look at myself in the mirror in front of me.

I shake my head, my fingers hovering over the keyboard on my phone.

Don't come, I type, but stop my thumb before I hit *Send*.

"You're probably right." Amy pulls the glass away and takes a drink. "Once I get started, I keep going, and since it's still early, I'll be passed out by eight."

But I don't say anything as she drones on. I stare at my phone, willing myself to hit the goddamn button. To tell Callum Ames that I don't want him to escort me tonight, because that's her place. That he means nothing more than a waste of my time.

All of this is a waste of time. I hate my hair. I don't even have to look to feel every strand pulled off my neck and away from my face, pinned into a tidy, boring little bun at the back of my head. The matte lipstick allows me to feel every dry patch on my lips, and I almost tell Amy to give me the damn drink in order to dull the pain of that dress on the hanger behind me.

"Is everything okay?" Jenny, the stylist, asks.

I squeeze my phone in my lap, not in the mood to lie, so I keep my mouth shut. I drop my eyes, staring at my screen and checking the volume again and my texts.

I don't care about my hair. I've called, texted . . . She doesn't answer. I go straight to voicemail every time, which means her phone is either off or I'm blocked.

I haven't had the courage to check social media yet. I want to throw up, because I know she's cut us off from each other there, too. Not knowing is better right now.

My chest shakes, and I let out a quiet sob.

"Ladies." Jenny pats my shoulders. "Let's go get them some refreshments."

The stylists leave, and I scroll through TikTok, seeing a video on Ruby's account of the play last night. Liv stands center stage, Mercutio's famous monologue hitting my heart like a brick. God, she can make you forget you're watching a play. I hope she didn't see me last night. My heart was in my throat the entire time.

Amy peers over my shoulder. "A few people are dragging her for her performance last night."

"Bullshit." Krisjen finishes her cocktail and checks herself in the mirror. "Word is, she nailed it. Lizbeth got snippy on Snap-chat, some loaded comment about 'someone' stealing the show, but everyone knows who she's talking about."

I want to ask Krisjen if she's seen her or talked to her. She's at their house a lot lately.

"And of course, everyone sticks up for the underdog," Amy adds, "doing that 'Hey, here's me and my token lesbian friend to show I'm woke and have the higher moral ground with my self-important opinions about world issues.'"

God, shut up. I squeeze my fists, silently telling her to shut her mouth, but I won't say it out loud, will I? Because I'm scared. I'm scared of that point of no return, but why? It's costing me Liv.

It's costing me everything.

Raising my eyes, I reach up and start unpinning my hair. I pull out the pins, the hair spray keeping it clumped together, but it falls down piece by piece until the entire work is undone.

"Hey," I hear Krisjen say.

Amy rises next to me. "Clay, what are you doing?"

I take everything out, shaking my head to loosen the locks, lazy curls spilling around me as I unscrew the diamond studs my grand-mother gave me to wear.

I'll wear the dress. I'll go to the ball. But that's it.

"No!" someone shouts.

I startle.

"Now, I said we aren't expecting any deliveries," Bernie snaps. "How did you get through the gate?"

Amy and Krisjen stand behind me, all of us with our eyes pinned toward the foyer, but whoever is at the door is out of sight.

But then a voice booms. "Clay Collins! Are you home?"

I bolt out of my chair, tightening my robe around me as I come into the entryway and see Iron Jaeger standing at my door. He's in his usual grease-smudged white T-shirt with sweat shining across his forehead. He holds two large boxes.

"A little help?" he chides me, glaring at Bernie, who won't let him pass.

"Bernie, it's okay." I move forward and take a box off his load. "What is this?"

"Fuck if I know." He barely takes three steps inside before he drops the other box on the floor in front of me. "You figure out the rest."

Spinning around, he leaves, the door hanging open after him as I stand there holding the bag, so to speak.

"That was weird," Amy says.

Did Liv send him? I look down at the box, Lavinia's name engraved in lavender in the center. It's taller than the other one, both of them different shapes.

"What is it?" Krisjen asks.

I kneel down to the floor and set it next to the one Iron dropped, opening his first.

Peeling back the lid, I spread open the tissue paper and see a white gown, the sleeveless bodice decorated with pearls and stunning blush pink orchids, the wires in the corset running vertical.

I hold it up, noticing that the fabric on the torso is damn near see-through, except for the cups of the breasts, of course. The rest of the gown is adorned with a spiral of white birds sewn in down the legs to the feet, and it's honestly one of the most beautiful things I've ever seen. The minimal petticoat is sewn in so the wearer doesn't have to deal with looking like a cupcake.

"What's in the other one?" Krisjen asks.

I set the gown back in the box and push off the lid of the taller one, peering inside.

Something bubbles up in my chest, and I can't help but smile.

"What's all this?" my mom asks, coming into the room.

But I don't answer. I reach inside and pull out the black top hat, a black silk ribbon adorned with a cluster of jewels on one side wrapped around the brim.

I'm dying to put it on.

Diving back into the box like a kid on Christmas, I find black pants, a white shirt, and a fitted jacket with tails. A black tie spills into my lap.

I laugh, hugging the tux to my body. What did she do?

"This is beautiful," my mother says, examining the gown. "Who's the tux for?"

Me. Liv's giving me a choice. I look between the dress and the suit. *I can do what I'm told or do what I want.*

I shake my head. I hurt her so badly. She deserves better.

She must've already had the clothes done and figured why waste them?

Because I was still blocked as of ten minutes ago.

I search the boxes but don't see a note. Footfalls hit the floor behind me, and my mother rises.

"What are you doing here?" she asks.

My father darts up to her, stops, and I look up at him as he looks down at me. "We'll see you at the banquet hall, okay?" he tells me. And then he looks at her. "I need to talk to you now."

"Not now." She keeps her tone quiet because everyone is listening, but she turns away from him and starts to leave.

But my dad pulls her back around and throws her over his shoulder.

I shoot to my feet, dropping the clothes. "Dad!"

"Ah, Jefferson!" my mom screeches. "Let me go!"

He carries her up the stairs, and I follow. "Dad?"

"Clay, the adults are talking now," he fires back.

Someone snorts behind me, and my mom flails. "Ugh, you let me go!"

But my dad wraps his arms around her tighter. "Never."

They disappear down the hall, and I jog after them, reaching their door just as it closes.

"How dare—" But my mom's voice cuts off, and I lean my ear to the door, hearing muffled moaning and breathlessness.

I smile to myself and walk away, leaving them to it.

Heading back downstairs, I feel my body warm as I lay my eyes on the tux and top hat again. God, everyone will look at me.

But . . .

And then I pause, noticing that the dress is gone. I look left to right and walk into the living room, seeing Amy spike another drink before she sips it.

"Where's Krisjen?" I ask her. "And the dress?"

"No idea," she says, drinking the glass half down. "You didn't want to wear it anyway, did you? This one's much prettier." And she points to the ugly one on the hanger I'd gotten weeks ago at Mimi's.

No, I don't want to wear it.

I'm not wearing a dress tonight.

I look over my shoulder at the tux and smile. And then I grab my phone and send the text to Callum.

31

Olivia

Tomorrow night.

I stare at Callum's text from this afternoon, holding my breath a little. He thinks we have a deal. I took Mercutio and the key, after all.

But I'm not going. What's he going to do? Force me?

And if he tries to retaliate, he's going to find that the Jaegers don't need to get violent to make him pay.

It's done. Over. Fuck 'em.

"Olivia!" Dallas shouts from downstairs.

I heave a sigh, just knowing he's going to ask me to bathe Dex or make dinner or go run an errand. I toss my phone onto my bed and hop up, opening my door.

Voices hit me immediately. "You can't just come over here anytime you want," Trace scolds. "I got other ladies to tend to."

I peer over the stairs, seeing Krisjen. "Oh, please. 'Tend to'?" she jokes. "I've started to carry my vibe in my purse for afterward."

Dallas and Iron burst into laughter, and I walk down the stairs, seeing Trace's mouth fall open a little. "Is that what you do in the bathroom for so long?"

But she doesn't answer, her eyes shifting up to me as soon as I stop at the bottom.

I fold my arms over my chest. "What are you doing here?"

She starts to say something, but Army steps into the open doorway she's blocking and nudges her.

She scrunches up her face in a scowl, but when she looks behind her, her face falls.

"In or out, kid," Army tells her.

"Um . . ."

She gapes at his bare chest, and I roll my eyes. I shoot forward, snapping my fingers in her face to bring her out of it. "Krisjen."

I mean, hooray for being sex positive, but the girl has a one-track mind sometimes. Seriously.

She turns her attention back to me. "Oh, right." She pulls up the box under her arm and hands it to me. "I brought your dress back."

My dress. Clay's dress? That I made for her?

Fine. I snatch the box away from her and toss it onto the floor in the game room.

I feel like an idiot for even trying, but lesson learned.

But Krisjen dives down and picks up the box again. "I don't mean that," she spits out. "I mean for you to wear."

"I'm not a debutante."

"No, but you could escort one," she retorts in a tone like she's mocking my stupidity. She looks around the room to my brothers. "Do we have to talk about this down here?"

I stay rooted in my spot. I may have done what I could to cut off communication, but Clay has known where to find me. There's no way in hell I'm making some grand gesture in a public place. She's the one who screwed up.

"She's dying on the inside," Krisjen says in a low voice.

I lift my gaze, meeting hers.

"She's dying without you."

My throat tightens, my chest constricts, and something stings inside me.

But I shake my head. "She broke it off with me."

"She made a mistake," Krisjen says, my brothers still standing around while Macon sits in the chair off to my left. "She's going to make lots of mistakes. She's spoiled, a little self-absorbed, angry about a lot of shit, but she's learning." Krisjen lowers her voice. "And she's yours."

My eyes burn.

"Your crazy, impulsive, wild, complicated girl," Krisjen tells me.

I press my lips together and drop my gaze, because I'm about to lose it. *My crazy, impulsive, wild, beautiful girl.*

My girl.

"There's no point, Krisjen," I say. "We're both graduating, leaving town—"

"None of that matters!" she growls. "Just be here now!"

I've stopped breathing, Krisjen's anger startling me.

"There's no tomorrow," she goes on. "What are you worried about? Just be here today!"

A tear spills down my face, and I feel like I'm being scolded by a mom I didn't really have.

I don't want to be hurt.

Maybe I love her. Maybe she'll break me again or I'll break her, or maybe we'll leave each other in August.

Maybe we'll never see each other again.

But maybe she's worth a few more months.

A few weeks.

One more day.

I look over at Macon, who watches me in silence, and I don't know what I see in his eyes, but I understand it.

This could be it.

I drop my gaze to the box in her arms, knowing that the dress will be a little small for me, not to mention my brothers will peal with laughter at me trussed up like Cinderella, but . . .

She didn't bring the tux back. Does that mean Clay's wearing it?

She pats the bag hanging around her neck. "I've got makeup, hair stuff . . . Let's do this."

I can't help but smile a little. I wonder how many times Clay's tried to call or text the past couple of days. Will she want me there?

Oh, fuck it. Fuck it all. There is no tomorrow.

Krisjen heads past me toward the stairs but stops and eyes Aracely. "Aracely, right?" she asks. "It's going to take two of us to get her boobs into this dress. I'd appreciate the help."

I laugh under my breath at Ara's pissed-off expression at a Saint ordering her around. Normally, I'd take her side over one of St. Carmen's, but Krisjen has the mettle to hang over on this side of the tracks.

I head up the stairs, both of them following behind me.

"So, uh . . . Army . . ." Krisjen starts.

But I cut her off. "No."

"What?"

What do you mean, what? I know what she wants. "I said no," I state again.

Army needs a woman badly, but I'm doing this as much for her as for him. He'll just turn the poor girl into a babysitter he sleeps with.

She groans as we dip into my room. "Fine."

32

Clay

The line rings in my ear, Liv not picking up now or the last ten times I've called since getting the packages this afternoon.

She's blocked me. I could start another social media profile—one she hasn't blocked—on TikTok, Instagram, and Snapchat, but I don't have time right now, and that would be a new level of low and pathetic.

I just want her to want to talk to me. I don't want to stalk her.

I'm going over there. I'm done. I need her, and she loves me. I know she does.

Standing up straight, I hold out the phone, snapping a selfie as I tip my hat with my other hand. I post it, tapping out the caption **This could be it. I won't let you go.**

She may have blocked me, but I haven't blocked her. She'll see it.

I post it just as a figure heads toward me out of the corner of my eye, and I look up, seeing my dad. He approaches in a black tux, his dark hair combed, and his crisp white shirt making his skin look tan. He smiles gently, carrying a clear case in his hand as his eyes fall down my matching tux. His eyebrows rise to his hairline.

"I know, I know," I mumble, hearing the hall fill up beyond the stairwell where I hide. "Mimi will freak when she sees me."

He leans into the wall next to me, and I know he wants to talk, but I have no ambition. We haven't really spoken since my phone call the other night, and even though I feel a little guilty, I don't know why.

Maybe because we're all in pain, and I expect my parents to be stronger than me. They aren't, and I'm still debating on how mad I should be about that.

I'm still not apologizing, though. I'll save that for Liv. She's the only thing that's important right now.

"Actually, I was thinking you don't look the same," he finally says. His eyes drop to the boutonniere in the box, his mind far away and his jaw tense. "I'm sorry, baby. I'm sorry that we just couldn't seem to pull it together. There's almost nothing worse than having your children see you completely fuck up."

My dad was around for a while, but the house felt less and less like a home, and my mother only wanted her grief. I understand how it hurt my dad. How he felt alone.

He just forgot I was there, too.

"We're supposed to show you how it's done," he whispers, and I can hear the tears choking his voice. "We broke, and I didn't know how to fix it." He turns his head toward me. "I didn't want to escape your mother. I wanted to love her."

"Do you still?"

He doesn't falter. "Still."

There's hope, then. I'm not the only one making mistakes, and no matter what, I still love my parents. Even now.

Maybe Liv still loves me.

Mrs. Wentworth saunters through the door, girls in their white gowns filling the hallway behind her, pulling on gloves, and squealing as they rush from one room to another, getting ready.

The director slows in her steps, looking me up and down. I stay there, *not* standing up straight.

"Your escort isn't here," she informs me, looking to my father as well.

My father is supposed to walk me into the room, but at the end of the stage, Callum is supposed to take over. The symbolism of a father passing the jewel of his house onto the next man in her life like you pass a well-baked pie . . .

"I don't have one," I tell her.

What are they going to do? Tell me I can't walk.

I actually appreciate the update from her. Callum hadn't texted back, so I wasn't sure if he got the message or perhaps decided to ignore it, as I expected him to do.

But he's not here. *Thank goodness.*

"Oh well, we have spares." She looks at her clipboard, pulling at the gold-and-pearl earring on her lobe. "Just a date, not a mate," she assures. "I'll send him up."

"No, thank you."

Her gaze flashes to mine, alarmed. There was a time when I wanted to paint that perfect picture, and perfect girls are escorted by proud young men, but that desire is now gone. Alone, no white dress . . . I won't look like anyone else, and while I'm not yet happy, I'm no longer trying to be something I never was.

Wentworth presses her lips together.

"She said no," my dad reiterates before the woman has a chance to argue.

Her spine straightens like she has a pole up her ass, and she nods, spinning on her heel and leaving. I almost smile. That'll give the Garden Club something to talk about this week.

My dad pushes off the wall and turns me to face him. He takes my tie, and I look up at him under the brim of my top hat as he fixes the knot.

"Now the full Windsor is appropriate for formal settings," he tells me, "but I like the Prince Albert myself. It looks good with more slender necks."

He hasn't asked about my outfit. I wonder if Mom told him everything.

I guess from the sound of it, they knew long before I did anyway.

He finishes, and I walk to the window, the light inside the stairwell making my reflection easily visible against the black night outside. "You're right."

I smooth down the slim tie and pop my collar, looking like a British gentleman from 1912. Fabulous.

But then Liv's words come back to haunt me as I study the tie. *I need a good handle on you.* I blush, hoping she likes it. She can drag me around by it for as long as she likes, I don't care.

Dad kisses my cheek and leaves, going to where the fathers stand, and my heart rate kicks up a notch, because I'm actually kind of wishing I weren't alone, after all. Everyone will be staring, and everyone else will be walking with their boyfriends or escorts, and I'll just be standing there, nothing to distract me from all the eyes.

I could just walk out now. Leave and let my parents deal with the embarrassment they kind of deserve, but I want to do this. I always did. It's tradition, and it's me coming out to the community as a member of society who will be working and contributing, and I want them to see that people of value won't always look like them.

Walking back into the hall, I head past eyes and whispers, and see Krisjen, but she's not dressed. She veers down another hallway, and I debate following her, but it's almost time.

Where did she take Liv's dress when she left my house?

I stand backstage, hearing Mrs. Wentworth test the microphone, and seeing my grandmother sitting down at a table near the stage. Have my parents warned her about my attire? Probably not. I have a sneaky feeling my mom wants to "surprise" her.

I close my eyes, the orchestra tuning. I still hold my phone in my hand.

What is she doing right now?

My stomach growls, and I lick my red lips, wishing I had water, but I don't care to look for some.

A figure appears at my side, a flash of white, and I look over, my mouth falling open and my stomach dropping as I do a double take.

Liv stands there, her hair in shiny, silky waves down her bare back, her body adorned in the gorgeous gown she'd sent me earlier today. Her breasts bulge out of the top, and I can't inhale a full breath.

"What are you doing?" I burst out.

She turns to look at me, and my eyes drop to her dark pink lips. I can't stop myself. I take her in my arms, breathing her in and staring at her mouth.

"You look . . ." I can barely find the words. "So beautiful."

"I hope so," she says, that easy bantering tone back in her voice like nothing has happened. "I'm not particularly comfortable. Did you know the average woman owns twenty pairs of shoes and only wears five regularly? Wanna bet all five are sneakers?"

And before I can even laugh at her little joke, I feel my body move without my consent. I grab her face and sink my mouth into hers, exhilaration shooting up my spine when her hands take my waist and hold me back.

"Lips, lips!" I hear Krisjen shout, panicked. "Oh, no. Guys, oh my God. Aracely! I need lipsticks!"

And she's gone, and I know people are looking at us, but it's honestly in the top three things I couldn't care less about right now. Tilting my head and sliding a hand around her waist, I deepen the kiss, feeling her body flush with mine, every inch of me so alive I'm ready to cry.

Is she really here? How . . . ? What . . . ?

"You said you loved me," she whispers.

I smile, kissing her mouth again and again, over and over. "I was wondering . . ." More kisses. "If you'd noticed that."

"I didn't say it back."

I stop, now reminded myself. I search her eyes, hoping she says it but almost wishing she doesn't speak at all. I just want a few more minutes with her if she's about to walk away.

"I didn't want you to know that you could break my heart." Her brown eyes, behind beautiful smoky eye makeup, glisten. "I didn't want Clay Collins to ever know that . . ."

She pauses, the eyes and whispers around us, my family in the audience, and Wentworth's booming voice onstage not nearly as loud as my heart.

"That she has always broken my heart," she tells me. "I love you."

My chest swells.

"I've only ever loved you." Her breath warms me from head to toe, and I've never felt happier. "My heart is yours," she says. "Shred it, burn it, I don't care. I want every minute I can get."

Yes.

I laugh, smile, and dive in, lost in her mouth for I don't know how long until we've lost control, and I've fallen into the wall, her body pressed to mine.

"Lipsticks!" Krisjen chides, coming over.

I pull away, cleaning her mouth as she cleans mine, and I'm dizzy. She takes the lipstick from Krisjen and tries to reapply mine, but I can't stand it. I take her face in my hands, needing another dose.

"I'm never letting you go," I whisper in her ear.

But she meets my eyes, something wicked in hers. "I kind of hope you try."

What?

"You spent years torturing me," she points out, pushing me into the wall and jerking her body into mine. "I might like returning the favor if you ever try to keep this from me again."

I groan as she grips my body and her warmth seeps through my clothes.

Please, God, take me to a car now. Jesus.

She hands everything back to Krisjen and looks at me. "So, you ready for this?"

To be with her wherever and whenever I want? "Hell yes."

She nods. "Then let's make a scene."

My father steps up behind us and Krisjen takes Liv's hand, pulling her away to get in position, and I watch her go, the dress on her unlike anything here tonight. She's the most beautiful.

"Ready?" My dad takes my hand, hooking it over his arm.

"For anything."

The music starts playing, the line forms behind the stage, and I'm tempted to push myself and my father back a few spaces so we're not front and center and dominating attention like my outfit no doubt will, but what's worth doing once is worth doing big. I'm not hiding another second.

"Please welcome the Daughters of St. Carmen in the Ninety-Ninth Annual Debutante Ball!" Mrs. Wentworth announces on the stage.

Three-two-one . . .

We walk, stepping out from behind the curtain together and keeping in time, slow and steady, as I come into view and the applause suddenly falters. My skin warms as everyone watches us, my dad and I both in suits, me in a top hat, and then the clapping turns to whispers, because I'm the only one in nearly a hundred years who's broken protocol. I snort, nearly failing at holding in my laughter, and I look up to Dad, seeing him look down at me with a wink. What are they going to do? This isn't even the fun part.

We descend the stage and stop in the middle of the dance floor, bowing to the crowd. A full curtsy is customary next, and I oblige, dropping to the floor and lowering my head.

The orchestra plays, and I rise, hoping Krisjen took care of the next part.

Finally, I hear it. "Uh . . ." Mrs. Wentworth clears her throat, composing herself. "Miss . . . um, Miss Clay Collins, escorted by . . ." I hear a heavy exhale. "Escorted by Olivia Jaeger."

A few claps, but I don't expect more and don't wait for it as I watch Liv walk around the dance floor and stop at my side, slipping her fingers between mine.

I gaze at her, the way the string of little flowers drapes off her shoulders and down her arm. The way the dress hugs her body and only complements, doesn't hide. How she looks fantastic in a little pink, and I know, in this moment, that I have no intention of looking into any other pair of eyes for the rest of my life.

I ignore the heat of my grandmother's anger I can feel somewhere in the room. The camera phone here or there that's probably documenting this. And anyone who might be whispering or laughing, because my mom's right.

There are people who will never be lucky enough to feel this.

I probably pull her too roughly, but I'm just too full of energy. We burst through the front doors, out onto the front walkway just before the circular drive, and I swing her into my arms.

"Well, that was fun," she teases.

I paw the back of her dress, pulling the tie to the corset as I breathe in the balmy air and bite her lips.

"These dresses suck," I growl in a low voice over her mouth.

"I agree," she groans. "I feel like meringue."

I laugh and grab her hand, both of us running to the parking lot and toward our limo. An hour was long enough, right? We stood our ground, danced, held hands, and now it's time to get out of Dodge before I have to subject her to my grandmother. That will happen eventually.

Tonight, she's mine. I back her into the car and press myself between her legs as I yank up her skirt and try to find her skin in all the fabric.

"School's going to be fun on Monday," I whisper.

"You scared?"

"No."

At this moment, not at all. And I don't think I will be when the time comes, either. I mean, I'm pretty sure most of Marymount knows by now. Someone in there tweeted and snapped a picture.

Which reminds me . . .

I pull out my phone as Liv sucks on my neck, sending shivers across my body. I switch off my phone and tuck it back inside my breast pocket.

I grab her and we both can't get close enough to each other.

"Get it!" someone calls out, followed by a whistle.

I scowl, looking over my shoulder. Krisjen stands with Aracely by the back door of the banquet hall, both of them smoking.

I roll my eyes and open the door, shoving Liv inside the limo. "Get in."

As I jump in after her, the driver snaps to, his snoring cut off as he wakes up.

"Take me home," I tell him, pressing the button to close the partition between us and pulling off my hat.

I see him nod before I lose sight of him. A moment later, the engine starts.

"Undo me," Liv pants, giving me her back as she turns her head and kisses me.

"God, I love you so much," I tell her, yanking the thread of the corset, loosening her gown, but unable to keep my mouth off her neck, shoulders, and lips.

Reaching back, she wraps her hand around the back of my neck. "Let's go to my house, instead," she says, kissing me. "I want you loud tonight."

Fine, okay. God, I don't care where we go. I just need her.

"You let that girl wear your jacket," I grit out, finally pulling her bodice down.

She scoots the dress off and shoves it to the floor. "Oh, calm down. You can't kill her."

I wrap one arm around her stomach, her tight corset keeping me from her skin. I stick my other hand down her panties. "Can I stick my tongue down your throat in front of her?"

She breathes out a laugh between kisses. "I like you jealous."

Reaching up, I press the intercom. "Take us to 2743 Devon Road, instead."

"Yes, Miss Collins," the driver replies.

"'Yes, Miss Collins,'" Liv mimics.

I release the button, take her in my arms, and eat up her mouth so fast I don't know if I can wait.

"God, drive faster," I beg the driver, too softly for him to hear.

I kiss her forehead and every inch of her face, learning her body like it's my home. Every curve. Every bone. Every patch of skin.

This is my girl. And I know I was made for her.

A screech hits my ears moments before the limo halts, and I grab onto Liv with one hand and the back of the seat with the other, keeping us steady.

What the hell?

The limo stops, and I don't have time to remove the partition to talk to the driver before the glass on the door shatters, and an arm reaches inside the car and unlocks it.

I gasp, every muscle hard as I pull Liv back. But I'm not fast enough.

The door whips open, and Callum is there in jeans and a hoodie, dark figures looming behind him.

He sticks his head inside, his eyes gleaming with delight when he sees her nearly naked body in my arms.

"Well, what do we have here?" he sneers.

"What the hell do you want?" Liv growls, shooting out her leg to kick him back, but he grabs her foot instead.

Milo bends down, peering inside the car. "Goddamn."

"Hey, what's going on?" someone shouts, and I realize it's the driver.

"Help!" I shout.

But Callum yanks Liv, and she screams. "No!"

I lunge, slamming my fists and trying to hit anything I can—his head, his arms, anything to loosen his hold.

But he has her. He sweeps her out of the car and away from me.

"No!" I cry.

"Ahhh!" Liv yells.

"Time to pay your dues, bitch!" Callum spits out, and throws her over his shoulder.

I go after her, but the door slams in my face. I pull the handle, slamming my body against the door, but I can see Milo leaning into it through the broken window.

"Livvy!" I scream.

"No!" I hear her muffled cry.

Finally, the door gives away, and I bolt through it, falling onto the road. I climb to my feet and spin around, seeing Callum's car and Milo running to the passenger side.

I run as they climb into the car, but Callum hits the gas, speeding in reverse and whipping the car around in a one-eighty, speeding off down Main Street.

"Liv!" Two other cars follow, the rest of their crew, but I don't know who it is. I didn't catch any other faces.

"I'm calling the police!" the driver exclaims.

But I shake my head. The police won't know where to find them, and even if they did, they'll show up before Liv's brothers can fuck Callum and Milo up. I don't want them in our way.

I pull out my phone and Google **Jaeger's Lawn Service**. A moment later, one of them picks up.

"Trace . . ." I cry.

33

Olivia

I breathe hard, sucking my hair into my mouth as he presses my face into the seat.

Someone else pins my hands behind my back, securing them with some kind of cloth, and then I'm hauled up and into Callum's lap as Delaney Cooper, who graduated last year and attends Vanderbilt now, drives. Wanna bet Callum's trying to impress his future frat brother?

I glare at Callum, seeing pure satisfaction gleaming in his eyes. I growl, slamming my forehead into his nose.

Motherfucker!

He winces, howling, and I try to see out the window behind us, but Clay is out of sight.

If he hurt her . . .

His grip eases, and he holds his nose with one hand, a trickle of blood spilling down. "Goddammit!" he spits out.

I flail and whip, and while I know full well I won't escape, maybe if I'm enough trouble, he'll toss me from the car. Does he have any idea what's going to happen to him if he hurts me? Does he care?

He wraps his arm around me and then grabs my neck, squeezing it.

A groan escapes as he cuts off my oxygen. "You sure you want to do this?"

"This was always how it was going to go," he whispers. "Especially since I know you weren't going to come tomorrow night anyway. You gave Macon the key, didn't you? To break into Fox Hill? To trash the painting? To crash our party tomorrow night and fuck us up?"

So he decided to surprise me a day early.

Well, he's only partially correct. There wasn't going to be any fight, and my brothers were never going to make an appearance. They did a lot more than Callum thinks they did that night when they burned the painting.

But this changes things. He stole me off the street. Out of a car. Macon won't let this go. He can hold his temper for a lot, but not this. And while Callum will get exactly what's coming to him, the police won't get lazy when a founding son goes missing. My family won't get away with anything for long.

Please, Clay, don't call them. Please.

This isn't how it was supposed to go. Shit.

I twist, screaming and thrashing as I try to reach for the door with my hands to throw myself out of the car if I get a chance to, but Delaney presses the gas, speeding up, and Callum digs his nails into my neck. "Stop," he grits out. "Or we'll go back and get Clay for this, too."

"What do you think you're doing?" I ask. "She saw you. She saw your faces." I look around at Milo, Delaney, and the other guy in the passenger seat I don't recognize. "She's calling the police by now."

"You think so?" he taunts. "What will the police do to me?"

I close my mouth, staring at him.

"I think she called your brothers instead, don't you think?"

My heart sinks a little. Her instinct would've been to get me back and to make Callum Ames pay. She wouldn't have trusted the police, given who his father is.

And he knows that. He knows exactly what's coming.

"That's what you want," I say quietly. "You're drawing them in. You want his attention."

He falls silent, but his eyes never leave mine. I always knew this wasn't about me. I just underestimated how far he would go.

"Unless you told them about the night we planned, then no one will know where to find you, so no . . ." he says. "I don't expect your brothers to actually show up. It's just us. I'm sure they'll find me in the days to come, though. After we're done."

Oh, God. I swallow down the vomit.

Would Clay know where they're taking me? She said she wasn't aware of any clubhouses.

No one is coming for me. My phone is somewhere in the limo, so no one can track me, and there are four of them. Panic seizes me. *Shit*.

We race onto the highway, speeding down the dark lane, and Del dips off to the left suddenly, taking the long, smoothly paved road up to Fox Hill.

The oaks on both sides provide a canopy from the moon and stars, and I can only make out the sheen in Callum's eyes as I stare at him and he stares back at me. Darkness consumes us, and he knows what's about to happen as well as I do.

I feel a sting on my neck and know his nail has cut my skin. "You will never come back from this," I murmur.

"I'm not worried about me."

"You should be," I say. "This is gonna hurt."

No one is really evil. And not many are crazy or sick.

He's angry. He won't always feel like this. Is he sure this is a road he wants to cross?

His eyes narrow, and I can tell he's thinking about it. Can he still let me go? Or has he gone too far and might as well finish?

Reaching behind me slowly, I slip off the gold strappy heels I put Clay in more than a month ago. I won't be able to run in them.

Del slams on the brakes, and the SUV screeches to a halt. I dart my gaze out of the window, seeing we're on the golf course, around the back of the field house. Aracely used to work the beer cart on the course, and I had to pick her up one time.

The doors open, the scent of wood, grass, and sweat hitting me as someone grabs me and pulls me out of the cab. Delaney spins me around and looks down at me as Callum tightens the band around my wrists. A smile lights up Del's eyes, and I'm not sure this guy has ever looked me in the eye or knew I existed when he was at Marymount, but he sure knows now.

His eyes trail down and then back up my body, and it hits me that I'm in my underwear. Panties and a little corset, my dress on the floor of the limo.

"What a waste," he gripes.

And his hands spread over my stomach, sliding to my back, and I fight, hollering until my throat is raw.

And then, all of a sudden, teeth sink into my ass, and I whip around. I kick Milo, not giving him time to fight back before I throw myself on top of him, both of us falling to the ground and my knee slamming into his groin.

"Ah!" he bellows.

I growl, he yanks my hair, pulling my head back, and then someone pushes me off him, and I land on the driveway on my back.

I bolt up, but Callum is there, pinning me down. He places a vial in front of my face. "You wanna remember this?"

I go still, my breath hitching for a moment.

I look at the drug and then back to him, my fingers smashed and hurting behind me. He said he didn't drug people. Would he really use that on me?

I swallow hard, nodding. If he forces that down my throat, I'll be unconscious. I won't be able to fight back, run, give a positive ID . . .

He doesn't want to give it to me. He wants a willing girl. He wants what he thinks we agreed to.

But he'll take it if he has to.

Motherfucker.

"I doubt I'll remember it anyway," I spit out, putting forth what pathetic fight I have left.

He simply chuckles, challenge accepted, and hauls me off the ground.

"Take her." He shoves me to Milo, who's rougher as he fists my hair and squeezes my arm.

They lead me inside the dark building, and I spot paintings on the walls in gilded frames and smell all the wood polish and leather furniture. They push me through a sitting area, tables and couches and a bar gleaming in the moonlight streaming through the windows, and after a moment, we're in a hallway.

My knees shake a little, and I feel tears threaten. I drop my eyes. *Please. God, please.* I don't want anyone to hurt me. Please.

I want my dad. I want Macon.

No one can touch me but Clay. This isn't happening. I'm still in the limo. I'm with her.

In her arms.

A sob escapes, but I push it down, burying it, and grit my teeth. Fuck him for this. I'm going to kill him.

"There are witnesses," I say, keeping my tone calm. "There were cameras on the streets."

"You'll go home in one piece," Callum replies. "We had an agreement. I want what you promised."

I spin around, getting in his face. "I never promised."

But he just growls in a low voice, "Walk. Walk and pay up, and this won't have to escalate. I know how to hurt you without laying a hand on you."

Milo pulls me back around, shoving me headfirst through a door. He grips me hard, holding me as I stumble down some stairs, another hallway, and into a room.

I smell water. Is this a basement? Those aren't common in Florida.

I spot a few more bodies in the room and instantly stop, dread coiling its way through my gut.

Two other men wait in the room, and a young woman leans against the back wall. Next to the pool table.

She cocks her head, taking me in, and I know that she's for me. Petite, blond, blue eyes . . . like Clay.

But not Clay.

Walking over, she smiles gently, her long, smooth hair falling over her left eye just a little, and her full red lips open to perfect white teeth. She's dressed conservatively in tight black pants and a short-sleeved tight black T-shirt, and I don't think she's more than a year or two older than me. Beautiful, young, soft . . .

But then she drops her gaze, noticing my arms behind my back. "Why is she tied up?" she asks.

Callum comes around to my front and looks between the girl and me. "This is Morgan," he tells me, ignoring her question. "Your date."

Her finger slips inside the hem of my panties, and I fire up. Shooting out my foot, I kick her in the stomach. "Ugh!"

She yelps, stumbling backward, and I steel every muscle, preparing.

"What the hell?" she blurts out, holding her middle and glaring at Callum. "You didn't tell me she wasn't into this."

"She's into it."

But she charges to the wall again, grabbing her bag as she continues to hold her stomach. She marches for the door. "I don't do shit like this."

And before I can follow, she's gone. She no doubt has a pimp they don't want to mess with.

I hold my head up and meet each of their eyes. "Looks like you'll have to do your dirty work yourself," I tell Callum as I try to work my hands free. "Come on. Who's first? It's my first dick, so I'd prefer a little one to start. Milo?"

I meet Krisjen's ex's eyes, and a snarl crosses his mouth.

"Come on," I chirp. "Blow my mind. Fuck me so good I go straight."

He charges up to me and grabs the back of my hair, shoving me onto the pool table. "Shut up."

My heart races, fear coursing through me, but I'm angry, too. I flip over, sitting up. "Come on, baby. Come on. Show me what a man is."

He reaches down, unfastening his belt and jeans and breathing hard, ready to show me what I've been missing, and I almost crack. Tears pool, but I shove them back down.

"Yeah, look at that thing," I grit out, biting my lip and staring down his pants. "It gets bigger when it gets harder, right? I can't wait to see."

He grasps my throat. "Shut. Up."

He's getting angry.

I tip my head back, laughing, and I know I sound crazy, but it's like I'm not in my body right now, and it's either this or cry.

I laugh harder, rolling my wrists and working the bandana or necktie or whatever they tied me with looser and looser. "Oh, come on, baby," I growl. "You wanna feel me? Huh? Wanna give it to me? Wanna show me how it's done? I know you can. I know it."

He shoves me back onto the table. Tears hang at the corner of my eyes, and I arch my back, moaning.

"I don't think you can," I groan, writhing. "I bet your dick is so soft, it's like a floppy, wiggly worm." I cackle wildly. "You'll have to turn me around so you don't have to look at my face. Isn't that right, Callum?" I look to his friend, standing back by the door. "Isn't that how you'll have to do me, too? Turn me around and jam that pathetic, droopy appendage inside me by pretending I'm him. By pretending I'm—"

"Shut up!" Callum yells.

Milo's hand whips across my face, but it doesn't wipe the smile from it. "I've got five of you motherfuckers at home!" I shout to the room. "Is that the best you got? Huh?"

Not that my brothers hurt me, but I've gotten used to rough-housing.

I work the tie, almost able to slide it over my knuckles, but Milo grabs the backs of my knees and yanks me down to the end of the table.

"You're such a man," I coo. "Come on. What are you gonna do? Huh? Do it. Come on, baby. Do it. Blow my mind."

He reaches inside his jeans, and I stare, feigning excitement when I just want to throw up.

"Oh, yeah," I say. "More, more. Come on, come on."

"Come on, Milo!" someone shouts, but his brow is etched in anger, and I can see his face flush with strain.

"So, is this it?" I laugh. "Is it happening now? Is this what I've been missing?"

A laugh bubbles up from my stomach so deep there's no sound as I shake. "He can't fucking get it up," I taunt.

He shoves me down and grips my throat, digging his fingers in, and I fight not to squeeze my eyes shut. He can't tell how badly my body is shaking in the struggle.

I work the tie again and again. *Come on. Please.*

"Is it happening yet?" I force out at the top of my lungs. "Come on, baby. Fuck me up. Come on!"

"Goddammit!" he shouts, throwing me off and stuffing his shit back inside his pants. "She won't shut the fuck up."

Del hands him a roll of duct tape, and I wiggle my hands out, sweat beading my brow. I pull my hands through the fabric, finally freeing them as Milo comes over. He bites off a strip of tape and moves for my mouth, but I launch up, grab the bar light over the pool table and yank it again and again, screaming at the top of my lungs.

It crashes down, right on top of Milo's head, disorienting him, and I move fast. Shoving him off, I bolt off the tables, run for the door behind me, and fucking pray it's not a closet.

I dive through, the hallway on the other side dark, but I spot a bit of light at the end and race for it. Shouts echo behind me, and I pass a small black table against the wall and shove it to the ground as they launch through the door after me. I run for the end of the hallway, diving into a great room, moonlight glowing through the window and across the floor.

"Ah!" someone bellows.

"Fuck!" Callum growls.

Grunts and crashes sound behind me, and I know they've stumbled over the obstacle in the hallway, hopefully fucking piling on top of each other.

Throwing open the front door, I leap outside, into the night, the sprinklers spraying in long, misty arches over the green.

Digging in my heels, I run for the tree line in my bare feet.

"Liv!"

And I recognize the voice instantly.

I whip around, seeing Clay run for me, and I catch her in my arms as she rushes me.

"Baby," I cry. I wrap my arms around her, burying my face in her neck.

"What did they do to you?" She kisses me—my cheek, my lips, my jaw, again and again.

"Shhh," I tell her, trying to calm her down. I spot Macon and Army just as Dallas pulls me toward the bushes, and we all crouch down. Iron and Trace run up from the service entrance road, and I look around at my family as Clay touches my face, her eyes scanning every inch of my body.

Her gaze locks on my cheek, and I register the sting still there from Milo's slap. It's probably red. "It's okay," I say. "They didn't do nearly as much as I did to them."

"Liv . . ."

I dart my eyes to Macon. "It's okay," I cut him off. "They didn't hurt me."

Not badly anyway.

Dressed in my underwear, I know what he's thinking. And I know exactly what he'd do if he knew what might've happened if I hadn't gotten out of there.

I kiss Clay again, pulling on the flannel Iron tosses me.

"How did you know they brought me here?" I ask her.

"I didn't."

I look up at Macon, but he's already walking. I shoot to my feet, seeing Callum and Milo run out of the field house, Del and the other two stopping dead when they see my brothers charge across the green and right for them.

I start after Macon. "No."

But Clay interjects. "Let them fuck them up," she tells me, handing me my phone I'd left behind in the limo.

Macon, Army, and Dallas head straight for the patio, Del and the other two backing away. They bolt, disappearing back into the clubhouse or out of sight.

I stare at Clay. "They won't win this and you know it. No fighting." And then to my brothers, "This wasn't the plan."

We're not Collinses or Ameses. We can get physical and keep up in a fight, but they can hurt us because we're poor.

She touches my face again, lightly. "Who hit you?" she whispers.

I close my mouth.

"Who was it?" she demands again. "Callum?"

I glance after Dallas for less than a moment before answering her. "No."

"Milo?" she presses.

I say nothing.

And she has her answer. She straightens, locking her jaw, and grabs the hunting knife Iron has strapped to his belt.

She charges off, Iron and Trace following her.

"Clay, no!"

"Fuckin' yes," Trace replies.

She goes, they follow, and I run after them all, trying to figure out who to stop first as I button up the flannel.

Milo pulls something out of his pocket, and Dallas swats it out of his hand. A phone goes flying, but Callum just takes a chair at a nearby lawn table and drops his ass down, unfazed.

Army grabs Milo from behind, Macon kicks his legs out from underneath him, and he falls to his knees.

"Stop," Clay calls just as Macon's fist rears back, ready to punch. "You'll get in trouble. I won't."

Milo chuckles, eyeing her and the knife in her hand, but then everything seems to happen all at once, his face falling. Clay approaches, Macon steps out of the way, and I watch her raise the blade to his face.

"Clay, no!" he screams. "Ah!"

He winces as she drags the knife across his cheek, from his temple down to the corner of his mouth, and I stand there, impressed, and a little scared I'm not more scared.

"Clay . . ." But I stop, the deed already done.

Milo gasps and sputters, blood dripping down his face and off his chin, and Clay squats down to make eye contact. I can hear the tears in her throat.

"Now, when you go to get stitches," she tells him, "you're going to tell them that you cut yourself shaving."

Macon watches her, and I squeeze my phone so hard the plastic whines.

"When your parents ask, you tell them you cut yourself shaving," Clay goes on. "And when the next woman in your life asks about your scar, you're going to remember that if I get even a hint that you have done this to anyone else, they won't find you with another scar. They won't find you at all." And then she raises her voice and presses the point of the blade to the other side of his face as Army holds him. "Don't you ever touch her again! Not a finger!"

"Okay! Okay!" Milo pleads. "Okay . . ."

Clay rises, Macon looming behind her and watching her intently.

Army lets Milo fall to the ground, and he grabs his bloody cheek as Clay moves over to Callum.

He sits there, slouching and knees spread, watching as if it's a show and he's not outnumbered.

"That was hot," he tells Clay.

His eyes flash to the side as Dallas moves behind him, and I watch my brother stare down at him, his eyes unreadable.

Clay steps in front of him, still holding the knife.

"You really want to do this?" he asks her. "Make all the threats you want. Promise to sink me in the swamps for the gators. You and I both know that what you can do, so can I."

I drop my eyes to my phone, slowly moving my thumb over the screen.

"You didn't learn, did you?" he asks her. "That's why you always pick on the weak, Clay. You can't beat me if the playing field is even."

And I press *Play*.

"*Did you know*," Callum's voice drifts through my phone, "*that a structure can be deemed a historical landmark and cannot be destroyed after it reaches one hundred years old?*"

Everyone turns to look at me, taking in the cell in my hand. Callum's eyes sharpen on me.

"*And while fucking for me will get you Mercutio, fucking me will get you a meeting with Raymond FitzHugh to push through your petition to protect the lighthouse? And, in effect, your land?*"

Macon's body turns rigid, and Dallas lets loose a snarl.

"*Fucking me good guarantees it, in fact.*"

I pause the recording, stepping up to Clay's side. "The playing field is . . ." I shake my head, loving the way his lips tighten and that fucking smile is gone. "Not even, Callum."

I feel Macon's heat rolling off him, and I know the wheels in his head are turning. He wants to do something, but maybe if I can get him out of here now, I can calm them all down.

"Not here," I whisper to my brother. *Not on their turf.*

Another time. Another day. Somewhere not with cameras everywhere.

Callum tips his chin up, knowing I have the upper hand right now.

"Get out of here," he finally tells us.

Clay stands there, and slowly, I take her hand, all of us backing away.

But my brothers stay, Dallas stepping toward Callum as Macon, Iron, and Trace flank him.

"Dallas, no," I warn.

But no one looks at me as Macon speaks. "Army, get the girls home. We'll be there soon."

"Macon . . ."

"Now!" Macon yells, ignoring me.

Callum laughs, shaking his head as my brothers approach him. "Four against one. That's no fair."

"It's just you," Dallas assures him, cracking his knuckles. "And me. Now get inside."

"And if I say no?"

Dallas explodes, whipping the back of his hand across Callum's cheek, and Callum's chair tumbles over with the force, sending him spilling to the ground.

I gasp as a line of blood flies out of Callum's mouth and he lands on his hands and knees. He grabs his face, red seeping through his fingers as he glares up at Dallas.

"Now that's a word I've never heard from you," Dallas bites out. "Try it out. See what happens next."

And for the first time, as worried as I am, I can't help but force back a smile. It's good to see Callum bleed.

"Now get inside," Dallas tells him again.

Callum's body shakes a little but his eyes and jaw harden as he rises. I wait for him to resist, to tell my brother no, but he doesn't. With a slight smile curling the corner of his mouth, he finally turns and heads toward the clubhouse.

Dallas follows. "Watch the doors," he says to Macon, Iron, and Trace.

Army pulls Clay and me away as I watch my brother disappear into the clubhouse with Callum.

"Stop them," I urge Army as we walk.

But he just chuckles. "Are you on glue? Not a chance."

Goddammit. We have what we need. We're safe.

Macon, Iron, and Trace linger outside the door, keeping watch as Dallas gives Callum everything he deserves and more.

"Are you sure you're okay?" Clay grabs me once we're clear. "They didn't . . ."

"I'll be fine." I kiss her.

"We have the footage," Army tells me. "You want me to erase it?"

I look up at my brother, knowing that when Clay called, he would know where they took me.

"Footage? What do you mean?" Clay inquires.

"Cameras," I tell her. "That's what Callum was talking about at Mariette's. About the break-in? He gave me the key to Fox Hill. If I played nice with one of their escorts, he would play nice, too. He would give me his role in the play."

"And you agreed to that?"

"Of course not." I take her hand, trying to calm down the worry in her eyes. "It was never going to happen. My brothers used the key to get in and plant cameras throughout the facility. Now we can stockpile enough secrets and footage to keep St. Carmen off our backs. Callum will have more parties. And I'm sure that's not even the worst of what's going on there."

"But you took the role?"

"Hell yes. He tried to take my dignity," I retort, "on many occasions in the last four years, Clay."

She closes her mouth, her eyes softening as I'm sure she realizes she did the same thing many times over the years. The comments, the looks, the snide smiles . . .

But she takes the back of my neck and presses her forehead to mine, closing her eyes, and I don't see any of that anymore. All I see in front of me is my favorite thing in the whole world.

After a moment, I look to Army, not sure I can ever watch what could've happened to me in that room, but it's the first log in the fire. We can't delete it. "Store the footage," I tell him.

I take her hand again, and we move, loading into one of the trucks.

"We should have Milo arrested at least," Clay says.

"You know the law will protect them," I point out. "We end it here, hopefully it stays that way. For us, secrets are a better weapon."

"And if not . . ." she adds, tossing the knife on the dash.

I just laugh, climbing into the cab behind her. "You really gonna sink him into the swamp with a pair of cement galoshes?" I tease.

But she just looks past me into the distance, serious and caging.

Oh, come on. She wasn't serious about them not finding his body if he ever did that again. I chuckle, but then stop when I see she's still not laughing.

"Clay?" I press. "Babe?"

She cocks an eyebrow, lifting her chin and focusing on the wondrous trees out the windshield like they're the most beautiful things ever and she can't fucking hear me.

Army laughs under his breath, approving of the newest addition to the family.

Fucking great.

34

Clay

I kiss the corner of her mouth, her warm breath soft and calm as she sleeps. I've barely slept. But it's okay. I'm so happy, I don't want to miss a moment.

I kiss the bruise on her cheek, reaching around and cupping her face to hold her close. I can't believe what almost happened to her. Callum deserves to be in jail. They all do, but I know hurting them would bring attention on the Jaegers, so maybe I'll just have to find another way to punish him.

In addition to what Dallas probably did to him after we left last night, that is. We saw the rest of her brothers—including Dallas—pull into the driveway a few hours after we got back, so thankfully, no one was arrested.

Callum is keeping his mouth shut.

But that doesn't mean he's even nearly paid for what he did. Liv likes to give the impression she's a fighter, and she is, but she's not steel, and thanks to a lot of people, including me, she's been abused long enough. I'm her armor now.

I kiss her temple and her jaw, skimming my mouth over to hers and take it oh so gently so she feels the love. Her breathing hitches, her body stirring, and I slide my hand down her body, under the sheet, between her legs.

I shiver at just the feel of her, and I hear her start to pant a little, her eyes still closed.

I watch her, working my fingers inside her, but I can't take it. I want to kiss her down there. Her thighs fall open, and I pull the sheet off, sliding myself down her body.

But then my phone rings, and I stop.

Dammit. I grab it off the floor, knowing Liv's awake already, but I don't want her disturbed.

She gives a little groan in protest, grabbing me back, but I just laugh. "Shhh . . ." I tell her.

I see my mom's name on the screen, and I answer. "Morning."

"Where are you?" she bursts out.

Liv pulls me into her arms, and I kiss her. "Still at Liv's," I say.

Liv takes my other hand, putting it back where it was between her thighs.

I keep my laughter quiet.

"Okay, since I know you two are dating now, this changes things," my mom tells me. "Are you sleeping in separate beds?"

Liv rears back, having heard that, and looks at me like she's wondering if I'm aware how dumb my mom is.

"Of course not," I say without shame. "You're being homophobic."

"Don't you use that word with me!" Mom growls. "If she were Callum, there's no way I'd allow it, either. Sex is a big deal, Clay. You can't just start treating this house like a hotel and practically living with your girlfriend!"

I roll my eyes, tipping my head back as Liv dives into my neck.

"I don't care if you're eighteen or not," Mom goes on. "I need to meet her. She's coming to dinner tonight. Do you understand?"

My body is throbbing, Liv so warm under my hand.

"Clay?" Mom yells. "Are you being safe? You are still under my roof, you know."

The room spins.

"Give me back the phone!" Mom cries. And then I hear my father's voice. "I'll handle your mother. Bring Liv to Coco's at seven, okay?"

I nod, excited because that's my favorite restaurant. "'Kay. Thanks, Dad."

"Love you." And he hangs up, letting me go.

I drop the phone and cover her body with mine, needing this more than food. "Let's stay in bed all day," I tell her.

"Just try to leave," she threatens.

I straddle her, sitting up, and I can't stop smiling. It's probably all over social media, so if nothing else, I'm going to enjoy this one day before everyone else does their damnedest to infiltrate my peace of mind.

I stare down at her and pull off my T-shirt—her T-shirt—and grab her leather jacket from the end of the bed. If she's going to see anyone naked in it, it's going to be me.

I pull it on, leaving it unzipped, a strip of my bare skin visible down the middle with the hint of the curve of my breasts. I pull my hair out from the back and let her look.

She kneads my hips, shifting underneath me as her heated gaze falls down my body. "You definitely need a leather jacket."

"We can go shopping later," I tell her.

Any excuse to go shopping . . .

But she shakes her head. "No. You'll wear mine."

Yes, I will. No more hiding our little trinkets of each other.

My eyes fall on the bruise on her cheek again, and I take her hands, holding them in mine. "You should've posted that audio."

She looks up at me, her smile slowly dissipating as a thoughtful expression crosses her face. "Maybe I will," she tells me. "Or maybe I want to see what happens next."

"What do you mean?"

"I mean Callum has slept in this house more nights than you. Did you know that?"

I freeze. What?

She inhales and exhales. "He and Dallas . . ." she almost whispers.

"What?" I exclaim, dumbfounded.

But she nods. "Last summer, for about a month."

I gape at her. He and Dallas what? Is she serious?

"Dallas broke it off," she tells me, "and Callum was not happy."

Oh my God. I think, trying to find any clues I had, but there are none. Nothing that I picked up on, except . . .

Is that why he targeted Liv? Because she was a Jaeger he had access to at school every day and could hurt?

"I didn't know Dallas was . . ."

"He's bi," she says. "But don't bring it up. Dallas doesn't like anyone in his business."

I'd gathered as much.

"Callum, I'm pretty sure, is not bi," she tells me, almost as if she's breaking some bad news. "Or straight."

"Fuck . . ." I breathe out, thinking about all his taunting and the other girls at school.

But then a thought occurs to me. Last summer, Callum would've been seventeen. Dallas was at least twenty then. Callum could've gotten him into a lot of trouble, but of course, he would've outed himself in the process.

So Callum went after Liv instead. It wasn't random.

"It doesn't excuse his behavior," she says, "but the more I look around at the world, Clay, the more I realize that villains are a lot more complicated than we want them to be. Sometimes, they're just people who are really afraid."

It definitely doesn't excuse anything.

"Everyone has a story, Clay." She glides her hands up and down my thighs. "Callum will sink himself on his own. Or swim. And while we wait to see which, we have the cameras secretly recording every day to make sure he behaves himself. I like having that lever-age over him."

Especially since he can still send Dallas to prison.

"But what about your land?" I ask her. "You could use that video to blackmail his father."

"Once they know we have footage, they'll find the cameras and remove them," she says. "We don't want to give up that ace yet. I was actually hoping your mom and dad could help with the land."

Oh?

"Did you know structures over a hundred years old can be pe-titioned to be protected as historical landmarks?" she taunts. "Your parents sit on the city council, right?"

I smile, leaning down, nose to nose. "Are you just dating me for my power?"

She flips me over and comes down on top of me. "I love having a powerful girlfriend," she whispers over my lips.

Goose bumps spread at the sound of that word. "I love that I'm your girlfriend."

She nibbles my ear, and I can't think about anything else any-more this morning. Just excited for dinner, and tonight, and more nights, and a whole summer of her smiling and hopefully in a bikini.

"I love you," I say.

"I love you, too." She bites me gently. "And I want our flag back. Don't think I've forgotten."

"Well, my parents need to attend a reunion for my father's old frat next weekend," I taunt her. "I'll be home alone. Doors locked. If you can get to me, you can have more than just the flag."

She laughs against my skin. "Maybe you forgot what my last name is, but I love a challenge. And I promise. You won't even hear me until I'm standing right behind you."

Tingles spread up my spine, wanting time to slow down but

excited for next weekend to get here. She'll have to chase me, but I look forward to when she catches me.

Spreading open my jacket, she sucks on my nipple, but then I remember something else and grab my phone.

"Wait." I stop her, bringing up the screenshot I took from something online. "Can we do this?"

I show her the pic of a splendid new position I want to try, and her eyes go wide. "Jesus, Clay . . ."

And I laugh as she covers my mouth with hers, groaning like I'm driving her insane.

T he next morning, I stand with Liv in front of the school under the tree as everyone exits cars and heads for the doors. I know people are looking, but I only stare at her hand in mine.

"You ready?" she asks quietly.

"They all already know." I caress her fingers. "At least there's that."

She pulls me along, both of us making our way down the sidewalk as eyes turn and voices quiet, the stairs to the doors looming above.

"They'll look," she assures me, squeezing my hand. "They'll talk. But every time they do, just remember they're not feeling this."

We climb the stairs, and I stop, my heart thumping, but it's more because I'm excited for people to know I love her than dreading the pushback.

"Don't worry," I say, leaning in close and making no effort to hide my arm wrapping around her waist. "I'll never not want to feel this."

I'll never let anyone else cost me what I love most in the world.

And we walk into school together.

35

Olivia

Three Weeks Later

Clay runs past me, and I start to charge her with my stick, but I stop, giving up. "You want to tell me why we're still practicing?" I shout as the team races around us. "Season's over."

She spins, running backward as she speaks. "We still have incoming freshmen to train this summer."

"And why did I agree to that?"

"Because you do everything I say."

She winks, a wicked smile spreading across her face, and a jolt hits my heart the way it always does at the sight of her.

"Actually, she promised you a massage," Krisjen adds, jogging past me.

Followed by Chloe. "A full-body one."

Oh, yeah. Now I remember. She caught me at a weak moment.

Girls run back and forth, Clay saving the ball from the goal, and I think she's going to miss this. Being captain, she told me, has been one of the best parts of high school, because she got to spend time with me.

I remember it a little differently. Body slams and extra workouts and her always hogging the ball. But she sure is trying to make up for it. She kept her word. She has been *so* pleasant.

I swoop in front of her as she charges toward me and flings the ball off to Krisjen just as Clay pushes me to the ground. She lands on top of me, smiling, but I roll us over.

I stare down at her. "I'm not sure I wouldn't rather just spend it on the beach instead," I tell her. "Hell, I'd rather be on an air boat with Trace gator hunting this summer than sweating my ass off on this field one more second."

"Why were you ever on the team?" she fires back, because she knows this is the last thing I want to be doing with my time.

But we both know exactly why I put up with this shit for so long, and it wasn't because athletics looked good on my college applications.

I cock an amused eyebrow, smirking a little.

She smiles like she didn't already know I was always here for her.

"And gator hunting doesn't start until August," she says.

"And he's not hunting. Is that what he tells you?" Krisjen pants next to us. "He just feeds them marshmallows and then we sneak onto Mark Chamberlain's houseboat, drink his beer, and have sex."

I groan, rolling off Clay. "Too much information, Krisjen."

I rise, pulling Clay up after me, and notice blood on her knee. She's wearing pants to prom, otherwise she'd be pissed about a scraped knee. I'm wearing a dress again, but this time it's thin silk, tight, and there won't be a stitch of underwear underneath. I enjoy making her sweat in public.

Squatting down, I take her leg and use my shirt to pat away the blood. Coos go off to my left, and I turn my head at the girls on the bench looking at me like puppy dogs as I take care of her.

I shake my head. Some people, as expected, were pricks about it all when Clay came out, but the advocates are louder, stronger, and much more vicious when they witness an injustice. Anyone who had shit to say soon found it was better to keep their stupid comments to themselves, unless they wanted to be immortalized on the internet forever.

If anyone wasn't a friend, they were at least quiet.

Callum has never made eye contact again. It's almost as if we don't exist at school. He never appears without a girl wrapped around him, and I'm not sure who he's trying to convince that he's living his best life—us or himself—but the bruises Dallas gave him that night have healed, and Callum behaves like nothing ever happened.

We stay out of his way. He stays out of ours. For now.

Milo mysteriously left school following Fox Hill. We'd see him around town here and there, but no matter how many times I ask Clay about it, she denies playing any role in having him finish the school year from home instead of anywhere near me.

Not that I don't appreciate her throwing her weight around to protect me. Her mother's help to protect the lighthouse—and essentially Sanoa Bay—worked like magic, after all. Her grandmother fought us on it, but her father backed off surprisingly quickly, even though he was one of the people who lost when the development deal fell through. I think he just lost the energy to do anything else that might make his family any more unhappy.

"What are you all doing here?" I hear someone exclaim.

We look up, seeing the coach in a sundress with her glasses pushed up on top of her head. She looks like she was passing by on her way back from the beach.

"I have no idea," I tell her, shooting Clay a look.

Coomer checks her phone. "Prom is in four hours, Clay!"

Everyone looks to Clay, my devious angel feigning innocence.

"All right, we're going," she laughs. "See y'all tonight! Get out of here!"

"Wooo!" a unanimous howl sounds.

Everyone grabs their gear, thunder cracking across the sky, and I rise, pulling Clay in for a kiss now that everyone is clearing out.

Her hands immediately go to my face, and I'm trying not to count the days left, but it's always in the forefront of my mind.

"Come on." She takes my hand. "Hair, makeup . . ."

"Shower," I tell her, implying all good things start there.

"I'll be at your house in an hour," Krisjen says to Clay.

"Okay."

We put away our gear and take our bags, and I notice Amy sitting on the benches packing up her stuff. Alone.

The first day after the ball, Clay and I ate by ourselves in the cafeteria until Krisjen and Chloe joined us. Over the next few days, others found their seats closer until eventually we were in the mix, no separation between our little party and everyone else. We're a part of things now, despite whispers here and there.

Amy never showed.

And while she's not alone at school, she looks lonely, because her pride won't let her grow up.

I eye Clay.

She narrows her eyes, following my gaze to Amy and then back to me. She shakes her head.

Yes, I tell her with my glare.

Enemies are a choice. A result of our egos. They happen when we've chosen to see sheep instead of sleeping lions.

Amy will be a lion. Like us. She just needs to wake up.

Clay holds my stare, finally rolling her eyes, because she doesn't give a shit about convincing Amy of anything, but she does whatever I say.

We have that in common.

She looks down at Amy, who keeps her eyes lowered like she doesn't know we're right here. "So, are you . . . getting ready at home tonight?"

After a moment, Amy nods.

"By yourself?" Clay asks.

Another nod.

Clay's eyes flash to me, and we both look at Amy, who still hasn't met her eyes.

"Oh, for crying out loud," Clay says, swinging her bag over her shoulder. "Just bring your stylist. Margaritas kick off in fifty-nine minutes."

Amy shoots her eyes up, excitement and a smile on her face. She looks between Clay and me, the disdain I used to see there now gone.

"Thanks," she says.

I have no idea if we can trust her, but I guess we'll find out.

I pull Clay along, our duffels hanging crossbody, as I rush us to my bike and hand over her helmet. Taking mine, I pull it over my head and climb on, Clay straddling behind me and wrapping her arms around my body.

"Shower," she whispers against my neck.

Shivers hit me, and I kick the bike into gear extra hard, speeding off.

I take us to her house, usually loving the feel of her too much to rush, but we're busy tonight, and I want her to myself before everyone gets here.

My dress is already in the living room, as well as some vanities set up for makeup and hair, and I can hear Clay's mom chattering away on the phone, her earpiece hanging in her ear, as we run into the house.

"Girls, slow down!" Gigi shouts as we race for the stairs. "You're all muddy!"

We kick off shoes on the marble floor. "Sorry, Mom!" Clay says, taking my hand.

Clay's mom holds a tray of beautiful white-frosting-covered little cakes with pink flowers decorated on the top.

I reach out to take one but stop myself. "I need to fit into my dress."

Gigi leans in. "Take it from me: Eat the cake."

Well, if she's going to twist my arm about it. I pluck a fancy little confection off the tray and let Clay haul me upstairs as I stumble and eat at the same time.

"Your mom looks good," I tell her over my mouthful.

She pulls me inside her room and slams the door. "I think she's feeling good, too."

"And your dad?"

She pulls off her shirt, her black sports bra looking fantastic on her, and walks to the window, spying outside. She shrugs. "It doesn't feel weird."

That he's moved out, she means. Despite the flames and love that still exist between her parents, Gigi decided she needed to be alone, and good for her. Their divorce is proceeding.

"I'm glad Henry isn't here to see it," Clay says, "but she's getting younger every day. You know?"

She peers out the window, down onto the patio, and I walk over, seeing her mother enter the small greenhouse she'd built—or had someone build—in the backyard below. She's discovered a love of gardening, I guess.

She's also looking into a photography course and teaching herself the stock market. At first, I thought she was trying to distract herself, but it seems to bring her joy. Learning how to grow again.

I sit in the window seat, pulling Clay down between my legs. Her head falls back into my shoulder, and I kiss her hair.

"I'm gonna miss you," I say quietly.

"Just be here," she whispers. "Let's not talk about it, okay?"

"I can't stop thinking about it, though." A painful lump stretches my throat. "Maybe I can get into Wake Forest. Or you can come to Dartmouth."

"Too cold." She shivers. "And I'm not going to Wake Forest."

Excuse me?

"I haven't told my parents yet," she says. "But after everything, I think they know better than to stand in my way."

"Where are you going, then?"

This is news. When did she decide this?

She pauses, threading her fingers through mine on her stomach. "I'm staying, actually."

"What?"

She draws in a breath and sits up, turning around to face me. "I've seen the world, Liv," she tells me. "I've met people. Dressed to impress. I've had the same conversations with people I don't like and networked with people I don't want relationships with. Everything that leaving home is supposed to give me, I've already had." She doesn't falter, gazing into my eyes and thoughtful. "I don't want to be in a sorority, where peer pressure will have me vomiting every carb or hiding how much I love you instead of some frat brother." She touches my face. "I know what I want."

I don't know if I'm unnerved or relieved. It's normal to worry about her meeting someone else. Insecurities come with being separated. She'd make new friends at college, perhaps find something or someone who could take her away from me forever. It seems less likely now that she's staying home and won't be in that environment day in and day out.

But if we're going to have a future together, I don't want her to feel like she missed out on anything, either.

"I want to have a relationship with my parents again," she tells me. "I'm going to intern with Mrs. Gates. Take my classes online. I want to be here."

"Are you sure?"

"The only thing I'm not sure about is how hard it will be to watch you go."

Pain stretches across my chest, and I almost wince. It's almost harder. Knowing she'll be here. I'll be able to picture everything. The places she's eating. The storms when I check the weather. Her path to the funeral home every day.

"But you have to leave," she tells me softly. "Dartmouth is your dream. You've earned it. You deserve it."

I don't want to leave. "Clay, things change . . ."

"If you don't go, you'll always wonder." She inches in, hovering her lips over mine and staring at my mouth. "I mean, you can stay, and we can get married since we're eighteen, but then what?"

I laugh, but then her words hit me, and I stop. It didn't occur to me before she said it, but the words sound so right. *I'm going to marry her.*

I see her chin tremble. "And if you come back . . ."

But I press my finger over her lips. "I'm coming home." And I take her face in my hands. "This doesn't end."

"I love you," she breathes out.

And I kiss her, letting her feel my heart so she never doubts it. *I'm going to marry her.*

EPILOGUE

Clay

Four Years Later

I*'m gonna be sick.*

I hover over the sink, seeing Macon through the window. He paces around the garage, working on my Bronco, and it seems like maybe I should wait to talk to him. He's already fixing my car for free. I'd hate to ask for more.

A slap lands on my ass, and I yelp, spinning around. Dex squeals, Cheeto crumbs all over his mouth, and then he runs away.

"Dex!" I growl as he disappears out of the Jaegers' kitchen.

No manners, and why should he? I've only spent more time with him the last four years than his aunt. He's absorbed nothing that I've tried to teach him.

I dust his crumbs off my jeans and blow out a breath, smoothing down my hair. I'm more nervous to speak to Macon than I am to Liv.

I take a couple more deep breaths and swipe the corners of my mouth, tidying up my lipstick, and head into the garage.

"Turn it up," Macon calls out.

Army sits on the stool at the worktable and reaches over, turning up the radio. Some Type O Negative song plays, and I hover at the doorway for a minute before I force myself down the steps.

"I'm not done yet," Macon says to me.

He bends over the hood, twisting a wrench, and I stand on the other side, shifting on my feet.

Can I speak to you in private?

No, don't say that. Adding occasion to this will just piss him off.

So, Liv and I . . . like since we're moving into the old lighthouse . . . I was like . . . wondering if . . .

Ugh. Why am I stuttering? After four years, I'm no more comfortable around this man than I ever was. Direct works best, but I feel like if I open my mouth and don't prepare myself, I'll puke.

I open my mouth and then close it, my skin vibrating, and a light sweat dampening it.

"Are you okay?" I hear someone ask.

I look up, seeing Macon frozen under the hood and watching me.

"Um, yeah. Why?"

He starts working again. "You look like you have something to say."

I swallow a few times to wet my throat, but I realize I'm wringing my fingers, and I stop immediately.

"I . . . um . . ." I can't catch my breath.

He stops again and looks up, and I sense that Army has stopped what he's doing as well, watching.

Just say it. Jesus.

I suck in a breath. "I would like to marry your sister."

He stands there, and he doesn't even look like he has a heartbeat as he stares at me.

My stomach roils, and I cough to stop myself from throwing up.

I mean, is he surprised? Liv and I have been together since high school. We've weathered separation, doubt, a few fights, uncertain futures, and where our careers would take us. She even left Dartmouth for a week and came home because we couldn't stand to be apart anymore.

Until I convinced her to go back, that is.

We just bought the lighthouse, and now we're renovating it. He knows we're in this forever.

"And you want me to what?" he asks. "Ask her if she likes you, but just don't tell her you like her unless I know she likes you first or something?"

Such an asshole. "I'm asking for your blessing."

"My permission, you mean?" he corrects, amusement lighting up his expression.

I clench my jaw, my stomach all right now, but my anger rises to take its place.

He laughs, glancing to Army and then back to me. "She doesn't come with goats or land or anything. We're poor people, Clay. I mean, you could probably get us to pay *you* to take her off our hands."

Army chuckles, and I cock a brow, losing my patience. "Macon . . ."

"I don't know, we might be able to stuff her arms with six-packs of Bud or something," he offers as her dowry. "Would that do?"

Army cackles louder.

Asshole! I tense up. "Would you shut up?" I bark at Macon. "This was supposed to be a beautiful moment, dammit."

I mean, excuse me for living. He's a southern man. I thought the gesture of asking for his sister's hand in marriage would be appreciated.

Fuck it. I'll just take her, then. "Are you going to create a stink if I marry your sister?" I growl.

He and Army finish laughing at the irony of an independent woman like myself, a successful business owner, asking for a man's permission for anything.

He calms down, sets down his tool, and walks around the Bronco to me. A thoughtfulness hits his eyes. "Be good to her?"

I square my shoulders.

"Be faithful and supportive," he tells me. "It was the only thing my father could do for my mother. It kept her alive."

I drop my eyes for a moment, knowing the mental illness that killed Trysta Jaeger years before she actually died. One of the hardest things to learn with my brother was that you couldn't always take away the pain of those you loved. *Just be there.*

"At the end of the day, that trust is all you need," Macon says.

I nod, a little surprised by the tears in my eyes.

He turns and heads back to the car. "If you fail her," he calls over his shoulder, "I feed you to the gators."

Army laughs, but I don't as I leave the garage and grip the ring in my pocket.

Macon doesn't make idle threats.

Macon sucks.

Olivia

I'm cooking tonight. She doesn't know, so I hope she doesn't have anything planned, but I'm sure she doesn't. She's been so busy at work, and it's kind of a double-edged sword to know what to think or feel when a funeral home is busy.

I mean, yeah, she's able to support us as I wait for royalty checks from indie films and invest everything else I have in my first theater production at a playhouse in Miami next summer, but it also means people suffered, losing loved ones. I'm glad she's doing well, though. The community trusts her, and Wind House has done well, taking her on as a partner.

I round the corner of the small market, searching for that wine she likes, but I see Mr. Collins standing in front of some canned goods, and I stop.

I take a step back, debating on trying to escape before he sees me.

But he twists his mouth to the side, looking unsure, and I don't leave.

We get along and all, but we're not usually alone together, either. Clay is better with the small talk.

"You look lost," I say.

He jerks his eyes over to me, and then he chuckles, kind of laughing at himself. "I'm cooking dinner tonight," he says. "For someone." He looks back at his choices and then shakes his head. "I should just order takeout and act like I cooked it."

Cooking for someone. Same as me.

I move to his side. "How about a . . . charcuterie board." I reach over to the cheeses in the oblong cooler behind him, pulling a wedge of brie, some aged cheddar, and smoked gouda. "It's easy and it looks really cultured and fancy, so I think you'll pass with it. You can eat it outside or in front of a fire . . ."

He smiles and takes the stuff. "Anything low on carbs." He murmurs his approval.

Yeah.

I pull him over to the produce, grabbing some crackers and French bread on the way. "Some tomatoes, grapes, cherries . . ." I dump the stuff into his basket. "Hit the deli and pick up some meats and then some wine, and you should be good."

He stares at his loot, looking impressed.

"It's a really easy way to look like you know what you're doing, and no cooking involved," I tell him.

"Thanks." But then a worried look crosses his face, and he looks around. "Oh, I need a board, right? I don't have one."

"Gigi does."

His gaze darts to mine, and I swear he looks like it was some big secret, and no one knew he's been dating his ex-wife.

Speechless for a moment, he finally just breathes out a laugh. "We were trying to keep it on the down-low," he says. "Does Clay know?"

"Everyone knows."

He rolls his eyes. "Awesome."

And I laugh. I can understand. The divorce was hard on them. Clay saw the home her brother grew up in become unrecognizable.

But it wasn't solely Mr. Collins's fault, either. Loss, abandonment, cheating . . . a lot of things happened to break up their marriage, but it didn't break up their family. Gigi sold the house, bought a lovely cottage on the beach, and found herself. Clay's closer to her parents apart than she was when they were together.

And now, after years, maybe he can make his ex-wife fall in love with him again. He's certainly up for the challenge, because it will be one. She's different now.

They were trying to keep it quiet, though. They didn't want to get Clay's hopes up until they knew it would last.

"This is a great idea," he tells me, gesturing to the food. "Thank you, honey."

"Anytime."

I head over to the wine, picking up the sauv blanc and hoping the refrigerator in our little house has decided to work today so it'll be chilled by the time she gets home. I check my phone for a call, just in case Macon doesn't finish with her car and I need to pick her up.

I drive to our home, loving to cross the tracks and loving that she's on the wrong side of them with me now, St. Carmen's little princess, a full-fledged swamp rat. I speed down the dirt road in an old Jeep I picked up a couple of years ago; my Ninja is at Macon's house.

The sea permeates the air, and I grab the groceries out of the back, tipping my head and looking up at the lighthouse. One of the many things on our list—and as funds allow—is to get the light functional again.

But first, dinner.

I open the old windows in the kitchen, spreading them wide

and letting in the September air as I switch on the music and start making the gumbo.

I feel the dust on the floor grind under my shoes, and no matter how much we clean, there always seems to be more dirt. The light-keeper's house is a shithole, but it's our shithole, and it's better than any mansion across the tracks. The old wooden beams above me smell like years of hurricanes and wind, and everything here is ours. Our stove, our table, our food, our bed.

The fireplace works, and if it ever gets so cold that I can't keep her warm, then a fire will.

We're going to have so much fun renovating this place and making every inch of it ours. Of course, we have to keep a certain aesthetic to maintain the historical landmark status, but that's no problem. We only want to make it comfortable and enhance what's already here.

I cut the stems of the flowers I bought at the market and stick them in a vase with water, placing it at the center of the table, and I spot headlights outside, just as the sun starts to set.

In a moment, the front door closes, and I feel arms slide around my waist.

"I have to talk to you," she whispers in my ear.

I damn near shiver, tilting my head into her breath more.

"Let me set this to simmer," I tell her. "Then we can 'talk.'"

I know what she wants.

She reaches over to my side, flipping open the old tin box I found this morning.

She holds up the old snapshot. "Archie?"

"Yeah." I nod, wiping off my hands. "Found it under a floor-board."

She sifts through the box, looking at pictures of the previous inhabitants. The corgi, Archie, and his human, the old lightkeeper.

"It's him." She smiles, finding the picture of the man in a torn cable-knit sweater and a beard.

"He looks just like I pictured," I say. "An old sea dog."

She searches through the pics in the box, looking again. "No girl, though."

I come around her and kiss her ear. "Someone was taking the pictures of him."

Her eyes light up, the mystery safe and sound that just maybe this cottage was a hideaway for two other lovers before us.

I hug her tight, determined to keep the tradition going.

I turn down the temp on the stove, and she takes my hand, but instead of leading me upstairs, she takes me outside.

"What are we doing?" I ask.

She remains silent, leading me over the dunes and down to the beach. I don't ask questions and don't ask permission when I sink to the sand and pull her down between my legs, holding her as we both look out to the endless horizon.

"So, what did you want to talk about?" I ask.

"Your car's extended warranty."

I bury my face in her neck, unable to not laugh. "Brat."

"Beautiful," she calls me, instead.

"Trouble," I counter.

"My pearl."

"Hellion," I bite out in her ear.

She turns her head, whispering, "Sunshine."

"Pain in my ass."

I smile and kiss her. I kiss her for a long time, the wind in our hair as the last light leaves us.

"Do you love me?" I ask against her lips.

She meets my eyes. "So much, I'll hurt if you don't marry me."

And before I know what's happening, she's slipping something on my ring finger, her gaze never leaving mine.

My heart stops a beat, and I can't speak, everything inside me swelling so big, my body can't contain it.

What?

I mean, yes. I . . .

I slam my mouth down on hers, trying to get the words out, but my voice is in my stomach, my heart is in my throat, and my head is somewhere twenty feet above my body.

God, I love her. I was ready to ask her, but she beat me to it.

"Mmmmm, wait," she tells me, pulling away and taking out her phone. "Before you say yes, I just want to make sure . . . We can do this when we get married, right?"

But I growl, pulling her phone—and whatever kinky sexual position she wants to try now—away as she giggles and I roll over on top of her.

"Handful," I grit out over her mouth right before I kiss her madly. "Hellion. Pain in my ass. Trouble."

"You're never going to get rid of me, you keep talking sweet like that."

And I dive in, biting her neck and making her squeal.

BONUS SCENE

This scene takes place a couple of months after Liv leaves for college. Clay has stayed in St. Carmen to reestablish a bond with her parents, intern with Mrs. Gates, and take online classes.

Clay

"Mom, just call Dad," I tell her, climbing out of my car.

"No."

I hold back my sigh as I slam the door and drop my keys into my bag. I hold my phone at my side as she talks into my earbuds and walk toward the bar—the *only* bar—in Sanoa Bay.

"He's not seeing her." I make my way across the dirt road. "He's not seeing anyone."

"You talked to him?"

I hear the break in her voice. It gives her away every time. She misses him.

But I know she's right. She was right when the decision was made last spring. If she took him back now, she'd be miserable, because she never got the chance to find out who the hell she was before they got married. Before being a wife and a mother distracted her from her unhappiness and lack of self-worth. She needs to find out some things before she can know if she can ever forgive him.

And maybe he needs to find out some things, too.

"I went to D.C. with him for a few days," I tell her. "He had to check out some real estate. We spent an entire day at the Smithsonian."

"Finally let him take you to the capital, huh?"

"I never said I wouldn't go." I stop, hearing the music inside the bar as the October wind caresses my bare arms. "I said I would only go if I could tour the White House, and there was no way I was stepping foot in that building while that prick still lived there."

"Clay . . ."

I almost laugh. She hates it when I curse. Still so prim and proper. You'd think being the only alum of South Florida's chapter of Omega Chi Kappa with a lesbian daughter would loosen her up. Time will tell, I guess.

I walk toward the bar again, the palms overhead blowing in the night sky. "Call Dad," I order her.

"I'll do it myself."

"No, you're going to hire someone to do it."

"Same thing."

I roll my eyes. "I'll send Iron over."

"No—"

"Mom," I blurt out, taking charge. "Contractors only see dollar signs when they look at St. Carmen housewives. What if Dad re-marries? You still going to take the alimony?"

She falls silent.

"You need to learn to be frugal," I explain.

Okay, not really. She has her own trust fund she's never really used, but still . . .

"Says the child who just purchased every color version of a fifty-dollar shirt at White House Black Market on her father's credit card."

And wheeeeeere did I learn that? As if she's not completely to blame for my shopping habit.

"I'll have Iron there in an hour," I tell her.

She groans a little. "Just send Trace. He's a lot easier to talk to."

He is. But I'm sure she only thinks so because he's the one she knows the best, since he's my grandmother's favorite. His hedge sculptures are a major delight for her. My mom is used to seeing him around over there.

But I look at the time on my phone, seeing it's almost nine. "Trace got off work three hours ago," I point out. "He'll be drunk by now."

"But isn't Iron the one who's always getting arrested?"

"Not for anything violent," I point out. "Or . . . not for anything violent against *women* anyway."

"Clay . . ."

"It'll be fine." I yank open the door to the bar. "Expect him soon." And I hang up before she can argue more.

Some Styx song plays on the jukebox, and the scent of smoke and fried food hits me. The bartender, Jilly, serves a beer and brandishes a new tattoo on her neck. She locks eyes with me, her disdain visible through the bleached-blond hair that hangs in her eyes.

I dial Iron. And redial every time the voicemail picks up. On my fourth try, he finally answers.

"I'm not driving your ass to the Bay," he says without a hello.

I laugh to myself, remembering our motorcycle ride at Night Tide.

"I'm already in the Bay." I head toward the bar. "Are you sober?"

"Yeah . . ."

Good. "You need to go to Palm Island," I tell him, "and install my mom's new washer and dryer set."

There's a click and the line goes dead.

I clench my teeth. *You little . . .*

I tap out a text instead.

Do it now or I'll tell Macon about the boat you
stole last week in the Glades.

He won't wonder how I know. I know everything.

His text rolls in. God, fuck you.

I arch a brow and wait another three seconds, seeing the next text.

Leaving now.

I smile wide. *That's right, you are.* I'm so badass.

Be nice, I tell him.

Just not *too* nice. I actually do want my parents back together after all their middle-aged growth-and-reflection shit is complete.

I plop my bag down on the bar and pull my hair out of its ponytail, shaking it out. Jilly is dressed in a miniskirt and a tank top with extra cleavage, but I just came from transporting three—*three*—bodies to the funeral home from the morgue, and I am not in the mood. My friends have been bitching on TikTok about trudging across campus for their nine a.m. classes and how their research papers are keeping them from the frat party of the year. Meanwhile I've been up since four thirty this morning, putting in the work for my online classes and the extra hours I'm doing at the Wind House.

Jeans and a sleeveless tee for me tonight. I don't need the tips anyway.

"Hey," I say, pulling out my AirPods.

Jilly spins, shooting me a glare as she pours a shot of Jack. "Do you know anything about tending bar?"

Well, you do it, so it can't be hard.

I shoot a lazy glance around the place. "Seems like mostly beer, shooters, and vodka and cranberries," I mumble. "I'll google anything else that comes up."

She could be nicer. I'm filling in so she doesn't have to pull a double shift.

"And why did Macon think you were the best choice to cover for Aracely tonight?"

"He's just trying to annoy you." I smile. "Because he *hates* you."

She cocks an eyebrow but shuts up. Aracely called in sick, so Macon called me yesterday, because I was literally the last resort. He knows I know that. No one else must've wanted the job tonight, but I'm still trying to get him to like me, so I agreed. I want to be able to sleep with his sister whenever I want.

"I'll show you the register," she says, walking away.

I follow, dipping behind the bar and keeping my trap shut as she walks me through how to ring up liquor and put orders in to the kitchen. The place is busier than usual, and I'm the only one on, but it's after dinner, so other than some appetizers, I'm hoping it's just mostly drink orders tonight.

Jilly sticks around, eats a basket of jalapeño poppers, and watches me for a few minutes, but then she leaves without a word. Probably dissatisfied I didn't make a mistake.

"A Corona, a mojito, and a shot of Patrón," some guy orders over the bar. "A *chilled* shot, please."

I empty the rest of the ice into the cooler and set the bucket down, aggravated he didn't at least wait to make eye contact before ordering me around, but then get distracted when I realize "How the fuck do you make a mojito?"

Shit.

I nod, flipping the top off the beer, hand it to him, and tap away on my phone for a mojito recipe.

I study it and then glance around me. Do they even have mint leaves here?

But then I open a cooler and see them in a tub of cold water. *Huh*, I guess the Swamps aren't completely unsophisticated.

Hurriedly, I mix the lime juice and sugar, then add the rum and soda water, kind of wanting to taste it to see if it's like the one I snuck at the resort with my parents a couple of years ago, but that's probably not a good idea.

I garnish with the leaves, hand him the drink, and then add the tequila to a shaker with some ice to chill before I pour it for him.

He smiles and takes the drinks, and I'm so excited that he's not calling me out for doing something wrong that I totally forget to charge him.

"Ugh," I groan, debating for a second whether to go confront him at his table, but that would be awkward. *Screw it.* Jilly drinks on the job all the time. Trace gives free drinks here and there. Macon won't know if every shot isn't accounted for.

Army comes in and out, grabbing food to go, and I'm half tempted to see if he'd run next door to get me some of Mariette's pie, but I promised Liv I wouldn't eat any without her, so . . .

Liv.

I usually stay busy enough to not feel paralyzed by not seeing her every day, but if I slow down long enough—especially at night—my head goes places it shouldn't.

I look down at my phone, still not seeing a reply from our text exchange yesterday. She'd left me hanging.

Please come, she wrote.

I will.

I miss you.

My throat tightens every time she says that. I miss you too. Can you just come home for the weekend?

I did in September, she'd argued. And I can hear how she's losing patience with me. I want you to come up here. Be a part of my life here. Meet my friends. See my room. It's just a visit, Clay.

I rub my forehead, wishing I'd handled it better yesterday. She's right. She came home last month after only being at school a matter of weeks, because the separation is torture. It's my turn to go to her now.

But I don't want to. I want to make you happy. I just . . .

She gave me time to find my words.

I'm worried I'll be jealous, I'd told her. I'll be intimidated.

But aren't you wondering? Wanting to
know what I do all day? Where I'm at?
Where I eat? Who I see?

                    Yes, but it's better than knowing.

Knowing what?

                    That you're creating a life without me in it
                    and sooner or later you'll want to be free
                    to keep going.

I knew we'd be here eventually. We wanted to follow each
other. She was willing to give up Dartmouth to stay with me, and
I wanted nothing more than to pack up my stuff, jump in that car,
and go with her. The two of us. On our own. Together.

But I couldn't let her change her dream for me, and if I tagged
along on hers, I'd just be my mother all over again. Knowing in
twenty years, I'd still not have a clue about who I was. Incapable of
standing on my own and being solid. If we were going to make it,
we needed to walk our own paths.

For now . . . I'd cried as I typed, thankful she couldn't see me. I
can pretend that you're not there. Making friends, having experi-
ences, discovering a whole world. In my head, you're not living somewhere else. You're just not here today.

She didn't respond. That was thirty-six hours ago.

I scroll up, seeing the pics I'd sent her in previous messages and
the ones she'd sent me. Thanks to video calls and sexting, the time
apart hasn't been completely awful.

I just had to go and put my foot in it yesterday. Why can't I just
jump on a plane and go? She's asking for so little, and I'm an asshole.

I go to her TikTok, not seeing any new updates, but I log on to Instagram and see a new post. My heart leaps at the picture in that way that makes me want to break into a smile and puke at the same time.

She's there in a black-and-white flannel, buttoned up to her neck in that nerdy way I love, sitting at a Dairy Queen with another girl next to her as they both tip their Blizzards upside down like they do when they give it to you to prove how thick it is.

Another girl stands behind them both, looking over her shoulder and jutting out her ass for the camera. I know they're her roommates—Mal and Bennett—but it's Bennett's arm around her neck that makes everything hurt. I know it's her, because Liv said she looks like me a bit. Blond.

I swallow. *They're friends.* Friends do that.

But why would she post this? She had to know it would hurt me. If I were a guy, and another man was putting his arm around her, would that be okay?

"Vodka and cranberry," someone pipes up.

It takes a minute, but I blink and look up. What?

Dallas stands there, leaning on the bar, his arms tan and bare in his sleeveless T-shirt, too, but his is black. It makes his green eyes look darker.

I glance behind him and see a table filled with his crew, and Amy sits there in the middle of all the attention.

The drink is for her. She must be home for the weekend. And she's certainly not twenty-one, but I know she has an ID that says she is because we bought them together.

I exhale, slamming my phone down as Dallas's gaze remains on me.

"Does she have a ride?" I ask, filling a glass with ice.

He smirks. "Several."

And the innuendo isn't lost on me. Liv told me about her coming out of Iron and Dallas's room one morning, and here she is now. Entertainment for a whole table.

I almost spit, the taste in my mouth is so damn awful. He's such a prick.

I pour a shot of vodka and grab the juice.

"So how are you, Clay?" he asks as I work.

I ignore him. For a minute this summer, I wanted a relationship with Liv's whole family. Not really anymore.

"And you and Livvy?" he goes on when I don't answer.

I plop the drink down in front of him; it sloshes onto the bar and I stick a straw in it.

He chuckles and takes a napkin, wiping off his hand. "You don't like me, do you?"

I stare at him. His hair has grown out a little. The Tryst Six tattoo peeks out of his shirt where it sits on his shoulder, between his chest and his arm.

"I'm not nice like Iron and Trace." He points out the obvious. "Or a big brother like Army and Macon."

"Because you're miserable."

"Because you're a problem," he retorts.

My gaze falters, but I steady myself. I'm not a problem. I'm a Saint, and I'll never be anything else to him. Same as Callum.

"You know it's only a matter of time." He cocks his head at me. "She'll get a part in a production with the theater at the university soon. Can't come home as much and eventually never, because she'll decide to volunteer her summers with a theater troupe or take a course in London or audition for a Shakespeare festival that takes up all her vacation time."

I inhale, and dig my toes into my shoes where he can't see.

"She'll make friends," he goes on. "You'll make friends. You'll both realize the loneliness is too hard or you'll meet people in your own circles—because let's face it, you're not in her circle—and you'll realize there are so many other people who are probably much better suited for you." His tone condescends. "I mean, the notion that your soulmate just happens to be born a few miles from you? Come on. It's a big fucking world, Clay."

I want to take the drink and throw it on him, but I'm shaking on the inside. All I can manage is "You're miserable."

"There are a lot of people out there, baby. Lots of pussy." He leans in again, and I can smell his body wash. I know it's his, because I've used their shower, and he's the only male in the house who doesn't use the bar soap. "Why don't you see what's out there?"

I have no interest in anything else but his sister. But that picture haunts me, just like everything about her life up north. Is she finding people more her pace? More stimulating in conversation and experience?

"Let's see what's out there." He nods at me, his voice unusually gentle. "Let's go to Miami. Tonight. You and me."

He says it like we're two buddies.

"They've got some great clubs," he tells me. "You don't have to sleep alone tonight."

I don't want to sleep alone a single night.

His eyes gleam. "I'll get a girl in your bed."

It hurts to swallow. "Was Callum a problem, too?" I ask him. "Is that why you ended it?"

His eyes thin to slits for a second, but then he recovers.

"He's doing well, you know?" I say. "At UPenn."

"I'll get you someone warm and soft," he continues as if I'm not talking. "Something good to suck on."

"Doing well, despite the beatdown he took last spring," I go on.

"The beatdown he deserved," he states.

"I agree. Thank you for that."

Some guy signals me, and I turn to pour him another draft.

"But I have wondered something about all that shit with

Callum last spring," I tell Dallas over my shoulder. "He wasn't really 'a problem' before you."

He remains silent.

"Not that anything excuses what he did," I point out, "but four years around Liv and he'd never pulled anything like that before. It's curious, isn't it?"

His jaw flexes; he inhales and exhales, and then pins me with a stare. "Let's go to Miami," he says, trying to take back the conversation.

But I'm loving the tension in his body.

"He will be back," I muse. "A man, richer, more powerful than his father . . ."

"Get in my car, Clay."

But I won't. I've found it. Dallas's kryptonite. I'm not scared of him anymore.

I hand the man his beer and come back to Liv's brother, smiling small. "He'll be back," I almost whisper. "I wonder what he'll do to you."

He rises, stiff like I've never seen him as he looks down at me. He takes the shooter sitting in front of the guy next to him and throws it back, swallowing it and looking at me the entire time.

He takes Amy's drink and turns away, finally leaving me alone. Hopefully for good.

Because he knows I'm right. What Callum will inherit employs at least twenty percent of Sanoa Bay.

But the Jaegers have leverage on St. Carmen with the surveillance at Fox Hill now, too. Unbeknownst to Callum.

I will never be on Callum's side, but I'm not exactly on Dallas's, either. I might just stand back and watch when the shit hits the fan.

I take a sip of my soda, momentarily pleased, until her face drifts through my head again and I reach for my phone.

But then I sigh and slam it back down. *Stop stalking her. Jesus.*

Why am I so worried? She's mine. We spent the whole summer barely a foot apart for more than a few hours at a time. Sleepovers and beach days and Disney World—I totally got her in some Mickey ears—and a road trip to Miami for a weekend and another one to New Orleans for a week.

Last year at this time, I could have any guy I wanted. I never checked up on Callum or obsessed about anyone else's daily activities. Loving her is like nothing I've been through before. I'm afraid of losing her.

And when she's not here, where I can be reassured every day that she's mine, my brain fucking tilts, and I want to bang my head into a wall.

The doubts overpower reason, and I don't know how to stop it.

I check the phone one more time and then toss it down on top of the beer cooler. I can't believe she hasn't called. Or texted back. It's so inconsiderate.

I order a basket of mozzarella sticks, but then I realize I have a bar full of people I'd rather not have staring at me while I cry into my junk food. I set them in front of Amy at her table instead to help neutralize the alcohol I'm illegally giving her.

Hours pass.

I learn how to make a sidecar, and someone asks for a lemmy—which is just a Jack and Coke, I guess. Wise-ass.

Thankfully, most of the evening is beers and shots, until some guy asks if I'm on the menu, too. He wants to take me home to his wife, because she's looking to "explore." His bed will fit all three of us, he says.

But then Trace grabs his earlobe and yanks his face down onto the bar so hard I hear his nose break, and then the guy is apparently "just kidding," he says.

And the cherry on top for the night? My tip jar holds almost enough for a swanky night at McDonald's.

Ugh. I'm honestly glad I agreed to help Macon out tonight. If for no other reason than to remind myself that while I'm kind of tired of being in school nearly all of my life so far, it will hopefully ensure I have some better choices. I almost feel sorry for Jilly.

And Aracely. This can't be their dream. Not that there's anything wrong with a good, honest job—I get that. The world needs every kind of worker, but . . . paying bills will always be a struggle for them. What would people be capable of without that on their shoulders, you know?

I'm a lucky girl. Luckier than I deserve.

Feeling suddenly—and rightly—guilty, I pick up my phone and dial Liv. I'm lucky to even have her. Too lucky. I should be doing everything I can to show her I know that.

But it doesn't ring. It goes straight to voicemail like she has it turned off. I falter, my worry spiking again. She never turns off her phone.

And when the line beeps, I just want to tell her that I'm an idiot and spoiled and stupid. *Let's go for it, babe.* I'd rather have a moment than nothing. A weekend, a day, an hour . . . rather than no part of her ever again.

But as the noise in the bar snakes into my ears and my head, and some guy shouts for a Coors, I stammer. "I . . ." I swallow and just blurt it out. "I miss you."

I hang up, actually thankful I am too distracted to go into some long, heartfelt monologue of lunacy.

"That register turns up short," I hear Macon yell, "it's coming off your credit card, Collins."

I glance up, arching a brow as Liv's oldest brother points at me and heads for the kitchen, probably just passing through to make his authority known.

I drop the phone down next to the register. "Yeah, that sixty-eight cents in there will really help me finally buy that personality I've been eyeing for you."

I hear Trace laugh, knowing that sound easily by now, as

Macon disappears into the kitchen. Liv looks the most like him. They both have brown eyes.

I check my phone. Still no call. Or text. I walk out from behind the bar.

I go over to Amy's table and steal one of the cold cheese sticks still left. I stuff it into my mouth, ignoring her look, and dig out a few bills from my pocket, dialing in about ten songs on the jukebox, starting with "Dearest Helpless" by Silverchair. Army and his eclectic taste in old music are rubbing off on me, apparently.

But even the music can't drown out the voices in my head. Every minute that passes, my conscious thoughts are consumed with her. I pour someone a beer. *She hasn't called.* I wash and dry a martini glass. *She hates me.* Someone orders wings. *She's avoiding me.*

Of course she would. I'm a basket case and completely unpleasant. She wised up.

Customers start to drift out. Dallas leaves a mess on the table, and I don't even bother to call him back to pay the bill he racked up treating all of his friends. Macon can deal with him.

There's a twenty-dollar tip on the bar from Trace, and I let Mr. and Mrs. Torres keep me fifteen minutes longer than necessary, since everyone is now gone, because they still aren't done in the bathroom.

I wash the dishes, wipe down the bar, and clean the tables, tossing my dirty cloth down next to the register as I grab my backpack because I need air. The kitchen staff will lock up, and Macon will be back to count the register.

I step outside, resisting the urge to grab my phone.

Resisting, resisting, don't do it, don't do it . . . It's only been almost two days. Just two days since she lacked the common courtesy of participating in the conversation I thought we were having.

I should ignore it.

But I don't want to let her ignore it. She's just going to try to call and act like "Oh, that?" And brush it off.

To hell with it. She's doing this on purpose. You can't even manage to return a text or a call, I type. I'm supposed to believe we'd spend time together if I were there?

I mean, hey . . . if she's so busy, then what's the point of me visiting there?

I don't think I'm overreacting. Some reassurance from time to time is expected and appreciated. I mean, what the fuck is she doing that she ignores me this long?

I told you this would happen, I type out. You're finding a world. I'm not important anymore.

I throw my backpack onto the passenger seat and climb into my car, starting the engine. I ignore the lights and music pouring out of Liv's house as I pass, knowing Macon's only allowing a party because Liv's gone now. I'm not sure if he tried to keep the house respectable when she lived there because she was in school and needed to study or because he wanted to protect her from bad behaviors and idiots.

Either way, he's drinking more now. Even if he still doesn't smile.

I drive, rolling down the windows and smelling the rain that's coming. Trying to cool off my brain. Clear my head. Calm the hell down. I'm cooking all this up in my head, and it's all Dallas's fault.

I mean, the notion that your soulmate just happens to be born a few miles from you?, he had said. *Let's go to Miami. Tonight. You and me. See what's out there.*

I drive, crossing the canal into St. Carmen, and up into the hills, thinking.

She'll make friends. You'll make friends, he'd taunted me.

I stop at the red light, breathing hard. What is she doing that she can't call or text?

The empty streets shine with the latest cleaning, and I kind of miss the dirt roads of Sanoa Bay. The chipped paint and overgrowth. The heat and the taste of her skin when she sweats for me.

I glance across the street and see Lavinia's, dark and locked up.

The lap dance I gave her drifts through my mind, and I shake my head. "Why am I letting him get to me?" I murmur to myself. "Olivia Jaeger's girlfriend is not a fucking coward. Liv Jaeger can't live without her. She thinks about her all the time. University, new people, culture . . . Hot roommates. It's no contest. She's obsessed with Clay. Nothing compares."

Or so I would've been able to convince myself six months ago, when I thought I was the shit.

The light turns green, I punch the gas, and tears fill my eyes as I make my way home. I lost Henry and survived. Why does this feel harder?

I park in my driveway, the house lit up, even though I know my mom is at her cottage tonight and I'm all alone.

But as soon as I step through the front door, my phone rings.

I pause, hating how my heart leaps that it could be her. Might be her.

God, I hope it's not her.

Pulling it out of my bag, I stare at her name on the screen. It takes a moment, but I answer it, holding it to my ear.

"What have you gone and done now?" she asks before I say anything.

I sniffle. "Worked myself into a tizzy."

My voice sounds like a guilty child who knows she screwed up. But I can hear the humor in her tone. "Yeah, no kidding."

"Well, I'm not wrong," I retort, the confidence building again now that I finally have her on the phone. "This is too hard, Liv. I'm just so . . ."

I can't say the word. It's stupid.

I just can't seem to control the feelings.

"So . . . ?" she presses.

"Jealous," I blurt out. "I'm jealous all the time. I hate it. The doubt that's always there. And I hate for you to see it, too."

My head starts going, and maybe I want it to go there, because

I miss her, and I'm upset. Maybe I want to sabotage this so I have an excuse to be the first to walk away.

Before she does.

"What are we doing?" Last spring, we were in it to win it. And now . . . "This is torture."

"So, you'll come to Dartmouth this weekend, then?" she asks.

"That's not what I was thinking."

"Then stop."

"Stop what?"

"Thinking," she deadpans.

If only . . .

Faith was never my strong suit. I've learned nothing is permanent. When I can't see her and know and be reassured, my head starts making up its own truth.

"I saw your post." I drift into the house, leaving the lights off. "You didn't tell me your roommate had an amazing ass."

"You like her ass?"

I lean back against the fridge, my messenger bag still looped over my shoulder. "Does she walk around naked?"

"Clay . . ."

That wasn't a no.

"Or in her underwear, maybe?" I press.

Liv says nothing, and wind rushes through her phone. She must be outside.

"She does, doesn't she?" I say, able to read her silences by now.

"What do you want from me?" she spits out. "It's her room, too."

I set my jaw, staring at my shoes, and try to keep my voice steady, but the tears spill down my face and I watch them dot the black hardwood floor.

She and those girls share a tiny space, talking every day, eating together probably, laughing, and falling asleep together and . . .

"I want you in your own room," I grit out.

"Fine, done," she spits out. "Will you be happy then? Will this be the end of it? Want me to eat alone, too? Not attend parties? Move to another seat if someone attractive sits next to me in class? What about acting roles? Should I stay away from any that make you feel threatened?"

I push off, gritting my teeth. This is unbearable. School rules force my girlfriend to have other women in her bedroom like that would be okay if they were the opposite sex. It wouldn't be.

She acts like she wouldn't feel the exact same way if I'd gone away to college. She would.

But . . . I know it would cost Liv money she doesn't have to pay more for a single dorm room. And there's no way she can afford an apartment. Not yet.

And her roommates are straight. Liv knows it, I know it, and for the first time in a long time—no thanks to me—she's not alone. Not an outsider. She has friends and an environment that makes her feel good.

She's right. I'm angry and scared for so many reasons, and her roommates aren't the problem. I will still miss her and be angry about it, no matter her roommate situation.

I calm my voice again, standing in the dark kitchen as rain patters the windows. "You fit there." That's what I saw in the picture on the post, not the other girls. "I knew it a long time ago, you know?"

"Knew what?"

"Years ago, when I knew I loved you," I answer, leaning over the island and speaking softly. "That's why I battled so hard, because I knew you were going to win. I already knew I'd lost you, even freshman year. The world was going to see how beautiful you are. What can I possibly give you now?"

"You know what you give me."

I stand up straight again, cutting off my scoff before she can hear it. "You're not stupid. Stop acting like it," I scold, knowing what we're good at. "When the sex gets old, you'll realize that's all that's between us."

And as soon as the words are out of my mouth, my jaw drops, and I want to snatch them back. Tears well until more spill over. I close my eyes. *Jesus, fuck.*

Her silence burns my ear, and I almost hang up, too mortified. What the hell is wrong with me?

"I'm sorry," I breathe out. "But see? I can still hurt you, after all, can't I?"

"Get in your car."

I go still. "My car?"

"The back seat," she tells me.

I want to.

I want to do everything she tells me, because for some reason, my conscience needed to put up a fight tonight, so when this ends, I can say, *I told you so*, but I never want it to actually end. I want her to reel me back in.

But sex isn't going to solve this.

"I'm not in the mood," I tell her. My voice is gentle, but I'm sure she can hear the fatigue. I just want to go to bed with my shame right now. "I shouldn't have said what I said just now. I didn't mean it."

"The back seat, Clay," she orders.

But I shake my head. "I don't want to. I just need to get off the phone."

And smash the damn thing with a hammer before I do anything else stupid.

"I'm hideous." Tears lodge in my throat, and I can only manage a whisper. "But I love you."

And I pull the phone away from my ear, but then I hear her voice.

"Do you remember our first time in your car?" she asks.

I stop, unable to answer right away. Images flood back, and I drop my head, almost blushing.

Prom night. My mom had reserved the penthouse suite at the Palmer for my friends and me to party after the dance. She knew Liv and I would be spending the night together, but with Krisjen calling it an early night when she got called home by her little sister for whatever reason and Amy passed out with some guy in the room next to ours, Liv and I didn't want to stay. A bed a thousand people had slept on (been there, done that). Cold furniture. Amy able to hear us from the next room.

We Ubered back to my house, got my car, and intended to take a blanket and sleep on the beach, but we stayed in the car instead.

"I thought we were going to die," I whisper. "It was so hot."

It was May and miserable.

"But we couldn't stop," she adds. "I could never stop."

My throat tightens, warmth building in my body again as the good slowly eases all of the damn ugly shit I'd been thinking tonight.

"It was so tight back there," she muses. "I was ready to scream, because I couldn't reach all of you. I couldn't kiss everything I wanted to kiss, but the . . . the need suspended time. Nothing else existed."

I nod to myself. "Wild," I add. "It was so wild. I thought you were going to bite me."

I hear her soft laugh, and I pick out my AirPods from my bag, fit them into my ears, unloop my bag from over my head, and set it on the floor.

I make my way for the front door, carrying my phone and listening.

"When I'm with you," Liv says in my ears, "I feel like I'm doing what I should be doing with all of my time. I feel you with every sense, Clay. I always have. Your taste, your scent, your whispers in my ears . . ."

Chills spread down my arms and legs, and I stand inside the front door, looking out through the sidelight at the driveway and my car.

"I'm glad you weren't my first," she goes on, "because at least I know you're another level."

My eyes sting.

"That's what you forget," she says. "You're not my first, but you're the first one I loved. There's a reason. It's not that good with you because of your body and what you can do with it. It's that good with you because we're connected. We're connected in places your hands and mouth can't reach. My head, my heart, and places deeper than that—you're always inside me, Clay."

My chest almost caves. She knows how to let me think I have the power here, and I'm grateful. Liv is a survivor. She might hate losing me, but she'd live. I'm not so sure I, on the other hand, could bear the pain.

"Get in your car," she whispers.

I swallow hard as sprinkles hit the glass panes. "It's raining."

"Good. Then no one will see you through the glass."

I peer outside, the driveway shining black. My car sits off to the side, the top up as water pours down the windshield.

I hesitate. "Why didn't you answer your phone tonight?"

But instead she orders me, "Lie down in the back seat."

"Liv?" I press.

"And take off your shirt."

She's playing with me. That used to be my job, but she floors me now. With her, I can't think straight.

Or I couldn't.

An idea runs through my head, and I hold back my smile. Opening the door, I step outside, close it, and walk to my car, the rain cooling my shoulders. I run my fingers through my hair, flipping it to one side as I open my car door and dive into the back seat.

I set my phone on the console, the dome light dims, and all I can hear is the downpour beating on the roof. Water spills down the windshield, obstructing the view outside until the trees and the lampposts around the driveway are like a pool of paint on a palette.

She sits in my ear, silent.

"I love you," I tell her.

"Take off your shirt."

I pull my T-shirt over my head, glancing around once more to make sure I'm completely alone. The house sits back far from the street and is surrounded by trees, far from the view of anyone driving by, but you never know.

I toss my shirt into the front seat.

"Until you're bare," she clarifies as if she can see me and knows I'm in a bra.

I ignore the tingle in my body.

Reaching behind me, I unhook my bra and pull it off, tossing it up front with my shirt. I lie down and kick off my shoes, one knee bent with my foot on the seat and the other planted on the floor of the car.

"I'm lying down," I tell her.

My breath already fogs the windows, remembering all the times we were on top of each other in here this past summer.

"Now take off your jeans," she orders.

"I'm not wearing underwear."

"You tended bar in the Bay tonight with no underwear on?"

I break into a smile, loving the scold I hear in her tone, but then . . . I hesitate. "How did you know where I was tonight?"

Macon called me yesterday. After I'd texted Liv. I hadn't had a chance to tell her yet.

One of her brothers must've mentioned it. I know she talks to Trace almost daily. Army and Iron at least once a week. Macon doesn't talk to anyone unless there's a point, and Dallas wouldn't talk about me to her unless it was to hurt us.

"Take them off," she demands.

But I play, touching my stomach and gliding my fingers over and down my neck to massage my breasts.

"I want you to watch me," I say as I squeeze.

"I am, baby."

"Don't kiss me anywhere or . . . or suck on anything," I pant, grazing my nipples until they're rocks. "Or lick anything."

"I like to watch you," she whispers.

I nod, thinking about the times I let her watch. The times I performed more than just a little dance.

"But I *love* to touch you," she states. "Now take off your jeans."

I slip my hand between my legs, over my jeans, and squeeze and massage myself with my hand.

"No," I say in a flat tone.

"Excuse me?"

"I said no."

I groan, feeling myself grow wet.

"You know, if I were there, you wouldn't be pulling this shit," she points out.

"But you're not here, are you?" I taunt.

She's silent, my nipples point to the sky, and I'm feeling strong again, because I know she likes how good I make her feel. That's something, at least.

"My jeans aren't coming off again until your hand is inside them," I inform her. "And then you can watch me."

She says nothing.

"Watch me come," I tell her. "Watch me make *you* come. Watch me between your legs and watch my hands between *my* legs."

She breathes into the phone.

"I'm going to have so much fun in my bed tonight all by myself, and when you see me, then you can have—"

Something slams right into the window, and I jerk, pulling my hands off myself.

What the hell?

I pop my head up, my lungs emptying. The wet palm of a slender hand presses into the glass, and the door opens just as I shoot upright.

Liv dips her head inside the car, calm with a smirk in her eyes as she looks me up and down. Her phone is in her hand. "I'm sorry, you were saying?"

"Liv?" I gasp. I don't know why it sounds like a fucking question, because she's right there, but I still can't believe it. "Oh my God!"

I reach for her, but I don't have to do much. She climbs in, takes my arms, and pushes me back down onto the seat, pinning my arms above my head.

The warm rain wets my bare feet where they dangle out the door.

"I'm sorry I didn't answer the phone," she says, staring down at me, and I just want her to kiss me. "I wanted to surprise you. And then I was on a plane."

Yeah. I was pretty sure there was a simple explanation, but I needed a reason to be mad, I guess.

She grips my wrists as her eyes trail down my body, lingering on my breasts. "But I'm kind of aggravated I wasted the time now. You're pissing me off tonight."

Yeah, I know that, too. She'd probably been on a plane as I was starting work tonight and all the dread and worry was for nothing. When we're frustrated, we want someone to be mad at. I need to work on that.

"So, what are you going to do about it?" I ask her, but don't wait for a reply. "Nothing, as usual?"

She breathes out a small laugh, fire lighting up her brown eyes. "Clay, I learned a long time ago with you that I can't make you sorry." She lowers her mouth toward my body. "But I can make you beg."

She flicks my nipple with her tongue, holding my eyes the entire time. I suck in a breath.

I know it's only been a few weeks, but tears hang at the corners of my eyes, because the distance has made me realize one thing. I feel best only with her.

"I love you." My body shakes, and I can't look at her. I stare at the roof.

She moves from one breast to the other, kissing and sucking so lightly my body erupts in chills, because all she's doing is teasing me.

Her face comes up to mine, and I don't even fight her hold as she brushes my nose with hers. "Do you think I don't worry, too?"

I open my mouth, trying to kiss her, but she holds back. "About what?"

"That, at any moment, you'll meet someone who makes you question if waiting for me is worth it."

I close my mouth again, watching her.

"And I worry, because you're doing something so amazing with your life," she tells me. "I may see a thousand places in college, Clay, but you're going to be a part of a thousand lives. More even."

"So will you."

She cocks her head like I'm so naïve. "But what do people say about actors at their funerals, you know? People will need you. That scares me, because some day you might think that my life's work is shallow and unimportant, and I never know if you're going to call me one night and tell me you've met someone else. You know how many first loves last?"

Rarely any.

"I think about it all the time." She takes my lips with hers, holding them softly. "What you're doing. Who you're seeing. If you still miss me. If life's just moving on here without me." She licks her lips, gazing down, and I see the tears in her eyes. "Part of me honestly hates it when I see your name on my caller ID. There's a moment when I'm so scared to answer it."

She releases my hands, and I don't hesitate. I take her ass in both hands, threading our legs, and lean up, taking her mouth.

We kiss, breathless, and the taste of whatever gloss is left on her lips sends my stomach fluttering.

"But no amount of panic is going to force this to last," she says. "If we want it, then it will."

I know that. I knew that months ago when I committed to letting her go without me and neither of us holding back for the other.

But I want her, and she wants me, so I need to step up. "I'll come up for Halloween," I tell her. "Okay?"

She smiles.

It's two weeks away. Our first Halloween as a couple. I want to be together for it. "I want to see your room, meet your friends, go to a party . . ." I tell her. "We could dress up as Daphne and Velma."

She kisses me again and again, moaning as my hands slip under her flannel and grope her breasts.

But then she pulls back and looks down at me. "No. How about Liv and Clay," she states. "The high school version. Catholic skirts and all."

Dress up as ourselves?

"And this time . . ." She pinches my chin. "I don't take your shit."

I can't contain myself. "This time . . ." I grip her ass. "Maybe I don't hold back what I really want from you. Take off your shirt, Jaeger."

She bites her lip, and I can tell she wants to smile. She's fucking excited.

But she doesn't want to show it.

Arching up, I thread my fingers through the back of her hair and kiss her hard and deep, slipping my tongue in and feeling her moan down my throat. I take her hand and put it to her chest.

"Unbutton it," I whisper over her lips. "Do it now."

Our breath mixes, her hair—longer in just a matter of weeks—is cool in my fist, and our eyes meet. Suddenly, we're back in high school, and she's going to do everything I want, because she wants me, too.

With one hand, she undoes each button from the neck on down, and as soon as the last button is unfastened, I tear off her shirt. "You're so beautiful."

In seconds, our jeans are crumpled onto the floor.

"Yeah, you're just being nice, because you want a piece of ass," she teases.

I wrap my arm around her waist and bite her breast. "I'm not just being nice." I sit up, pull her over my lap backward, pushing her forward between the front seats over the console, and bend her knees at my side. My clit throbs as I scoot down and fit us together like a scissor and take her panties in my fist.

"Clay," she gasps, startled.

"You are beautiful," I continue. "I had the prettiest girl at prom and they all knew it."

Clutching her underwear in one hand, I see her grab the console with both hands to hold on just before I yank hard, ripping her little white panties off her.

Holding her hips, I tip my head back, sweat already glistening across her back and my chest. "Fuck me, baby. Fuck me now."

Her ass starts to move and I'm lost. God, I'm lost. Her hips roll in and out like a wave, her cunt rubbing on mine so good, the friction feels like little pricks on the raw flesh of my pussy.

Slow at first and then faster, she grinds on me, looking back into my eyes as I push the hair out of her face, the windows layering with fresh fog, and the sound of the rain is drowned out by the sounds of breathing and moaning.

"God," I grit out, bringing my hand down and taking a fistful of her ass as she works me harder and harder. "God, baby."

The long hair down her beautiful back. The soft, olive skin. Her gorgeous body and how she looks at me like I'm the most important thing she'll ever see.

I love her so much.

"You like that, Clay?" she taunts.

I watch her ass move in and out, fucking me good.

"Yeah."

I reach out and take a breast in my hand, keeping her ass in the other.

"You dream about me?" she goes on.

And I move one hand into her hair, gripping it, and the other I slip between us and then slide two fingers inside her. She shudders when I go deep, her eyes rolling as she tips her head back. "Oh . . ." she moans.

"I dream about you in five years, straddling me like this in your wedding dress," I tell her.

That's what I dream about.

She shakes as I crook my fingers inside her. We rub so hard and fast that it's like little jerks as we chase our orgasms.

"Oh, God," she groans. "Clay."

"Fuck, Jaeger," I cry. "Fuck, don't stop. Ah!"

We come, and it billows into my thighs and spreads through my stomach as sparks rise up my arms and head until I swear that I can feel every pore on my body. The world tilts a little, and I'm suddenly so glad my mom is gone tonight.

"Clay," she whimpers.

I breathe hard. "I know." My mouth is so dry I can't swallow. "I know."

I know. This has to last. There's no way around it. Even if I lost her, she'd be back someday. One look again and we wouldn't be able to stay away from each other. I may not have any experience to compare to, but . . . *she does.*

I lean forward, pressing my forehead into her back and wrapping my arm around her. *She knows this is it.*

"No, I mean my hair," she whines.

Which . . . Liv never does.

And that's when I realize one of my hands is still fisted at her scalp. Tightly.

"Oh." I pull it out, releasing her. "Sorry."

She laughs and then I do, too.

She collapses back onto me, turning her head and kissing me. "Halloween, then?"

"Halloween."

And she dives in for another quick peck. "And I love you, too."

Well, fucking finally. I've only said it five hundred times tonight.

ACKNOWLEDGMENTS

To the readers—Again, I want to thank you so much for all the help and support over the years. I love being online with you, having fun and socializing, but social media has a funny way of sucking me in, and before I know it, it's noon! Not that it's time wasted, by any means, but I realized that I'm more successful about reaching my goals and staying organized and on schedule the more disciplined I am about how my time is spent. Thank you to those of you who put up with my long spells offline. You understand that just because someone isn't constantly posting doesn't mean that great things aren't happening.

To my family—my husband for taking over so much in the past year. Seriously. Roles have certainly changed between us since we met, and I'm so grateful you're here to handle so much so I can make good use of my time to do the work I love.

To Dystel, Goderich & Bourret LLC—Thank you for being so readily available and helping me grow every day. I couldn't be happier.

To the PenDragons—Gosh, I've missed you all. There were so many days, especially a month into quarantine, that I was desperate to spend some time with you. I needed people, and I really appreciate that you're my guaranteed happy place. Thanks for giving me a community and validating the stories I love.

To Adrienne Ambrose, Tabitha Russell, Tiffany Rhyne, Kristi Grimes, Lee Tenaglia, and Claudia Alfaro—the amazing Facebook group admins! Not enough can be said about the time and energy you give freely to make a community for the readers and me. You're selfless, amazing, patient, and needed. Thank you.

To Vibeke Courtney—my indie editor who goes over every move I make with a fine-toothed comb. Thank you for teaching me how to write and laying it down straight.

To Elaine York and Christine Porter—the gifts from the gods who are always on call, work hard, and reply quickly whenever I need them. Thank you for editing, formatting, and going above and beyond with being available.

To all the wonderful readers, especially on Instagram and Tik-Tok, who make art and videos for the books and keep us all excited, motivated, and inspired—Thank you for everything! I love your vision, and I apologize if I miss things while I'm offline.

To all of the bloggers and bookstagrammers—there are too many to name, but I know who you are. I see the posts and the tags, and all the hard work you do. You spend your free time reading, reviewing, and promoting, and you do it for free. You are the life's blood of the book world, and who knows what we would do without you. Thank you for your tireless efforts. You do it out of passion, which makes it all the more incredible.

To every author and aspiring author—Thank you for the stories you've shared, many of which have made me a happy reader in search of a wonderful escape and a better writer, trying to live up to your standards. Write and create, and don't ever stop. Your voice is important, and as long as it comes from your heart, it is right and good.

Keep reading for a special preview of

FIVE BROTHERS

by Penelope Douglas

Krisjen

I take the shot Iron holds up in front of me, all of us tapping our drinks in a toast before we shoot it. Peppermint burns my throat, and I close my eyes, feeling the music under my skin. I lean back into a body I know is Iron's.

He reaches around me with one arm and picks up his drink, his other hand on my hip. "Go," he tells Trace. "She's with me tonight."

I look over at Trace, his eyes flashing to me and then his older brother. I turn around, facing Iron. "I'm with you? When was that decided?"

"In the cooler yesterday." He cocks his head. "I could've had you then."

Trace passes by, leaving us to it. I'm not with him, either.

Iron watches me with those eyes, and my cheeks feel like he's touching my face, but he's not.

I raise my chin a little higher.

"If you're not interested . . ." He starts to back away. "You better tell me now. I plan on getting laid tonight. I'd like it if it were you."

My eyes catch on fire, and the laughter bubbling up is about to pop out of my pores. Is he serious?

"Sure, absolutely," I taunt. "Let's do it now. Upstairs or in your car? I'll just climb on and start bouncing." I start to walk and pull him along. "If we do it quickly, you might have time to fit in another girl. Or two. Come on. We can be back before the beer runs out."

I drop his hand and keep walking, leaving this fucking party. What a mistake. *Asshole.*

But he grabs me.

I pull against his grip as he yanks me in. "I'd like it," he grits out, "if it were you."

Why?

I jerk free as people around us turn to look. Maybe I want him with me tonight. Maybe it would've been easy to seduce me into staying. In a dark hallway. Up against a quiet wall. As he kissed me and slid into me nice and slow, over and over for an hour, and then took my smell with him tomorrow.

It wouldn't have been hard to get me to stay. I knew that when I walked in here tonight. That doesn't mean I don't enjoy being seduced.

I tip my chin at him. "Truth or dare?"

His mouth twitches with a smile as he remains quiet for a moment. Then he replies, "Truth."

"How would you fuck me?"

His eyebrows twitch in surprise, and I see a guy next to me falter in his dancing to look at me.

Iron squares his shoulders. "I want you to ride me. On the pool chair outside."

Someone close by laughs, and others around us stop, taking notice of our confrontation.

Iron takes one step toward me. "Truth or dare?"

"Dare."

"Open your vest," he tells me.

Not *take off your jacket* or *remove your hat*. He's going straight for skin.

I undo the three buttons holding the vest closed over my bare chest, watching him the whole time.

But he's not looking at my eyes. He stares at the open sliver, an inch wide, appearing from sternum to stomach and revealing only a tease of the mounds still covered.

The hair on my arms rises, and I can't hear the music anymore. All I feel are his eyes like a tongue running up that slice of skin. "Truth or dare?" I ask him.

"Truth."

"Are you big?"

People laugh, Iron smiles. "Ask your friend," he tells me. "What was her name again?"

Amy.

I fist my right hand. He's going for broke tonight. Seeing how far he can push me.

"Truth or dare?" he says.

"Dare."

"Take off your hat."

I do, tossing it behind the recliner in the corner.

I steel my spine. "Truth or dare?"

"Truth."

"Will I come with you?"

A few more people have stopped to watch us and are snorting their appreciation.

Iron steps, closing the distance between us and looking down at my open vest. Sweat dampens my skin, and my nipples harden against the fabric.

"You're almost coming right now," he says.

I arch a brow.

"Truth or dare?" he asks.

"Dare."

"Drop your jacket."

But it's a whisper, and desire pools inside me.

Holding his gaze, I pull the Mad Hatter's fitted red jacket off my shoulders and let it slide down my arms to the floor.

"Truth or dare?"

"Truth," he replies.

"Do you go down?"

A woman behind me expels a breath.

Iron grins. "I always return a favor."

More laughter.

"Truth or dare?" he challenges.

My heart skips a beat. I'm taking off something important now. But I get in his face anyway. "Dare."

He stares at me, something playing behind his eyes. Probably the knowledge that this won't end how he wants it to if he asks me to get naked in the middle of this party.

But he doesn't. Instead, he squats down in front of me, slides his hands up my thighs, underneath my skirt, and I let him pull my panties down.

It feels like no one in the room is breathing. I step out of my lacy black underwear while he looks up at me and slips them into his pocket.

"Truth or dare?" I ask.

He smiles. "Truth."

I reach down where he still squats in front of me and touch his face. I want to memorize it. "Are they going to be okay without you?" I ask.

His smile falls.

I faintly register the whispers, and I can feel Trace off to my right, clearing his throat.

Iron rises, the fun over, and he's not amused now because he wants to get laid. It's his own fault that it has to be tonight or nothing.

"Tryst Six . . ." I muse, pushing him some more. "Tryst Five when Liv left. Now it'll be Tryst Four, I guess, without you."

"Ohhhh," someone goes off.

People shift nervously. They can tell Iron's pissed.

"Dare," he grits out, changing his answer.

"Fine. What do you want to do?"

"Tape your mouth shut," he growls.

I smile, my chest bubbling with excitement. I look up, toying with him. "If you had bothered to seduce me instead of taking for granted that I was a sure thing, I would've let you tape up my wrists, too." I bite my bottom lip, watching his eyes drop to my mouth. "Because, Iron, my favorite part isn't the fucking. Color me shocked that you're the one who understands that the least. What a disappointment."

Laughter and howls explode around us, and Iron cocks an eyebrow. At least Trace indulged some foreplay.

"Or is that why you go after teenage girls?" I ask. "Because we're just that easy."

A woman laughs quietly next to Trace, and I look over to see him and Aracely smiling, amused.

Iron tosses him a glare, his younger brother throwing up his hands in defense. "I love you. I'm on your side."

Iron turns back to me, and I notice his hand is still in his pocket with my panties.

"Hey, Army?" he calls out, but his eyes don't leave mine.

"Yeah?" Army replies from somewhere behind me.

"We still got any red paint?" Iron asks him.

Excited laughter and chatter sound around the room as if that means something. I shoot my eyes left and then right.

Then back to Iron. The corners of his lips tilt up. "I think it's time for a few rounds of Red Right Hand."

Everyone starts moving, someone's hands shooting into the air while a woman lets out a squeal.

Red Right Hand?

Army passes me, coming up to his brother. "That is the best idea I've heard in a while."

Penelope Douglas is a *New York Times*, *USA Today*, and *Wall Street Journal* bestselling author. Their books have been translated into twenty languages and include the Fall Away series, the Hellbent series, the Devil's Night series, and the stand-alones *Misconduct*, *Punk 57*, *Birthday Girl*, *Credence*, and *Tryst Six Venom*.

VISIT PENELOPE DOUGLAS ONLINE

PenDouglas.com

PenelopeDouglasAuthor

PenDouglas

Penelope.Douglas

LEARN MORE ABOUT THIS BOOK
AND OTHER TITLES FROM
NEW YORK TIMES BESTSELLING AUTHOR

PENELOPE DOUGLAS

SCAN ME

or visit
prh.com/penelopedouglas